ANCIENT HAUNTINGS

MORE WILDSIDE CLASSICS

Please see www.wildsidepress.com for a complete list!

ANCIENT HAUNTINGS

Edited by

R. Reginald
and
Douglas Melville

WILDSIDE PRESS

Dedicated to Al & Joe Sanders,
with thanks and appreciation.

ANCIENT HAUNTINGS

This edition published in 2006 by Wildside Press, LLC.
www.wildsidepress.com

CONTENTS

THE ENSOULED VIOLIN.

I.

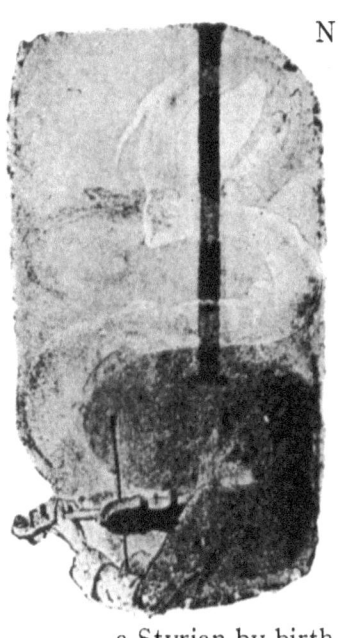

N the year 1828, an old German, a music teacher, came to Paris with his pupil and settled unostentatiously in one of the quiet faubourgs of the metropolis. The first rejoiced in the name of Samuel Klaus ; the second answered to the more poetical appellation of Franz Stenio. The younger man was a violinist, gifted, as rumour went, with extraordinary, almost miraculous talent. Yet as he was poor and had not hitherto made a name for himself in Europe, he remained for several years in the capital of France—the heart and pulse of capricious continental fashion—unknown and unappreciated. Franz was a Styrian by birth, and, at the time of the event to be presently described, he was a young man considerably under thirty. A philosopher and a dreamer by nature, imbued with all the mystic oddities of true genius, he reminded one of some of the heroes in Hoffmann's *Contes Fantastiques*. His earlier existence had been a very unusual, in fact, quite an eccentric one, and its history must be briefly told—for the better understanding of the present story.

Born of very pious country people, in a quiet burg among the Styrian Alps ; nursed " by the native gnomes who watched over his cradle " ; growing up in the weird atmosphere of the ghouls and vampires who play such a prominent part in the household of every Styrian and Slavonian in Southern Austria ; educated later, as a

THE ENSOULED VIOLIN

H. P. Blavatsky

student, in the shadow of the old Rhenish castles of
Germany ; Franz from his childhood had passed through
every emotional stage on the plane of the so-called
" supernatural." He had also studied at one time the
" occult arts " with an enthusiastic disciple of Paracelsus
and Kunrath ; alchemy had few theoretical secrets for
him ; and he had dabbled in " ceremonial magic " and
" sorcery " with some Hungarian Tziganes. Yet he
loved above all else music, and above music—his violin.

At the age of twenty-two he suddenly gave up his
practical studies in the occult, and from that day,
though as devoted as ever in thought to the beautiful
Grecian Gods, he surrendered himself entirely to his art.
Of his classic studies he had retained only that which
related to the muses—Euterpe especially, at whose altar
he worshipped—and Orpheus whose magic lyre he tried
to emulate with his violin. Except his dreamy belief in
the nymphs and the sirens, on account probably of the
double relationship of the latter to the muses through
Calliope and Orpheus, he was interested but little in the
matters of this sublunary world. All his aspirations
mounted, like incense, with the wave of the heavenly
harmony that he drew from his instrument, to a higher
and a nobler sphere. He dreamed awake, and lived a real
though an enchanted life only during those hours when
his magic bow carried him along the wave of sound to
the Pagan Olympus, to the feet of Euterpe. A strange
child he had ever been in his own home, where tales of
magic and witchcraft grow out of every inch of the soil ;
a still stranger boy he had become, until finally he had
blossomed into manhood, without one single characteristic of youth. Never had a fair face attracted his attention ; not for one moment had his thoughts turned from
his solitary studies to a life beyond that of a mystic

Bohemian. Content with his own company, he had thus passed the best years of his youth and manhood with his violin for his chief idol, and with the Gods and Goddesses of old Greece for his audience, in perfect ignorance of practical life. His whole existence had been one long day of dreams, of melody and sunlight, and he had never felt any other aspirations.

How useless, but oh, how glorious those dreams! how vivid! and why should he desire any better fate? Was he not all that he wanted to be, transformed in a second of thought into one or another hero; from Orpheus, who held all nature breathless, to the urchin who piped away under the plane tree to the naiads of Calirrhoë's crystal fountain? Did not the swift-footed nymphs frolic at his beck and call to the sound of the magic flute of the Arcadian shepherd—who was himself? Behold, the Goddess of Love and Beauty herself descending from on high, attracted by the sweet-voiced notes of his violin! . . . Yet there came a time when he preferred Syrinx to Aphrodite—not as the fair nymph pursued by Pan, but after her transformation by the merciful Gods into the reed out of which the frustrated God of the Shepherds had made his magic pipe. For also, with time, ambition grows and is rarely satisfied. When he tried to emulate on his violin the enchanting sounds that resounded in his mind, the whole of Parnassus kept silent under the spell, or joined in heavenly chorus; but the audience he finally craved was composed of more than the Gods sung by Hesiod, verily of the most appreciative *mélomanes* of European capitals. He felt jealous of the magic pipe, and would fain have had it at his command.

"Oh! that I could allure a nymph into my beloved violin!"—he often cried, after awakening from one of his day-dreams. "Oh, that I could only span in spirit flight the abyss of Time ! Oh, that I could find myself for one short day a partaker of the secret arts of the Gods, a God myself, in the sight and hearing of enraptured humanity ; and, having learned the mystery of the lyre of Orpheus, or secured within my violin a siren, thereby benefit mortals to my own glory ! "

Thus, having for long years dreamed in the company of the Gods of his fancy, he now took to dreaming of the transitory glories of fame upon this earth. But at this time he was suddenly called home by his widowed mother from one of the German universities where he had lived for the last year or two. This was an event which brought his plans to an end, at least so far as the immediate future was concerned, for he had hitherto drawn upon her alone for his meagre pittance, and his means were not sufficient for an independent life outside his native place.

His return had a very unexpected result. His mother, whose only love he was on earth, died soon after she had welcomed her Benjamin back ; and the good wives of the burg exercised their swift tongues for many a month after as to the real causes of that death.

Frau Stenio, before Franz's return, was a healthy, buxom, middle-aged body, strong and hearty. She was a pious and a God-fearing soul too, who had never failed in saying her prayers, nor had missed an early mass for years during his absence. On the first Sunday after her son had settled at home—a day that she had been longing for and had anticipated for months in joyous visions, in which she saw him kneeling by her side in the little church on the hill—she called him from the foot of the stairs. The hour had come when her pious dream was to be realized, and she was waiting for him, carefully wiping the dust from the prayer-book he had used in his boyhood. But instead of Franz, it was his violin that responded to her call, mixing its sonorous voice with the rather cracked tones of the peal of the merry Sunday bells. The fond mother was somewhat shocked at hearing the prayer-inspiring sounds drowned by the weird, fantastic notes of the " Dance of the Witches " ; they seemed to her so unearthly and mocking. But she almost fainted upon hearing the definite refusal of her well-beloved son to go to church. He never went to church, he coolly remarked. It was loss of time ; besides which, the loud peals of the old church organ jarred on his nerves. Nothing should induce him to submit to the torture of listening to that cracked organ. He was firm, and nothing could move him. To her supplications and remonstrances he put an end by offering to play for her a " Hymn to the Sun " he had just composed.

From that memorable Sunday morning, Frau Stenio lost her usual serenity of mind. She hastened to lay her sorrows and seek for consolation at the foot of the confessional ; but that which she heard in response from the stern priest filled her gentle and unsophisticated soul with dismay and almost with despair. A feeling of fear, a sense of profound terror, which soon became a chronic state with her, pursued her from that moment ; her nights became disturbed and sleepless, her days passed in prayer and lamentations. In her maternal anxiety for the salvation of her beloved son's soul, and for his *post mortem* welfare, she made a series of rash vows. Finding that neither the Latin petition to the Mother of God written for her by her spiritual adviser, nor yet the humble supplications in German, addressed by herself to every saint she had reason to believe was residing in Paradise, worked the desired effect, she took to pilgrimages to distant shrines. During one of these journeys to a holy chapel situated high up in the mountains, she caught cold, amidst the glaciers of the Tyrol, and redescended only to take to a sick bed, from which she arose no more. Frau Stenio's vow had led her, in one sense, to the desired result. The poor woman was now given an opportunity of seeking out in *propriâ personâ* the saints she had believed in so well, and of pleading face to face for the recreant son, who refused adherence to them and to the Church, scoffed at monk and confessional; and held the organ in such horror.

Franz sincerely lamented his mother's death. Unaware of being the indirect cause of it, he felt no remorse ; but selling the modest household goods and chattels, light in purse and heart, he resolved to travel on foot for a year or two, before settling down to any definite profession.

A hazy desire to see the great cities of Europe, and to try his luck in France, lurked at the bottom of this travelling project, but his Bohemian habits of life were too strong to be abruptly abandoned. He placed his small capital with a banker for a rainy day, and started on his pedestrian journey *viâ* Germany and Austria. His violin paid for his board and lodging in the inns and farms on his way, and he passed his days in the green fields and in the solemn silent woods, face to face with Nature, dreaming all the time as usual with his eyes open. During the three months of his pleasant travels to and fro, he never descended for one moment from Parnassus ; but, as an alchemist transmutes lead into gold, so he transformed everything on his way into a song of Hesiod or Anacreon. Every evening, while fiddling for his supper and bed, whether on a green lawn or in the hall of a rustic inn, his fancy changed

the whole scene for him. Village swains and maidens
became transfigured into Arcadian shepherds and
nymphs. The sand-covered floor was now a green
sward; the uncouth couples spinning round in a
measured waltz with the wild grace of tamed bears became priests and priestesses of Terpsichore; the bulky,
cherry-cheeked and blue-eyed daughters of rural Germany were the Hesperides circling around the trees
laden with the golden apples. Nor did the melodious
strains of the Arcadian demi-gods piping on their
syrinxes, and audible but to his own enchanted ear,
vanish with the dawn. For no sooner was the curtain
of sleep raised from his eyes than he would sally forth
into a new magic realm of day-dreams. On his way to
some dark and solemn pine-forest, he played incessantly,
to himself and to everything else. He fiddled to the
green hill, and forthwith the mountain and the moss-
covered rocks moved forward to hear him the better, as
they had done at the sound of the Orphean lyre. He
fiddled to the merry-voiced brook, to the hurrying river,
and both slackened their speed and stopped their waves,
and, becoming silent, seemed to listen to him in an en-
tranced rapture. Even the long-legged stork who stood
meditatively on one leg on the thatched top of the rustic
mill, gravely resolving unto himself the problem of his
too-long existence, sent out after him a long and strident
cry, screeching, " Art thou Orpheus himself, O Stenio ? "

It was a period of full bliss, of a daily and almost
hourly exaltation. The last words of his dying mother,
whispering to him of the horrors of eternal condemnation,
had left him unaffected, and the only vision her warning
evoked in him was that of Pluto. By a ready association
of ideas, he saw the lord of the dark nether kingdom
greeting him as he had greeted the husband of Eurydice

before him. Charmed with the magic sounds of his violin, the wheel of Ixion was at a standstill once more, thus affording relief to the wretched seducer of Juno, and giving the lie to those who claim eternity for the duration of the punishment of condemned sinners. He perceived Tantalus forgetting his never-ceasing thirst, and smacking his lips as he drank in the heaven-born melody ; the stone of Sisyphus becoming motionless, the Furies themselves smiling on him, and the sovereign of the gloomy regions delighted, and awarding preference to his violin over the lyre of Orpheus. Taken *au sérieux*, mythology thus seems a decided antidote to fear, in the face of theological threats, especially when strengthened with an insane and passionate love of music ; with Franz, Euterpe proved always victorious in every contest, aye, even with Hell itself !

But there is an end to everything, and very soon Franz had to give up uninterrupted dreaming. He had reached the university town where dwelt his old violin teacher, Samuel Klaus. When this antiquated musician found that his beloved and favourite pupil, Franz, had been left poor in purse and still poorer in earthly affections, he felt his strong attachment to the boy awaken with tenfold force. He took Franz to his heart, and forthwith adopted him as his son.

The old teacher reminded people of one of those grotesque figures which look as if they had just stepped out of some mediæval panel. And yet Klaus, with his fantastic *allures* of a night-goblin, had the most loving heart, as tender as that of a woman, and the self-sacrificing nature of an old Christian martyr. When Franz had briefly narrated to him the history of his last few years, the professor took him by the hand, and leading him into his study simply said :

"Stop with me, and put an end to your Bohemian life. Make yourself famous. I am old and childless and will be your father. Let us live together and forget all save fame."

And forthwith he offered to proceed with Franz to Paris, *viâ* several large German cities, where they would stop to give concerts.

In a few days Klaus succeeded in making Franz forget his vagrant life and its artistic independence, and re-awakened in his pupil his now dormant ambition and desire for worldly fame. Hitherto, since his mother's death, he had been content to receive applause only from the Gods and Goddesses who inhabited his vivid fancy ; now he began to crave once more for the admiration of mortals. Under the clever and careful training of old Klaus his remarkable talent gained in strength and powerful charm with every day, and his reputation grew and expanded with every city and town wherein he made himself heard. His ambition was being rapidly realized ; the presiding genii of various musical centres to whose patronage his talent was submitted soon proclaimed him *the one* violinist of the day, and the public declared loudly that he stood unrivalled by any one whom they had ever heard. These laudations very soon made both master and pupil completely lose their heads.

But Paris was less ready with such appreciation. Paris makes reputations for itself, and will take none on faith. They had been living in it for almost three years, and were still climbing with difficulty the artist's Calvary, when an event occurred which put an end even to their most modest expectations. The first arrival of Niccolo Paganini was suddenly heralded, and threw Lutetia into a convulsion of expectation. The unparalleled artist arrived, and—all Paris fell at once at his feet.

II.

Now it is a well-known fact that a superstition born in the dark days of mediæval superstition, and surviving almost to the middle of the present century, attributed all such abnormal, out-of-the-way talent as that of Paganini to "supernatural" agency. Every great and marvellous artist had been accused in his day of dealings with the devil. A few instances will suffice to refresh the reader's memory.

Tartini, the great composer and violinist of the XVIIth century, was denounced as one who got his best inspirations from the Evil One, with whom he was, it was said, in regular league. This accusation was, of course, due to the almost magical impression he produced upon his audiences. His inspired performance on the violin secured for him in his native country the title of "Master of Nations." The *Sonate du Diable*, also called "Tartini's Dream"—as every one who has heard it will be ready to testify—is the most weird melody ever heard or invented: hence, the marvellous composition has become the source of endless legends. Nor were they entirely baseless, since it was he, himself, who was shown to have originated them. Tartini confessed to having written it on awakening from a dream, in which he had heard his sonata performed by Satan, for his benefit, and in consequence of a bargain made with his infernal majesty.

Several famous singers, even, whose exceptional voices struck the hearers with superstitious admiration, have not escaped a like accusation. Pasta's splendid voice was attributed in her day to the fact that, three months before her birth, the diva's mother was carried during a trance to heaven, and there treated to a vocal concert of seraphs. Malibran was indebted for her voice to St.

Cecilia, while others said she owed it to a demon who watched over her cradle and sung the baby to sleep. Finally, Paganini—the unrivalled performer, the mean Italian, who like Dryden's Jubal striking on the " chorded shell " forced the throngs that followed him to worship the divine sounds produced, and made people say that " less than a God could not dwell within the hollow of his violin "—Paganini left a legend too.

The almost supernatural art of the greatest violin-player that the world has ever known was often specu-lated upon, never understood. The effect produced by him on his audience was literally marvellous, overpower-ing. The great Rossini is said to have wept like a sentimental German maiden on hearing him play for the first time. The Princess Elisa of Lucca, a sister of the great Napoleon, in whose service Paganini was, as director of her private orchestra, for a long time was unable to hear him play without fainting. In women he produced nervous fits and hysterics at his will ; stout-hearted men he drove to frenzy. He changed cowards into heroes and made the bravest soldiers feel like so many nervous school-girls. Is it to be wondered at, then, that hundreds of weird tales circulated for long years about and around the mysterious Genoese, that modern Orpheus of Europe. One of these was especially ghastly. It was rumoured, and was believed by more people than would probably like to confess it, that the strings of his violin were made of *human intestines, according to all the rules and requirements of the Black Art.*

Exaggerated as this idea may seem to some, it has nothing impossible in it ; and it is more than probable that it was this legend that led to the extraordinary events which we are about to narrate. Human organs are often used by the Eastern Black Magician, so-called,

and it is an averred fact that some Bengâlî Tântrikas
(reciters of *tantras*, or "invocations to the demon," as a
reverend writer has described them) use human corpses,
and certain internal and external organs pertaining to
them, as powerful magical agents for bad purposes.

However this may be, now that the magnetic and
mesmeric potencies of hypnotism are recognized as facts
by most physicians, it may be suggested with less danger
than heretofore that the extraordinary effects of Paganini's violin-playing were not, perhaps, entirely due to
his talent and genius. The wonder and awe he so easily
excited were as much caused by his external appearance,
"which had something weird and demoniacal in it,"
according to certain of his biographers, as by the inexpressible charm of his execution and his remarkable
mechanical skill. The latter is demonstrated by his
perfect imitation of the flageolet, and his performance of
long and magnificent melodies on the G string alone.
In this performance, which many an artist has tried to
copy without success, he remains unrivalled to this day.

It is owing to this remarkable appearance of his—
termed by his friends eccentric, and by his too nervous
victims, diabolical—that he experienced great difficulties
in refuting certain ugly rumours. These were credited
far more easily in his day than they would be now. It
was whispered throughout Italy, and even in his own
native town, that Paganini had murdered his wife, and,
later on, a mistress, both of whom he had loved passionately, and both of whom he had not hesitated to sacrifice to his fiendish ambition. He had made himself
proficient in magic arts, it was asserted, and had succeeded thereby in imprisoning the souls of his two
victims in his violin—his famous Cremona.

It is maintained by the immediate friends of Ernst

T. W. Hoffmann, the celebrated author of *Die Elixire des Teufels*, *Meister Martin*, and other charming and mystical tales, that Councillor Crespel, in the *Violin of Cremona*, was taken from the legend about Paganini. It is, as all who have read it know, the history of a celebrated violin, into which the voice and the soul of a famous diva, a woman whom Crespel had loved and killed, had passed, and to which was added the voice of his beloved daughter, Antonia.

Nor was this superstition utterly ungrounded, nor was Hoffmann to be blamed for adopting it, after he had heard Paganini's playing. The extraordinary facility with which the artist drew out of his instrument, not only the most unearthly sounds, but positively human voices, justified the suspicion. Such effects might well have startled an audience and thrown terror into many a nervous heart. Add to this the impenetrable mystery connected with a certain period of Paganini's youth, and the most wild tales about him must be found in a measure justifiable, and even excusable ; especially among a nation whose ancestors knew the Borgias and the Medicis of Black Art fame.

III.

In those pre-telegraphic days, newspapers were limited, and the wings of fame had a heavier flight than they have now.

Franz had hardly heard of Paganini ; and when he did, he swore he would rival, if not eclipse, the Genoese magician. Yes, he would either become the most famous of all living violinists, or he would break his instrument and put an end to his life at the same time.

Old Klaus rejoiced at such a determination. He rubbed his hands in glee, and jumping about on his lame leg like a crippled satyr, he flattered and incensed his pupil, believing himself all the while to be performing a sacred duty to the holy and majestic cause of art.

Upon first setting foot in Paris, three years before, Franz had all but failed. Musical critics pronounced him a rising star, but had all agreed that he required a few more years' practice, before he could hope to carry his audiences by storm. Therefore, after a desperate study of over two years and uninterrupted preparations, the Styrian artist had finally made himself ready for his first serious appearance in the great Opera House where a public concert before the most exacting critics of the old world was to be held ; at this critical moment Paganini's arrival in the European metropolis placed an obstacle in the way of the realization of his hopes, and the old German professor wisely postponed his pupil's *début.* At first he had simply smiled at the wild enthusiasm, the laudatory hymns sung about the Genoese violinist, and the almost superstitious awe with which his name was pronounced. But very soon Paganini's name became a burning iron in the hearts of both the artists, and a threatening phantom in the mind of Klaus. A few days more, and they shuddered at the very mention of their great rival, whose success became with every night more unprecedented.

The first series of concerts was over, but neither Klaus nor Franz had as yet had an opportunity of hearing him and of judging for themselves. So great and so beyond their means was the charge for admission, and so small the hope of getting a free pass from a brother artist justly regarded as the meanest of men in monetary transactions, that they had to wait for a chance, as did so many others. But the day came when neither master nor pupil could control their impatience any longer ; so

they pawned their watches, and with the proceeds bought
two modest seats.

Who can describe the enthusiasm, the triumphs, of
this famous, and at the same time fatal night! The
audience was frantic; men wept and women screamed
and fainted; while both Klaus and Stenio sat looking
paler than two ghosts. At the first touch of Paganini's
magic bow, both Franz and Samuel felt as if the icy
hand of death had touched them. Carried away by an
irresistible enthusiasm, which turned into a violent, unearthly mental torture, they dared neither look into each
other's faces, nor exchange one word during the whole
performance.

At midnight, while the chosen delegates of the Musical
Societies and the Conservatory of Paris unhitched the
horses, and dragged the carriage of the grand artist home
in triumph, the two Germans returned to their modest
lodging, and it was a pitiful sight to see them. Mournful and desperate, they placed themselves in their usual
seats at the fire-corner, and neither for a while opened
his mouth.

"Samuel!" at last exclaimed Franz, pale as death
itself. "Samuel—it remains for us now but to die!
. . . Do you hear me? . . . We are worthless!
We were two madmen to have ever hoped that any one
in this world would ever rival . . . him!"

The name of Paganini stuck in his throat, as in utter
despair he fell into his arm chair.

The old professor's wrinkles suddenly became purple.
His little greenish eyes gleamed phosphorescently as,
bending toward his pupil, he whispered to him in hoarse
and broken tones:

"*Nein, nein!* Thou art wrong, my Franz! I have
taught thee, and thou hast learned all of the great art

that a simple mortal, and a Christian by baptism, can learn from another simple mortal. Am I to blame because these accursed Italians, in order to reign un-equalled in the domain of art, have recourse to 'Satan and the diabolical effects of Black Magic ? ''

Franz turned his eyes upon his old master. There was a sinister light burning in those glittering orbs ; a light telling plainly, that, to secure such a power, he, too, would not scruple to sell himself, body and soul, to the Evil One.

But he said not a word, and, turning his eyes from his old master's face, gazed dreamily at the dying embers.

The same long-forgotten incoherent dreams, which, after seeming such realities to him in his younger days, had been given up entirely, and had gradually faded from his mind, now crowded back into it with the same force and vividness as of old. The grimacing shades of Ixion, Sisyphus and Tantalus resurrected and stood before him, saying :

" What matters hell—in which thou believest not ? And even if hell there be, it is the hell described by the old Greeks, not that of the modern bigots—a locality full of conscious shadows, to whom thou canst be a second Orpheus.''

Franz felt that he was going mad, and, turning instinc-tively, he looked his old master once more right in the face. Then his bloodshot eye evaded the gaze of Klaus.

Whether Samuel understood the terrible state of mind of his pupil, or whether he wanted to draw him out, to make him speak, and thus to divert his thoughts, must remain as hypothetical to the reader as it is to the writer. Whatever may have been in his mind, the German enthusiast went on, speaking with a feigned calmness :

"Franz, my dear boy, I tell you that the art of the accursed Italian is not natural; that it is due neither to study nor to genius. It never was acquired in the usual, natural way. You need not stare at me in that wild manner, for what I say is in the mouth of millions of people. Listen to what I now tell you, and try to understand. You have heard the strange tale whispered about the famous Tartini? He died one fine Sabbath night, strangled by his familiar demon, who had taught him how to endow his violin with a human voice, by shutting up in it, by means of incantations, the soul of a young virgin. Paganini did more. In order to endow his instrument with the faculty of emitting human sounds, such as sobs, despairing cries, supplications, moans of love and fury—in short, the most heart-rending notes of the human voice—Paganini became the murderer not only of his wife and his mistress, but also of a friend, who was more tenderly attached to him than any other being on this earth. He then made the four chords of his magic violin out of the intestines of his last victim. This is the secret of his enchanting talent, of that overpowering melody, that combination of sounds, which you will never be able to master unless . . . ."

The old man could not finish the sentence. He staggered back before the fiendish look of his pupil, and covered his face with his hands.

Franz was breathing heavily, and his eyes had an expression which reminded Klaus of those of a hyena. His pallor was cadaverous. For some time he could not speak, but only gasped for breath. At last he slowly muttered:

"Are you in earnest?"

"I am, as I hope to help you."

" And . . . and do you really believe that had I only the means of obtaining human intestines for strings, I could rival Paganini ? " asked Franz, after a moment's pause, and casting down his eyes.

The old German unveiled his face, and, with a strange look of determination upon it, softly answered :

" Human intestines alone are not sufficient for our purpose ; they must have belonged to some one who had loved us well, with an unselfish, holy love. Tartini endowed his violin with the life of a virgin ; but that virgin had died of unrequited love for him. The fiendish artist had prepared beforehand a tube, in which he managed to catch her last breath as she expired, pronouncing his beloved name, and he then transferred this breath to his violin. As to Paganini, I have just told you his tale. It was with the consent of his victim, though, that he murdered him to get possession of his intestines.

" Oh, for the power of the human voice ! " Samuel went on, after a brief pause. " What can equal the eloquence, the magic spell of the human voice ? Do you think, my poor boy, I would not have taught you this great, this final secret, were it not that it throws one right into the clutches of him . . . who must remain unnamed at night ? " he added, with a sudden return to the superstitions of his youth.

Franz did not answer ; but with a calmness awful to behold, he left his place, took down his violin from the wall where it was hanging, and, with one powerful grasp of the chords, he tore them out and flung them into the fire.

Samuel suppressed a cry of horror. The chords were hissing upon the coals, where, among the blazing logs, they wriggled and curled like so many living snakes.

"By the witches of Thessaly and the dark arts of Circe!" he exclaimed, with foaming mouth and his eyes burning like coals; "by the Furies of Hell and Pluto himself, I now swear, in thy presence, O Samuel, my master, never to touch a violin again until I can string it with four human chords. May I be accursed for ever and ever if I do!" He fell senseless on the floor, with a deep sob, that ended like a funeral wail; old Samuel lifted him up as he would have lifted a child, and carried him to his bed. Then he sallied forth in search of a physician.

IV.

FOR several days after this painful scene Franz was very ill, ill almost beyond recovery. The physician declared him to be suffering from brain fever and saie that the worst was to be feared. For nine long days the patient remained delirious; and Klaus, who was nursing him night and day with the solicitude of the tenderest mother, was horrified at the work of his own hands. For the first time since their acquaintance began, the old teacher, owing to the wild ravings of his pupil, was able to penetrate into the darkest corners of that weird, superstitious, cold, and, at the same time, passionate nature; and—he trembled at what he discovered. For he saw that which he had failed to perceive before—Franz as he was in reality, and not as he seemed to superficial observers. Music was the life of the young man, and adulation was the air he breathed, without which that life became a burden; from the chords of his violin alone, Stenio drew his life and being, but the applause of men and even of Gods was necessary to its support. He saw unveiled before his

eyes a genuine, artistic, *earthly* soul, with its divine
counterpart totally absent, a son of the Muses, all fancy
and brain poetry, but without a heart. While listening
to the ravings of that delirious and unhinged fancy
Klaus felt as if he were for the first time in his long
life exploring a marvellous and untravelled region, a
human nature not of this world but of some incomplete
planet. He saw all this, and shuddered. More than
once he asked himself whether it would not be doing
a kindness to his "boy" to let him die before he returned to consciousness.

But he loved his pupil too well to dwell for long on
such an idea. Franz had bewitched his truly artistic
nature, and now old Klaus felt as though their two lives
were inseparably linked together. That he could thus
feel was a revelation to the old man ; so he decided to
save Franz, even at the expense of his own old and, as
he thought, useless life.

The seventh day of the illness brought on a most
terrible crisis. For twenty-four hours the patient never
closed his eyes, nor remained for a moment silent ; he
raved continuously during the whole time. His visions
were peculiar, and he minutely described each. Fantastic, ghastly figures kept slowly swimming out of the
penumbra of his small, dark room, in regular and uninterrupted procession, and he greeted each by name as
he might greet old acquaintances. He referred to himself as Prometheus, bound to the rock by four bands
made of human intestines. At the foot of the Caucasian
Mount the black waters of the river Styx were running.
. . . . They had deserted Arcadia, and were now
endeavouring to encircle within a seven-fold embrace
the rock upon which he was suffering. . . .

"Wouldst thou know the name of the Promethean

rock, old man ? " he roared into his adopted father's ear.
. . . "Listen then, . . . its name is . . . called
. . . Samuel Klaus. . . ."

"Yes, yes ! . . " the German murmured disconso-
lately. "It is I who killed him, while seeking to con-
sole. The news of Paganini's magic arts struck his
fancy too vividly. . . . Oh, my poor, poor boy ! "

"Ha, ha, ha, ha ! " The patient broke into a loud and
discordant laugh. "Aye, poor old man, sayest thou ?
. . . So, so, thou art of poor stuff, anyhow, and
wouldst look well only when stretched upon a fine
Cremona violin ! . . ."

Klaus shuddered, but said nothing. He only bent over
the poor maniac, and with a kiss upon his brow, a caress
as tender and as gentle as that of a doting mother, he
left the sickroom for a few instants, to seek relief in his
own garret. When he returned, the ravings were following another channel. Franz was singing, trying to
imitate the sounds of a violin.

Toward the evening of that day, the delirium of the
sick man became perfectly ghastly. He saw spirits of
fire clutching at his violin. Their skeleton hands, from
each finger of which grew a flaming claw, beckoned to
old Samuel. . . . They approached and surrounded
the old master, and were preparing to rip him open . . .
him, "the only man on this earth who loves me with an
unselfish, holy love, and . . . whose intestines can
be of any good at all ! " he went on whispering, with
glaring eyes and demon laugh. . . .

By the next morning, however, the fever had disappeared, and by the end of the ninth day Stenio had
left his bed, having no recollection of his illness, and no
suspicion that he had allowed Klaus to read his inner
thought. Nay ; had he himself any knowledge that

such a horrible idea as the sacrifice of his old master to his ambition had ever entered his mind ? Hardly. The only immediate result of his fatal illness was, that as, by reason of his vow, his artistic passion could find no issue, another passion awoke, which might avail to feed his ambition and his insatiable fancy. He plunged headlong into the study of the Occult Arts, of Alchemy and of Magic. In the practice of Magic the young dreamer sought to stifle the voice of his passionate longing for his, as he thought, for ever lost violin. . . .

Weeks and months passed away, and the conversation about Paganini was never resumed between the master and the pupil. But a profound melancholy had taken possession of Franz, the two hardly exchanged a word, the violin hung mute, chordless, full of dust, in its habitual place. It was as the presence of a soulless corpse between them.

The young man had become gloomy and sarcastic, even avoiding the mention of music. Once, as his old professor, after long hesitation, took out his own violin from its dust-covered case and prepared to play, Franz gave a convulsive shudder, but said nothing. At the first notes of the bow, however, he glared like a madman, and rushing out of the house, remained for hours, wandering in the streets. Then old Samuel in his turn threw his instrument down, and locked himself up in his room till the following morning.

One night as Franz sat, looking particularly pale and gloomy, old Samuel suddenly jumped from his seat, and after hopping about the room in a magpie fashion, approached his pupil, imprinted a fond kiss upon the young man's brow, and squeaked at the top of his shrill voice :

" Is it not time to put an end to all this ? " . . .

Whereupon, starting from his usual lethargy, Franz echoed, as in a dream :

" Yes, it is time to put an end to this."

Upon which the two separated, and went to bed.

On the following morning, when Franz awoke, he was astonished not to see his old teacher in his usual place to greet him. But he had greatly altered during the last few months, and he at first paid no attention to his absence, unusual as it was. He dressed and went into the adjoining room, a little parlour where they had their meals, and which separated their two bedrooms. The fire had not been lighted since the embers had died out on the previous night, and no sign was anywhere visible of the professor's busy hand in his usual housekeeping duties. Greatly puzzled, but in no way dismayed, Franz took his usual place at the corner of the now cold fire-place, and fell into an aimless reverie. As he stretched himself in his old arm-chair, raising both his hands to clasp them behind his head in a favourite posture of his, his hand came into contact with something on a shelf at his back ; he knocked against a case, and brought it violently on the ground.

It was old Klaus' violin-case that came down to the floor with such a sudden crash that the case opened and the violin fell out of it, rolling to the feet of Franz. And then the chords, striking against the brass fender emitted a sound, prolonged, sad and mournful as the sigh of an unrestful soul ; it seemed to fill the whole room, and reverberated in the head and the very heart of the young man. The effect of that broken violin-string was magical.

" Samuel ! " cried Stenio, with his eyes starting from their sockets, and an unknown terror suddenly taking possession of his whole being. " Samuel ! what has happened ? . . . My good, my dear old master ! " he called out, hastening to the professor's little room, and throwing the door violently open. No one answered, all was silent within.

He staggered back, frightened at the sound of his own voice, so changed and hoarse it seemed to him at this moment. No reply came in response to his call. Naught followed but a dead silence . . . . that stillness which, in the domain of sounds, usually denotes death. In the presence of a corpse, as in the lugubrious stillness of a tomb, such silence acquires a mysterious power, which strikes the sensitive soul with a nameless terror. . . . The little room was dark, and Franz hastened to open the shutters.

.   .   .   .

Samuel was lying on his bed, cold, stiff, and lifeless. . . . . At the sight of the corpse of him who had loved him so well, and had been to him more than a father, Franz experienced a dreadful revulsion of feeling, a terrible shock. But the ambition of the fanatical artist got the better of the depair of the man, and smothered the feelings of the latter in a few seconds.

A note bearing his own name was conspicuously placed upon a table near the corpse. With trembling hand, the violinist tore open the envelope, and read the following :

MY BELOVED SON, FRANZ,

When you read this, I shall have made the greatest sacrifice, that your best and only friend and teacher could have accomplished for your fame. He, who loved you most, is now but an inanimate lump of clay. Of your old teacher there now remains but a clod of cold organic matter. I need not prompt you as to what you have to do with it. Fear not stupid prejudices. It is for your future fame that I have made an offering of my body, and you would be guilty of the blackest ingratitude were you now to render useless this sacrifice. When you shall have re-placed the chords upon your violin, and these chords a portion of my own self, under your touch it will acquire the power of that accursed sorcerer, all the magic voices of Paganini's instrument. You will find therein my voice, my sighs and groans, my song of welcome, the prayerful sobs of my infinite and sorrowful sympathy, my love for you. And now, my Franz, fear nobody! Take your instrument with you, and dog the steps of him who filled our lives with bitterness and despair! . . . Appear in every arena, where, hitherto, he has reigned without a rival, and bravely throw the gauntlet of defiance in his face. O Franz! then only wilt thou hear with what a magic power the full notes of unselfish love will issue forth from thy violin. Perchance, with a last caressing touch of its chords, thou wilt remember that they once formed a portion of thine old teacher, who now embraces and blesses thee for the last time. SAMUEL.

Two burning tears sparkled in the eyes of Franz, but they dried up instantly. Under the fiery rush of pas-sionate hope and pride, the two orbs of the future magician-artist, riveted to the ghastly face of the dead man, shone like the eyes of a demon.

Our pen refuses to describe that which took place on that day, after the legal inquiry was over. As another note, written with the view of satisfying the authorities, had been prudently provided by the loving care of the old teacher, the verdict was, " Suicide from causes un-known "; after this the coroner and the police retired, leaving the bereaved heir alone in the death-room, with the remains of that which had once been a living man.

.   .   .   .

Scarcely a fortnight had elapsed from that day, ere the violin had been dusted, and four new, stout strings had been stretched upon it. Franz dared not look at them. He tried to play, but the bow trembled in his hand like a dagger in the grasp of a novice-brigand. He then determined not to try again, until the portentous night should arrive, when he should have a chance of rivalling, nay, of surpassing, Paganini.

The famous violinist had meanwhile left Paris, and was giving a series of triumphant concerts at an old Flemish town in Belgium.

V.

ONE night, as Paganini, surrounded by a crowd of admirers, was sitting in the dining-room of the hotel at which he was staying, a visiting card, with a few words written on it in pencil, was handed to him by a young man with wild and staring eyes.

Fixing upon the intruder a look which few persons could bear, but receiving back a glance as calm and determined as his own, Paganini slightly bowed, and then dryly said :

" Sir, it shall be as you desire. Name the night. I am at your service."

On the following morning the whole town was startled by the appearance of bills posted at the corner of every street, and bearing the strange notice :

On the night of . . . , at the Grand Theatre of . . . , and for the first time, will appear before the public, Franz Stenio, a German violinist, arrived purposely to throw down the gauntlet to the world-famous Paganini and to challenge him to a duel—upon their violins. He purposes to compete with the great " virtuoso " in the execution of the most difficult of his compositions. The famous Paganini has accepted the challenge. Franz Stenio will play, in competition with the unrivalled violinist, the celebrated " Fantaisie Caprice " of the latter, known as " The Witches."

The effect of the notice was magical. Paganini, who, amid his greatest triumphs, never lost sight of a profitable speculation, doubled the usual price of admission, but still the theatre could not hold the crowds that

flocked to secure tickets for that memorable performance.

.   .   .   .

At last the morning of the concert day dawned, and
the "duel" was in every one's mouth. Franz Stenio,
who, instead of sleeping, had passed the whole long
hours of the preceding midnight in walking up and
down his room like an encaged panther, had, toward
morning, fallen on his bed from mere physical exhaustion. Gradually he passed into a death-like and dream-
less slumber. At the gloomy winter dawn he awoke,
but finding it too early to rise he fell asleep again. And
then he had a vivid dream—so vivid indeed, so life-like,
that from its terrible realism he felt sure that it was a
vision rather than a dream.

He had left his violin on a table by his bedside, locked
in its case, the key of which never left him. Since he
had strung it with those terrible chords he never let it
out of his sight for a moment. In accordance with his
resolution he had not touched it since his first trial, and
his bow had never but once touched the human strings,
for he had since always practised on another instrument.
But now in his sleep he saw himself looking at the
locked case. Something in it was attracting his attention, and he found himself incapable of detaching his
eyes from it. Suddenly he saw the upper part of the
case slowly rising, and, within the chink thus produced,
he perceived two small, phosphorescent green eyes—
eyes but too familiar to him—fixing themselves on his,
lovingly, almost beseechingly. Then a thin, shrill voice,
as if issuing from these ghastly orbs—the voice and orbs
of Samuel Klaus himself—resounded in Stenio's horrified ear, and he heard it say:

"Franz, my beloved boy. . . . Franz, I cannot, no, *I cannot* separate myself from . . . . *them!*"

And "they" twanged piteously inside the case.

Franz stood speechless, horror-bound. He felt his blood actually freezing, and his hair moving and standing erect on his head. . . .

"It's but a dream, an empty dream!" he attempted to formulate in his mind.

"I have tried my best, Franzchen. . . . I have tried my best to sever myself from these accursed strings, without pulling · them to pieces . . ." pleaded the same shrill, familiar voice. "Wilt thou help me to do so? . . ."

Another twang, still more prolonged and dismal, resounded within the case, now dragged about the table in every direction, by some interior power, like some living, wriggling thing, the twangs becoming sharper and more jerky with every new pull.

It was not for the first time that Stenio heard those sounds. He had often remarked them before—indeed, ever since he had used his master's viscera as a footstool for his own ambition. But on every occasion a feeling of creeping horror had prevented him from investigating their cause, and he had tried to assure himself that the sounds were only a hallucination.

But now he stood face to face with the terrible fact, whether in dream or in reality he knew not, nor did he care, since the hallucination—if hallucination it were—was far more real and vivid than any reality. He tried to speak, to take a step forward; but, as often happens in nightmares, he could neither utter a word nor move a finger. . . . . He felt hopelessly paralyzed.

The pulls and jerks were becoming more desperate with each moment, and at last something inside the case snapped violently. The vision of his Stradivarius, devoid of its magical strings, flashed before his eyes, throwing him into a cold sweat of mute and unspeakable terror.

He made a superhuman effort to rid himself of the incubus that held him spell-bound. But as the last supplicating whisper of the invisible Presence repeated: "Do, oh, do . . . . help me to cut myself off——" Franz sprang to the case with one bound, like an enraged tiger defending its prey, and with one frantic effort breaking the spell.

"Leave the violin alone, you old fiend from hell!" he cried, in hoarse and trembling tones.

He violently shut down the self-raising lid, and while firmly pressing his left hand on it, he seized with the right a piece of rosin from the table and drew on the leather-covered top the sign of the six-pointed star— the seal used by King Solomon to bottle up the rebellious djins inside their prisons.

A wail, like the howl of a she-wolf moaning over her dead little ones, came out of the violin-case:

"Thou art ungrateful . . . very ungrateful, my Franz!" sobbed the blubbering "spirit-voice." "But I forgive . . . for I still love thee well. Yet thou canst not shut me in . . . boy. Behold!"

And instantly a grayish mist spread over and covered case and table, and rising upward formed itself first into an indistinct shape. Then it began growing, and as it grew, Franz felt himself gradually enfolded in cold and damp coils, slimy as those of a huge snake. He gave a terrible cry and—awoke; but, strangely enough, not on his bed, but near the table, just as he had dreamed, pressing the violin case desperately with both his hands.

"It was but a dream, . . after all," he muttered,

still terrified, but relieved of the load on his heaving breast.

With a tremendous effort he composed himself, and unlocked the case to inspect the violin. He found it covered with dust, but otherwise sound and in order, and he suddenly felt himself as cool and as determined as ever. Having dusted the instrument he carefully rosined the bow, tightened the strings and tuned them. He even went so far as to try upon it the first notes of the " Witches " ; first cautiously and timidly, then using his bow boldly and with full force.

The sound of that loud, solitary note—defiant as the war trumpet of a conqueror, sweet and majestic as the touch of a seraph on his golden harp in the fancy of the faithful—thrilled through the very soul of Franz. It revealed to him a hitherto unsuspected potency in his bow, which ran on in strains that filled the room with the richest swell of melody, unheard by the artist until that night. Commencing in uninterrupted *legato* tones, his bow sang to him of sun-bright hope and beauty, of moonlit nights, when the soft and balmy stillness endowed every blade of grass and all things animate and inanimate with a voice and a song of love. For a few brief moments it was a torrent of melody, the harmony of which, " tuned to soft woe," was calculated to make mountains weep, had there been any in the room, and to soothe

. . . even th' inexorable powers of hell,

the presence of which was undeniably felt in this modest hotel room. Suddenly, the solemn *legato* chant, contrary to all laws of harmony, quivered, became *arpeggios*, and ended in shrill *staccatos*, like the notes of a hyena laugh. The same creeping sensation of terror, as he had before felt, came over him, and Franz threw the bow away. He had recognized the familiar laugh, and would have no more of it. Dressing, he locked the bedevilled violin securely in its case, and, taking it with him to the dining-room, determined to await quietly the hour of trial.

VI.

THE terrible hour of the struggle had come, and Stenio was at his post—calm, resolute, almost smiling.

The theatre was crowded to suffocation, and there was not even standing room to be got for any amount of hard cash or favouritism. The singular challenge had reached every quarter to which the post could carry it, and gold flowed freely into Paganini's unfathomable pockets, to an extent almost satisfying even to his insatiate and venal soul.

It was arranged that Paganini should begin. When he appeared upon the stage, the thick walls of the theatre shook to their foundations with the applause that greeted him. He began and ended his famous composition "The Witches" amid a storm of cheers. The shouts of public enthusiasm lasted so long that Franz began to think his turn would never come. When, at last, Paganini, amid the roaring applause of a frantic public, was allowed to retire behind the scenes, his eye fell upon Stenio, who was tuning his violin, and he felt amazed at the serene calmness, the air of assurance, of the unknown German artist.

When Franz approached the footlights, he was received with icy coldness. But for all that, he did not feel in the least disconcerted. He looked very pale, but his thin white lips wore a scornful smile as response to this dumb unwelcome. He was sure of his triumph.

At the first notes of the prelude of " The Witches " a
thrill of astonishment passed over the audience. It was
Paganini's touch, and—it was something more. Some—
and they were the majority—thought that never, in his
best moments of inspiration, had the Italian artist himself, in executing that diabolical composition of his, exhibited such an extraordinary diabolical power. Under
the pressure of the long muscular fingers of Franz, the
chords shivered like the palpitating intestines of a dis-
embowelled victim under the vivisector's knife. They
moaned melodiously, like a dying child. The large blue
eye of the artist, fixed with a satanic expression upon the
sounding-board, seemed to summon forth Orpheus himself from the infernal regions, rather than the musical
notes supposed to be generated in the depths of the violin.
Sounds seemed to transform themselves into objective
shapes, thickly and precipitately gathering as at the evo-
cation of a mighty magician, and to be whirling around
him, like a host of fantastic, infernal figures, dancing the
witches' "goat dance." In the empty depths of the
shadowy background of the stage, behind the artist, a
nameless phantasmagoria, produced by the concussion
of unearthly vibrations, seemed to form pictures of
shameless orgies, of the voluptuous hymns of a real
witches' Sabbat. . . . . A collective hallucination
took hold of the public. Panting for breath, ghastly, and
trickling with the icy perspiration of an inexpressible
horror, they sat spell-bound, and unable to break the
spell of the music by the slightest motion. They experienced all the illicit enervating delights of the paradise
of Mahommed, that come into the disordered fancy of
an opium-eating Mussulman, and felt at the same time
the abject terror, the agony of one who struggles against
an attack of *delirium tremens*. . . . . Many ladies

shrieked aloud, others fainted, and strong men gnashed their teeth in a state of utter helplessness. . . .

Then came the *finale*. Thundering uninterrupted applause delayed its beginning, expanding the momentary pause to a duration of almost a quarter of an hour. The bravos were furious, almost hysterical. At last, when after a profound and last bow, Stenio, whose smile was as sardonic as it was triumphant, lifted his bow to attack the famous *finale*, his eye fell upon Paganini, who, calmly seated in the manager's box, had been behind none in zealous applause. The small and piercing black eyes of the Genoese artist were riveted to the Stradivarius in the hands of Franz, but otherwise he seemed quite cool and unconcerned. His rival's face troubled him for one short instant, but he regained his self-possession and, lifting once more his bow, drew the first note.

Then the public enthusiasm reached its acme, and soon knew no bounds. The listeners heard and saw indeed. The witches' voices resounded in the air, and beyond all the other voices, one voice was heard—

> Discordant, and unlike to human sounds ;
> It seem'd of dogs the bark, of wolves the howl ;
> The doleful screechings of the midnight owl ;
> The hiss of snakes, the hungry lion's roar ;
> The sounds of billows beating on the shore ;
> The groan of winds among the leafy wood,
> And burst of thunder from the rending cloud ;—
> 'Twas these, all these in one. . . . .

The magic bow was drawing forth its last quivering sounds—famous among prodigious musical feats—imitating the precipitate flight of the witches before bright dawn ; of the unholy women saturated with the fumes of their nocturnal Saturnalia, when—a strange thing came to pass on the stage. Without the slightest transition, the notes suddenly changed. In their aerial flight of ascension and descent, their melody was unexpectedly altered in character. The sounds became confused, scattered, disconnected . . . . and then—it seemed from the sounding-board of the violin—came out squeaking, jarring tones, like those of a street Punch, screaming at the top of a senile voice:

" Art thou satisfied, Franz, my boy ? . . . . Have not I gloriously kept my promise, eh ? "

The spell was broken. Though still unable to realize the whole situation, those who heard the voice and the *Punchinello*-like tones, were freed, as by enchantment, from the terrible charm under which they had been held. Loud roars of laughter, mocking exclamations of half-anger and half-irritation were now heard from every corner of the vast theatre. The musicians in the orchestra, with faces still blanched from weird emotion, were now seen shaking with laughter, and the whole audience rose, like one man, from their seats, unable yet to solve the enigma ; they felt, nevertheless, too disgusted, too disposed to laugh to remain one moment longer in the building.

But suddenly the sea of moving heads in the stalls and the pit became once more motionless, and stood petrified as though struck by lightning. What all saw was terrible enough—the handsome though wild face of the young artist suddenly aged, and his graceful, erect figure bent down, as though under the weight of years ; but this was nothing to that which some of the most sensitive clearly perceived. Franz Stenio's person now entirely enveloped in a semi-transparent mist, cloud-like, creeping with serpentine motion, and gradually tightening round the living form, as though ready to engulf him. And there were those also who discerned in this tall and ominous pillar of smoke a clearly-defined figure, a form showing the unmistakable outlines of a grotesque and grinning, but terribly awful-looking old man, whose viscera were protruding and the ends of the intestines stretched on the violin.

Within this hazy, quivering veil, the violinist was then seen, driving his bow furiously across the human chords, with the contortions of a demoniac, as we see them represented on mediæval cathedral paintings !

An indescribable panic swept over the audience, and breaking now, for the last time, through the spell which had again bound them motionless, every living creature in the theatre made one mad rush towards the door. It was like the sudden outburst of a dam, a human torrent, roaring amid a shower of discordant notes, idiotic squeakings, prolonged and whining moans, cacophonous cries of frenzy, above which, like the detonations of pistol shots, was heard the consecutive bursting of the four strings stretched upon the sound-board of that bewitched violin.

.   .   .   .

When the theatre was emptied of the last man of the audience, the terrified manager rushed on the stage in search of the unfortunate performer. He was found dead and already stiff, behind the footlights, twisted up into the most unnatural of postures, with the " catguts " wound curiously around his neck, and his violin shattered into a thousand fragments. . . .

When it became publicly known that the unfortunate would-be rival of Niccolo Paganini had not left a cent to pay for his funeral or his hotel-bill, the Genoese, his proverbial meanness notwithstanding, settled the hotel-bill and had poor Stenio buried at his own expense.

He claimed, however, in exchange, the fragments of the Stradivarius—as a memento of the strange event.

THE END.

THE WHITEFRIARS PRESS, LTD., LONDON AND TONBRIDGE.

THE GREEN STAIRCASE

Gilbert Campbell

THE GREEN STAIRCASE.

CHAPTER I.

A SICILIAN HOME.

FROM the days of old, Sicily has been more or less connected with tales and traditions of the supernatural. The straits of Messina were the terror of ancient mariners owing to the dangers of Scylla and Charybdis, whilst the conquered Titan Enceladus lay in his fiery grave beneath the weight of Etna, breathing forth volumes of smoke and sulphurous flame. But in addition to these well-known legends, the woods, valleys, and forests of the island had each and all its mystical inhabitants, fauns, satyrs, and wood nymphs; and as the more graceful superstitions of the classic age faded away, the solitudes were reported to be peopled with a more hideous and more brutish race of monsters, and the prettily toned stories turned into ghastly legends of crime and bloodshed.

Poetic in their temperament, the Sicilians drew deeply upon the treasures of their imagination in the relation of the tales of their beloved island, but it is a fact that strange and weird occurrences have taken place which it is beyond the power of the human mind to explain or fathom.

Some miles from Messina is the small inland town of

Caromo, which lies so far away from the usual tourist track that it has lost but few of its ancient characteristics. The streets are narrow and ill-paved, and the houses which line each side are quaint and bare-looking, with their lower windows defended by a strong network of iron bars. The inhabitants of the little town are full of prejudices and superstitions, and look upon all foreigners with the gravest suspicion, considering them as heretics, whose souls must eventually sink to the lowest pit of perdition. The women were a little given to flirting, and, as the men were extremely jealous, the nocturnal sounds of the guitar were often interrupted by the clash of steel, and the rough stones of the streets were frequently crimsoned by the blood of an assassinated man. Lofty hills clothed with gloomy pine forests surrounded the town, and on various commanding sites amongst the mountains could be seen the residences of the Sicilian aristocracy, which the inhabitants of Caromo dignified by the name of palaces, but which seemed more worthy of the title of prisons.

And yet it was to this strange home of prejudice and superstition than an English family came to take up their abode. Mr. Frederic Bellingham had some six years ago inherited a palace situated in the great square of Caromo from a cousin who had married a Sicilian gentleman, and who, finding herself left alone in the world without children or relatives, bethought her of her distant cousin in England, and bequeathed him a small sum in money and the great gloomy house in Çaromo. Mr. Bellingham, who was at that time in the enjoyment of a large income, did not attach much importance to the unlooked-for legacy, and it was not until a sudden reverse of fortune compelled him to look closely to the expenditure of every penny, that he thought of utilizing the bequest by taking up his residence in the little Sicilian town.

Mr. Bellingham was a widower, with a daughter Isabel,

who was nineteen years of age, and little Dulcie, who was born late in his married life and had not yet attained the ripe age of six. Collecting together the relics of his past grandeur, and after some communications with the British Consul at Messina, the ruined gentleman and his two daughters travelled by the cheapest mode of conveyance to that town, and from thence to Caromo. Mr. Bellingham, and his daughter Isabel, were both good Italian linguists, and the former felt sure that little Dulcie would soon pick up the language of the country in which she was to make her future home.

Upon their arrival at Caromo the travellers put up at the principal inn in the place, known by the title of "The Dancing Lizard," until the house could be put into proper order for their reception. Procuring the keys, which had been left at the office of the Syndic of the town, Mr. Bellingham and Isabel sallied forth to inspect their new abode, leaving Dulcie in charge of the English nurse who had accompanied them.

"You will find the house rather gloomy, Signore," observed the official as he handed over an imposing bunch of keys to the new owner. "I could not get any one to live in it, for our people do not like to reside away from their own homes ; but it has been well looked after for all that, as I am sure you will find."

Mr. Bellingham thanked him for his courtesy, and he and his daughter crossed the square under the guidance of a saturnine Sicilian who appeared, from the sour expression of his face, to be in constant dread lest the English heretics should endeavour to convert him to the creed of their church upon the spot. Halting before a tall gateway set between two massive pillars, he selected the proper key, inserted it in the lock, then throwing open the door he pocketed the gratuity which Mr. Bellingham slipped into his hand, and turning on his heel, crossed the square with the air of a man who was glad that he had completed a disagreeable task.

"Why, papa, it is quite a palace," exclaimed Isabel, as they passed through the great gateway and found themselves in a wide courtyard. "We shall be utterly lost in it."

The house, which was of a massive if not ornamental style of architecture, faced them as they entered; and the side structure, at right-angles with the main building, comprised the stables and servants' offices. The house had a very gloomy appearance, as all the shutters were closed, and there were no signs of life about the place save a few pigeons which sat solemnly upon the projecting stonework with which the roof was ornamented.

"I had certainly no idea that the house was of such a size as this," returned Mr. Bellingham. "Why, it will take a host of servants to keep the place in anything like order. But let us go in and see what the interior is like."

After some trouble the key was discovered that fitted the front door, and Mr. Bellingham and his daughter found themselves in a large entrance-hall paved with squares of black and white marble. There were two long oaken tables upon each side, and the walls were covered with antlers and trophies of rusting arms. At the farther end was a wide staircase, with heavy balustrades which had formerly been richly gilded, but which now had only a few traces of their former grandeur remaining on them.

"Let me open the windows," remarked Mr. Bellingham, "as we go along; the place has been shut up so long that there is quite an unhealthy savour about it."

"It is a little ghost-like," returned Isabel, with a light laugh. "But what a splendid place this hall will be for Dulcie to play about in when the weather is wet."

The Englishman and his daughter went from room to room. They found long reception-rooms, with full-length portraits of the dead-and-gone members of the old Sicilian family fastened upon the walls in quaint frames of gilded plaster. The rooms were full of strange spindle-legged furniture, which the slightest touch would send crashing to the ground ; whilst the long corridors which ran through the house from end to end were filled with cabinets containing choice specimens of china. Behind the house stretched extensive pleasure-grounds, extending as far as the ancient wall which still surrounds a portion of the town of Caromo. A portion of the grounds were thickly wooded with clumps of tall trees, which threw a funereal gloom for many yards beyond their stems ; whilst the remainder was laid out in the hideous Dutch fashion, with closely-cropped hedges, and leaden effigies of gods and goddesses standing in rockwork grottoes or dried-up fountains.

Facing the garden, on the first floor of the house was a long picture-gallery, in which powdered gentlemen stood side by side with fair dames in widely-hooped petticoats, whilst stalwart warriors glared grim defiance at sleek-looking ecclesiastics. This gallery ran the whole length of the house, and had fourteen windows, all looking into the pleasure-grounds. The bedrooms were great rambling barns, with wardrobes in them of such a size that, as Isabel remarked, not only a single robber, but a whole horde of banditti could conceal themselves within their recesses.

At length, when every portion of the house had been explored, the father and daughter came to a low doorway situated in an oddly-formed corner of one of the upper corridors.

"Where can this lead to, I wonder?" demanded Mr. Bellingham.

"We will soon see that," returned Isabel, bending forward with the bunch of keys in her hand. But her efforts were all in vain, for a strong plate of iron had been securely screwed over the keyhole, and no orifice had been left for the insertion of the key. "This is curious," said the girl, dropping upon her knees so as to look more closely into the method by which the door had been made secure. "And see, papa," she added, as she examined the plate more narrowly, "there are some words engraved on it."

Mr. Bellingham carefully wiped his glasses, and bending down his head, tried what he could make of the words to which Isabel had alluded.

"'La Scala Verde,'" read he. "Why, what on earth can that mean?"

"The Green Staircase, of course," returned his daughter. "But why should there be a staircase here? and where does it go to?"

Mr. Bellingham took a few minutes to consider, stepped across the corridor to one of the windows, and glanced downwards.

"The corridor," remarked he, after a short further consideration, "is exactly over the picture-gallery, so that this curious staircase which we have discovered must lead into it. Odd, though, we never saw any door in the gallery except the one by which we entered."

"Why are you so positive that it must go into the picture-gallery?" demanded Isabel.

"Because the entrance-hall is open up to the roof, and the flooring of the picture-gallery is visible from it. It would therefore be impossible for any staircase to pass it without its being visible from beneath," returned Mr. Bellingham.

"I suppose you are right, papa," answered Isabel, making a slight grimace. "However, I will allow that it gives me rather a creepy feeling when I think that I am living in a house that has a staircase we cannot go up or down, and which apparently leads to nowhere."

"Pooh, pooh! Isabel," answered Mr. Bellingham; "you are too fond of letting your imagination run away with you.

I dare say, after all, the solution of the mystery is a most simple one. But mind you do not put any foolish ideas into Sarah Hartley's head; she is an Essex woman, and full of foolish ideas and superstitions."

"Really, papa, you must think me as silly as Sarah, when you consider it necessary to give me such a caution," answered Isabel, with an air of offended dignity; for since her mother's death she had been entrusted with the conduct and guidance of the household.

"There, Isabel," replied Mr. Bellingham, a little testily, "don't get into one of your tantrums. I think that we have been all over the house now, and had better return to our hotel, and see about getting our luggage conveyed over here. Dear me, dear me," he added, with a sigh, "we shall want at least three servants to look after this great rambling barrack. I hope to goodness wages are not high in this outlandish part of the world."

They returned to the hotel, and then Mr. Bellingham's troubles began. All his efforts to obtain servants were utterly futile. The landlord assured him that the girls of Caromo could not bear the idea of service in a dull, quiet household, and preferred lower wages and a more cheerful abode; whilst the Syndic, to whom he applied in his despair, gravely declared that the inhabitants of the island were too haughty and proud to accept menial service, and advised him to procure his domestics from Reggio, on the other side of the straits, as the Italians were more accustomed to be commanded than the freeborn Sicilian.

In the end a compromise was effected, and an arrangement entered into by which the landlord of "The Dancing Lizard" agreed to send in all the meals of the Bellingham family, and a discharged soldier and his mother were found, who for a trifling consideration agreed to live in the house and do the rough work.

"My mother is old, Excellenza," remarked the soldier,

philosophically, "and won't last much longer, so a little
fright more or less will not cause her much injury. As
for me, I have quarrelled with the Church in the shape of
my padre ; so as I am certain—so he assures me—to fall
into the clutches of Satan, it matters little whether I asso-
ciate with heretics and phantoms during the remainder of
my life on this earth."

In the course of a week the Bellinghams had taken
possession of their new home, which was known as the
Palazzo Spordese. Mr. Bellingham was delighted to find
that living in Caromo was both cheap and good, and that
small as his income now was, it compared favourably with
that of the neighbouring gentry. The fact of all his family
having been members of the Church of Rome also told
considerably in his favour, and by degrees he began to find
the doors of society opening to him. Isabel, who was a
perfect type of a fair-haired English beauty, found numerous
admirers amongst the dark-skinned scions of noble Sicilian
families ; and for a time the daily life of the Bellinghams
was a constant round of innocent enjoyment and harmless
gaiety.

Sarah Hartley was the only one of the family who did
not look upon her surroundings with a very pleasant eye.
Her mother had been what is termed "a notable woman "
in a sequestered Essex village, and the young woman had
from her earliest youth imbibed a wonderful amount of
weird tales and strange superstitions. She was therefore
very nervous at being compelled to thread the dark, dimly-
lighted passages of the Palazzo after nightfall, and had a
habit of uttering suppressed shrieks, and dropping plates
and dishes, under the impression that the shadows she
caught sight of were spectral visitants. Little Dulcie,
however, was charmed with her new abode, and rambled
over the great house without displaying a symptom of fear.
The picture-gallery was, however, her chosen resort. She

would convey her playthings thither, and would hold long
imaginary conversations with the pictured ladies and gentlemen upon the walls. The leaden gods and goddesses
in the Dutch garden were a source of constant admiration,
and she would pass many hours in rapt contemplation of
them.

The visitors at the Bellinghams' used at first to put many
veiled questions as to whether the English family had experienced any annoyance in their new abode, but as the
questions were always answered in the negative, these
queries ceased to be put.

At first Isabel had been much exercised in her mind in
regard to the closed door with the strange inscription upon
it, and had even gone so far as to consult Lorenzo Spaleto,
the military domestic, on the subject; but the ex-soldier,
however much of a freethinker he might be considered in
ecclesiastical matters, was a firm believer in matters supernatural, and gave his opinion with the greatest gravity—
that doubtless an evil spirit was shut up behind the door,
and that it would be an act of utter madness to let him out
to vex the house, and to disturb the dwellers in it by his
uncanny presence.

Things had gone on thus peacefully for some time, and
the exquisite Sicilian summer had now set in, so that many
were the little parties that assembled after the heat of the
day was over in the extensive gardens of the Palazzo
Spordese. It was after one of these reunions that Sarah
Hartley sought the chamber of her young mistress. The
woman was evidently a prey to some violent agitation, and
Isabel, who was always a kind and considerate mistress, told
her to be seated, and begged her to tell her what was the
cause of her trouble.

"Well, Miss Isabel, if you must know," replied Sarah, "it
is because my heart is clean breaking. I can't stay in this
gloomy hole, which is as full of ghosts as an egg is of meat,

though you all pretend that you see nothing of them. Then there's that blessed child Dulcie — how can I leave the sweet darling? though it goes to my heart to see her flacking about the great lonesome rooms, and, above all, making a point of staying in the picture-gallery. I'm sure all those ladies and gentlemen follow me with their eyes; and then Miss Dulcie says in her innocent way, 'Don't you be afraid of them, Sarah—they are all very good to little Dulcie;' and with that she'll up and speak to them in a way that makes the very blood run cold in my veins. I can't stand it any longer, Miss Isabel; and so, if you please, send me home to Malden, where, if there are ghosts, they have respectable English ways, and stick to one place, and don't come out in sneaking foreign fashion, flustering one's very soul out of their body."

"I really don't understand you, Sarah," returned Isabel. "You seem in a most uncomfortable frame of mind. Have you seen anything to frighten you?"

"Don't you ask me any such questions," answered Sarah, mysteriously. "I wouldn't frighten you or make you as nervous as I am for heaps of untold gold; but all I know is that I can't abide these dark passages any longer. When I go up to bed it seems as if there was a something walking behind me, and when I do pluck up courage to look round, then it starts up in front of me, and sends a regular chill right through my marrow. I shall have to stick close to my room, Miss, and not come down any more, or I shall go clean dazed with the horrors."

"But surely, Sarah, Lorenzo would see you through the passages, and then you wouldn't feel so frightened," suggested Isabel.

"He, the silly clown!" retorted the nursemaid with much contempt. "I beg your pardon, Miss Isabel, but he makes things worse. He's always talking about that trumpery quarrel of his about the fat pullet that was missing from

Father Anselm's poultry-yard, and saying that he is so utterly beyond the pale of salvation, that his very presence would be sufficient to invoke every demon and goblin within the next fifty miles. A nice sort of protection is Lorenzo."

"Well, Sarah, of course if you must go, I can't prevent your doing so," returned her mistress; "but I tell you plainly that poor Dulcie will cry out her pretty little eyes at your loss."

"And that's what frets me, too, Miss Isabel," returned Sarah. "I can't bear the thoughts of parting with the pretty lamb. Ah, if that handsome young Count Monteleone would make up his mind and take you and she and me to the handsome villa they say he has at Palermo, I wouldn't think of going back to Essex for all the rest of my life."

Isabel blushed, for certainly Count Alberto Monteleone, a handsome young Sicilian of twenty-four years of age, and as rich as he was good-looking, had been rather particular in his attentions for the past few weeks.

"Hush, Sarah," said she, gently, "you must not talk like that. If you like, I will speak to papa to-morrow; but I wish you would think over the matter during the night, for you know how much we shall all miss you. And now good-night. Do you think you can get to your room alone, or shall I come with you and take care of you?"

"The idea, Miss," replied the nursemaid valiantly. "I'm not afraid up here, not a mite. Good-night. I wish I could make up my mind to stay, or that Count Monteleone would make up his mind to take you away."

She walked away bravely enough, and evidently reached her room without much cause of alarm, for beyond a stifled shriek, the crash of a falling candlestick, the hurried sound of footsteps and the hasty slamming and bolting of a door, were the only apparent signs of her progress to her sleeping apartment.

Left alone to herself, Isabel thoughtfully placed aside the book which she had been perusing at the moment of Sarah Hartley's entrance.

"Can there be anything in what the girl says," thought she ; "and have the strange forebodings some real foundation after all—the sense of some weird horror that, though invisible, appears to be ever present, and, as Sarah describes, seems to be following close behind me through these long echoing corridors? I have mentioned these feelings to my father, but he has always laughed at me, and at his command I have striven to crush down the fear into the innermost recesses of my heart. But it is useless, and Sarah's words have roused them all again. How often have I awoke in the silent watches of the night, bathed in a cold perspiration, and feeling that a hideous something was standing within a few feet of my bed, ready to spring upon me with a terrible cry ; then again, how the words 'On the Green Staircase' haunt me, without my being able for a moment to fathom their meaning. I will speak to my father to-morrow, for I feel that my brain will give way under this continued pressure."

Rising from her seat, she threw herself upon her knees by her bed, and sought refuge in prayer from the harm that she felt was closing round her.

CHAPTER II.

IN THE PICTURE-GALLERY.

THE prayer she had breathed seemed to refresh her, for Isabel sank into a refreshing sleep, and the next morning awoke in a much calmer state of mind. She had scarcely completed her toilet when Sarah Hartley entered the room. "If you please, Miss," began she, before Isabel could utter a word, "I have been thinking over what I said last night, and I had rather that you would not say a word to the master about it.   I dare say I shall get used to this remarkable old house presently; and after I got to my room I laid out the cards, and there plain enough was a 'removal from a great house with a fresh settlement,' which I take it means that pretty villa near Palermo that I was talking about last night——"

"Sarah," interrupted Isabel, "have you forgotten that I forbade you to speak on that topic again?"

"All right, Miss Isabel; but I suppose I may tell you that he is here?"

"He; whom are you talking about, Sarah?" returned Isabel, endeavouring to throw an air of serenity into her pretty features.

"Why, of Count Alberto Monteleone, of course," replied the nursemaid, with a roguish smile.   "He is sitting on the terrace smoking cigarettes with the master, and Mr. Bellingham sent me up to you to say that he would be glad if you could manage to come down directly."

"Very well; go and tell papa that I will be with him almost immediately," replied Isabel, to whose cheek a delicate pink flush had risen at the mention of Alberto Monteleone's name.

The girl hastened from the room, and Isabel, after a farewell glance at the mirror, followed her without further delay.

Alberto and her father were seated at a small table which had been placed in the veranda which covered a portion of the terrace, and Lorenzo was just placing some covered dishes upon it.   There was an expression of extreme contentment upon the face of Mr. Bellingham, and the young Count's features were radiant with happiness.   Both rose to their feet as the young girl made her appearance, and at the conclusion of the meal Mr. Bellingham, rising from his seat and excusing himself on the plea of having letters to write, left her and Alberto alone together. For a few seconds they remained without uttering a word, and then the Count spoke.

"Will you not come for a stroll through the grounds, Signorina Isabella?" said he. "The sun is hot, but there is plenty of shade underneath the trees."

Isabel put on a broad-brimmed straw hat which lay upon a chair by her side, and accepted the arm which the young man gaily offered her.

"You seem in excellent spirits to-day, Count," remarked she, after they had reached the grateful shade of the tall trees.

"And well I may be," answered Alberto, "for I feel that I am the happiest man in the world."

"Then you occupy a very enviable position," retorted Isabel, playfully. "Pray can you not tell me how I can attain to a similar one?"

"It is my earnest wish to do so," replied the Count, with a sudden gravity, "but I am half afraid to tell you how."

"Why should you be so?" replied Isabel, opening her eyes in extreme surprise.

"Though our acquaintance has been a brief one, I feel that we can talk like old friends already. I have been speaking to your father."

"That is a simple recipe," returned Isabel; "and if the doing so is your sole secret, I ought to be the happiest girl in the world, for I do so every day."

"Pray be serious for a moment," answered Monteleone. "Shall I tell you the subject of our conversation?"

"If you please," answered Isabel, casting her eyes upon the ground with a sudden access of shyness.

"Do you not know that I love you?" cried the young Sicilian, bursting out with all the impassioned fervour of his race. "Can it be that my passion for you has passed unnoticed, and that I have not succeeded in touching your heart? To-day I told all to your father, and it was his reply that gave me such intense happiness, and now it remains for you to place the last stone upon the pinnacle of my hopes. Isabel, dearest Isabel, have you no tender feeling for me, and do you not think that you could pass your life with me in one long dream of happiness?"

He had made himself master of her hand as he was speaking, and was covering it with impassioned kisses, gazing into her eyes with an expression of the deepest affection.

Isabel did not attempt to withdraw her fingers from his grasp, but she uttered no word.

"Have I offended you, *caressima mia?*" continued the young man. "Have I been too sudden? Will you not let your heart speak one little word in response to all that I have said? The Signore Bellingham offers no objection to our union; our faith is the same; and though you are a child of cold Britain, yet you have the tongue and the vivacity of a daughter of the sunny South."

No woman, innocent though she may be, is ignorant of the feelings of admiration that she has inspired in a man's heart, and Isabel had for some time realized the love that the young Count bore her. Her own heart, too, had spoken, and it was with a feeling of the deepest happiness that, looking down into her lover's face, she answered with perfect confidence, "Yes, Alberto, I *do* love you, and I fully share your happiness."

With a bound the young man sprang to his feet, and grasping the unresisting form of Isabel in his arms, pressed a fond kiss upon her lips.

Then they wandered arm in arm under the leafy arcade of the trees, indulging in all those airy castles of the future which lovers delight in piling up. The hours passed away, and found the lovers still conversing; but they had now found a more matter-of-fact topic of conversation, and Isabel was confiding to her lover the strange feelings of fear that had recently crept over her.

"It is a curious old house, certainly," answered Alberto, thoughtfully. "I presume you knew nothing of the Castrucci family into which your cousin married?"

"No," replied Isabel. "All communication with her ceased soon after her marriage, and it was not for some time after her death that we heard of her having left us this old house."

"She lived very happily with her husband—at least, so I have heard," remarked Alberto, "and was deeply affected by his sudden decease. But there have been strange stories with regard to other members of the family in times gone by, and there is a terrible legend connected with Baldassare Castrucci, the grandfather of your cousin's husband."

"Indeed!" cried the girl, gazing eagerly into her lover's face; "and pray is that legend in any way connected with the Green Staircase?"

"How did you hear anything about that?" exclaimed Monteleone, starting back in surprise. "I know that all your Sicilian friends have carefully abstained from mentioning it to you."

"We found a closed doorway with that name inscribed upon it the first day that papa and I went through the house," exclaimed Isabel; "but, oddly enough, we could find no other communication with it on the floor below."

"I think that I could show it to you," replied the Count, with a quiet smile.

"Will you tell me the story about Baldassare Castrucci? I should like to know the worst," said Isabel.

"It is a sad tale," returned Monteleone, "but perhaps it is best that you should hear it—though I hope that you will not much longer remain within reach of the evil influence which is unquestionably at work within these walls."

Isabel blushed at the meaning glance with which he accompanied these words, and permitted him to lead her to a bench, when, taking his seat beside her, he commenced his story.

"Baldassare Castrucci was the owner of this old Palazzo at the time when the French troops, under the command of General Regnier, were carrying fire and sword through the island, and was one of the staunchest supporters of Queen Caroline. He was a man, so I have heard, of a sombre and saturnine disposition, and but a sorry companion for the young and beautiful wife he had taken to himself, Agneta Paltozzi. Baldassare was too old a man to offer himself as a member of the *Masse*, as the volunteer force which had been raised to defend the island from French aggression was termed; but he was a wise counsellor, and had the command of plenty of money, and was consequently a good deal absent from home on various missions of the greatest importance to the national cause. It was reported that his young wife chafed and fretted a good deal at the solitary life she led, and at the frequent taunts which her husband hurled at her head with regard to the conduct of her brother, who was reported to be favourable to the annexation of Sicily by the French. Matters went on in this uncomfortable manner for some time; but one evening, after a brief absence on public affairs, Baldassare Castrucci suddenly shut up the Palazzo, and dismissed all his servants, alleging as his reason for doing so that his wife and he could no longer live comfortably together, and that she had gone over to stay with some distant relatives on the mainland, until some definite understanding could be arrived at between them. Servants, however, will gossip, and some of them spoke to having heard angry words between their master and mistress, whilst the gardener declared that he had seen a man let himself down from the Signora's window just as his master entered her chamber. The country, however, was in too great a state of ferment to occupy itself with the quarrels of the lord and lady of the Palazzo Spordese, or even with the total disappearance of the fair châtelaine, and so the matter was permitted to drop.

" Baldassare Castrucci did not long survive the destruction of his matrimonial happiness, for Miguel Paltozzi the brother of the missing Agneta, who had now openly joined the invading forces, rode up one day to the Palazzo at the head of a detachment of French Dragoons, and finding Baldassare at home, hung him over his own door as an encourager of sedition. It is reported that Miguel offered the prisoner his life if he would tell what had become of his sister, but Baldassare sternly refused. ' She was as false to her husband, as her brother has been to his country,' said he, ' and whatever her fate was she fully merited it.'

" 'She was never false to you, Castrucci,' retorted the young man, ' though your harshness and severity might have led many another woman to forget the vows she had plighted at the altar.'

" ' It is a lie ; I saw her lover descend from her window when I returned home somewhat unexpectedly,' answered Castrucci, with an angry scrowl.

" ' It is you who lie !' exclaimed the young man furiously, ' for it was I whom you saw. I was hunted by a party of the Masse, and sought an asylum with my sister ; but when she heard of your return she urged me to fly, for she knew your savage and vindictive temper too well to trust her brother's life in your hands.'

" But Baldassare Castrucci remained obstinate, and died without divulging his secret.

" Miguel Paltozzi remained for a few moments contemplating the body of his brother-in-law as it swung backwards and forwards, and then thrusting it aside entered the house, calling upon half-a-dozen of the dragoons to follow him and search the premises. After a strict peregrination through the

rooms on the ground-floor they ascended to the great
drawing-room, which is now used as the picture-gallery, and
from which a private way, known as the Green Staircase, led
to the floor above.   Casting a hasty glance round the room,
Miguel Paltozzi, who was well acquainted with the premises,
advanced to the door behind the hangings which led to
the Green Staircase.   As he threw it open, a pestilential
vapour issued forth which caused him to stagger back with
a faint cry of surprise.   In an instant, however, followed by
two of the soldiers, he darted up the stairs, and found the
dead body of Agneta Castrucci stretched upon the first
landing, with a deep sword-wound in her bosom and Baldassare Castrucci's silver-hilted rapier lying by her side, with
its blade blackened and discoloured.   The beautiful face of
the young woman was discoloured by the hue of decompo-
sition, and in the fingers of her right hand was clutched a
lock of iron grey hair which had once evidently grown upon
the head of the late Baldassare Castrucci.

"Whilst the brother was standing gazing upon the murdered
body of his sister, and even the rough soldiers who had
followed him could hardly restrain their emotion, the loud
blast of a trumpet was heard, followed by pistol shots and
the clashing of steel.   Rushing back to the drawing-room,
they saw their comrades retreating backwards into the house
followed by a dense crowd of armed peasantry.   The
Frenchmen, with Paltozzi at their head, made a desperate
attempt to cut their way through the foe, but it was a vain
one, and not a man amongst them escaped.   The con-
querors left them where they fell, and it was not until some
months afterwards, when the country had become a little
quieter, and the kin of Baldassare Castrucci came to take
possession of his property, that the skeleton form of Agneta
was found lying where she had been struck down upon the
landing-place of the Green Staircase.

" The remembrance of the tragedy which had been enacted

almost within the four walls of the drawing-room made it
distasteful to the new possessor, and it was turned into a
picture-gallery, whilst the door of the staircase which opened
on to the upper floor of the Palazzo was nailed up, and the
ill-omened stairs never again used as a means of communication."

Alberto Monteleone paused and passed his handerchief
across his forehead ; he had told the terrible tale with all the
vivacity of his southern blood, and the effort had been a
severe one.

"No wonder I have felt uncomfortable in a house where
such a sad tragedy has taken place," murmured Isabel,
laying her hand softly upon the Count's arm. "But, Alberto
dear, can you guess what is occupying my mind at present?
I do not think you can ; it is so frivolous that I am half
ashamed to confess it. I should so dearly like to know
where the door of the Green Staircase is, for in spite of
the many times I have been in the picture-gallery, I have
never yet seen any signs of it."

"Your curiosity on that hand can easily be satisfied,"
answered Monteleone, with a smile. "If you dare to
venture with me into the gallery, I will show it to you at
once. Evening has not yet set in, so that I do not think
you need fear risking a visit there."

"As if I could have any fear whilst I am with you!"
answered the girl, with a bright smile of confidence. "Come
along ; really I shall feel much more at ease when I have set
my mind at rest upon this point."

Together they left the shade of the trees, and crossing the
open space entered the wide hall, which seemed strangely
cool after their long sojourn in the open air ; and then
ascending the staircase, pushed open the red-baize door and
entered the picture-gallery. Though the sun was still high
in the heavens there were always gloomy nooks and deep
shadows in the gallery, and Isabel could not repress a

shudder as she fancied that the eyes of the portraits that hung upon the walls followed her movements with a glance of reproof, as if to censure the idle curiosity that had led her to intrude upon their solitude.

Monteleone led her about half-way down the long gallery, and then pausing before a half-length portrait of the size of life, whispered, in impressive accents, "*Baldassare Castrucci.*"

Isabel started violently, and then bending forward, took an attentive survey of the canvas before her. It represented an elderly man with a sallow complexion and sharp irregular features ; the thin cruel mouth was hardly hidden by a scanty moustache, but it was the expression of the eyes that attracted the girl's attention the most. They were filled with spite and malignancy, and blazed with a lurid fire.

"This picture moves on hinges," continued Monteleone, "and behind it is the door leading to the Green Staircase. Shall I make the spring work ?"

"Not for worlds !" answered the girl, as she clung timidly to her lover's arm. "I should expect to see something terrible behind it. Let us go away, Alberto."

As she spoke, however, she still kept her eyes riveted on the portrait as though it exercised some strange power of fascination over her, and did not attempt to move from the spot.

"How dark it has suddenly grown !" exclaimed the Count ; "and dear me, who would have expected this cold wind, which seems to chill the very marrow in my bones ?"

Receiving no answer from Isabel he turned towards her, and was horrified at the change that had taken place in her appearance. She was gazing over her shoulder with eyes widely dilated with terror, and her lips parted as if at any moment a pent-up shriek might burst through them, and every fibre and muscle in her body was quivering and vibrating with the intensity of her emotion.

She too had perceived the sudden darkness, and had felt

the icy chill, but in addition she had heard a sound behind her resembling a soft though deep-drawn sigh, and turning rapidly round to ascertain the cause of it, had been confronted by the exact counterpart of the portrait standing a few paces behind her.

Yes, there stood Baldassare Castrucci exactly as the painter's art had traced his features upon the canvas. There was the same hard, cruel smile upon the lips and the same lurid glow in the eyes, but the rest of the form was wavering and indistinct. For a few seconds the thing remained there, striking terror into her inmost soul, and then vanished away as suddenly as it had appeared, whilst Isabel, with a wild shriek which rang through the old Palazzo, sank senseless into her lover's arms.

Monteleone had not seen the apparition, but his quick perception descried that something was wrong, and clasping her to his breast he bore her swiftly from the gallery.

At the door he was met by Mr. Bellingham and Lorenzo, who had been alarmed by her shrill cry, whilst the pale face of Sarah Hartley could be discerned bending over the banisters with little Dulcie in her arms.

By slow degrees Isabel came back to life, and as soon as she was able gave her father an exact account of the terrible apparition that had appeared to her. Mr. Bellingham, however, was not at all given to superstitious leanings, and prided himself on being able to account for the strangest and most unheard-of events by natural causes.

"My dear child," said he, "do not give way too much to the follies of imagination. You had been listening to a most lugubrious story which Alberto was silly enough to relate to you, and from hearing it you go straight to the picture-gallery and gaze intently upon the ugliest portrait on the walls—that of Baldassare Castrucci. What is the result? Why, simply that the old scoundrel's portrait is firmly imprinted upon the retina of the eye, so that when you turn

round you see him for a few seconds as distinctly as if the
canvas were still before you.   If you brought common sense
to bear upon every ghost story you hear, you would find them
as easily explained away as the present one."

"Oh, indeed, sir!" exclaimed Sarah Hartley, who had
descended the stairs and was standing close by.   "Then
will you please account for how it was that a night or two
ago I woke up and missed that blessed child Dulcie from
my side? At first I was properly scared, as you may imagine,
but then all of a jump it came to me that the dear little
creature had been winnicking about having left her doll in
the picture-gallery, and wanted me to go down and fetch it.
You may be sure I wasn't going to do anything of the kind,
but gave her a sweet cake and told her she should have it
again to-morrow.   She fretted a great deal, but after a time
cried herself to sleep.   Now I felt sure that the artful little
puss had only waited until I had dropped off, and had then
crept down to fetch dolly.   I bundled a few clothes on, and
though I felt my heart going like a mill-race I stole down to
the gallery, for I was determined that my poor lamb should
not come to any harm if it was in my power to prevent it.

"When I opened the door I fairly gave a jump, for the
whole place seemed a blaze of light—not a right-down honest
one, but a greeny sort of glare, which, however, lighted up
every nook and corner in the room.   Right in the middle
of it was my little lambkin in her nightdress, toddling along
on her bare tootsies hugging dolly to her breast.   Then, to
my surprise, I saw that there was a sight of finely-dressed
ladies and gentlemen bending over the little pet and making
as if they would fondle and caress her.   I thought it main
wrong for them to encourage the little tyrant to be running
about the house at that hour, and so I up and says in
my best Italian: 'I really think, ladies and gentlemen,
that——' when all at once I glances round and I see all the
frames empty, and that the fine ladies and gentlemen were

only the pictures a-walking about as if they were alive. I make no more bones, but I runs forward and catches up the little angel and makes off for the nursery as fast as my legs would carry me, and as I done so out goes the light and there is a little titter of a very strange kind of laughter. Can you account for that, sir?"

"Of course I can," answered Mr. Bellingham, calmly. "You ate a good supper, did you not, Sarah, before you went to bed that night?"

"I mostly do, sir," was the reply.

"Then you dreamed it all," retorted her master, decisively. "It was just a nightmare dream, and nothing more. Take care and not eat so heartily again, my girl, or you may have biliousness for it."

"I didn't make a hog of myself," answered the indignant nursemaid.

"And the proof that what I am saying is the truth," continued her master, "is, that little Dulcie was not a bit frightened, and did not know a word about it the next morning," went on Mr. Bellingham.

"No, sir; the aggravating little toad, when I told her if she went there any more she would be eaten by ghosts, just said, 'Who toasts?'" answered the aggrieved Sarah, turning away in high dudgeon.

"Stop, Sarah!" exclaimed Mr. Bellingham, as the nursemaid reached the nursery door. "Perhaps it was not eating too much that caused this."

"And what was it then, sir?" inquired Sarah, turning round.

"Drinking too much of that red wine," returned her master, pleasantly. "Take care, Sarah; it is stronger than you—— "

But the rest of his words were drowned in the slam of the door, as the indignant damsel took refuge in her own domain.

"I think I have laid both your ghosts," remarked Mr. Bellingham. "And now, my dear Count, see if you cannot persuade my daughter to give you a little music before dinner."

His assured manner, and the confidence with which he spoke, for a time made Isabel believe that she must have been the victim to some strange optical delusion, and the remembrance of her newly-found happiness chased away the clouds that had been closing around her ever since she had taken up her residence in the ill-fated Palazzo Spordese. She played and sang with her customary taste and execution, and during dinner chatted upon various subjects with her usual ease and fluency; and it was not until after she and her father had accompanied the Count to the great gateway, and the magic spell which his presence had appeared to cast around the place had faded away, that the feeling of depression began again to surround her, and her mind once again reverted to the sad fate of Agneta Castrucci, the details of which had been so graphically related by her lover during the hours that she had passed with him beneath the trees in the old-fashioned garden.

As she passed by the closed door of the Green Staircase on her way to her sleeping-chamber, she could not avoid pausing for a moment and listening intently. Her imagination was wrought up to the highest pitch, and she almost fancied that she could hear sounds of stifled altercation proceeding from within, then a faint shriek, a heavy fall, and the sound of ascending footsteps. She waited for no more, but with terror lending its aid to her feet, fled away in the direction of her chamber, and, after carefully securing the door, stayed for a moment palpitating and trembling, as if she momentarily expected some spectral summons to give admission to a something which she felt it would be death to gaze upon. Nothing of the sort, however, occurred, and after the first spasm of alarm had passed away, she once again took refuge in prayer, and rose from her knees with a calmer mind, as she had done on the previous night.

Her slumber was not, however, of a peaceful nature, and when she awoke again it was still dark, and she lay awake trembling until at last the welcome beams of the morning dispelled, to a great extent, the hideous phantoms of the night. To-day she would see Alberto again; to-day she would hear the music of his voice; and perhaps in a few brief weeks she would be enabled to leave the Palazzo Spordese, and all the spectral inhabitants that made a sojourn within its walls a kind of long-protracted agony.

CHAPTER III.

THE COMING OF HYMEN.

THE sun rose bright and gloriously, and the young Count Alberto Monteleone visited the Palazzo Spordese as soon as the rules of etiquette would permit of his doing so. Fortunately in Sicily, and especially in a little town like Caromo, early visits are not forbidden, and by ten o'clock Isabel had the happiness of seeing her lover arrive. To-day they did not at first go into the garden, but sat in one of the half-lighted drawing-rooms, and, with hand clasped in hand, discussed the future of the life that was about to open before them. Their pleasant conversation was disturbed by a tapping at the door, and, on permission being given, the ex-soldier Lorenzo Spaleto entered.

"It is no use, Signorina," began he, plunging at once into the subject; "I shall have to turn out of the most comfortable quarters that I have been in for many a long day. You see, though I am an out-and-out reprobate and have no hopes of future bliss, yet I have some regard for the old woman, and as she won't stay here any longer, out I must go too."

"What do you mean?" asked Isabel. "And pray why will not your mother remain with us?—it is only a day or two ago that she was telling me how comfortable she was."

"And so she was; and I am sure that she will always speak of you and the Signore Bellingham as the kindest people that she has ever met with, and that she had no idea that the *forestieri* could be so nice. But I knew how it would be. You see we are getting on to the 17th of June, and of course everything that keeps about the old place is all up and about."

"You are forgetting yourself, Lorenzo," remarked the Count, severely. "Was it not an agreed thing that nothing was to be said about——"

"Yes, yes, Excellenza, I know," returned the man, raising his hand to his forehead after the style of a military salute; "but you see that the 17th is near, and when that comes they will be as nice as every one else; besides, old Baldassare Castrucci has begun his pranks earlier than usual this year."

"Lorenzo," said Isabel, assuming an air of authority, "of course if you insist upon leaving you must do so; but I think you ought to tell me your reasons for so doing. You need not be alarmed at committing yourself, for I am perfectly acquainted with what you are alluding to."

"Well, then, if you must have it, Signorina," answered the man, twirling his fingers one over the other in great embarrassment, "you must. You see, the dear old madre is very anxious about me, and spends all her time in thinking how she can get me out of my scrape with the Church——"

"Your scrape with the Church, indeed, you idle vagabond!" retorted Alberto, with a laugh. "Why all that Father Anselm ever said was that there was a fine chicken missing from his poultry-yard, and that as you had been

seen loitering near, he expected you had been playing some
of your old soldier's tricks, and going on a foraging expedition.   And upon this you have built up your fable of being
cast out of the Church; more, I think, for the purpose of
avoiding paying your religious dues than anything else."

"It is all very well for you, Excellenza, to make fun of a
serious matter," returned Lorenzo, with an affectation of deep
grief; "but I know what I heard, and so does my poor old
mother.   Well, as I was saying, she is always trying to do
something for her wicked son, and last night she went out
to a late service, and when I found that she didn't come
home I went out to look for her, and found the dear old
thing shivering outside the great gate, crossing herself as
fast as she could, and reeling out *aves* and *credos* by the
yard.   I asked her why she did not come in, and after
a great deal of difficulty I managed to get out of her that
just as she was raising her hand to knock at the gate it
opened of its own accord, and old Baldassare Castrucci
came out, glared at her for a moment, and then deliberately
hung himself up on the old iron hook which still remains
there, and swung about, beating the door with his feet, and
with his eyes and tongue protruding, just as they did when
Miguel Paltozzi and his French dragoons hauled him up
like a dog.   Well, Signorina, you can imagine the old
woman's terror; she ran back to what she considered a safe
distance, and, falling on her knees, began to call with all
her might upon the saints for protection.   She declares that
the horrid thing kept swinging and dangling there for more
than half an hour, and then when it vanished as suddenly
as it had appeared, she was too terrified to venture through
the gateway lest she should again encounter the same grisly
apparition."

Isabel turned so pale at this narrative, that the Count
angrily called upon the man to cease.

"You blockhead!" exclaimed he; "do you not see that

you are frightening the Signorina into fits with your silly stories? Why, your old mother is nearly in her dotage; and it is only kind people like the Englishman and his daughter who would be bothered with such a useless old bundle of grumbling. She fancied the whole thing, for what with religion and ghosts her brain is fairly addled."

"Whether her brains are addled or not, Signore Count," answered the man sulkily, "she insists on going, and so do I. If the develries are beginning so early this year, no one can say what sort of a 17th of June we shall have."

"What does he mean by the 17th of June?" whispered Isabel.

"It was the day upon which Agneta Castrucci was murdered," returned her lover, in the same tone.

The deadly pallor which had spread over the girl's face now gave way to a bright scarlet as the blood rushed to her brain, and for a moment almost deprived her of her senses. By a powerful effort, however, she recovered the mastery of them, and informed Lorenzo that she could not undertake to decide in so important a matter, and that he must go to Mr. Bellingham, who was in the library at that moment.

The man retired somewhat sullenly, and then, with a scared face, Isabel turned to her lover, saying—

"Can this be true; and is this old place the haunt of the denizens of the other world at a certain time of the year? Why, if I had seen what old Teresa Spaleto says she witnessed, I should have gone entirely out of my mind."

"Well, to tell you the truth," answered Alberto, "ever since the terrible events which I related to you, it has been the custom of the Castrucci family to leave the Palazzo Spordese for a few days before and after the 17th; and I shall, if you will permit me, suggest to your father that it will be well for him to follow the custom of the family."

"Oh, do please try and persuade him," exclaimed Isabel, eagerly. "Why, gloomy and uncomfortable as the chambers at 'The Dancing Lizard' were, they would seem like Paradise to me after the terrors that I have endured here."

" I certainly should not suggest your taking up your residence at 'The Dancing Lizard;' that old thing Giuseppe Lambri made quite enough out of you during the few days you stayed there; besides, I know of a place that you would be happier in, humble though it may be," returned Alberto, with a smile.

" I do not care how humble it is, provided it is far enough away from this dreadful place, and that there is sufficient accommodation," answered Isabel.

" It is some ten miles away on the road to Messina," observed the Count, with the same quiet smile pervading his features, " and is a place which I think you ought to be acquainted with, for it will exercise a certain influence over your future life. It is pretty well known, and is called the Castello Monteleone——"

" For shame, Alberto ! you should not tease me like that. But do you really intend to ask us to visit you in that grand place of which I have heard so much, but which you occupy so little ? "

" I used to like the villa at Palermo best, but since the arrival of a certain young English lady at Caromo, the Castello Monteleone has seemed to me the preferable one of the two. But now, my dearest, I will go to your father, and see if we cannot settle this matter at once."

He rose from his seat beside her, and was about to put his project into execution, when the door opened suddenly, and Mr. Bellingham entered the room. He face was flushed and his manner excited, and after a brief word of welcome to the Count, he proceeded to address his daughter.

" Did that fellow Lorenzo lie, or did you send him to me ? "

" Certainly I sent him, papa," replied Isabel. " I thought that it was best to do so."

"And you acted quite rightly, my dear child," returned her father; "and I am not at all angry with you, but with that *facchino* Lorenzo for coming and upsetting you with a cock-and-bull story about mothers and ghosts and seventeenths of Junes. I hope you paid no attention to what he said."

"I have always found poor Teresa so truthful," answered Isabel, "that I confess I was a good deal startled by the strange tale she told her son, and it has made me feel nervous and uncomfortable."

"Of course it has," returned her father, triumphantly—"it could do nothing else; but I have hit upon the very means to remove all such feelings for ever and a day."

"You dear, good papa!" exclaimed Isabel, throwing her arms round her father's neck, and kissing his cheek affectionately, "tell me the sure means you have hit upon to put your little girl's fears at rest?"

"My idea is very simple," answered Mr. Bellingham, with the air of a man who had found a satisfactory solution to a riddle. "To-day is the 15th of June; well, instead of leaving the Palazzo to the ghosts, as Lorenzo tells me has ever been the custom of the Castrucci family on the 17th of June, I propose not only remaining here, but also giving a ball in honour of my daughter's marriage with Count Alberto Monteleone—and that, I think, will settle the question of the ghosts completely, for when the guests and the servants find that there are no spectral visitors, we shall have no more of these silly tales."

Isabel turned so ghastly pale at this announcement that Alberto, fearing she would faint, stepped forward to catch her in his arms.

"Are you serious, sir?" said he, addressing Mr. Bellingham. "I do not think that you will get your friends to attend your ball, for there is a very strong feeling here on the necessity of closing the Palazzo on that unlucky date; and I was going to propose that you, your daughter, and her little sister, should honour me by visiting Castello Monteleone, and making my betrothed familiar with it during that time."

" The idea is an excellent one, my dear Alberto, but unfortunately it is one that cannot be carried out," returned Mr. Bellingham, decisively. " I am not a man given to talk, but I heard all about the 17th of June shortly after I came here, and then made up my mind to crush down an idiotic superstition which injures the value of my property considerably; and I am perfectly sure that I have hit upon the best means of doing so. Besides, I sent out all the invitations last night, and so, my dear Count, you see that I am utterly unable to accept your offer."

" But, my dear Signore, consider your daughter's feelings," urged Alberto ; " she is really in a very nervous state, and I greatly fear that if too great a strain is put upon her, she will break down."

" When you know me better, Count," observed Mr. Bellingham, a little stiffly, " you will find that when once I have made up my mind to any suited plan, nothing upon earth can induce me to deviate from the path that leads to its accomplishment; therefore you will oblige me by saying nothing further on the matter. My daughter Isabel will, I am sure, do her utmost to carry out her father's wishes—will you not, my dear child ? " he added, turning affectionately towards her.

" Yes, papa," answered the poor girl, submissively, but her voice faltered and the tears stood in her eyes at the prospect of the terrible ordeal that was before her.

" I intend to convert the picture-gallery into a ball-room," continued Mr. Bellingham, complacently.

" The picture-gallery ! " repeated Monteleone, aghast at such foolhardiness. " Why, my dear Signore, do you not know that the Green Staircase opens into the present picture-gallery, which used to be the principal drawing-room ? "

"No, I did not know it," returned Mr. Bellingham; "but if such is the case, all the more reason for doing as I propose, for it will strike at the very root of the foolish belief."

"You are mad!" returned Monteleone, who was unable to comprehend such dogged obstinacy.

"You forget yourself, Count," returned the Englishman, angrily; "but there, I cannot be angry with you. And listen—after I have carried out my idea, I will not delay the marriage, which, if you choose, can take place as soon as my daughter will consent, and therefore I leave you to fix the time between yourselves."

At any other time Isabel would have thanked her father with the utmost effusion, but the knowledge that she was not going to escape from the Palazzo as she had anticipated, had thrown a damp over her spirits, and she could only turn to Alberto with a faint smile.

"We had better say nothing, dear Alberto," remarked she, "about our marriage until the 17th is past; then, if all goes well as my father seems to anticipate, we shall have ample leisure to discuss the matter. Excuse me for a little, but I must go, as I always do, and pay Dulcie a visit at her dinner hour."

She glided from the room, looking so pale that she resembled more one of the ghosts of the Palazzo than the fresh English girl who had so recently taken up her residence within its walls, and left her father and lover alone.

"Poor girl, she has been terribly upset by all these idle tales," remarked Mr. Bellingham; "but you will see, my dear Count, that the heroic remedy I propose will not only cure her, but also half the good people of Caromo, of their silly belief in the supernatural. And now you must do me a good turn: go round amongst your friends and relatives, and urge on them the acceptance of my invitations; tell them that it is a matter of greater import than they think, and, above all, allude to the fact that the *festa* is given in honour of your betrothal to my daughter, and that they cannot refuse to take part in it without acting discourteously both to her and you. You think I am obstinate and pig-headed, I know, my dear boy; but humour me in this, and I promise you that for the future both you and Isabel shall find me the most indulgent of fathers."

"I will do as you wish," returned the young man, sadly, "but I wish that you would be persuaded to give up this scheme of yours; be sure that no good will come of it——"

"There, my dear Count, that is sufficient," returned the owner of the Palazzo Spordese; "you will find it quite impossible to turn me from my purpose. You Sicilians have been brought up in such an atmosphere of superstition that you are not content with having a family ghost, but actually as ready at any moment to leave your house in order to permit it to indulge in its freaks without let or hindrance. My plan, however, will, I think, show that if a ghost persists in becoming a member of the family, it must to a certain degree conform to rule, and not make itself more objectionable than the due performance of its duty renders absolutely necessary."

The Count Alberto endeavoured to force a smile at Mr. Bellingham's proposal for dealing with ancestral apparitions; but it was with a heavy heart he took a farewell of Isabel when she returned to the room, and mounting his horse, which he had left at "The Dancing Lizard," cantered away in the direction of Castello Monteleone with the foreboding that some dreadful calamity was hanging over himself and Isabel.

CHAPTER IV.

THE OPEN DOOR.

THE preparations for the ball at the Palazzo Spordese were pushed on by Mr. Bellingham with the utmost energy. The worthy gentleman was constantly on the move, now running up ladders and superintending the decorations of the picture-gallery, and again driving to the outskirts of Caromo to purchase flowers from the market-gardeners; then falling like a thunderbolt upon a man-cook who had been sent for from Messina, and who stoutly avowed that he had no fear of ghosts, and would convert his satanic majesty into a ragout if he got the chance; and in another moment holding a colloquy with the man who had engaged to supply the many hundred little oil-lamps with which the courtyard was to be illuminated.

The Count Monteleone had not been idle, and by re-peatedly asserting that if the invitations were not accepted he should consider himself personally slighted, had con-trived to get up a fair muster amongst his more considerate friends. Some of the dare-devil *cavalieri* of the neighbour-hood came with the hopes of seeing some sensational incident, whilst many fair dames laid aside their terror of the supernatural in their ardent desire to exhibit their fine feathers at one of the grandest fêtes which had been given at Caromo for many a long day.

Isabel tried to interest herself in the preparations, and strove, but in vain, to catch a spark of her father's enthusiasm.

Lorenzo, who sincerely repented his defection from the flesh-pots of Egypt, hung about the great gate, and saluted Mr. Bellingham with unfailing regularity whenever that gentleman passed in or out, with the faint hope of being again employed; but the Englishman was too angry at the annoyance he had caused him to pay the slightest notice of him beyond a distant nod of the head.

The tradesfolk were much interested, anticipating a rich harvest, and even the editor of the local paper felt that he could fill a column or two of his paper with perfect ease, in giving a dilated account of the grand doings at the Palazzo Spordese.

Even Sarah Hartley seemed to have got over her fear
of the ghosts, and busied herself in preparing her young
mistress's ball-dress ; and Dulcie was thoroughly delighted
at all the bustle and fuss which was going on, and revelled
in the thoughts of all the delicacies which would fall to her
share at the supper-table.

Alberto Monteleone was a constant visitor, and perhaps
had never had so good an opportunity of being alone with
his betrothed ; for they would contrive to steal away unnoticed into the more distant portions of the pleasure-
grounds, and there, seated beneath the trees, he would do
his utmost to rouse Isabel from the strange lethargy which
seemed to have crept over her. She was very quiet and
gentle, but she did not appear to take an interest in anything except the passing away of the much-dreaded seventeenth of June. By the time, however, that that day
dawned, everything was ready : the festoons of coloured
lamps had been suspended in the courtyard and garden,
ready to be lighted at the approach of night ; the ball-room
was a mass of flowers, artistically arranged in devices of all
kinds, and the frames of the portraits of the Castrucci
family almost disappeared beneath the mass of floral decorations. The harsh, repulsive features of Baldassare Castrucci,
whose portrait Mr. Bellingham had positively refused to
remove from the scene of the festivities, were encircled by a
wreath of roses and river-lilies, which, however, only made
their ugliness stand out in bolder relief.

By nine o'clock the guests began to arrive, and were
received in the principal drawing-room by Mr. Bellingham
and his daughter. Isabel looked very beautiful in her soft
diaphanic robes, with her fair hair crowned by a wreath of
silver oak-leaves which made her look like the priestess of
some ancient fane. She was very pale, but even her pallor
won the admiration of the gentlemen, forming as it did so
striking a contrast with the olive-cheeked women of their

own land. When some fifty guests had assembled, the soft
sounds of music from the ball-room warned them that the
moment for dancing was at hand ; and Mr. Bellingham,
taking the hand of a little shrivelled Marchesa glittering
with diamonds, led the way to the old picture-gallery. A
burst of admiration broke from all the assembled guests at
the appearance of the room, which seemed a perfect bower
of flowers ; and as the music rang out in a lively measure,
the gay Sicilians gave themselves up to the enjoyment of the
hour, and the terrible seventeenth of June and its ghostly
reminiscences were entirely effaced from their recollections.

As a betrothed maiden, Isabel's hand was not often
solicited for the dance, though many were the congratulations offered to her and Alberto as they sat together at one
end of the long room.

At about eleven o'clock, Sarah Hartley made her appearance to take little Dulcie to bed. Ordinarily Dulcie was
the quietest of children, and one the least prone to rebel
against the decrees as to her doings, but to-night at the
appearance of the nursemaid she raised a loud wail, and
positively declined to be removed to bed. " I was promised
to tay up to tupper," sobbed she in her pretty baby lisp.

" But, Miss Dulcie," urged Sarah, "there are all sorts of
lovely things which have been sent up, awaiting for you in
the nursery, and a beautiful barley-sugar birdcage which the
good man who have come all the . way from Messina made
for your special self. Won't you come with poor Sarah like
a dear good child ? "

" No, I oon't," returned the child, who had picked up a
few of nurse's provincialisms ; and again the tears rolled forth,
and the sobs became more and more violent.

" What is the matter, Dulcie dear ? " asked Isabel, who,
attracted by the disturbance, now joined the little group
which had gathered round the refractory child.

" I ton't want to go bye-bye ; I want to tay up to tupper,"
sobbed Du'cie.

"But you know you are to have, oh, such a nice supper in the nursery," remonstrated Isabel, "and that if you stayed up much later you would be tired, and perhaps sick, and then you would not be able to enjoy them half so much. Come, let your sister take you, my pet."

As she spoke she raised the child in her arms, and Dulcie, who appeared to feel the weight of the last argument that had been advanced, threw her little arms round her neck, and rested her tear-stained cheeks upon her shoulder.

"Now say good-night all," said Isabel, as she stood for a moment in the doorway.

"Dood-night all!" cried Dulcie, waving her chubby little hand, as her sister held her up to say her farewell.

A very fair picture did Isabel Bellingham present as she stood framed in the doorway, her soft robe floating round her and her head crowned with its silver leaves, holding up the laughing child, who had now recovered her usual spirits. Many who witnessed this scene, when in bygone years they recalled the last time they had seen Isabel Bellingham could hardly restrain their tears, for not a soul had ever imagined the strange and terrible calamity that was about to fall upon the Palazzo Spordese.

Isabel did not find it so easy a task as she had anticipated to leave her little sister Dulcie. The child insisted upon her taking her seat at the supper-table, and helping her to each of the various delicacies which the good-natured *chef* had sent up for her refection; and at last, when, by the united efforts of her sister and Sarah, she was persuaded to permit herself to be put to bed, she embraced the former with such vehemence that her hair and wreath were sadly disarranged.

Sarah scolded the laughing child, and offered her assistance in repairing the damages, but Isabel declined her offer.

"Get Dulcie to bed," whispered she, "whilst she is in the

humour. I will go to my room and put all right in a few minutes."

She gave Dulcie a last kiss, and, cautioning her to be a good girl, passed through the long corridor that led to her sleeping apartment. Far away in a distant part of the house she could hear the melody of the band, the hum of conversation, and the rythmical tread of the dancers' feet, all softened and rendered half indistinct by the distance. She paused for an instant to listen to this strange mixture of sounds, and as she did so she was conscious of a curious kind of rustling, as if some one or something was moving close beside her. She glanced timidly round, and discovered that she had been standing in immediate proximity to the closed door of the Green Staircase.

With a faint cry of terror she sped away from a spot which of late she had learned to look upon as one of ill-omen, and in a few seconds had reached her own chamber. It did not take her very long to repair the damage which the playful hands of Dulcie had inflicted on her *coiffure*, but when this was completed she did not immediately retire to the ball-room, but sat, with her elbows resting upon the dressing-table, gazing out into the night. The moon was high in the heavens, and the stars were shining like so many diamonds; a gentle breeze was moving the branches of the trees with a soft rustling wind inexpressibly soothing, and beyond the high wall which surrounded the grounds could be seen the tall spires and massive towers of Caromo, standing out sharp and distinct against the night sky.

For some minutes she gazed upon a scene in which all seemed peace, and the thought crossed her mind that perhaps, after all, the trouble that she had been for so long anticipating might be averted, and that her life might again be bright as it had been before.

All at once the whole fair scene disappeared as though a

thick curtain had been drawn across the window, and glancing up in sudden alarm she saw that a dark cloud had spread over the face of the heavens, completely shrouding the moon and the stars. A high wind, which had evidently swept this cloud before it, now burst through the trees, and howled mournfully round the stone projections of the Palazzo, whilst heavy drops of rain fell with a pattering sound. The change from peace and quiet to storm and tempest was almost instantaneous.

Isabel gave a little shiver of affright. " How suddenly the change came," murmured she. "I must not stay here alone any longer, or I shall go mad. Where, oh where shall I find refuge from my own thoughts ! Come, let me see if I cannot cast them aside, for—and yet I cannot, for I feel that the blow is about to fall."

She rose from her sitting posture and gazed fearfully around her, as if she expected to see some terrible form behind her, but there was nothing. She pressed her right hand upon her heart, and uttered a suppressed gasp. "I must have company," murmured she. "I shall die of fright if I am left alone any longer. I feel that it is coming, but what *is* it ? I am not far from Sarah Hartley ; she would hear my voice, and yet I dare not call out. Let me see if I cannot get to her ; she will take me back to Alberto."

She tottered across the room, and then, as a sudden sound struck upon her ears, uttered a half-stifled shriek and remained motionless. It was only the clocks of the different churches and public buildings of Caromo chiming the midnight hour.

As the sound, however, rang out above the howling of the storm, a sudden change manifested itself in the young girl's chamber. The flame of the numerous wax candles with which it was lighted dwindled away into mere luminous threads, and a strange dull yellow glare permeated the whole apartment; the door flew open, and from every side was heard a whisper which uttered in tones low and distinct the words " *Come, come !* "

Isabel made one frantic effort to cast off the spell which appeared to have been cast around her.   Her lips endeavoured to formulate a prayer, but no sound passed through them.   Her fingers turned and twisted in vain efforts to make the sign of the cross, and at last, with a tottering step in which there was no sign of life or elasticity, she began to move like an automaton propelled by some cunning device of clockwork across the chamber.

Through the door she passed and out into the broad corridor, which was bathed in the same spectral yellow light, while the whispered words "Come, come !" still murmured distinctly on all sides of her.

A few steps brought her to the door of the Green Staircase, before which she paused, and gazing upon it with the eye of a hunted animal, uttered a hoarse gasping cry, as she perceived that it stood wide open, whilst from the dark depths below came the same mysterious sounds of invitation.

With an expression of blank despair upon her face the unhappy girl threw up her arms above her head, and peered eagerly into the darkness; then with a swift movement she approached the door, but with a violent effort shrank back again before her feet had crossed the threshold.   The struggle that was going on between herself and some unseen power was evidently a tremendous one, and for more than a couple of minutes she stood swaying backwards and forwards as either side alternately gained the mastery.

At last, however, victory declared itself on the side of the unseen power, and with another cry of anguish in which there was nothing human, she plunged forward into the darkness, the door closing upon her as noiselessly as it had opened.

   *   *   *   *   *   *

As twelve o'clock struck, a footman, throwing open the great folding-doors at the end of the gallery, announced that supper was served. The music ceased at the same instant, and the dancers formed little groups in different parts of the room.

"Where is Isabel?" asked Mr. Bellingham, rising from a table where he had been playing whist with an old Barone and two titled dames. "Where has my daughter gone to?"

"Yes, yes; where is the Signorina?" cried several voices. "She and the Count must show us the way into the supper-room, and then we will drink to their future health and happiness."

"She went up with Dulcie," said Monteleone, stepping forward; "the little puss would not let the English *camarista* take her to bed, and so, like a good sister, she went up with her."

"She ought to be here now," said Mr. Bellingham, looking at his watch; "she knew that supper would be served at twelve punctually. Where is your mistress?" he added, turning to Sarah Hartley, who at that moment appeared with some other servants at the other end of the room.

"Miss Dulcie pulled her wreath about her ears, sir," answered the woman, "and she went to her room to put herself a bit to rights before she came down again."

"Go up and ask her to come down as soon as she conveniently can," returned Mr. Bellingham.

"No, no," exclaimed a handsome Sicilian girl, "I and my sister will go up and fetch her. Wait a minute or two, ladies and gentlemen, and we will bring down the shy little bird to receive our congratulations!"

With a light laugh the two girls darted away, whilst the friends wiled away the time in pleasant conversation until the heroine of the ball should again make her appearance.

In about ten minutes' time, the young ladies appeared with rather a puzzled expression of countenance.

" Well! where is she?   Where is the fair Inglése? " exclaimed a chorus of voices.

"I don't know," answered the elder girl; "she is not in her room, nor yet in the nursery, where little Dulcie is wide awake with a plateful of bonbons by her side. We hunted about, but finding no signs of her, concluded she had reached the ball-room by some other way."

" This is very strange," exclaimed Mr. Bellingham. " Excuse me for a few moments, and I will see if I cannot be more successful."

" And I, with your permission, will accompany you," cried Monteleone, whose heart was full of all manner of mournful forebodings for which he could in no way account.

"Certainly, Alberto ; I shall be glad of your assistance," answered the master of the Palazzo Spordese, and the old and young man quitted the room together.

But now when they were thus again left alone, the sound of mirth and laughter was hushed amongst the guests· Heads were placed close together, and ominous whispers circulated in which the words, "An act of folly," "The 17th of June," could be plainly distinguished. A sudden chill seemed to have fallen upon the gay assembly. Pleasure and revelry seemed to have taken to themselves wings, and sadness and despair to have usurped their places. The infection seemed even to have spread to the servants, who, with scared faces and pallid cheeks, crowded in the doorway, making audible comments upon the strange event that had occurred.

Meanwhile Mr. Bellingham and the Count proceeded straight to Isabel's chamber, not pausing for a moment until they reached it; but here there were no signs that could give any clue to the young girl's whereabouts. Everything was in perfect order; there were no traces of any struggle or foul play, and the door was open as if she had hurried away to join her guests and neglected to close it.

" This is strange, very strange," muttered Mr. Bellingham.
" I am at a loss what to do."

" Do? " cried the young man, impetuously. "Why, do
not lose a moment; let every available person get lights,
and search the house from garret to cellar. Oh, my dear
Signore, I fear that you will bitterly repent your obstinancy
in having persisted in remaining in this accursed house
during a seventeenth of June! Haste, do not lose a
moment; my heart is heavy with the most cruel forebodings,
and I fear the worst!"

As he spoke he darted from the room, followed with
almost equal celerity by Mr. Bellingham, who was now half
distracted with terror as he thought of what fatal consequences his having given way to his prejudices might have
caused. Hardly had Count Monteleone proceeded a few
steps down the corridor than he stopped short as though
the hand of a giant had been placed upon his breast, and
then, starting back a pace, clutched the arm of his companion with a grasp which made the old man wince.
"Look ! " exclaimed he, hoarsely, "look there ! "

The unhappy father endeavoured to follow with his eyes
the direction of Alberto's finger, but emotions had rendered
his sight dim, and he could see nothing.

" What is it? " he faltered. "I can see no signs of her;
tell me what you have discovered, and do not leave me
longer in suspense."

The sole reply of the Count was to drag the old man up
to the door of the Green Staircase, before which he had
come to a halt, and in suppressed tones of the deepest
mental anguish again to repeat the monosyllable "Look!"
Jammed in the door the father recognized, with a feeling
of sickening terror, a portion of the diaphanous material
which had formed the ball-dress of his daughter not many
hours before.

For an instant he hardly realized the fatal truth, and

then, as the terrible reality dawned upon him, he sprang like a maniac at the door, and tore at it until the blood streamed from his lacerated fingers.

"It is hopeless," said the Count, in accents of the keenest despair. "A smith, with all the implements of his trade ready to his hand, would be some hours battering down that formidable barrier. I know another means of exit," and half leading, half dragging the half-crazy old man with him, he made his reappearance in the ball-room.

Just as he did so there was a violent crash, followed by a cry of alarm, and a cloud of dust rose up hiding what had occurred.

In a few moments all was explained; the portrait of Baldassare Castrucci had become in some way detached from the wall, and had fallen upon a group which was standing just beneath it, severely injuring several of those who composed it.

The fall of the picture disclosed a narrow door, and Alberto Monteleone, pushing his way towards it, after passing his hand for a few seconds over the frame, appeared to have discovered what he was seeking for, and pressing heavily against it, the door slid into the wall with a strident shriek.

In an instant, as if the four winds of heaven had been let loose in the chamber, every light was extinguished, and in the yellow light which filled the staircase upon which the door opened could be seen two shadowy forms upon the first landing, the one a woman upon her knees, and the other a man with a rapier in his hand in the attitude of delivering a deadly thrust at the supplicating figure before him.

But there was something lying at the foot of the staircase which was no shadowy form from beyond the grave, but a terrible bodily reality, a fair young English girl, with such a look of horror on her face as the lookers-on at this extraordinary scene hoped never again to witness.

For a few brief moments, which seemed ages to the spectators, the shadowy forms remained, then they vanished like a vision of the night ; the glare died away, leaving the Green Staircase in total darkness. The lights in the great chandelier and the candelabra sprang up again, and all that was left was the dead body of Isabel Bellingham lying at the foot of the stair with the distracted form of Alberto Monteleone bending over her.

Suddenly there was a loud cry of "Fire, fire!" and from half-a-dozen quarters the flames burst forth, and volumes of smoke poured out from every quarter. The terrified guests fled in all directions, and after a wild glance around him Alberto followed them, bearing the dead body of his lost love in his arms.

Sarah Hartley, who could be brave enough when there was nothing supernatural in the question, contrived to save little Dulcie, but the house and its contents were entirely destroyed, and the blackened remains of poor Mr. Bellingham were found amongst the ruins.

Alberto Monteleone took charge of little Dulcie, and retained the services of the faithful Sarah ; but his heart was broken, and all the love that he was capable of lies buried beneath the stone under which lie the remains of Frederic and Isabel Bellingham.

WARD, LOCK, AND CO., LONDON AND NEW YORK.

THE HAUNTED HANSOM

Howell Davies

THE HAUNTED HANSOM.

BY HOWELL DAVIES.

CHAPTER I.

SOME twelve months before the date of my story I had been fortunate enough to secure a junior partnership in the house of Campbell and Merrivale, stock and share-brokers, who were known in the City as an eminent and old-established firm.

John Campbell had been a dear school and college friend of my father's, was a trustee under my father's will, and had given still further proof of his friendship by readily promising my mother, on her deathbed, that he would look after me as though I had been his son.

I was then a lad at school; and the death of my parents left me in possession of a modest competency, which during my minority was carefully and judiciously "nursed" by my excellent guardian. In short, he kept his sacred promise so faithfully that at twenty-eight years of age I found myself in the very comfortable position I have intimated. I liked my work, had plenty of friends (as prosperous men always have), and had no just cause of quarrel with my lot in life.

I am not by any means a superstitious man. The mysterious influences under which some folks seem to exist, and from which they profess to derive a melancholy pleasure, have no part in my busy life. Morbid fancies have no affinity with active occupations.

When a man has to secure the necessary sustentation for the physical existence of himself and family by elbowing his way through the unsympathetic, unscrupulous crowds who dog the steps of the fickle goddess, his imaginative powers are pretty certain to be kept under healthy control. Such has been my experience; and I want my readers to bear this in mind, if they care to peruse the strange story I have to tell.

Whether it be deemed interesting or not, it is certainly a fresh confirmation of the well-worn aphorism that "truth is stranger than fiction."

Some four years ago, on a certain twenty-third of December, I was sitting in my cosy bachelor quarters, alone, with the indispensable pipe in my mouth, having a "good think."

By the way, what a wonderful assistance to the process of thought is the fragrant weed !

I sometimes try to imagine what the life of a lonely man who doesn't smoke must be like. I've tried to contemplate the abstruse question from every point of view, and with as little prejudice as it is possible for an inveterate smoker to feel, but I am bound to confess that hitherto the problem has baffled me.

Why are so many bachelors hurried perforce into ill-assorted marriages every year ?

Simply because they've never learnt what an amount of unselfish companionship and calm philosophy is to be found in the bowl of a well-coloured meerschaum.

On the day in question I had been detained at the office rather later than usual, as the next three days were holidays; so that when I got home, and had disposed of a substantial dinner, with eminent satisfaction to my inner man, I wasn't at all sorry to draw up my snug arm-chair to the fire that blazed cheerily in the grate, light my pipe, and fall back upon my "inner consciousness" for a quiet meditation.

Christmas was at hand, with all its probing memories redolent of sunnier days. Time was—and not so very long ago—

when the weird season was indeed a festival for loving hearts and smiling faces who sat at the hospitable board in our old house at home. Then an indulgent father's cheery greeting welcomed my return from school, and the warm caresses of a tender mother's lips made sweeter the benediction of that holy time.

Ah! those were happy days. Why is it that we poor mortals, in our pitiful blindness, never see the full beauty of such times and seasons until they are for ever gone? Did the sweetness that haunts us in the after years have a real existence then?—or is it that memory, by some fanciful trick, concentrates all the illumination of intervening years upon that far-off glorified spot?

I cannot tell. I only know that, young, prosperous, esteemed as I was, on that chill December evening, I would have readily—ay, cheerfully—given up all those coveted possessions for

> " But one touch of a vanished hand,
> And the sound of a voice that is still."

However, I've my story to tell, and mustn't stay to moralize now.

In the midst of my meditations there came a knock at my door, which effectually aroused me, and the servant entering, placed in my hands a telegram.

Now, although the receipt of that masterpiece of modern science was a matter of the commonest occurrence during business hours, I must plead guilty to a feeling of considerable surprise, almost amounting to trepidation, as I hastily tore it open.

I needn't have alarmed myself, for its perusal gave me nothing but satisfaction. Was that strange thrill which shot through me at sight of the familiar brick-coloured envelope the mere effect of being suddenly awakened from a gloomy train of thought, or was it a premonition of the awful task which a relentless destiny was forcing upon me, and which I was powerless to repel? Who shall say?

Have not the wisest and best of us experienced this inexplicable emotion at some time or other—this strange sense of a cold, cruel hand clutching at our heart-strings, or a grim shadow of impending evil crossing our path?

Napoleon Bonaparte felt it at every crisis of his marvellous life, and it made that hard-headed hero as superstitious as the veriest school-girl.

Well, something of that sort came upon me as my trembling fingers tore open the telegram, but the next moment I laughed at my stupid folly.

The message ran as follows :—

" T. Lawrence, The Priory, Southfield, to Martin Bennett, 116, George Street, Hanover Square, London.
" Have just arrived home. Come down to us for Christmas. Shall expect you by first train in the morning."

Dear old Tom! this was just like him, impetuous and warm-hearted as ever. As a lad he was the same—always left everything to the last moment, and then, by some unaccountable witchery, always did the right thing, and made everybody comfortable once more.

He and I were at school together, and from the first the thickest of "chums"—foremost in every conceivable piece of mischief, and, as a natural consequence, always in "the heel of the hunt," where intellectual pursuits and scholarly attainments were concerned.

At the conclusion of that happiest time of one's life, we drifted apart, as schoolboys do. Tom went into the army; I embarked on the treacherous waters of the Stock Exchange. In the usual course of his military life, Tom was ordered abroad, and, at the date of my story, had returned on leave, after having spent three years at the Cape.

We had written to each other, perhaps, half a dozen times during that absence, and Tom's last letter contained a vague hint of the likelihood of his being in the old country again before very long. Nothing more definite than that; so that his telegram was really no surprise to me. As I say, it was just Tom's *modus operandi* in all he did.

Now, this kind invitation came just in the nick of time. I had one or two places "open" for Christmas, where I knew I should be heartily welcomed, for (pardon the conceit, dear reader!) I was not altogether an ineligible *parti*; and fond mammas, from the most disinterested motives, generally met me with smiling faces and gracious words.

Yet there were few places where I felt that I could spend a really "Happy Christmas." Indeed, I had more than half determined — misanthropist as I was — to spend the festive day alone, relying upon the unfailing companionship of my books for entertainment that would, at any rate, possess the advantage of unobtrusiveness.

Tom's genial, unsophisticated invitation drove this half-formed resolution out of my mind at once, and on the spur of the moment, yielding to the rush of sunny memories borne in upon my heart, I has-tened to prepare for my journey into the country. There was ample time; the train didn't leave Paddington until 10.40, and it was now eight o'clock.

My roomy portmanteau was soon packed, my cigar-case well filled, my mystified land-lady informed of my sudden freak, and myself comfortably ensconced in Hansom cab No. 00911.

Amongst my numerous peculiarities, all more or less characteristic of a fidgety bachelor, is a habit I contracted long ago of always looking at the number of a cab before getting into it.

"How absurd!" exclaims the easy-going reader.

Perhaps so, my friend. The sequel will show.

CHAPTER II.

As soon as I was seated, and had placed my rugs and small portmanteau by my side, I lit a choice Havanna, and under its soothing influence allowed my mind to wander back, over the haunted ground of memory, to the old days when dear Tom and I shared our school-boy triumphs and consoled each other under its griefs.

What halcyon days they seemed *now*, and, ah, how far away! We had both ex-changed the mimic warfare of the play-ground for the real, earnest, cruel battle of life—the awful fight going on from day to day, in which so many good and true men go down fighting bravely to the last.

What immortal honours are won on this field! But as the crowning of these heroes takes place beyond our human ken, we make no note of it. And so the world rolls on!

Musing thus, I had drifted quite away from present surroundings, and was lying back in the cab, with closed eyes, lazily puffing at my cigar. The ceaseless roar of that most mysterious of all oceans—London life—seemed a fitting accompaniment to my dreamy thoughts.

Suddenly I was awakened from my reverie by a terrible feeling of chilliness, as though a blast from a northern ice-field had swept by me. At the same time, a deep, blood-curdling groan close to my ear caused me to look quickly round. Great heavens! what a sight met my fascinated gaze! On the seat beside me sat a ghastly figure, that I instinctively knew belonged not to the bustling, noisy world around me.

The apparition was that of a young and handsome man, little more than a lad, in fact. Round the high white fore-head clustered masses of short golden curls; on the upper lip was a slight moustache that marked the borderland between youth and manhood; every fea-ture was as delicately chiselled as a woman's, and yet the face bespoke the promise of great manliness and high courage.

But it was the eyes that first riveted my attention. They were of a deep in-tense blue, and under happier circum-stances must have been veritable foun-tains of laughter and love. As they slowly turned upon me, their wild, appeal-ing, hunted look was terrible to behold. I candidly declare that I never thought or could have believed it possible for human eyes to have held such a burden of horror in their depths. Agony, remorse, entreaty, despair—all were depicted in that soul-consuming glance.

Heaven forbid that my eyes should ever look upon such a sight again! After the first shock of fright, which was succeeded by an unnatural calmness, such as animals are said to manifest under the transfixing orbs of the serpent, I noted that my super-natural companion wore evening dress.

On one of the delicate, high-bred hands sparkled a diamond ring, and in the centre of the shirt-front a single stone of great purity flashed and shimmered in the flitting lights of the Edgware Road, through which we were being driven.

But what is the meaning of that crimson stain on the snowy linen? Horror! it is a stream of blood, which is oozing from a wound under the left breast, and is steadily trickling over the white expanse, cut clean through, as if from a quick stab!

I saw it all in a moment then. A cruel murder had been committed, and this poor restless spirit was claiming inquiry and vengeance at my hands.

But why at *mine?* I had never seen that beautiful, boyish face before. I knew nothing of its melancholy history.

Again the supplicating eyes were turned upon me; the rigid lips moved with a con-vulsive twitch, and forth from between them issued a groan of mortal anguish that paralyzed my throbbing brain, and made my very heart stand still. I lost consciousness. The next thing I remember was the cheery, matter-of-fact voice of my Jehu, exclaiming, "'Ere ye are, sir! Pad-din'ton, sir!"

I got out as one in a dream; saw a porter taking things from the very spot where my awful visitor had sat, without any remark beyond the stereotyped question "Where for, sir?"

I answered him quite as mechanically,

nd turned to pay the cabman. To this
ay I don't know what I gave him. It must
ave been something handsome, for it drew
rth from that representative of a useful
ut frequently discontented class a fervent
"Thank ye, sir. A merry Christmas to
ou."

As he turned to drive off, the number of
ie cab again caught my eye. Yes: there
was, a simple row of five figures; nothing
iore. Yet to me, at that moment, those
umerals were as terrible and fateful as
as the mystic writing on the palace walls
) the Assyrian monarch. They burnt
iemselves into my bewildered brain, never
) be erased whilst memory held sway.

With a strong effort I pulled myself
)gether, walked into the booking-office,
id took my ticket for Southfield.

The busy scene around me served, in some
ieasure, to draw me out of myself, and to
issipate the effects of the horrible ex-
erience through which I had recently
issed.

I tried to argue with my own heart on
ie absurdity of allowing myself to believe
iat I had really seen a ghost. I, a man
ithout an atom of superstition in my
hole moral economy, and generally
edited among my daily acquaintances
business with the possession of more
an an average share of shrewdness
id hard common sense—I to be tormented
th a visit from a disembodied spirit! It
is too absurd! Why, I must have fallen
leep, and had a bad dream, and there was
end to it! So said common sense—or,
tner, that childish fear of being thought
olish which we frequently designate com-
)n sense.

Still, argue as I would, I knew the dread
ystery was no vision in sleep, and an infinite *something* within me stopped the
credulous sneer at my own weakness that
s rising to my lips.

In this frame of mind I entered a well-
hted first-class carriage, and having
ide myself thoroughly comfortable, com-
inced my long railway journey. For I
ist tell you that Southfield was a long
y from London. It nestled in snug
irement on the far-off western coast, on
iranch line, twenty miles from its junc-
n with the main line. So I had plenty
time for thought, if I'd wished to think.
at, however, was just what I didn't want
do.

Before leaving my warm bachelor quar-
s, I had comforted myself with the as-
ance that I should sleep soundly all the
y down from Paddington. Being a
erably experienced traveller I could in-
iably manage that. For once I had

reckoned without my host, or, more strictly
speaking, my *guest*.

There was to be no sleep for me that
night, nor the next either, if I'd only known
it.

Do what I would, that agonized face, with
its story of a hidden crime, rose before my
mental eye, and drove away all inclination
to rest.

Must I confess it? *Fear* kept me broad
awake. Fear, lest if I closed my eyes, I
should find on opening them again, that
same awful presence before me. We laugh
at the terror a little child displays in the
presence of some forbidding-looking
stranger, and yet what abject cowards,
what veritable infants, the wisest and
strongest of us are when we come face to
face with the supernatural or the inexplicable. Heaven help us, then! for our
vaunted reasoning powers offer but sorry
consolation.

My journey, however, was not interrupted by any further adventure; and on
reaching Southfield, I had sufficiently recovered from my fright to be able to conceal all traces of anything extraordinary
having occurred.

In the gray dawn of the chill December
morning we glided into the silent little
station, where a sleepy porter and an un-
happy-looking boy were the sole repre-
sentatives of authority at that early hour.

I was glad enough to reach my destina-
tion, you may be sure, and still more
pleased to see my old schoolfellow on the
diminutive platform, though I should
hardly have recognised him had it not
been for the cheery tones in which he welcomed me, and in which I could not fail to
detect the old happy ring of the voice I had
heard so often in the bygone days.

CHAPTER III.

THE PRIORY was distant some three miles
from Southfield, and as we drove through
the High Street of the sleepy little town
there was hardly a soul in sight. A
mongrel cur at the door of the principal
inn, annoyed at our unlooked-for appearance at such an unearthly hour, saluted us
with a noisy protest on behalf of the slum-
bering inhabitants; whilst a half-awakened
ostler at the same establishment ceased his
out-door ablutions to give us a surly recognition as we rattled by.

The rising sun gave promise of a bright
cold, genuine mid-winter day—a promise
that was amply and beautifully fulfilled
by-and-by.

How delightful the country looked as we
drove briskly through it that fair morning!

All nature seemed to smile a merry Christmas welcome, as if conscious of the sweetly solemn season. At least so it seemed to me, just released from Babylon and its jarring sounds and murky canopy of fog. How vast a store of misery and crime, of heroic endurance and greedy cunning, of brave Christian helpfulness and more than fiendish vice that same grim canopy covers! I felt like one transported into a new world that morning. Under the bracing influences of the weather, our brisk drive, and Tom's lively conversation, I rapidly regained my wonted elasticity of spirits, and the hideous events of the previous night lost their hold of me for the time being.

"There's the dear old place!" said Tom, as we turned a sharp corner, and came in view of a fine old mansion situated on a gentle slope facing the sea.

I have little or no architectural knowledge; and even had I possessed ten times the amount I did at that time, it would have puzzled me to say which of the various orders prevailed in the construction of The Priory. There were corners and gables of every conceivable form, and in all imaginable positions. Yonder loomed out a broad bay-window, and beside it an ancient Gothic light. Here a low French window opened upon the bright, smooth lawn, whilst, far above it, quaint dormer panes admitted the day.

Perhaps my best description of the house would be to call it a perfect specimen of the eminently-comfortable order. It certainly was that.

I have visited it many times since that eventful morning, and each succeeding visit has but served to confirm my first impression as to its sweet homeliness, its quiet, inviting comfort. Never have I seen a place which so thoroughly realized my idea of what a true English home should be.

No wonder in our boyhood's days Tom used to speak of it with such tenderness and affection. It was indeed a home that any lad might be proud of. Moreover, it had been in his family for generations, and was intimately interwoven with all its traditions.

Little did I think, as I entered its friendly portal, that my coming would produce the effects it did.

On entering, I was at once shown to the rooms that had been set aside for me in the very pleasantest part of that very pleasant house. As soon as I had removed the grimy traces of my all-night journey, I found my way down to the breakfast-room, where Tom and a young lady stood at the low window feeding some hungry little birds gathered in a chirping crowd on the lawn.

Lawrence at once introduced me to the young lady as his sister Beatrice.

Now, I'm not going to attempt a description of the most indescribable thing in nature—a bright and beautiful girl. In all my reading I have never yet come across a word-picture that did anything like justice to such a subject.

We read of girls graceful as Hebe and lovely as Venus, and how much the wiser are we? What do you or I, dear reader, know of those mythical, and probably overrated, females of antiquity? I wager you that we have in these degenerate days many a maiden in our quiet English homes before whom the gods of old would have bowed with a lower reverence and a wilder passion than was ever evoked by their own æsthetic damsels in their palmiest days!

I have a shrewd suspicion that in my heart of hearts I considered Beatrice Lawrence one of these incomparable beauties.

She gave me a frank and hearty welcome to The Priory, so that I sat down to our comfortable breakfast in a very happy frame of mind, and with an exceedingly voracious appetite for the good things set before me.

Mrs. Lawrence did not put in an appearance at the early meal; but later in the day I was presented to her, a sweet, matronly old lady she was. Her face must have been wonderfully handsome in its youth; now there were deep lines on it, which gave it a look of intense, almost painful melancholy—lines that it was easy to see had not been carved by the patient hand of Time, but that seemed rather to have been rudely chiselled by the cruel strokes of some stupendous sorrow.

Withal it was a grand, sweet face, and one that commanded love and esteem from all.

The day passed off pleasantly but quietly. Tom had so much to tell me and so many questions to ask, that the hours flew by on rapid wings as we strolled about the fine old park, or wandered on the beach near by.

Of course, the stables were inspected, the dogs introduced, with a due acknowledgment of all their exceptional merits, and the gun-room overhauled.

So the day wore on, and evening came, with its quiet comforts.

When we were in the drawing-room, awaiting the announcement of dinner, Beatrice seemed unusually gloomy and *distrait*.

Rousing herself with evident effort, she

"WHERE TOM AND A YOUNG LADY STOOD AT A LOW WINDOW." (See p. 40.)

turned to me, and with one of her rare smiles, said, "I'm very much afraid you find us dull company to-night, Mr. Bennett. But it has been an inflexible rule of my mother's, for some years now, to spend Christmas Eve as quietly as possible. So you must make the best you can of a stupid family party!" she added, gaily.

But as she turned away from me, I fancied I saw her lip quiver and her lovely eyes fill with something suspiciously like tears. Could I have been mistaken?

We shall see.

Though we were but four, the dinner was not by any means a dull affair. Indeed, it would be impossible to feel gloomy in the presence of Beatrice Lawrence's fascinating face and ways. Without at all approaching that *bête noir* of young manhood — a blue-stocking — she had read enough to be able to join in a conversation, which would have been a Chinese riddle or a Dutch conundrum to the majority of young ladies.

She possessed a keen wit, and had a certain charming way of "putting a fellow down," that to my infatuated mind and heart was sweeter than any flattery I'd received from other lips.

Yes, we were a quietly happy little circle that evening round the amiable widow's dinner-table. How short and deceitful was the calm!

I have heard it said that at certain times there falls upon the beautiful Bay of Naples a calm unwonted even in that sunny clime. There is no rustle in the fragrant myrtle groves; the olive-trees cease their graceful swaying to and fro; the vine hangs heavy on the trellis; there is no voice of bird, or insect, or whispering breeze; the very waters hush their murmur as they touch the silent shore. Then the dwellers in that delectable land know that Vesuvius is gathering all its fierce artillery together for one of its wild *feux de joie*.

So is it in our lives, whatever our lot may be. So was it in that peaceful home-circle at The Priory that Christmas Eve.

Shortly after we had joined the ladies in the drawing-room, a company of carol singers stationed themselves on the lawn beneath the window, and charmed our ears and touched our hearts with their simple, plaintive music.

What memories those strains awakened in my heart! what emotions stirred my breast!

Our voices were hushed, our conversation was dropped in a moment.

Suddenly the silence in the room was broken by a stifled moan, expressing the keenest agony of soul, followed by bitter sobbing.

Looking round, I saw Mrs. Lawrence hurrying from the room, weeping profusely. With a hastily-whispered apology, her daughter followed her, and Tom and I were left alone.

And up through the clear, silent, frosty night came the voices of the singers, in softened harmony. How well I remember to this day the pathetic words they chanted to a plaintive tune — words that wrung those anguished sobs and tears from that patient mother's heart.

How much she had suffered I was soon to know!

CHAPTER IV.

"COME into the billiard-room, Martin," said Tom, in a moment or two. "We sha'n't see mother or Beta again to-night. Whilst we smoke, I've something to tell you, though it will cost me no little pain.

"Dear old friend," I replied, taking him by the arm, "if the telling of it, whatever it may be, will cause you a pang, I would rather it remained for ever untold."

"Generous and thoughtful, as in the old days," he answered, with a sad smile; "but it is due to you, as my guest and oldest friend, that some explanation of this evening's occurrences should be given you."

When we'd reached the billiard-room, and had seated ourselves, one on each side of its merry sea-coal fire, I again urged Lawrence to consider his own feelings rather than a fancied duty to me; but it was no use.

So having lighted our cigars, we sat and smoked in silence for a few minutes. As I watched my companion's face, I could see that he was struggling with strong emotions, and in my heart I pitied him, for I knew the womanly tenderness of his brave disposition.

At last he broke the spell, and looking me steadily in the face, began his absorbing story.

"You must have noticed, Martin, that my dear, good mother is prematurely aged, and that all to-day she has been under the cloud of an unusual melancholy; the carol-singers brought it to a climax to-night, and you must have wondered why their homely strains should have so utterly broken down my mother's self-possession. She is naturally of the brightest, happiest disposition. Heavens! how she has suffered though, and yet lived through it all.

"My father's death left her with the heavy charge of a young family on her hands. But even then, tenderly as she mourned her beloved partner, she kept up the cheerfulness of the dear old home, and lived only for her childrens' happiness and well-being. Ah, her great sorrow hadn't come upon her *then*,—the sorrow that whitened her locks with the snows of an untimely winter, and drove the light and gladness from her bosom!

"We were three children. I was the eldest, then Beta, and next to her Charlie, the pride and darling of the household. How we petted and did our best to spoil him from morning till night! The dear mother loved us all very truly and tenderly; but Charlie, her youngest born, was as the very breath of her life.

"He grew up a fine, handsome lad, and chose the medical profession. So at nineteen he was articled to an eminent London doctor.

"I need not tell you how sadly he was missed from the home-circle. He went up to town in May of that year, and from time to time wrote us in his happy boyish style, glowing accounts of his pleasant London life, and the delight he took in his professional studies. Very often he would add a postscript that he knew would bring the happy tears to the mother's eyes. 'How glad I shall be when Christmas comes, for I shall be *home* then.'

"Christmas did come round at last; and just a week before, Charlie wrote that he would leave London by the 10.40 train on the evening of the twenty-third. He couldn't get off until that day, and by leaving his journey until the last train, he would be able to attend Lady Southfield's dinner-party that evening. The Southfields have that handsome place on the hill which we passed in driving from the station yesterday; but since Lord Southfield's death her ladyship declares that she cannot exist out of London.

"Well, the twenty-third of December came, and every preparation was made for the reception of the pet of the household. My poor mother's excitement was intense. I never saw her in such spirits—I've never seen her look happy since!

"All that night she lay awake, longing for the daylight that should bring her boy to her. As I drove off in the breaking dawn to the station, she drew aside her window-blind to see me start.

"Alas! alas! it was all in vain—all in vain!

"I reached Southfield platform some ten minutes before the train was due. How long those minutes seemed!

"At length the train came lumbering in, and I scanned each carriage as it passed.

"Strange! I could see nothing of Charlie, nor get any tidings of him. I turned into the station disappointed and sore at heart, yet comforting myself with the thought that he would be in by a later train."

Tom's voice broke, and with the tears coursing down his bronzed, handsome face, he sobbed out, "Martin, *we never saw our dear lad again.*

"I hurried up to town by the last train that afternoon, when I found he didn't come and had sent no word. I didn't know what to fear.

"He was ill, perhaps dying, and even now I might be too late. I was indeed too late, but not in the way I supposed. I would to Heaven it had been so!

"As soon as I reached Paddington, I made careful inquiry of the officials, *and found Charlie's luggage (labelled for Southfield) in the cloak-room.* It had been brought there by a messenger, early in the evening of the twenty-third. That was all I could gather, except that no first-class ticket for Southfield had been issued on that or the succeeding day.

"I then drove direct to my brother's rooms in the Albany, only to find that he had sent his portmanteau, &c., to Paddington by a trusty messenger, who had returned and handed him the cloak-room ticket just as he was getting into the cab to drive to Lady Southfield's, in Grosvenor Square.

"It was now nearly ten o'clock on Christmas morning, and away I posted to her ladyship's residence, in the hope of seeing her before she went out to morning service.

"I knew her sufficiently well to be sure she would forgive the intrusion at such an hour; and I was not mistaken.

"I made an attempt to conceal my agitation as my kind old friend came forward, and shook me warmly by the hand; but she saw at once, with a woman's keenness, that there was something wrong.

"'What is it, Tom? What's wrong? Has anything happened to Charlie? You've not come to tell me that our handsome, darling boy is ill?'

"And the kindly Dowager's eyes filled with tears.

"You see, Martin, they all loved our dear lad and his sunny ways. Lady Southfield had always been as a second mother to Charlie and me from our infancy. She had no children of her own, so she lavished all her affection upon us.

"I told her of the mysterious disappearance of Charlie, and asked her whether he had dined with her, as he intended doing.

"'Yes; he came amongst the first,' she exclaimed—'to have a nice chat with me, he said, before the "lions" arrived. He begged me to excuse his leaving at ten o'clock, as he was going home for Christmas, and wouldn't miss his train for the world. He seemed in unusually high spirits, and at table was the gayest of the gay. He confided in me that it was *all* because he should so soon be with the loved ones at The Priory.'

"And so we talked and speculated, and the darkness in our hearts deepened.

"Then Lady Southfield sent for the footmen who were in the hall when Charlie left.

"They both remembered his going away. One of them had called a hansom cab for him, and heard him tell the driver 'Paddington.'

"Well, Martin, dear friend, to shorten my painful story, from that point I lost all trace of my brother, for whom I would have given my life. I advertised, and searched, and inquired; I employed a keen and skilful detective; but all in vain.

"Four years have passed away—for it happened at the time when you were in South America; but we have heard nothing of him who is worse than dead.

"When I went abroad with my regiment, I took his last photograph with me, vainly hoping that I should some day come across someone who could give me news of 'the loved and lost.'

"Disappointment has been my lot, hope deferred my dreary company, since that terrible time.

"So now you can understand the strange occurrences of this evening, and the reason why there was no company invited to meet you."

Long before Tom had finished his strange and startling narrative, I was as excited as he was himself, and felt the deepest, acutest sympathy for my old schoolfellow and those who had suffered with him.

I clasped his hand, and comforted him with all the consolation I could find words to express. I am afraid it wasn't much, though.

After a long and painful silence, which I felt was too sacred to be disturbed, Tom drew from his breast-pocket a photograph-case, and handed it to me, remarking, in a broken tone, "That's all we have left."

I took it from his hands with reverential touch, and opened it with all tenderness.

As the light fell upon its contents, it dropped from my paralyzed grasp.

It was the face I had seen in the hansom!

CHAPTER V.

WITH a great cry of terror and amazement, I started to my feet, and confronting my astounded companion, gasped out, as if every word would choke me, "Tom—I—saw—him—last—night!"

Lawrence's hands gripped my shoulders in an iron grasp; his face became ghastly in its excitement, as he hissed out between his clenched teeth, "Saw *him*?—you saw *Charlie*?—and last night, too? Where? In Heaven's name, *where*?"

Then the reaction came, and I told him all.

There were no tears in the fierce eyes that glared upon me as I finished my horrible narrative. There was no tremor in the hard, cruel voice, so unlike Tom's cheery accents, that fell upon my ears after a momentary pause.

The whole man was changed in that brief space of time. In the place of the loving, emotional, heart-sick brother stood the stern and pitiless avenger of a brother's blood!

"He has been murdered—foully, cruelly murdered, poor lad!" said the harsh voice. "And all these weary years his blood has been crying aloud for vengeance, and yet *I* knew it not!—I, his brother! Oh, my God, it is hard—it is pitiful! But he shall be avenged *now*; for I swear, by my hope of heaven, never to rest until I have discovered his murderer, and brought him to his doom!"

"Come!" he exclaimed, hurrying from the room; "there isn't a moment to be lost. You and I will go up to town at once. A quick train passes through Southfield a little after midnight. In the meantime, I must take Beatrice partly into my confidence. She is a clear-headed little darling, as well as a warm-hearted one, and will find some good excuse to satisfy the dear, heart-broken mother."

We hastened to our respective dressing-rooms, and were soon in travelling costume.

I went back to the drawing-room, where Tom had agreed to join me.

In a few moments he appeared, with his sister at his side, pale and trembling, but making a brave fight, as only a woman can, to conceal the emotions under which she was labouring.

She came quickly towards me, and, in tones that thrilled through my whole being, cried, "Oh, Mr. Bennett, Tom tells me you have brought him some news of

Charlie, our darling, handsome boy! Have you seen him? Is he alive? Is he ill, or in want? Tell me all you know; do, please! I am his sister, his *only* sister. I ought to hear all, whatever it may be. He loved me very, very dearly, did Charlie!" she sobbed. "And, oh, how I idolized him!"

What could I say in reply? Was my hand to be the one to demolish all her hopes, and realize her worst fears at one fell stroke?

No one knows the anguish that tore my heart at that moment.

Before I had time to frame a soothing reply to her passionate questionings, a servant entered, and requested her presence in her mother's room.

Thus I escaped.

Tom and I reached London in the gray dawn of Christmas morning, and as the train drew up to the platform at Paddington I saw my excited companion shudder. Was it some sudden memory of that other Christmas morning, when he had come up to pursue his futile search for him who was the sunshine of that loving home-circle where his glad smile beamed never again, and the music of his laughter was heard no more?

We drove at once to Scotland Yard, and placed our supernatural evidence before one of the shrewdest officers of the Detective Department.

As I told my story, I could not fail to notice the grim smile that stole over the man's impassive features.

He evidently looked upon me as a timid, superstitious fool, who had mistaken incipient *delirium tremens* for an important revelation of crime. But when I mentioned the number of the cab, his expression changed, and by the time he had had Tom's version of the mystery which had enshrouded his brother's disappearance, he had become as interested and excited as either of us.

You see, these professional stoics are very human after all!

Detective Sandell lost no time, but set to work at once.

He found his task a much easier one than he had anticipated. In less than a week he brought us news which confirmed our worst fears. Charlie had indeed been foully murdered, *and his murderer discovered!*

The detective laid the whole story before us.

He had gone first to the owner of Hansom No. 00911, and had made cautious inquiries as to the men in his employ. Those inquiries elicited the fact that the man who

drove the cab in question, at the time of the supposed murder, had disappeared from amongst the fraternity of "Jehus" altogether.

Oddly enough, his disappearance occurred in the spring of the following year, when he stated that he had been left a little money by a distant relative. The cab-owner had remembered it well, because of that somewhat unusual circumstance, "as legacies wasn't much in a cabby's line."

"Yes; Jim Bullen was a decentish sort of fellow. Steady as a clock, but a rum temper. Where did he live? Somewhere down in Stepney. Couldn't remember the name of the street. Married? No, sir. Lived all by hisself. His pals on the rank used to call him the 'Hermit.' Hope there's nothing wrong. Should be sorry to hear Jim had got into trouble."

Sandell then found one of Jim's old chums on the rank, who recollected "the ''Ermit's' luck ven 'e dropt into that bit o' tin. 'Adn't seen much of 'im for a long time arter that, but 'spotted' 'im t'other day doing 'sandwich' at the corner o' Tott'n'am Court Road. Hawful seedy 'e looked, too. Got thro' all 'is quids long ago, and was 'anging out somewhere about Vitechap'l now,

For some two days and nights after this, the detective had hung about Whitechapel and its unsavoury surroundings, scouring all its likeliest dens in search of his man.

At length he ran him to earth in a miserable garret, questioned him as to his past life, and, to make a long story short, got out of the wretched creature sufficient to justify his arrest, on suspicion of having caused the death of Mr. Charles Lawrence.

The poor whining, half-starved wretch was removed in custody that evening, and locked up, pending the magisterial investigation in the morning. But when Sandell and the policeman in charge entered the cell early next day, they found their prisoner raving in a paroxysm of insanity.

Medical aid was at once called in, but too late to save him.

Drink and destitution, aided by the unsleeping pangs of conscience, had done their ghastly work all too surely.

As the afternoon gloom deepened, he passed beyond the jurisdiction of earthly tribunals, dying with a mad imprecation upon his lips.

It was during those frenzied moments in which the day passed that he acted over again the awful tragedy of that Christmas

Eve, four years before. Piece by piece it all came out, down to the smallest incident, forming an unconscious confession of one of the most cowardly and cold-blooded crimes ever committed by the hand of man—the cruellest, the most diabolical of all animals!

Here is the narrative in brief :—

As Charles Lawrence stepped into the hansom, on that fatal night, the glitter of his diamond stud and ring caught Jim Bullen's covetous eye. He longed to possess what appeared to him to represent fabulous wealth. Longing gave place to the murderer's reckless determination.

Swiftly and cautiously lifting the little trap-door in the head of the cab, he struck his unsuspecting victim a sharp, well-directed blow upon the head with a heavy iron " spanner."

With a stifled cry, the handsome, innocent lad fell back stunned.

The murderer wheeled his horse round, and drove like a fury to his lonely hovel in one of the lowest quarters in Stepney.

Once there, he felt that he was safe from detection and consequent punishment. He bore his unconscious but still breathing victim into the dark, solitary cottage, and snatching up a knife from the one ricketty table, plunged it into the heart of the lad, for whom mother, and sister, and brother were at that moment waiting, with loving solicitude, in a far-away country mansion.

Hastily divesting the beautiful corpse of every valuable, the villain hid it away in a corner of the hovel until he should return. Shortly after midnight he got back, and locking himself in with his ghastly accuser, he carefully barricaded door and window. He then stripped the bruised and lacerated body, and buried it deep beneath the hearthstone of his miserable hut.

When the "hue and cry" for the missing lad had pretty well died out, his brutal murderer disposed of the valuable jewellery, for a considerable sum of money, to a notorious thieves' " fence," from whose hands of course it speedily passed.

The criminal then took to the inevitable resource in all such cases, and sought to drown, in the madness of intoxication, the stings of a conscience that could never know rest again.

He succeeded in some measure whilst his ill-gotten funds lasted ; but when they gave out, hope died within his haunted brain, and a constant agonizing fear of retribution took its place.

And so he sank lower and lower, until it wanted but the knowledge that his awful crime had been discovered to crush him into the grave.

This was the substance of the detective's story.

Lawrence sat as one petrified, until the distressing, harrowing tale was all told ; then he sprang to his feet with a terrible oath, and whilst the knotted veins seemed to start from his forehead, he gave vent to the rage and disappointment consuming his heart.

" My God! Foiled—foiled, and within reach of vengeance, too! I would have staked my soul for one chance of cursing the wretch ere he went to his doom! The murderer of our brave, bright boy to die uncursed, unpunished! Oh, it's terrible!"

" Ah, sir," said the detective, "if you'd seen the awful end he made of it, even *you*, sir, wouldn't wish him a worse fate than that!"

CHAPTER VI.

LITTLE more remains to be told. Under the supervision of the police, a search was made for the remains of Charlie Lawrence in the place where the miserable house of his murderer formerly stood ; and there we found the ghastly skeleton—all that was left of that which once was so bright and beautiful.

That same evening Tom left for home, to break the harrowing intelligence to the fond mother and sister. In the morning I followed with the remains, which were laid by loving hands to rest in the family vault at Southfield.

I returned to London and its business worries, as one who had been suddenly awakened from a hideous nightmare.

In little more than a month, I was again summoned to the house of my boyhood's friend.

Once more it was a house of mourning.

The mother's loving heart, unable longer to sustain its agonizing load of grief, had given up the fight and gone to rest.

I found Beatrice and her brother plunged in the profoundest sorrow. Ah, there is no human desolation to be in any way compared to a mother's place suddenly left vacant!

It is, indeed, *the* one irreparable loss, in a world of change and disaster.

As the earliest and purest love of our hearts entwines itself around her who bore us, so the bitterest tears that can ever bedim our eyes fall upon her grave.

I remained for nearly a fortnight at The Priory, and then with difficulty tore myself away from its grief-stricken inmates.

One of them had crept, all unconsciously, into my heart, and brought me thrilling glimpses of new and sweet possibilities.

＊　　＊　　＊　　＊　　＊

My last visit to the dear old English home was made in the early summer of this present year of grace. Need I detail the object of my journey?

Let it suffice that when I left its hospitable roof Tom alone remained in charge.

Here in my cosy suburban home I find the hurrying feet of Time move far too quickly.

But I musn't stay to moralize, for Beatrice is waiting to be taken out, and she is an awful little tyrant in her way.

It is such a sweet way, though!

THE VIAL-GENIE AND MAD FARTHING

[Frederic de la Motte Fouquè]

VIAL-GENIE AND MAD FARTHING.

CHAPTER I.

A YOUNG GERMAN ARRIVES AT VENICE. WHO BID HIM
WELCOME THERE. A SPANISH CAPTAIN
AND HIS VIAL-GENIE.

It was a fine evening of summer, when a young German merchant whose name was Richard, quite a wild and jovial spirit, entered Venice, the far-famed commercial city of Italy. Just at that period, owing to the Thirty Years' War, there were continual disturbances throughout Germany; and in consequence of this state of things, the young merchant, glad to embrace the opportunity of enjoying himself, esteemed it a most fortunate circumstance, that his affairs called him for some time to Italy, where the tumults of war were little felt, and where, as he had been informed, he would meet with wines of the finest flavour, and many of the most delicious fruits, not to mention crowds of women of exquisite beauty, of whom he was a passionate admirer.

On this evening of his arrival, wishing to enjoy the customary amusement of Venice, he stepped aboard a gondola, and was rowed about on the canals, which there supply the place of our paved streets. He took great pleasure in viewing the beautiful houses, and, what were much more attractive, the forms and features of the females, whom he frequently saw gazing from the balconies. At length, as he came opposite a magnificent edifice, at whose windows appeared ten or twelve girls in the bloom of beauty, the gallant young blade said to one of the gondoliers, who were rowing his boat:

" Would to heaven I were so happy as to know those beautiful creatures up there!—that I were allowed to speak only two words to one of them!"—

"Why," said the gondolier, "what can be more easy? you have only to step ashore, and go boldly up to them. Your two words will keep you there but a few moments."

But young Richard replied: " You take pleasure, no doubt, in imposing upon strangers, and think you have found in me a rustic, who is simpleton enough to follow your advice, and then get laughed at above there in the palace, with perhaps a clever drubbing into the bargain."

" Do not think, Sir, to teach me the customs of this country," rejoined the gondolier. " Only do as I have advised you, in case you really wish to enjoy that pleasure, and if they do not open their beautiful white arms and bid you welcome, then I am willing to forfeit my fare."

Supposing the gondolier not to have misrepresented matters, this appeared to our novice well worth the trying. So he landed and went up.

The bevy of girls, that appeared so charming to the stranger, not only received him with the greatest courtesy, but one of the number, she whom he considered the handsomest of them, was still more civil: she conducted him to her own room, where she regaled him with cordials and delicacies, and even gave him the welcome of many a kiss; nay more, he had no single wish remaining, of which she did not grant him at last the complete accomplishment. He could not avoid, every now and then, thinking within himself: " I have assuredly reached the most delightful and extraordinary country in the world: at the same time, however, I cannot be too thankful for my attractions of mind, manners, and person, which render me so acceptable to these foreign ladies of quality."

But when he was on the point of departing, this beauty of his required of him the modest sum of fifty ducats; and as he seemed to be astonished at this demand, she said to him: "Why pray, young gentleman, do you expect to share the favours of the fairest courtesan in all Venice for nothing? Let me advise you to pay with alacrity, for he who makes no agreement beforehand, must rest contented with whatever another may ask him. But, should you come again, then mind and be more prudent, and for the same sum it has cost you this evening, you can pass a whole week in every kind of enjoyment."

What severe mortification was this! especially for one, who, supposing he had made conquest of a princess, discovered that she was a mere woman of the town, and had tricked him too out of so considerable a sum of money! The young fellow showed, however, less indignation than most men would have done. Personal indulgence seemed to be more his object, than distinguished name or excellence of character; and so, after making the payment demanded, he ordered his boatmen to proceed with him to a wine-tavern, where he might drink away his confusion and chagrin.

Our German spark, having thus entered upon a career of dissipation, failed not to have a large number of merry companions. He went on with his revels and riots for a considerable time, and among none but convivial associates: there was one exception, however, to this class of characters, and this was a Spanish captain, who was present indeed at all the jollities of the wild set, to which young Richard had abandoned himself, but almost always without deigning to waste a single word among them, and wearing a strong expression of distress upon every feature of his dark countenance. Still they were willing to endure the gloom of his presence, as he was a person of wealth and respectability, who made nothing of defraying the expenses of the whole band many evenings in succession; and this was an event of no rare occurrence.

Notwithstanding this liberal spirit in the captain, and although young Richard no more suffered himself to be so grossly over-reached, as on the day of his arrival at Venice, still his money began at length to fail, and he could not without deep concern reflect upon the fact, that a life so delightful must for him soon come to an end, should he be so prodigal as to lose all he possessed.

His companions perceived his melancholy, and at the same time detected its cause, — as they had frequently witnessed in their circle occurrences of a like nature, — and they cracked their jokes upon the spendthrift, who, though drained in purse and depressed in spirit, could not refrain, with the remnant of his money, from tasting the sweet poison of dissolute living.

At this time it was, that the Spaniard took him aside one evening, and with an air of unusual kindness, led him into a rather solitary quarter of the city. Our exemplary young gentleman became somewhat alarmed at this, but after a moment's reflection he said to himself: "My companion is well aware, that I have but little more with me to lose ; and as to any personal violence, if such be his aim, he must first hazard his own safety, which he will perhaps value at a rate too high to seek an encounter of that kind."

But the Spanish captain, seating himself upon the foundation of an old ruined building, pressed the young merchant to sit down beside him, and began addressing him as follows :

"I strongly suspect, my dear young friend, that, owing to your inexperience, you are in want of precisely the same power, which to me is above all measure a burden,— the power, I mean, of procuring at any moment a sum of money to whatever amount you may choose, and the ability to continue doing so at will. This power of securing wealth, and many other gifts that the world prizes, I am willing to sell you for a small sum of money."

" But how can more money be of any importance to you, when you wish to dispose of your means of producing it ? " asked Richard.

" The thing is embarrassed with the following condition," answered the captain. " I know not whether you are acquainted with certain diminutive creatures, called vialgenies. These manikin imps are little black devils enclosed in vials. He who possesses one of them, can obtain from him whatever gratification he may wish for in life, but more especially countless sums of money. In return for these, the imp requires the soul of his possessor for his master Lucifer, should the possessor die without having transferred him to other hands. But this transfer can be effected only by sale, and beside he must receive from him a less sum than he gave. My demon cost me ten ducats ; if you are willing to give me nine for him, he is yours."

While young Richard was yet deliberating what to do, the Spaniard went on: "I have the power indeed of imposing upon a person, and of putting the imp into his hands in room of some other vial or play-thing, just as an unprincipled trader put me in possession of him. But I mean to burden my conscience no more, and I offer you the purchase honourably and openly. You are yet young and attached to life, and will doubtless have numerous opportunities of getting rid of the thing, should it ever become oppressive to you as it now is to me."

"My dear Sir," said Richard in return, "you must not take it ill, if I am somewhat slow to believe such wonders, for, since coming to this city of Venice, I have been more than once imposed upon already."

"Why, you foolish young fellow," cried the Spaniard in anger, "you have only to remember my entertainment of last evening, to satisfy yourself whether I would deceive you for the paltry pittance of nine ducats."

"He who is lavish in banqueting, must be lavish also in expenditure," modestly observed the young merchant; "and it is not coffers of gold, but the labour of the hands, that secures to us an unfailing mine of wealth. Now supposing you last night spent the only ducats you had remaining, no doubt my nine, the last but one that I possess, would be very welcome to you."

"Excuse my not stabbing you to the heart," cried the Spaniard, withdrawing his hand from the dagger he had grasped. "Perhaps I break the laws of honour by this forbearance, but I am influenced by a powerful motive: I hope you will relieve me of my genie of the vial, and thus aid me in my resolution to do penance, while such an act of violence would only aggravate my crime."

"Will you give me with the vial, then, some proofs of its value?" the young merchant cautiously asked him.

"How is that possible?" answered the captain. "It remains with him alone, and affords assistance to him alone, who has first fairly bought it with cash."

Young Richard now became anxious and alarmed; for the lonely place, where they sat together in the darkness, appeared dismal, although the captain was prompt to assure him, that, owing to the penance he purposed, he would by no means compel him to embrace his offer. Still all the enjoyments, which would surround him on the acquisition of the vial-demon, seemed at once hovering before him. So he resolved to hazard on the purchase half of all the ready money he possessed, though he first made trial whether he could not reduce the high price somewhat lower.

"You are a fool!" exclaimed the captain with a laugh more grave than gay: "It is for your advantage, and the advantage of those who make the purchase of you, that I ask the highest price: my motive is, that no one may soon buy the vial for the smallest of all the coins in the world, and thus irretrievably become the devil's property, because he would then no longer have the power of selling it."

"Ah, say no more, leave that to me," said Richard in a tone of friendly acquiescence: "Believe me, I shall be in no hurry to dispose of that wonderful thing. Could I have it then for five ducats" ———

"For my own sake I accept the offer," replied the Spaniard. "Should you make your little black devil work out his whole term of service, even to the last moment, a human soul, alas, will be lost too soon."

Receiving the sum offered, he then handed to the young German a slender glass vial, in which Richard saw by the starlight something black leaping wildly up and down.

To prove the worth of his purchase, he at once required in thought the sum he had expended, to be doubled in his right hand, and swift as the wish he felt the ten ducats to be there. He then joyfully returned to the public house, where the rest of his clan were still carousing, and they were all in the highest degree astonished, that their two companions, who had just left them with an air so disconsolate, now re-entered with faces so brightened. But the Spaniard took a hasty leave without remaining to share the rich and sumptuous entertainment, which Richard, although the night had far advanced, ordered to be brought in, — paying the mistrustful landlord beforehand, while through the power of his manikin genie both his pockets chinked anew, with ducats, the very moment he formed the wish to have them.

CHAPTER II.

INCIDENT OF THE BROOK. SIN AND SUFFERING. DANCE OF
VIALS. DEVIL'S CHANT. THE DOCTOR AND HIS
RARE REMEDY. LAWYER'S TRICK.

THOSE persons who would like to get possession, themselves, of such a genie as Richard had obtained, will best
be able to imagine the life, which this jovial youngster led
from this day forward, unless indeed they would choose to
devote themselves to the excesses of avarice. But even
a provident and better disposed mind may easily conceive,
that his course of conduct all savoured of the wildest prodigality. His first concern was, that the beautiful Lucretia, — for by this name his late sharper-courtesan had not
scrupled to call herself, — should by uncounted sums of
money be secured wholly to himself; after which he purchased a palace and two villas, and surrounded himself
with all the imaginable splendour of the world.

It happened one day, that he was sitting with Lucretia
in the garden of one of his country-seats, on the border of
a deep and rapid stream. A good deal of raillery and
laughter had passed between these two young fools, when
at length Lucretia unexpectedly saw and seized the imp-
vial, which Richard had attached to a small chain of gold,
and carried in his bosom under his vest. Before it was in
his power to prevent her, she had torn the delicate chain
from his neck, and now sportively held up the slender vial
toward the light. At first she laughed at the wonderful
gambols of the little black within, and all at once shuddered and screamed with affright : "Foh! it is a
perfect toad !" and she threw chain, vial, and demon into

the stream, which instantly whirled them all from their view.

The poor young fellow strove to conceal his terrour, lest his mistress should press him too closely with questions, and at last bring him before the tribunal of justice on the charge of sorcery. But he represented the thing as a curious toy, and as soon as he thought it discreet, relieved himself of Lucretia's company, in order to deliberate by himself what was now best to be done. He was still in possession of his palace, as well as his country-seats, and a glorious heap of ducats must remain in his pockets. But he was agreeably surprised, when, feeling for his money, he held in his hand both vial and devilkin. The chain was lying perhaps at the bottom of the brook, while the vial and wishing genie had safely returned to their owner. "Why, how is this?" cried he in a transport: "I possess a treasure, then, of which no power on earth can deprive me!" and he would no doubt have kissed the vial, had not the little gamboling black within looked rather too horrible.

Wild and as extravagant as Richard's career had hitherto been, he now made it ten times more so. He looked down with pity and contempt upon all the princes and potentates of the earth, convinced that no one of them could enjoy half so delightful a life as his. Scarcely an individual, in the rich commercial city of Venice, could bring together such rare viands and choice wines, as he demanded for his sumptuous banquets. Whenever any friendly person reproved or warned him in relation to these, he was wont to reply: "Richard is my name, and my riches are so inexhaustible, that no expenses can make any impression upon the sum." Often too did he laugh immoderately at the Spanish Captain, who sought to rid himself of a treasure so invaluable, and who, as he was told, in addition to such folly, had retired into a monastery.

But every thing earthly is of brief continuance. This truth was our young libertine, as well as the rest of the world, compelled to experience, and no doubt the sooner, as he abandoned himself to every species of sensual pleasure with the most unbounded indulgence. A deathlike weariness fell upon his exhausted body, notwithstanding his wishing genie, whose assistance, the first day of his illness, he called for ten times — in vain. One weary hour followed another: still he became no better, and moreover, he that night had a strange dream.

It seemed to him, that one of the vials of medicine, that stood by his bed, began the merriest fandango ever danced, and with ceaseless din kept clinking and tinkling against the tops and sides of the rest. When Richard examined the matter more narrowly, he saw it was the vial that contained his demon, and he exclaimed : " Why, you gallows-bird, you gallows-bird, you not only refuse to help me, in defiance of your duty, but are spilling and destroying the medicines provided for my cure." The fiend, however, sang hoarsely from his vial in reply :

> " Why, Richard dear, why, Richard dear,
> No endless pains torment you here ;
> But when you hell's fierce tortures share,
> You'll feel the gentlest patience there.
> To cure your ails I craft have none,
> For death no healing herb has grown,
> It joys me, — you are now my own."

Thus chanting his devil's' doggerel, he stretched himself out into a long and slender shape ; and fast as Richard held the vial, he crawled out between his thumb and the sealed stopple, and became a huge black figure, that hideously danced about, and at the same time made a swift whirring with his bat-like wings, and finally pressed his hairy breast upon the breast of Richard, and his grinning face upon his face, so firmly and so closely, that Richard felt as if he already began to resemble him, and shrieked out in terrour: "A mirrour ! a mirrour ! bring me a mirrour ! "

He woke in the cold sweat of agony, while it still seemed to him, as if a black toad were running nimbly down his bosom into the pocket of his night-robe. Shuddering, he thrust his hand into it, but brought nothing out except the vial, wherein the little black was now lying, as if wearied out and dreaming.

Alas, how endless to the sick man appeared the remainder of this night ! He would no longer trust himself to sleep, fearing it would bring the black miscreant upon him again ; and still he hardly ventured to open his eyes, fearful that the monster might be actually lurking in some corner of the room. If he again closed them, he thought the form had come creeping close upon him by stealth, and once more started up in terrour. He rung the bell for his attendants, but they continued sleeping as soundly as if they were deaf or dead, and Lucretia, since his illness, had never once appeared in his chamber. Thus then was he obliged to lie alone in his anguish, which became still more aggravated, as this reflection was continually forced upon him : "Ah, my God, if this night seem so long, how long will be the perpetual night of hell !" and he resolved, should God spare his life until the morrow, to employ all the means in his power of freeing himself from his fiend.

When morning at length came, and he was somewhat enlivened and strengthened by the early light, he set about considering whether he had as yet derived as much advantage from his purchase, as it would be wise to do. His palace, villas, and every variety of splendour appearing insufficient, he instantly required a great quantity more of ducats under his pillow ; and the moment he found the heavy bag there, he began calmly to deliberate, to whom he could best sell his vial. His physician, he knew, was fond of collecting all the strange creatures, that are preserved in spirit, and he hoped to pass off his genie to him for one of these, because the doctor, being a religious man, would make no improper use of it. To be sure, it would be playing him a scurvy trick, but he reasoned himself into the measure thus : " It is better to expiate a smaller sin in purgatory, than to yield yourself up to Lucifer irrevocably. Besides, every man is most interested in his own destiny, and my danger of death admits of no delay."

Thus the matter rested. He offered the imp to the physician. It had just become lively again, and was gamboling in its vial right merrily ; so that the learned man, wishing to examine such a production of nature more closely, (for in that light it was he considered it) said he should like to buy it, if the price were not too high. With a view to ask enough to satisfy his conscience, in some

degree at least, Richard set the price as high as he could,—
four ducats, two thalers, and twenty groschen, German
money. But the doctor was not willing to give more than
three ducats at most, and decided at last, that if he could
not have it for that, he must think of it a few days. Then
the horrour of death again fell upon the poor young sin-
ner; he let him take it for three ducats, and ordered his
servants to distribute them among the poor. He kept his
bag of money under his pillow, however, now purposing,
in the best manner he could, to found upon it all his future
fortune, — whether weal or woe.

The young merchant's illness, meantime, became extremely severe. He lay almost continually in a delirium
of fever; and had he still felt on his heart the distress occasioned by his vial-fiend, he would no doubt have per-
ished with anguish of soul. But that being removed, he
at length gradually recovered, and a single circumstance,
alone, was all that retarded his perfect restoration: this
was the anxiety, with which he every moment thought of
the ducats he had placed under his pillow, and which
from his first lucid interval he had searched for there in
vain. He felt unwilling, at first, to ask any one respecting them; but when he at last did so, no one chose to
know any thing of the matter. He sent to Lucretia, who
in the most dangerous hours of his unconsciousness would
be about him, and had now returned home again to her
former companions. But she ordered his messenger to
carry back this answer to his inquiries : 'That there was
no use in troubling either her or himself about the ducats;
for had he ever mentioned them either to her or any other
person? and if no one knew any thing about them, his
impression must doubtless have been all produced by the
frenzy of fever.'

While he was rising with a weight of sadness on his
mind, the thought struck him, that he could convert his
palace and country houses into money. But several persons came in soon after, who brought deeds of all his possessions, which they had bought and paid for; they were
signed and sealed by himself, for in the season of his pride
and prodigality he had given blank-bonds to Lucretia, to
make whatever use of them she might chuse; and he was

now compelled, in his reduced state, to scrape together the miserable fragments of his fortune, in order to set himself up as little more than a beggar.

In addition to this calamity, came the physician who had cured him, with a solemn countenance. — " Why, doctor," exclaimed the young prodigal, fretfully accosting him, " if, after the practice of all your tribe, you have come with your bill drawn out as long as your arm, then give me a poison-powder into the bargain ; for the consequence of paying such a demand, I well know, would be my ruin ; my last bread would be baked, since I should have no money to buy any more."

" Not so," replied the physician with much gravity ; " I remit to you my whole charge for your cure. But I bring you a rare remedy, which I have already set away in that cupboard, and which you may take for your future strengthening, as occasion may require ; — for this you must allow me two ducats. Would you like to have it ? "

" Yes, with all my heart ! " cried the delighted merchant, and gave him the money. The doctor then left the chamber with as much speed as possible. But hardly had Richard put his hand into the cupboard, when his genievial already stood snugly between his fingers. A small billet was twisted about it, in which were the following rhymes :

" Your body I sought to cure,
    My soul you sought to kill ;
Soon warned by deeper lore,
    I knew your scoundrel will.

Preferring you to all, —
    How pat the countermine ! —
I here to worthier hands
    Your devilkin resign.

Be a gallows-rope
A gallows-bird's hope,
And a devil's friend
Have a devil's end."

Young Richard was certainly in extreme terrour, when he found that he had purchased the vial-fiend again, and for so small a sum. But still there was joy mixed with the terrour. He purposed to be soon rid of the imp again,
11*

and he was not embarrassed with the least scruple in regard to the way, so determined was he, by means of it, on being revenged upon the vile cheat, Lucretia.

And he undertook the business in the following manner. He first wished his pockets replenished with double the number of ducats, that he had placed under his pillow, and he immediately almost sunk to the ground beneath their weight. The whole of this enormous sum he deposited with the nearest advocate, and took such receipt or security as the law requires, reserving only about a hundred and twenty pieces of gold, with which he repaired to the residence of the dissolute Lucretia. There he again gave himself up to intemperance, gaming, and every species of folly, as he had done some months before, and Lucretia showed exceeding kindness to the young merchant, — in consideration of his money. From time to time he played every variety of ingenious juggling tricks by means of his vial-genie, and told his astonished mistress, that it was a thing of the same kind as that, which she had once thrown into the water, and that he was in possession of several of them. Like other women, she too was eager to possess a plaything so curious, and when, as if he were in sport, he demanded money for it, she without hesitation gave him a ducat. The bargain being closed, Richard left the house as soon as possible, in order to get from the advocate a part of the sum intrusted to his care. But not a stiver could he obtain there ; the lawyer opened his eyes as wide as an owl, and appeared to be exceedingly surprised : he was a perfect stranger, he said, to the young gentleman. When Richard would have produced a testimonial from his pocket, he found it nothing but an unwritten piece of white paper. The advocate had written his document with that kind of ink, which fades away in a few hours, and leaves no vestige of the words. By this manœuvre, so contrary to all expectation, the young blade saw himself again impoverished ; and he would have been a beggar, had he not still retained in his pocket about thirty ducats of his lavish expenditure with Lucretia.

CHAPTER III.

OUR HERO REDUCED TO A PEDLAR. RICHARD HIMSELF
AGAIN. RESUMES HIS GRAND STYLE OF LIVING.
HIS THREE GROSCHEN.

HE whose bed is too short, must lie crooked ; he who
has no bed at all, must make shift to sleep on the floor ;
he who is unable to pay for a carriage, must ride on horse-
back ; and he who has no horse, must go on foot.

After some days of idle indecision, Richard saw clearly,
that in this lounging kind of life his money would soon be
exhausted, and that he must resolve at once to sink for a
time from merchant to pedlar. So making inquiry for a
small trunk, suitable to his humble employment, he found
one to his mind : he bought a box also to hold the remnant of
his money, while for every little article he put into his
trunk, he paid on an average about four groschen, German
money.

Alas, what a change was here ! how irksome he found
the task of bending over the strap, and offering his trinkets
for sale in those very streets, where, only a few weeks
before, he had flaunted with all the airs of lordly insolence !
He however got through the day with a pretty cheerful
mind, as purchasers came for the most part running to
meet him, and frequently offered him more than he
had ventured to ask. — " The city after all is very good,"
he thought within himself, " and if things go on in this
way, a short period of hardship will again raise me to the
condition of a wealthy man. I will then return to Germany, and shall be so much the more able to realize the

comforts of home, since having been in the clutches of the cursed vial-genie, I have had sense and consideration enough to escape out of them."

With musings of this nature he flattered and comforted himself that evening at the inn, where he had just set down his trunk. Some inquisitive guests were standing about the bar-room, and one of them asked him: "What strange animal is that, friend, which you have in that vial there, and which is tumbling and shooting about so comically?"—Richard darted a look of alarm that way, and now for the first time perceived, that among other trinkets of his trade he had unawares possessed himself of the vial-demon again. Without a moment's delay, he offered it to the stranger who made the inquiry, for three groschen,—he had just given four for it himself,—and with the same haste he offered it to all the guests at the same price. But they were disgusted with the odious black creature, for which he was unable to tell them the least use,—or none that he dared tell them; and as he kept pressing his worthless toy upon them, never ceasing to interrupt their talk, they turned their troublesome companion, together with his trunk and black jumper, out of the house.

In perfect agony of soul, he hurried to the man who had sold him the box containing the vial, and would have forced upon him the little Satan for a lower price than he gave. But the man was drowsy, and absolutely refused to have any thing to do with the matter; and he ended by saying, that if he was determined to restore the hateful vial to its first owner, he must go with it to the wench Lucretia; she had sold him the thing, together with several other trifles. But for himself, he begged to be allowed to sleep in peace.

"Ah, most gracious God!" sighed Richard from the depth of his soul, "how is it possible for him to sleep thus peacefully!" While he was hurrying across a great square, in order to reach the residence of Lucretia, he felt the certain conviction, that somebody was running and making a rustling behind him in the darkness, and every now and then grasping him by the neck. Trembling with terrour, he entered Lucretia's apartment by a back door, formerly quite familiar to him. She was still seated at a

merry supper with two of her paramours, who were strangers to him. At first she did not know who he was, and
reproved the insolent pedlar with severity. Her sparks
however purchased nearly all the articles he had, as pres-
ents for the courtesan, who thus coming to know him,
began laughing him to scorn. But as for the vial-genie,
no one was disposed to buy it. When he repeatedly made
them the offer of it, Lucretia cried out :

"Foh! away with the offensive thing! I have already
been the owner of it once, and endured the abomination a
whole day. I then sold it for several groschen to a miser-
ly sharper resembling its present owner, this huckster, who
had himself persuaded me to give him a ducat for it."

"It was for your own temporal advantage," cried the
young merchant in deep distress : "you know not, Lucretia, what a treasure you are thrusting from you. Let me
speak but five minutes alone with you, and you will not
fail to purchase the vial."

She stepped a little apart with him, and he fully disclosed to her the strange secret of the wishing genie. But
she only began to scream and revile him. "Do you still
take me for a fool, you rascally beggar ? " she cried.
"Were your story true, you would certainly require Satan
to give you something of more value, than that trunk and
that strap. Pack off! And even should you speak false-
ly, I will denounce you as a sorcerer and wizard ; and then
you will be burnt, senseless braggadocio that you are."

In addition to this abuse, the two profligates, in order
to recommend themselves to their mistress, fell upon the
young stripling, bewildered and alarmed as he was, and,
after pommeling him without mercy, pitched him down
stairs ; so that although enraged at this ignominious treatment, he was so horribly afraid of being burnt for sorcery,
that he did nothing but hurry from Venice with all the
speed in his power. By the next day at noon he had left
its boundaries, when he turned and cursed it from its borders, as the cause of all his misery.

At this moment Richard saw the vial-genie peering from
his pocket, and while he chanced to observe the creature's
wild jumps and gambols, he exclaimed: "Well, this is
fortunate, you worthless miscreant ; you shall still prove of

some service to me, and aid me too in the more expeditiously getting rid of you." And he instantly wished himself again a countless sum of money, much more than at the last time ; and now, with difficulty supporting his heavy pockets, he stole along into the nearest town. There he bought a brilliant chariot, hired lackeys, and hastened to plunge into the vortex of dissipation, — the pomp and luxury of the great metropolis, Rome, — fully persuaded that there, amid the confusion of so many men of diverse wishes and manners, he should get rid of the foe of his peace. Meanwhile, as often as he spent his ducats, he required his imp to make good the sum expended, so that after the sale of the vial he might still have the whole undiminished. This appeared to him no more than a just recompense for the misery he endured ; for it was not enough, that almost every night the demon assumed again the hideous black figure of his first dream, and lay upon his breast ; — he saw also when wide awake, that the fiend continually danced about in his vial with such a frenzy of delight, as if he were now sure of his prey, and were exulting in prospect of the speedy accomplishment of his term of servitude.

Hardly had his wealth and profusion introduced him into the most distinguished society of Rome, ere his terrour, ever awake, allowed him no leisure to wait for convenient opportunities of selling his enemy. To every man he addressed, he without distinction, offered the vial for three groschen, German money, and was soon viewed as a strange madman, the universal derision of the city. Money indeed inspires courage and gains us friends. He was everywhere, too, very desirous of making a display of his riches ; but the instant he began to speak of his vial and three groschen, German money, all nodded to him with much courtesy, and then with a smile made haste to disengage themselves from his company. This treatment led him often to remark : " There is only one thing prevents men's selling themselves to the devil, and that is, alas !.... they are more than half his already ! "

CHAPTER IV.

JOINS A TROOP IN DESPAIR. SKIRMISH. ADVENTURE
OF SOLDIERS IN A WOOD.

Our hero was at last seized with such a feeling of despair, that he could bear to remain in the beautiful city of Rome no longer; so he formed the resolution of taking his chance in war, to see whether he could not deliver himself from his vial-demon there. Hearing that two of the small states of Italy were engaged in hostilities, he seriously prepared to attach himself to one of the parties. Provided with a coat of mail ornamented with gold, a hat waving with plumes, a choice pair of horse-pistols, a sword as bright as a mirrour, and two costly daggers, he rode from the gates on a Spanish charger, followed by three well-armed attendants on stout horses.

Would not a warriour so well equipped, and who was willing beside to serve without pay, receive a warm welcome from any captain of horse whatever? The bold Richard saw himself at once enrolled in a brave troop, and for a long while fared so well, and lived so pleasantly in the camp, that he seemed to be less sensible to his severe distress arising from his genie, and the stifling dreams with which he was all night persecuted. Gaining wisdom from his experience at Rome, he now became more cautious how he offered his unwelcome article with too much importunity. As yet, indeed, he had avoided mentioning it to any of his comrades; and this he did, that he might effect his purpose the more easily, and, as it might seem, in sport.

One fine morning, about this time, some scattering reports of fire-arms came cracking from the neighbouring mountain. The troopers, who happened at the moment to be playing dice with Richard, paused and listened; soon after the trumpets blew a blast, summoning all to muster throughout the camp. They mounted their horses in haste, and moved rapidly and in good order toward the plain, at the foot of the mountain. On the mountain side they already saw the foot-soldiers of both armies enveloped in vapour and smoke; the enemy's horse formed on the plain. Richard felt in high spirits, as his Spanish war-horse neighed and pranced under him, his weapons produced an inspiring clang, the leaders shouted, the trumpets blew. A troop of horse, belonging to the enemy, advanced toward them, with a view, as it appeared, to prevent their ascending the mountain, but soon sheered off and retreated before the superiour force; and Richard, with his attendants, was by no means among the last, who pressed them hard at full gallop, and who were greatly amused in becoming themselves the pursuers and objects of alarm. All at once they heard a whizzing in the air over their heads. The horses started; then came the whizzing a second time, and a horseman, struck by a cannon-ball, rolled with his horse in blood.

Now Richard thought within himself, "the greater the number the greater the safety," and he was on the point of scouring off, when to his astonishment his own troop came pouring on close in his rear, resolving to advance upon the foe, almost in the very face of the artillery. Richard kept with them for a while; but when the balls began to tear up the ground near him, on the right and left, and the enemy's horse were pushing forward in great numbers, the thought flashed upon him: "Why, where am I? How have I been guilty of such madness, as to rush into peril like this! On this meadow I am much nearer death, than on the bed of sickness; and should one of these cursed whizzers hit me, I am the booty of the imp and his master Lucifer forever." — And hardly had the thought darted through his mind, when his Spanish courser turned, and rushed with uncontroulable swiftness toward a wood not far off.

So long and so wildly did he spur forward beneath the lofty trees, and so perfectly regardless was he of path or direction, that at last his horse stood stock-still through exhaustion. Overwearied himself, he then dismounted, disengaged himself from his cuirass and shoulder-belt, and his horse from his head-stall and saddle, and said, as he flung himself upon the grass: "Why, good Heaven! how little I am fitted for a soldier, at least with the vial-fiend in my pocket!"—He was now about to deliberate what his next move should be, but in doing so he fell into a deep slumber.

When he had slept a considerable time, it may have been many hours, a murmur like that of human voices, and the sound of the trampling of men's feet, came crowding upon his ear. But as he lay stretched upon the cool turf of the forest, he tried to keep out of his mind the bustle, and to sink deeper and deeper into the lethargy of sleep, until a voice of thunder burst upon him: "Are you already dead, in the devil's name? Speak, speak instantly, or we crack away upon you, and burn our powder for nothing."—Our hero, thus roused with so little ceremony, looked up and saw a musket levelled at his breast. The man who held it, was a grim-looking foot-soldier, whose companions stood around, having already taken possession as well of his weapons as of his horse and portmanteau. He begged for quarter, and cried above all in the greatest agony of spirit:

"If you *will* shoot me, do at least first buy this small vial in the right pocket of my doublet."

"Buy it! you stupid fellow," replied one of the soldiers with a laugh; "I will not buy it, but as sure as fate I will have it." And while speaking, he seized the vial, and tucked it into his bosom.

"In God's name," cried Richard, "take the creature, if you are only able to keep him. But unless you buy him, he will not stay with you."

The soldiers laughed, and marched off with horse and booty,—giving themselves no more trouble about a man, whom they looked upon as half crazy. But feeling in his pocket, and finding his fatal genie snug in his place again, he shouted after them, and held up the vial. The soldier who had taken it from him, in astonishment thrust his hand in his bosom, and, not finding it there, ran back to get it a second time.

"I tell you of a truth," said Richard in distress, "it will never remain with you, unless you buy it. Pray give me only a few groschen for it."

"Ay, you conjurer!" replied the soldier with a laugh; "never think to chouse me after that fashion, — I am not to be fooled out of my hard-earned money so easily." And he ran after his comrades, carefully holding the vial in his hand. But stopping suddenly, he cried:

"The devil! the thing has slipped through my fingers in spite of all my care."

While he was hunting for it among the grass, Richard shouted to him: "For heaven's sake do only come here. It has got into my pocket again already."

When the soldier became sensible of the nature of the animal, he for the first time felt a real inclination for the sportive thing, which, — as it was wont to do, when it was sold, — showed the highest glee and delight; for whenever it changed its master, it of course drew nearer to the end of its slavery. — But the three groschen he asked for it, appeared to the soldier to be too much, at which Richard said impatiently:

"Well, you stingy fellow, if you think so, we will not chaffer about trifles. I shall be satisfied, if you are. Give me a single groschen then, and take the thing." So the bargain was closed, the money paid, and the little Satan delivered up.

While the soldiers continued standing a little way off, observing and laughing at this whimsical sale and purchase, Richard reflected upon his future fate. He now stood there with a light heart, indeed, but at the same time with pockets as light, and with no fair prospect of improving his condition; for he could not venture to return to his company of horsemen, where his attendants yet remained with weapons, horses, and a large sum of money. This was partly owing to shame on account of his disgraceful flight, and partly because he feared being shot as a deserter according to martial law. Then the thought occurred to him, whether it would not be wise to change sides, and

go at once with these soldiers to their army. He had
learned from their talk, that they belonged to the other
party, where no one would know him ; and having disposed of his demon, he was now well pleased, destitute
as he was of money, and unlucky as his experiment in
war had been, to hazard his life on any adventure of promise. He expressed his desire, they consented to what he
proposed, and he went with his new companions to their
camp.

CHAPTER V.

THE captain made little or no difficulty in receiving a
young fellow of so fine a form and so muscular a frame,
as Richard, and he now passed his life for some time as
a foot-soldier. But still he was often a prey to dejection
and grief. Ever since the last engagement, the two armies had lain inactive over against each other, as a treaty
of peace was on foot between the two states. He was
not now, to be sure, exposed to the danger of death, but
at the same time he had just as little opportunity of plunder and booty. He was obliged to live within the camp
in peaceful inaction, his pay very slender, and his portion of
food equally small. In addition to these circumstances,
most of the soldiers had possessed themselves of considerable plunder during the progress of the war; and Richard,
who, as a merchant, had fared so sumptuously as almost
to rival the luxury of kings, was now compelled to make
shift, as it were, with the scanty subsistence of a beggar.
This was a kind of life, of which he was naturally enough
soon weary; and when he one day held in his hand his
pittance of wages for a month, — too little to support him
in comfort, too much to hazard for nothing at all, — he
resolved to go to the sutler's tent, and see whether dice
would not be more propitious to him, than business and
war had hitherto been.

Richard's course of playing discovered the usual vari-

ety of fortune : now winning, and then losing, he continued at the gaming table till late at night, by which time
he had become not a litle intoxicated. But at last every
throw of the dice went against him in his present condition; his month's wages were all played away, and no
one would give him credit for even a half-penny. He then
rummaged all his pockets, and finding them empty, he
at last opened his cartridge-box, where was nothing but
cartridges. He produced these, and offered them as a
stake; they were accepted, and the moment the dice
rolled upon the table, the tipsy Richard saw for the first
time, that the same soldier had thrown upon them, who had
some time before purchased his imp-vial of him, and who
without doubt would now become the winner of them.
He would have cried out, "Hold!" but the dice were
already thrown, and had decided in favour of his oppo-
nent. He left the company with curses on his lips, and
returned toward his tent amid the darkness of night. A
comrade, who had also lost his money in gambling, but who
had kept himself more sober, took him by the arm.

As they walked along, the man asked him whether he
still had cartridges provided in his tent. "No," cried
Richard, almost maddened with rage; "had I the means
yet in my power, be assured I would return and play
longer."

"Ah, is that the case?" replied his comrade; "then
you must contrive to buy some more, for should the
commissary come to the review, and find a paid soldier
without cartridges, he would order him to be shot."

"Thunder and lightning!" exclaimed Richard, cursing
himself, "how was it possible for me to be so stupid! I
have neither cartridges, nor money to buy any."

"Why," rejoined his companion, "the commissary
does not come these four or five months."

"Oh, then all is safe," thought Richard; "before that
time I receive my pay again, and shall be able to buy
cartridges to my heart's content." Upon this they bade
each other good night, and Richard lay down to sleep off
the excesses of the evening.

But he had not lain long, ere the corporal came and
shouted before the tent : " Holla within there ! tomorrow

12*

is muster day ; the commissary will be in camp at day-break."

Richard's slumber was instantly broken. Though quite bewildered by intemperance, he still felt the loss of his cartridges blending with the confusion of his senses. He went round to his comrades of the tent, and anxiously inquired, whether any one would lend them, or sell them to him on trust. But they cursed him for a night-revelling tippler, and sent him back to his straw. In extreme anguish, through fear of being shot in the morning, he searched for money in every garment he possessed, but was unable to find among them all more than five half-pence. With these he now ran stumbling from tent to tent amid the obscurity of night, and tried to buy cartridges. Some laughed, others abused him, but no one gave him so much as an answer to his request.

At length he came to a tent, from which the voice of the soldier, who had won his cartridges an hour or two before, saluted him with curses. " Comrade," cried Richard in a moving accent, " either you can assist me, or no one. You took my all last evening, and aided others before in plundering me. Should the commissary find me without cartridges in the morning, he would give orders for my being shot. You are the cause of all my misery. Give them to me then, or lend them to me, or sell them to me, whichever you will."

" Either to give or lend, is what I have sworn never to do," replied the soldier ; " but, to be freed from the trouble of you, I will sell you the cartridges. How much money have you ? "

" Only five half-pence," answered Richard in a mournful tone.

" Well," said the soldier, " that you may see I am a friendly fellow, there you have five cartridges for your five half-pence, and now to bed again, and leave me and the camp in quiet."

Saying this, he reached him the cartridges out of the tent, while Richard handed him in the money, and then with a mind relieved he went back, and slept undisturbed till morning.

The inspection took place, and Richard got through

with his five cartridges; toward noon the commissary
departed, and the soldiers returned to the camp. But the
sun burnt insupportably through the canvass tent, and the
companions of Richard went to the sutler's, while he remained himself sitting at home with empty pockets, and
gnawing a piece of the commissary's crust, faint and ill
with the excess of the preceding day and his fatigue of
the present.

"Ah," said he with a sigh, "would to Heaven I had
only one ducat, — only *one* of all those I have squandered
in a way so thoughtless and wasteful!" when hardly had
he breathed the wish, and a bright ducat lay in his left
hand. Thought of the vial-genie now shot through
his mind, embittering all his joy, as he felt the heavy piece
of gold in his palm. That instant his fellow-soldier, who
had let him have the cartridges in the night, entered the
tent all in a flurry, and said: "Friend, you know that
vial with its little black tumbler; — you must remember I
some time ago bought it of you in the wood; — it has
disappeared. Did I give it to you unawares instead of a
cartridge? I had wrapped it in paper like my cartridges,
and laid it away with them."

Richard searched his cartridge-box in alarm, and the
very first paper he took up and unwrapped, contained the
slender vial and his fearful slave.

"Well, that is lucky," cried the soldier, "I should have
been very sorry to lose him, glum as he looks; it always
seems to me, that he brings me extraordinary good luck
at play. There, comrade, take your half-penny again,
and give the creature to me." Richard, with all the haste
in his power, complied with his request, and the soldier
hurried well pleased to the tent of the sutler. But the
unhappy Richard, from the moment he had seen the vial-
fiend again, held him in his hands, and carried him about
with him, endured a misery amounting to horrour. Such
was his dread, that he thought the demon must be grinning
at him from every fold of the tent, and while he was unaware, might strangle him in his sleep. The ducat, which
only a wish had called into his possession, he threw from
him in his agony of alarm, however extreme his need of
refreshment might be; and at last the fear that the genie

might be nestling so near him again, drove him far out of
the camp, and by evening twilight he had hurried into the
darkest recesses of a wood, where, exhausted by terrour
and fatigue, he sunk down on a desert spot.

"Oh miserable man!" he sighed, parched with thirst,
"would to God I only had a canteen of water to keep me
from fainting!" And a canteen of water stood by his
side. Scarcely had he, too eager to be conscious of the
act, swallowed a few draughts of it, ere he asked himself
whence it could have come. The wishing genie then flashed
across his mind again; with intense emotion he thrust his
hand into his pocket, and feeling the vial there, he sunk
back, overpowered by terrour into a deep swoon.

During this swoon-sleep, the horrible dream, with which
he had been afflicted before, returned upon him; and the
demon, rising taller and taller from his prison, lay grinning
on his breast with the weight of lead. He would have
struggled against the fiend, and disclaimed all connexion
with him, but the fiend cried with a hollow laugh: "You
have bought me for a half-penny; you must now sell me
for less; otherwise the bargain will not hold good."

Richard sprung upon his feet in a cold horrour, and
again imagined he saw the shadowy form, just as it was
snuggling into the vial in his pocket. Half distracted, he
hurled it down the precipice of a rock, but the moment
after felt it in his pocket again.

"O woe! woe!" he screamed aloud, till the forest rung
amid the gloom of night; "once I viewed it as my peculiar happiness, my blessed fortune, that the vial was sure
to return to me even from the waves and deep waters;
now it is my misery, alas, it may be, my eternal misery!"
and he began to run through the dark thickets of the wood,
rushing against tree and rock in the obscurity, and at every
step he heard the vial clink, clink in his pocket.

He left the forest by dawn of day, and came out upon a
bright, cheerful, and cultivated plain. His heart was
deeply oppressed with melancholy, but he began to indulge the hope, that all this wild turmoil of his might be
no more than a dream of frenzy or delusion; possibly he
might find the glass in his pocket of a different kind, and
such as was quite common. Drawing it forth, he held it

up to the morning sun. Ah, God of heaven! there the little black devil was dancing away between him and the pleasant light, and stretching toward him as usual his small misshapen arms like tongs. With a loud scream he let the vial drop, but only to hear it the moment after cuddle clinking into his pocket again.

What could he do ? The sole and engrossing object of his life must now be to search for a coin of less value than a half-penny, but with all his searching he could nowhere find any. So that every hope of selling his detested slave, who now threatened soon to become his master, vanished. He determined to demand nothing more of this terrible demon, for every time he attempted to do so, a fearful agony took from him both strength and recollection, and thus then he went begging up and down throughout Italy. As he now discovered the wildest discomposure in his air, and besides, while wandering on from town to town, continually kept asking for farthings, he was everywhere considered as crazy, and was called nothing but the Mad Farthing, by which name he was soon distinguished far and wide.

CHAPTER VI.

A RED HORSEMAN AND HIS BLACK HORSE. DUSKY RAVINE.
MONSTER AND PRINCE. BLACK FOUNTAIN.
THE DEVIL OUTWITTED.

IT is said of vultures, that they sometimes pounce upon
the necks of young deer or of other wild animals, and thus
pursue their poor victim even to death, clinging to him
and attacking him with the most determined fierceness, as
in his flight of fear and torment he rushes through bush and
brake, forest and ravine. In like manner fared the unhappy Richard with his imp of Satan in his pocket; but
since it would be too painful and excite too much com-
miseration to dwell upon the excess of his sufferings, I
shall say nothing more to you respecting his long and
helpless flight, but relate only what happened to him
many months afterward.

One afternoon, having lost his way on the southern
ascent of a wild mountain tract, he was sitting silent and
sorrowful on the margin of a small stream, whose waters,
trickling down among the bushy undergrowth, seemed to
have a feeling of sympathy and compassion for him, and
to be urging on their course to soothe and refresh him;—
when all at once he started, as if thrilled by an electric
shock, for the powerful tramp of a horse came sounding
over the stones and rocks of the mountain, and, riding on
a high, black, wild-looking courser, appeared a man of gigantic figure, his countenance hideous in the extreme, his
garments magnificent, and of a blood-red colour. He approached the spot where Richard was sitting.

"Why so disconsolate, friend?" cried he, accosting the

young man, whose very soul trembled with alarm and a presentiment of calamity. "I should take you for a merchant. Have you bought any goods too dear?"

"Alas no, quite the contrary; my purchase has been too cheap," answered Richard in a low trembling voice.

"So also it appears to me, my dear merchant," cried the horseman with a frightful laugh. "And you have, it may be, a small article to sell me this evening, called a vial-genie? Or do I mistake, when I suppose you to be the famous MAD FARTHING?"

Hardly could the poor young fellow return answer, with blanched lips and in a subdued tone, "Yes, I am he:" he shuddered as if he were expecting every moment to see the horseman's mantle take the form of blood-dropping wings, and his charger expand his broad vans covered with feathers black as night, and illumined by the flames of hell, and himself, wretched man, be borne swiftly away to the abode of eternal torment.

But the horseman went on with a voice somewhat softened and gestures less terrible: "I see plainly for whom you take me. Pray be comforted; I am not he. So far from it, I may perhaps deliver you from his power, for I have been these many days in quest of you, with a view to make purchase of your vial-treasure. You gave, it is true, but a cursed small piece of money for it, and I know not myself where to find a smaller. But listen, and mark what I say to you. On the northern side of this mountain lives a prince, a young man of extravagant habits. Tomorrow morning, when he goes out to hunt, I shall drive a horrible monster upon him, the very instant I succeed in withdrawing him from his train of attendants. Do you, meantime, remain here till midnight, and then, — exactly at the moment the moon rises over that jagged rock yonder, — set off at a moderate pace eastward, along that dusky ravine to the left. Neither loiter nor hurry, and you will arrive at the place, just when the monster has the prince in his clutches. Do you ask what next? You have only to seize the beast with a fearless grasp, and he will be forced to yield to you, and tumble headlong before you down the steep crags of the sea-shore. Then, while the prince is warm with gratitude, request him to allow you to coin a

few farthings, exchange two of them with me, and for one
of them the vial-genie shall be mine."

Thus spoke the terrible horseman, and, without waiting
to receive an answer, rode slowly into the thickets of the
mountain.

"But where shall I find you, when I get the farthings?"
Richard shouted after him.

"At the Black Fountain!" shouted the horseman in
return. "Every nurse in the district can tell you where
that lies."

And with slow, but far reaching strides, the huge steed
bore off his hideous burden.

For a person, who is almost the same as completely
ruined, there can be no more room for choice or hesitation;
Richard resolved therefore, in the misery of his despair, to
comply with the advice of the terrible horseman.

Night came on, the moon rose, and with its reddish lustre at length stood over the craggy cliff that had been
pointed out. The pale wanderer then moved forward,
trembling, and entered the dusky ravine. All within appeared joyless and gloomy; seldom was a moonbeam admitted over the lofty summits on either hand; and there
was a vapour in this confined passage, like the effluvia of
the tomb, but he met with nothing else to annoy him.
Faithful to the horseman's instructions, Richard was careful neither to linger nor hasten, but resolved that through
no fault of his own would he lose his hold on that slender
thread which as yet connected him with light and hope.

After the lapse of many hours, some faint rays of morning light beamed upon his obscure passage, while cool airs
with a comforting influence came breathing in his face.
But just as he emerged from the deep pathway, and began
to enjoy the freshness of the woodlands, and the glimmer-
ing of the blue sea, that lay only a short distance from him,
a cry of distress broke in upon his enjoyment. Looking
round, he saw where a monstrous beast had thrown a
young man in a rich hunting suit upon the ground, and
was standing over him. Richard's first impulse, indeed,
was to run and afford assistance; but when he fixed his
eyes directly upon the beast, and saw that he resembled a
fierce baboon of monstrous size, and that his head was

armed with the prodigious horns of a hart, his courage all
forsook him, and he felt tempted, notwithstanding the
fallen stranger's cry of distress for help, to creep back into
his ravine again. Then it was, that he seemed first to
remember what the horseman had said; and impelled by
fear of eternal perdition, he rushed upon the monster-ape
with his knotted club. The beast was just seizing the
hunter in his forepaws, in order, as it appeared, to throw
him up into the air, and then catch him upon his horns.
But the moment Richard drew near, he dropped his prey,
and scampered off with a hideous whistling and croaking;
while Richard, now grown fearless, pursued him, till he
pitched headlong from the cliffs overhanging the sea, (still
grinning at him as he fell,) and then disappeared beneath
the waves.

The young adventurer now returned in triumph to the
hunter whom he had rescued, and who before long made
himself known as the reigning prince of the country, pro-
claiming his protector a hero, and entreating him boldly to
claim from him the highest recompense he had the power
to bestow.

"May I indeed thus presume?" cried Richard with
the inspiration of hope; "can you be serious? and will
you on your princely honour aid me, as you can, in relation
to a request I shall make?"

The prince cheerfully renewed his promise, and gave
him all the assurance he could desire.

"Well then," cried Richard with impassioned eager-
ness, "pray, for God's sake allow me to coin a few farthings, good current money, even if not more than two."

While the prince was yet looking upon him in perfect
astonishment, some of his train came up, to whom he related all that had happened; and one of them immediately
knew Richard to be the MAD FARTHING, whom he had
formerly seen.

On receiving this information, the prince began to laugh,
and the unhappy Richard embraced his knees with the
most intense anguish, and appealed to heaven for the truth
of what he said, that without the farthings he should be a
lost man.

13

But the prince replied, still laughing : " Rise, my friend, dismiss all fear ; you have my princely word, and if you persist in making this request, I permit you to coin as many farthings as you please. But were it equally agreeable to you, instead of these, to get a piece of money worth one third of a penny, you would have no occasion for coining ; for the neighbouring states complain, that the half-pence of mine are so light, that three of them pass for two common ones."

" I should be but too happy to get a few of those half-pence, were I only sure of their inferiour value," said Richard, in doubt.

" Why," replied the prince, " you are the first person, that ever considered them as worth too much. But notwithstanding this, should you light upon any such, then I give you my solemn word, before these witnesses, to permit you to coin still worse, . . . if indeed we can suppose that to be possible."

Saying this, he commanded an attendant to give Richard a whole purse of the half-pence of the country.

Thus provided, he ran, as if the evil one were in pursuit of him, to the bordering frontier of the prince's territory, and was a happier man than he had been for a long period, when, at the first public house of the neighbouring state, he received, though not without some difficulty and delay, two common half-pence for three of the prince's, which he got exchanged merely to ascertain their current value.

He now in a hurried voice inquired for the Black Fountain, when several children who were playing in the common apartment for guests, ran screaming from the room. The host informed him, though almost shuddering himself as he spoke, that this place was notorious as one of a very bad and alarming character, from which many evil spirits were wont to go forth into the land, and which few men had ever personally seen. He knew it well himself: the entrance leading to it, was not far distant from where they were, a cave with two dead cypresses before it, and he could not miss the way, if he entered there, — but from that peril might God preserve him and all true Christians !

It must be acknowledged, that, on hearing this account, Richard became extremely alarmed again; but still, come monster, come fiend, he was resolved to hazard the adventure, and therefore set off to achieve it. While he was yet afar off, the cave looked very dark and dismal; it almost seemed as if the two dead cypresses over the horrible abyss, which disclosed to him as he approached a wonderful rock at its opening, had been withered and killed with terrour. This rock appeared full of faces, distorted, long-bearded, and baboon-like, some of which bore a strong resemblance to the ape-monster he had encountered on the cliffs of the sea shore. And when he looked directly in, nothing was visible but jagged and cracked veins of rock. The poor fellow stepped in, trembling, beneath these fearful forms. The vial-fiend in his pocket now became so heavy, that it seemed to be pulling him back. But this only inspired him with a new rush of courage; "for," thought he, "just what my enemy would *not* desire, that must I strive to do."

Deeper within the cave, so thick a darkness met his view, that he soon lost sight of the frightful figures entirely. To avoid plunging down some unknown and abrupt descent, he cautiously felt his way before him with a staff; he found nothing, however, but a soft, smooth, moss-grown bottom; and had not a strange whistling and croaking now and then sounded through the cavern, he would have been preserved from every semblance of alarm.

At length he got through the passage. A desolate scene, resembling a deep mountain chasm or crater, inclosed him in on every side. On the left hand, he saw the huge and terrific black steed of the giant who promised to purchase his wishing genie, standing unfastened, with head high-raised, like a brazen statue, neither feeding nor moving. On the right hand, flowed a fountain from the rock, in which the horseman was washing his head and hands. But the evil stream was as black as ink, and possessed the same colouring quality; for as the giant turned toward Richard, his hideous countenance was that of a perfect blackamoor, and formed a fearful contrast with the richness of his splendid crimson attire.

"Do not tremble, my young hero," said the dreadful form. "This is one of the ceremonies, which I am forced to perform to please the devil. Every Friday I am obliged to wash here in this manner, in defiance and mockery of Him, whom you call your gracious Creator. In the same manner, too, I am compelled to tinge the purple of my red robe, whenever I have occasion for a new one, with a devilish deal of my own blood, little less than a bucketful, — from which it acquires its wonderfully gorgeous hue, — and this is the most burdensome condition of all. What is yet worse, I have so firmly signed and sealed myself over to him, body and soul, that it is impossible to think of any deliverance. And do you know what the curmudgeon gives me for all this? A hundred thousand pieces of gold a year. I cannot subsist upon this pittance, and this is the reason I wish to purchase your gentleman of the vial, just to serve the old niggard a clever trick. For observe, he is sure of my soul already, and the little devil in the vial, after his long period of slavery, must hereafter return to hell without having in the least accomplished his purpose. Then what a rage will seize the grim dragon! and what a glorious cursing-bout will he have!" And he set up such a shout of laughter, that the rocks rebellowed, and even the black horse, that stood so motionless, shrunk and shuddered at every explosion.

"Well," he asked, again turning to Richard, "have you brought your farthings, partner?"

"I am no partner of yours," answered Richard, half in fear and half in bravado, while he opened his purse.

"Ah, don't affect so much superiority," cried the giant purchaser. "Who drove the monster upon the prince, that you might gain the victory?"

"All that bustle and hobgoblin business were unnecessary," answered Richard; and he related how the prince had not only promptly consented to let him coin fourths of a penny, but had provided him with thirds that were coined already.

The red man appeared to be chagrined, that he had given himself the needless trouble of conjuring up the monster. He nevertheless exchanged two good half-pence for three of the bad ones, gave back Richard one of the latter, and received the vial instead of it: the vial fell from his pocket with its excessive weight, and the imp lay at the bottom in deep dudgeon, miserably doubled together neck and heels. Upon this the buyer raised another shout of laughter, and exclaimed: "All this can afford you no help, Satan; gold, gold here, as much as my black courser can carry beside myself." And instantly the monstrous beast groaned beneath a heavy burden of gold. Still he received his master also, and then, like a fly that goes up the wall toward the ceiling, he went directly up the perpendicular rock, but at the same time with motions and distortions so horrible, that Richard could not help fleeing swiftly from the spot, and rushing back into the cavern, that he might see nothing more of him.

As soon as he had come out again, on the eastern side of the mountain, and run on a great distance from the abyss, his whole soul was filled with the rapturous feeling of his deliverance. He felt in his heart, that he had made expiation for the grievous offences, which he had committed since leaving his home, and that henceforward no vial-fiend could any more embitter his being. He threw himself for joy among the high grass, played caressingly with the flowers, and kissed his hand to the sun. His heart, relieved from its paroxysm of terrour, was again serene and lively within him, but, at the same time, he neither cherished nor discovered aught of his former shameless levity and proneness to evil. Although he could now boast, and with some justice, that he had outwitted the devil himself, this was a feat on which he was far from priding himself. Yes, he was a true penitent: he directed the whole energy of his renovated powers to the grand purpose of existence, how he should henceforth pass his life in the world as a pious, respectable, and cheerful man. He succeeded so well in effecting this purpose, that, after some years of laborious exertion, he was able to return home to his dear Germany an opulent merchant, where he married a wife, and in his blessed old age often related to his grandchildren and great-grandchildren the story of his accursed vial-genie, as a warning full of instruction.

13*

THE METEMPSYCHOSIS

Robert McNish

THE METEMPSYCHOSIS

Dr. Robert McNish

A SLIGHT shudder came over me as I was entering the inner court of the college of Göttingen. It was, however, but momentary; and on recovering from it, I felt both taller and heavier and altogether more vigorous than the instant before. Being rather nervous, I did not much mind these feelings, imputing them to some sudden determination to the brain or some unusual beating about the heart, which had assailed me suddenly, and as suddenly left me. On proceeding, I met a student coming in the opposite direction. I had never see him before, but as he passed me by he nodded familiarly—"This is a fine day,Wolstang." "What does this fellow mean?" said I to myself. "He speaks to me with as much ease as if I had been his intimate acquaintance. And he calls me Wolstang—a person to whom I bear no more resemblance than to the man in the moon." I looked after him for some time, pondering whether I should call him back and demand an explanation; but before I could form any resolution, he was out of my sight.

Thinking it needless to take any further notice of the circumstance, I went on. Another student, whom I did not know, now passed me. "Charming weather, Wolstang." "Wolstang again!" said I; "this is insufferable. Hollo, I say! what do you mean?" But at this very moment he entered the library, and either did not hear my voice or paid no attention to it.

As I was standing in a mood between rage and vexation, a batch of collegians came up, talking loud and laughing. Three, with whom I was intimately acquainted, took no notice of me; while two, to whom I was totally unknown, saluted me with, "Good-morning, Wolstang." One of these latter, after having passed me a few yards, turned round and cried out, "Wolstang, your cap is awry."

I did not know what to make of this preposterous conduct. Could it be premeditated? It was hardly possible, or I must have discovered the trick in the countenances of those who addressed me. Could it be that they really mistook me for Wolstang? This was still more incredible, for Wolstang was fully six inches taller, four stone heavier, and ten years older than I. I found myself in a maze of bewilderment in endeavoring to discover the cause of all this.

While meditating as in a reverie on these events, I was aroused by approaching steps. On looking up, I beheld the most learned Dr. Dedimus Dunderhead, provost, and professor of moral philosophy of the college. He was a man about five feet high; but so far as rotundity of corporation went, noways deficient. On the contrary, he was uncommonly fat, and his long-waisted velvet coat of office, buttoning over a capacious belly, showed underneath a pair of thick, stumpy legs, cased in short small-clothes and silk stockings, and bedizened at the knees with large buckles of silver. The doctor had on, as usual, his cocked-hat, below whose rim at each side descended the copious curls of an immense bob-wig. His large carbuncle nose was adorned with a pair of spectacles, through which he looked pompously from side to side, holding back his head in grenadier fashion, and knocking his long silver-headed baton to the earth as he walked with all the formal precision of a drum-major.

Now be it known that it is binding on **every student** who attends the University of Göttingen to doff his cap on meeting this illustrious personage. It may be guessed, then, what was my degree of stupefaction when I saw Dr. Dunderhead approach—when I heard his baton striking upon the ground, responsive to his steps —when I saw his large eyes, reflected through the spectacles, looking intently upon me—I say my stupefaction may be guessed, when, even on this occasion, my hand did not make one single motion upward toward my cap. The latter still stuck to my head, and I stood folded in my college gown, my mouth half open, and my eyes fixed upon the doctor in empty abstraction. I could see that he was angry at my tardy recognition of his presence; and as he came nearer me, he slackened his pace a little, as if to give me an opportunity of mending my neglect. However, I was so drowned in reflection that I did not take the hint. At last he made a sudden stop directly in front of me, folded his arms in the same manner as mine, and looked upward in my face with a fixed glance, as much as to say, "Well, master, what now?" I never thought the doctor so little, or myself so tall, as at this moment.

Having continued some time in the above attitude, he took off his hat, and made me a profound bow. "Mr. Wolstang, I am your most humble servant." Then rising up, he lifted his baton toward my cap, and knocked it off. "Your cap is awry," continued he. "Excuse me, Mr. Wolstang, it is really awry upon your head." Another bow of mockery, as profound as the first, followed this action, and he marched away, striking his baton on the ground, holding back his head, and walking with slow, pompous step down the college court.

"What the devil is the meaning of it all?" said I. "Wolstang again! Confusion, this is no trick! The

provost of the college engage in a deception upon me
—impossible! They are all mad, or I am mad! Wolstang from one—Wolstang from another—Wolstang
from Dr. Dedimus Dunderhead! I will see to the bottom of this—I will go to Wolstang's house immediately." So saying, I snatched up my cap, put it on my
head, and walked smartly down the court to gain the
street where he lived. Before I got far, a young man
met me. "By-the-by, Wolstang, I wish you would let
me have the ten gilders I lent you. I require them
immediately." "Ten gilders!" said I; "I don't owe you
a farthing. I never saw your face before, and my name
is not Wolstang; it is Frederick Stadt."

"Psha! But, Wolstang, laying jesting aside," continued he, "I must positively have them."

"Have what?"

"My dear fellow, the ten gilders."

"Ten devils! I tell you, I don't owe you a farthing."

"Really, Wolstang, this joke is very silly. We know
you are an odd fellow, but this is the most foolish prank
I ever saw you play."

"Wolstang again!" said I, my heart boiling with indignation. "I tell you, sir—I tell you, sir, that—that
——" I could not get out another word, to such a degree had indignation confounded me. Without finish-
ing my sentence, I rushed into the street, but not without hearing the person say, "By Heaven, he is either
mad or drunk!"

In a moment I was at Wolstang's lodgings and set
the knocker agoing with violence. The door was opened
by his servant girl Louise, a buxom wench of some
eighteen or twenty.

"Is Mr. Wolstang in?" I demanded, quickly.

"Mr. who, sir?"

"Mr. Wolstang, my dear."

"Mr. Wol—Mr. who, sir?—I did not hear you."

"Mr. Wolstang."

"Mr. Wolstang!" re-echoed the girl, with some surprise.

"Assuredly, I ask you if Mr. Wolstang is within."

"Mr. Wolstang!" reiterated she. "Ha, ha, ha! how droll you are to-day, master!"

"Damnation! what do you mean?" cried I, in a fury, which I now found it impossible to suppress. "Tell me this instant if Mr. Wolstang, your master, is at home, or by the beard of Socrates, I—I——"

"Ha, ha! this is the queerest thing I ever heard of," said the little jade, retreating into the house, and holding her sides with laughter. "Come here, Barnabas, and hear our master asking for himself."

I now thought that the rage into which I had thrown myself had excited the laughter of the wench, whom I knew very well to be of a frolicsome disposition, and much disposed to turn people into ridicule. I therefore put on as grave a face as I could—I even threw a smile into it—and said, with all the composure and good humor I could muster: "Come now, my dear— conduct me to your master—I am sure he is within." This only set her a-laughing more than ever; not a word could I get out of her. At last Barnabas made his appearance from the kitchen, and to him I addressed myself. "Barnabas," said I, laying my hand upon his arm, "I conjure you, as you value my happiness, to tell me if Mr. Wolstang is at home."

"Sir!" said Barnabas, with a long stare.

I repeated my question.

"Did you ask," replied he, "if Mr. Wolstang was at home? If that gentleman is yourself, he is at home. Oh, yes, I warrant you my master is at home."

"In what place is he, then?" I inquired.

"Wherever you are, he is not far off, I warrant you, master."

"Can I find him in his study?"

"Oh, yes," continued Barnabas; "if you go to his study, I warrant you he'll be there. Will you please to walk in, sir?" and I could see the fellow put his finger to his nose and wink to the girl, who kept tittering away in a corner. As soon as I was in the study she burst into a loud laugh, which ended by her declaring that I must be mad—"Or drunk," quoth the sapient Barnabas, in his usual dry manner.

On entering the room, no person was to be seen; but from behind a large screen, which stood fronting the fire, I heard a sneeze. "This must be Wolstang," thought I; "but it is not his sneeze, either—it is too sharp and finical for him; however, let us see." So on I went behind the screen, and there beheld, not the person I expected, but one very different—to wit, a little, meager, brown-faced, elderly gentleman, with hooked nose and chin, a long, well-powdered queue, and a wooden leg. He was dressed in a snuff-colored surtout, a scarlet waistcoat, and black small-clothes buckled at the knee; and on his nose was stuck a pair of tortoise-shell spectacles, the glasses of which were of most unusual dimensions. A dapper-looking cocked-hat lay upon the table, together with a large open snuff-box full of rich rappee. Behind his ear a pen was stuck, after the manner of the counting-house, and he seemed busily pouring over a book in manuscript.

I looked a few seconds at this oddity, equally astonished and vexed at being put into what I naturally supposed the wrong room. "I am afraid, sir," said I, as he turned his eyes toward me, "that I have intruded upon your privacy. I beg leave to apologize for the mistake. The servant led me to believe that Mr. Wolstang, with whom I wished to speak, was in his chamber."

"Don't talk of apology, my dear sir," said the little

gentleman, rising up and bowing with the utmost politeness. "Be seated, sir—be seated. Indeed, I am just
here on the same errand—to see Mr. Wolstang—eh (a
sneeze)—that rappee is certainly very strong. Do me
the honor to occupy the seat opposite. I understand
from the servants that he is expected soon." (Another sneeze.)

For the first five minutes I did not form a very high
opinion of this new acquaintance. He seemed to have
all the fidgety politeness and intolerable chit-chat of a
French petit maître of the old school. He bored me
with questions and apologies, hoped I felt myself comfortable; and every interval of his speech was filled up
by intolerable giggling and sneezing. In order, as it
were, to increase the latter, he kept snuffing away at a
preposterous rate; and when he addressed me, his
mouth was drawn up into a most complacent smile, and
his long nose and chin, which threatened each other
like nut-crackers, thrown forward to within a foot of
my face.   However, in the next five minutes he im-
proved upon me, from some very judicious observations
which he made; and in five more I became convinced
that he was far from being an ordinary man. I found
that he had a complete knowledge of the philosophical
systems of the day; among others, that of my favorite,
Kant; and on the merits of the school in the north of
Germany, founded by this great metaphysician, his
opinions and mine tallied to a point. He also seemed
deeply conversant with the mathematics.

Let it not be supposed that all this was advanced with
the formal pomp of a philosopher; on the contrary, he
preserved throughout his frivolousness of manner, apol-
ogized for everything he said, hoped I was not offended
if he differed in opinion from me, and concluded every
position with a sneeze.

"By-the-by," said I, "what do you think of the doctrine of Gall and Spurzheim? I am inclined to believe there must be some truth in it; at least, I have seen it verified in a number of heads, and among others in that of Cicero, which I saw a few years ago in the sculpture-gallery of the Louvre. It was a beautiful head."

"You are right there, my dear friend," replied he. "The head, phrenologically considered, is extremely beautiful. I believe I have got it in my pocket." (A sneeze.)

"You have got the head of Cicero in your pocket!" cried I, with surprise.

"Oh, no! not absolutely the head of Cicero," said he, smiling—"Mark Antony disposed of that—but only his bust—the bust that you saw."

"You mean a miniature of that bust?"

"No—not a miniature, but the real bust. Here it comes—how heavy it is!" And, to my amazement, I saw him take out of his pocket the identical bust, as large as life, of the Roman orator, and place it on the table before me.

"Have you any more heads of this description about you?" said I, not a little marveling how he was able to stuff such a block of marble into his pocket.

"I have a few others at your service, my dear friend. Name any one you would wish to see, and I shall be most happy to produce it."

"Let me see, then, the head of Copernicus." I had scarcely spoken the word when he brought out the philosopher and put him beside Cicero. I named successively Socrates, Thales, Galileo, Confucius, Zoroaster, Tycho Brahé, Roger Bacon, and Paracelsus, and straightway they stood upon the table as fresh as if they had just received the last touch of the sculptor's chisel. I must confess that such a number of large heads emanating from the pockets of the little meager man in the snuff-colored surtout would have occasioned me incredible wonder, had my stock of astonishment not been exhausted by the previous display of his abilities.

"And do you," I demanded, as the last-named was brought forth, "always carry those heads about with you?"

"I generally do so, for the amusement of my friends," answered he. "But do not think that my stock is exhausted; I have still a few more that I can show you—for instance, Pythagoras."

"Pythagoras!" exclaimed I; "no, don't produce him. He is the last of all the philosophers I would wish to see."

"My dear friend," said the little man, with unusual gravity, "you do not say so?"

"I do say so. Pythagoras was a fool, a madman, an imposter."

"You don't speak thus of the divine Pythagoras?" returned he, putting his bust upon the table.

"No, not of the divine Pythagoras, for such a person never existed. I speak of Pythagoras the Samian—him of the golden thigh, the founder of what is called the Pythagorean philosophy."

"And the most rational system of philosophy that ever existed. Begging your pardon, I think it goes far beyond that of Plato or the Stagyrite."

"If you mean that it goes beyond them in being as full of absurdity as they are of wisdom, I really agree with you," said I, my anger rising at hearing the divine doctrines of Aristotle and the disciple of Socrates so irreverently spoken of.

"Pray, what were its absurdities?" asked he, with the most imperturbable good nature.

"Ah, well, did he not forbid the use of animal food to his followers? and, to crown all, did he not teach the monstrous doctrine of transmigration of souls—sending the spirits of men, after death, to inhabit the bodies of dogs, and cats, and frogs, and geese, and even insects?"

"And call you this a monstrous doctrine?"

"Monstrous!" I exclaimed with surprise—"it is the ne plus ultra, the climax of fatuity, the raving of a disordered imagination."

"So you do not believe in metempsychosis?" asked he, with a smile.

"I would as soon believe in demonology or magic. There is nothing I would not rather credit. But perhaps you are a believer." He shrugged up his shoulders at this last remark, stroked his chin, and, giving me a sarcastic look, said, with a familiar nod and smile, "Yes, I am a believer."

"What!" said I, "you—you, with your immense learning, can you put faith in such doctrines?"

"If I put faith in them," said he, "it is my learning which has taught me to do so."

"And do you really go all the length of Pythagoras?" I demanded.

"I not only go all his length, but I go much farther. For instance, he believed that the soul never left the body until the latter was dead. Now, my belief is that two living bodies may exchange souls with each other. For instance, your soul may take possession of my body, and my soul of yours, and both our bodies may be alive."

"In that case," said I, laughing heartily, "you would be me, and I would be you."

"Precisely so, my dear friend," replied the little gentleman, laughing in his turn, and concluding with a sneeze.

"Faith, my good sir," my reverence for his abilities

somewhat lessened by this declaration, "I am afraid you have lost your senses."

"I am afraid you have lost something of more importance," returned he, with a smile, in which I thought I recognized a tinge of derision. I did not like it, so, eyeing him with some sternness, I said, hastily, "And pray, what have I lost?" Instead of answering me, he burst into a loud fit of laughter, holding his sides while the tears ran down his cheeks, and he seemed half stifled with a flood of irresistible merriment. My passion at this rose to such a pitch that had he been a man of any appearance I should have knocked him down; but I could not think of resorting to such an extremity with a meager, little, elderly fellow, who had, moreover, a wooden leg. I could therefore only wait till his mirth subsided, when I demanded, with as much calmness as I could assume, what I had lost.

"Are you sure you have not lost your body?" said he.

"My body!" answered I, with some surprise; "what do you mean?"

"Now, my dear friend, tell me plainly; are you sure that this is your own body?"

"My own body—who the devil's can it be?"

"Are you sure you are yourself?"

"Myself—who, in Heaven's name, could I be but myself?"

"Ay, that is the rub," continued he; "are you perfectly satisfied that you are yourself, and nobody but yourself?" I could not help smiling at the apparent stupidity of this question; but before I was able to compose myself, he had resumed his query—"Are you sure you are—that you are——"

"That I am who?" said I, hurriedly.

"That you are Frederick Stadt?"

"Perfectly."

"And not Albert Wolstang?" concluded he.

A pang shot through my whole body at this last part of his question. I recalled in an instant all my previous vexation. I remembered the insults I had met with, not only from the students of Göttingen and Dr. Dedimus Dunderhead, but from the domestics of Wolstang; and lastly, I recollected the business which had brought me to the house of the latter. Everything came as a flash of lightning through my brain, and I was more perplexed than ever. At length, arousing myself from my stupor, I put the following question to him:

"Did you ask me if I was sure that I am not Wolstang?"

"I did sir," answered he, with a bow.

"Then, sir, I must tell you that I am not that person, but Frederick Stadt, student of philosophy in the University of Göttingen." He looked incredulous.

"What, sir," said I; "do you not believe me?" He shrugged up his shoulders.

"It is impossible, sir," said I, "that you can mistake me for Wolstang—seeing that, on my entry, you told me you expected that gentleman in a short time, and desired me to be seated till he came in." At this he seemed a little disconcerted, and was beginning to mutter something in explanation, when I interrupted him— "Besides, sir, Wolstang is a man at least six inches taller, four stone heavier, and ten years older than I."

"What an immense fellow he must be, my dear friend! At that rate, he ought to stand six feet eight inches, and weigh twenty stone."

I could hardly retain my gravity at this calculation. "Pray, what do you take my stature and weight to be?"

"I should take you," replied he, "to be about six feet two inches high, and to weigh about sixteen stone."

This admeasurement raised my merriment to its acme, and I laughed aloud. "Know, then, my good little man, that all your geometry has availed you nothing, for I only stand five feet eight and never weighed more than twelve stone." He shrugged up his shoulders once more, and put on another of his incredulous looks.

"Eh, eh—I may be mistaken—but I—I——"

"Mistaken!" exclaimed I; "zounds, you were never more egregiously mistaken, even when you advocated the Pythagorean doctrine of metempsychosis!"

"I may be wrong, but I could lay five gilders that I am right. I never bet high—just a trifle occasionally."

"You had better keep your gilders in your pocket," said I, "and not risk them so foolishly."

"With your permission, however, I shall back my pieces against yours"—and he drew five from a little green silk purse, and put them on the table. I deposited an equal number.

"Now," said I, "how is this dispute to be settled? Where can I get myself weighed?"

"I believe," answered he, "there is a pair of scales in the room hard by, and weights, too, if I mistake not." He accordingly got up and opened the door of the adjoining chamber, where, to my surprise, I beheld a pair of immense scales hanging from the roof, and hundred and half-hundred weights, etc., lying around. I seated myself on one of the scales, chuckling very heartily at the scrape into which the little fellow had brought himself. He lifted up weight after weight, placing them upon the opposite scale. Eleven stone had been put in, and he was lifting the twelfth. "Now," says I, eyeing him waggishly, "for your five guilders." He dropped the weight, but the beam never moved, and I still sat on the lowest scale. Thirteen were put on, and my weight yet triumphed. With amazement I saw fourteen and fifteen successively added to the number, without effect. At last, on putting down the sixteenth, the scale on which I sat was gently raised from the ground. I turned my eyes upward toward the needle, which I saw quivering as if uncertain where to stop; at last it paused exactly in the center, and stood erect; the beam lay perfectly horizontal, and I sat motionless, poised in middle air.

"You will observe, sir, that my calculation was correct," observed my companion, taking a fresh pinch of snuff. "You are just sixteen stone. Nothing now remains but to measure your height."

"There is no occasion for that," I replied, rising slowly from the scale. "If you can contrive to make me weigh sixteen stone, you can readily make me measure six feet two inches." I now threw myself down on a seat in the study, which both of us had re-entered, placed my elbows on the table, and buried my face in my hands, absorbed in deep reflection. I thought and thought again upon every event which had befallen me since the morning. The whole formed a combination which I found myself utterly unable to comprehend. In a few minutes I looked up, exhausted with vain thought. All the heads were gone except that of Pythagoras, which he left lying in its place. He now took up his snuff-box and deposited it in his waistcoat pocket; drew an old-fashioned watch out of his fob, and looked at the hour; and, lastly, laying his hand upon the ten gilders, he dropped them one by one into his green purse. "I believe," said he, with a smile, "the money is mine." So saying, he snatched up his little cocked-hat, made me half-a-dozen of bows, and bade me adieu, after promising to see me at the same time and place two days after.

Again did I bury my face in my hands; again did my fit of meditation come on; I felt my bosom glowing with perplexity. It was now the scales which occupied my thoughts, to the exclusion of everything else. "Sixteen stone!—impossible, I cannot believe it. This old rascal has cheated me. The weights he has put on must be defective—they must be hollow. I will see to it in a moment, and if there has been any deception, I shall break his bones the first time I set my eyes upon him, mauger his wooden leg; I will at least smash his spectacles, trip up his heels, and pull his hook nose." Full of these resolutions, I proceeded to the adjoining room. Guess of my amazement when, instead of the great machines in which I had been weighed but ten minutes before, I beheld nothing but a small pair of apothecary's scales, and a few drachm, scruple, and grain weights scattered upon the floor.

Not knowing what to make of this, I returned to the study, when, happening to look into a mirror placed behind the chair on which I had been sitting, I beheld (joyous sight) the reflection of Wolstang. "Ah, you have come?" said I, turning round to receive him, but nobody was to be seen. I looked again through every part of the room; no Wolstang was there. This was passing strange; where could the man have gone in such a hurry? I was now in a greater fright than ever, when, casting my eyes a second time upon the mirror, he again made his appearance. I instantly looked round—no one was present; in another instant I turned to the glass, and there stood the reflection as before. Not knowing what this phenomenon could be, and thinking perhaps that my eyes were dazzled by some phantom, I raised my hands, and rubbed them; Wolstang did the same. I struck my forehead, bit my lip with vexation, and started back, when, marvelous to relate, the figure in the glass repeated all my gestures. I now got alarmed, and, shrinking away from the apparition, threw myself upon the chair. In a few minutes, my courage being somewhat revived, I ventured to face the mirror, but without any better success—the same object presented itself. I desisted, and renewed the trial three several times, with the like result. In vain was my philosophy exerted to unfold this mystery. The doctrines of Aristotle, the dreams of alchemy, and the wonders of the Cabala presented themselves in succession to my disordered fancy. All was in vain; nothing could account for the present occurrence; nothing in mystical or scientific lore bore any analogy to it.

In this perturbed state of mind my eye caught the bust of Pythagoras. This was a flood of light to my understanding. I instantly remembered what the old fellow had hinted about the transmigration of souls; I remembered what he said about me being myself or another person. Then connecting this with the previous events of the day, with the Göttingen students, with Dr. Dedimus Dunderhead, with Wolstang's domestics, and lastly with the reflection in the looking-glass—I say, coupling all these thing together, I came to the horrible conclusion that I was not myself. "There must be some truth in the Pythagorean doctrine, and I am laboring under a metempsychosis."

It would be a vain attempt for me to describe the horror I endured at this dreadful transmogrification. After the first burst of dismay was over, I wept bitterly, bewailing the loss of my dear body, which I now felt convinced was gone from me forever. "And poor Wolstang," cried I, lamentably, "you are no longer yourself. You are me, and I am you; and doubtless you are deploring your misfortune as bitterly as your unhappy friend Stadt."

Night was now coming on, and it became necessary that I should resolve upon what ought to be done in my present state. I soon perceived that it would serve no purpose to say that I was myself; no one would have believed me, and I would run the risk of being put in a strait-jacket as a lunatic. To avoid these evils, there was no resource but to pass myself off upon the community as Wolstang.

In order to cool my heated brain, I went out into the open air and wandered about the streets. I was addressed by a number of persons whom I did not know; and several of my acquaintances, to whom I inadvertently spoke, did not know me. With the former I was very short, answering their questions at random, and getting off as soon as possible. To the latter I could only apologize, assuring them that they had been mistaken by me for other persons. I felt my situation most unpleasant; for, besides the consciousness of no longer being myself, I was constantly running into the most perplexing blunders. For instance, after strolling about for a considerable period, I came, as it were, by a sort of instinct, to my own lodgings. For a time I forgot my situation, and knocked at the door. It was opened by my domestic, from whom I took the candle which he held in his hand, and, according to wont, walked into the study. "Mr. Stadt is not in, sir," said the man, following me; "perhaps you will sit till he comes; I expect him soon." This aroused me from my reverie, confirming too truly the fact that I was changed. I started up from the seat into which I had dropped, rushed past him and gained the street. Here I made up my mind to return to Wolstang's lodgings, which I accordingly did, in a mood which a condemned criminal would hardly envy.

I kept the house for the whole of next day, employing myself in writing, in order that the servants might at least see some cause for my confinement. Notwithstanding this, it was easy to observe that they perceived something unusual about me; and several remarks which escaped them convinced me that they considered my head touched in no slight degree. Although I did all that I was able to compose myself, it was impossible that I could think like Wolstang, and still less that I could know a hundred private and household matters on which the pert Louise and sapient Barnabas made a point of consulting me. Whenever I was spoken to concerning things that I knew, my answers were kind and condescending; but on any point about which I was ignorant, I utterly lost temper, and peremptorily forbade them to repeat it. Both shook their heads at such inconsistent behavior; and it was soon bruited among the neighbors that Mr. Albert Wolstang had parted with his senses.

The second day arrived, and found me in the same state of mind. The amazement which succeeded the discovery of my metamorphosis had indeed given way, but my feelings were still as imbittered as ever, and I ardently longed for death to put an end to such intolerable misery. While brooding over these matters, the door of the study opened. Thinking it was one of the domestics, I paid no attention to it; but in a moment I heard a sneeze, which made my flesh creep, and in another the little man with the snuff-colored surtout, the scarlet waistcoat, and the wooden leg made his appearance. Since I last saw this old fellow, I had conceived a mortal hatred against him. I thought, although the idea was wild enough, that he had some hand in my metempsychosis—and the affair of the scales and the marble busts, together with his Pythagorean opinions, his vast learning, his geomancy and astrology, gave to my idea a strong confirmation. On the present occasion his politeness was excessive; he bowed almost to the ground, made fifty apologies for intruding, and inquired, with the most outré affectation of tenderness, into the state of my health. He then seated himself opposite to me, laid his cocked-hat upon the table, took a pinch of snuff, and commenced his intolerable system of sneezing. I was never less in a humor to relish anything like foppery; so throwing myself back upon the chair, putting on as commanding a look as I could, and looking at him fiercely, I said: "So, sir, you are back again; I suppose you know me?"

"Know you, my dear friend—eh—yes, I derived great pleasure in being made acquainted with you the day before yesterday. You are Mr. Frederick Stadt—that is to say, you are Mr. Albert Wolstang." (A sneeze.)

"Then you know that I am not myself?"

"My dear friend," replied he, with a smile, "I hinted as much the last time I saw you."

"And pray how did you ascertain that?"

"You don't ask me such a question," said he, with an air of surprise; "I knew it by your own signature."

"My own signature! I know not what you mean by my signature."

"Eh—eh—the signature, you know—that is, the compact you made with Wolstang."

"I know of no compact," cried I, in a passion; "nor did I ever make one with any man living. I defy either you or Wolstang to produce any such instrument."

"I believe it is in my pocket at this very moment. Look here, my dear sir." And he brought out a small manuscript book, and, turning up the leaves, pointed to view the following words:

"I hereby, in consideration of the sum of fifty gilders, give to Albert Wolstang the use of my body, at any time he is disposed, provided that, for the time being, he gives me the use of his.—Frederick Stadt."

"It is a damnable forgery," said I, starting up with fury; "a deceptio visûs at least—something like your scales."

"What about the scales, my dear friend?" said he, with a whining voice.

"Go," replied I, "into that room, and you shall see."

He accordingly went, but returned immediately, saying that he observed nothing remarkable. "No!" said I, rising up; "then I shall take the trouble to point it out to you." My astonishment may be better conceived than described when, instead of the small apothecary's scales, I beheld the immense ones in which I had been weighed two days before. I felt confounded and mortified, and returned with him to the study, muttering something about deceptio visûs, necromancy, and demonology.

"Well," continued I, after recovering a little, "what about this compact—when and where was it made?"

"It was made some three days ago, at the Devil's Hoof Tavern. You may remember that you and Wolstang were drinking there at that time."

"Yes, I remember it well enough; but I understood that I was putting my name to a receipt for fifty gilders which he paid me. I never read the writing; I merely subscribed it."

"That was a pity; for really you have bound yourself as firmly as signing with a person's own blood can do."

"Did I sign it with my own blood?" said I, alarmed.

"Exactly so. You may recollect of cutting your finger. I had the pleasure of stanching the blood, sufficient of which was, nevertheless, collected to write this document."

"Then you were present," said I—"yes, I have a recollection of your face, now that you mention the circumstance. You were then dressed as a clergyman, if I mistake not."

"Precisely."

"And what," continued I, "are the conditions on which I hold this strange existence? Suppose Wolstang dies?"

"Then you keep his body till the natural period of your own death."

"Suppose I die?"

"He then keeps your body."

"Then, if he dies, my body is buried and goes to decay, while I am clogged up in his body till relieved from it by death?"

"Precisely."

This announcement struck me with terror. "And shall I never," said I, weeping, "see my dear body again?"

"You may see it if ever Wolfstang comes in your way."

"But shall I never possess it—shall I never be myself again?"

"Not unless he pleases."

"The villain!" exclaimed I, in an agony of grief; "I am then undone—the tool of a heartless, unprincipled miscreant. Is my case hopeless?"

"Oh no, my dear friend," said the little man, "not at all hopeless; there is nothing simpler than the remedy. Only put your name here, and you will be yourself in a minute. The fellow will then lose all power over your body." I seized with avidity the pen which he presented to me, dipped it in a vial of red ink, and was proceeding to do as he directed, when the writing above caught my eye. It ran thus:

"I hereby engage, after my natural decease, to give over my soul to the owner of this book."

"Zounds!" said I, "what is this?"

"It is nothing at all; just a form—a mere form of business, of no intrinsic meaning. If you would just write your name—it is very easily done."

"Has any other person signed such a deed?" demanded I.

"Many a one. Here, for example, is Wolstang's name attached to a similar contract. It is, in fact, by virtue of this that he has the power over your body.

The deed which you have signed would have availed him nothing without this one."

"Then," said I, "if you relieve me from my present condition, you break faith with Wolstang, seeing that you deprive him of his stipulated power."

"I deprive him of his power over you, but I give him in return power over some other person, which will answer his purpose equally well. I think you had better sign."

"No, you old villain!" said I, wrought up to a pitch of fury at the infernal plan which I saw he was meditating, "I will never sign your damnable compact. I have religion enough to know the value of my soul, and sufficient philosophy to bear with any wretchedness I may endure under my present form. You may play the devil if you choose, but you shall never get me to act the part of Dr. Faustus." I pronounced these words in a voice of thunder; but, so far from being angry, he used every endeavor to soothe me—made a thousand apologies for having been the unwilling cause of such a commotion; then, snatching up his hat and making a profound bow, he left the room.

A glow of conscious virtue passed over me on his departure. I found that I had resisted evil, and gloried in the thought; but this triumphant feeling gave way to one of revenge against the author of my calamity. After reflecting for a short time, it occurred to me that the best way to punish him would be to commit some outrage which might stamp him with infamy, and render him miserable if he ever thought of resuming his body. "I shall at least have him expelled from the university. This shall be the first blow directed against his comfort. He will in time become weary of my body and will find very little satisfaction in his own when he takes it into his head to make an exchange." Full of these ideas, I entered the college court, where the first object that met my eyes was Dr. Dedimus Dunderhead coming toward me—his baton of office in his hand, spectacles on his carbuncle nose, and his head thrown back as he strutted along à la militaire. Without a moment's hesitation I advanced up to him and knocked off his cocked-hat; nor did I stop to see how he looked at this extraordinary salutation, but walked deliberately on. I heard him distinctly call after me, "You shall hear of this, sir, by to-morrow." "When you please, doctor," was my answer. "Now, Master Wolstang," said I to myself, "I have driven you from Göttingen college, and wish you much joy of your expulsion." Such were my thoughts, and the morrow verified them; for, a meeting of the Senatus Academicus being summoned by the provost, that learned body declared Albert Wolstang unfit to be a member of the university, and he was accordingly placarded upon the gate and expelled in terrorem.

This circumstance, being just what I wanted, gave me no uneasiness; but a few days thereafter an event arose out of it which subjected me to much inconvenience. Having unwittingly strolled into the college, I was rudely collared by one of the officers, which so enraged me that I knocked down the fellow with a blow of my fist. For this I was apprehended the same day by three gendarmes, and carried before the Syndic, who condemned me to suffer two weeks close confinement, and to be fed on bread and water. This punishment, though perhaps not disproportioned to the offence, was, in my estimation, horribly severe; and now, for the first time, did I feel regret for the absurdity of my conduct. I found that in endeavoring to punish Wolstang I was in truth only punishing myself, and that it was a matter of doubt whether he would ever submit to a corporeal change, seeing that my fortune was much more considerable than his own, and that he would come at it in the course of six months. This, I had no doubt, was the chief consideration that induced the fellow to bring about such a metamorphosis.

On getting out of prison I was the most miserable wretch on earth. The fierce desire of vengeance had formerly kept up my spirits; but this was now gone, and they sank to the lowest pitch. I found that I was spurned by those very persons who were before most anxious to cultivate my friendship. Barnabas and Louise had left me, resolving no longer to serve one who had undergone the punishment of a malefactor. In order to clear up matters, I frequently called at my own house to inquire if I myself was at home—for so was I obliged to speak of the miscreant who had possession of my body; but on every occasion I was answered in the negative. "I had gone out to see a friend in town;" "I had gone to the country;" "I was expected soon." Never by any possibility could I get a sight of myself. All this convinced me that the case was hopeless, and that I must make the best of my deplorable situation.

In consequence of the peculiar opportunities which I enjoyed, I soon discovered that Wolstang, whom I had long thought rather highly of, was in reality a very bad character. Some persons of the worst description in Göttingen appeared to have been his associates. Times without number I was accosted as an acquaintance by gamblers, pickpockets, usurers, and prostitutes; and through their means I unravelled a train of imposture, profligacy, and dissipation in which he had been long deeply involved. I found out even worse than this—at least what I dreaded much more. This was a forgery to an immense amount, which he, in concert with another person, had committed on an extensive mercantile house. The accomplice, in a high state of trepidation, came to tell me that the whole was in a fair way of being blown, and that if we wished to save our necks an instantaneous departure from the city was indispensable. Such a piece of intelligence threw me into great alarm. If I remained, my apprehension would be inevitable; and how would it be possible for me to persuade any one that I was not Wolstang? My conviction and execution must follow; and though I was now so regardless of life that I would gladly have been in my grave, yet there was something revolting in the idea of dying for a villain, merely because I could not show that I was not myself. These reflections had their due weight, and I resolved to leave Göttingen next day, and escape from the country altogether.

While meditating upon this scheme, I walked about three miles out of town for the purpose of maturing my plans undisturbed by the noise and bustle of the streets. As I was going slowly along, I perceived a man walking about a furlong before me. His gait and dress arrested my attention particularly, and after a few glances I was convinced that he must be myself. The joy that pervaded my mind at the sight no language can describe; it was as a glimpse of Heaven, and filled me with perfect ecstasy. Prudence, however, did not forsake me, and I resolved to steal slowly upon him, collar him, and demand an explanation. With this view I approached him, concealing myself as well as I could, and was so successful that I had actually got within ten yards of my prey without being discovered. At this instant, hearing footsteps, he turned round, looked alarmed, and took to his heels. I was after him in a moment, and the flight on one side and pursuit on the other were keenly contested. Thanks to Wolstang's long legs, they were better than the short ones with which my antagonist was furnished, and I caught him by the collar as he was about to enter a wood. I grasped my body with Herculean grip, so terrified was I to lose it. "And now, you villain," said I, as soon as I could recover breath, "tell me the meaning of this. Restore me my body, or by Heaven I will——"

"You will do what?" asked he, with the most insolent coolness. This question was a dagger to my soul, for I knew that any punishment I inflicted upon him must be inflicted upon myself. I stood mute for a few seconds, still holding him strongly in my grasp. At last, throwing pity aside, by one vast effort I cried out, "I declare solemnly, Wolstang, that if you do not give me back my body I shall kill you on the spot."

"Kill me on the spot!" replied he. "Do you mean to say that you will kill your own body?"

"I do say so," was my answer. "I will rather destroy my dear body, than it should be disgraced by a scoundrel like you."

"You are jesting," said Wolstang, endeavoring to extricate himself.

"I shall show you the contrary," rejoined I, giving him a violent blow on the nose, and another on the ribs. These strokes almost drew tears from my eyes; and when I saw my precious blood flowing, I certainly would have wept aloud, but for the terrible energy which rage had given me. The punishment had its evident effect, however, upon Wolstang, for he became agitated and alarmed, grew pale, and entreated me to let him go. "Never, you villain, till you return me back my body. Let me be myself again, and then you are free."

"That is impossible," said he, "and cannot be done without the agency of another person, who is absent; but I hereby solemnly swear that five days after my death your body shall be your own."

"If better terms cannot be had, I must take even

these, but better I shall have; so prepare to part with what is not your own. Take yourself back again, or I will beat you to a mummy." So saying, I laid on him most unmercifully—flattened his nose (or rather my own), and laid him sprawling on the earth without ceremony. While engaged in this business, I heard a sneeze, and, looking to the quarter from which it proceeded, whom did I see emerging from the wood but my old acquaintance with the snuff-colored surtout, the scarlet waistcoat, and wooden leg. He saluted me as usual with a smile, and was beginning to regret the length of time which had elapsed since he last had the pleasure of seeing me, when I interrupted him. "Come," said I; "this is not a time for ridiculous grimace; you know all about it; so help me to get my body back from this scoundrel here."

"Certainly, my dear friend. Heaven forbid that you should be robbed of so unalienable a property. Wolstang, you must give it up. 'Tis the height of injustice to deprive him of it."

"Shall I surrender it, then?" said Wolstang, with a pitiable voice.

"By all means; let Mr. Stadt have his body."

In an instant I felt great pains shoot through me, and I lay on the ground, breathless and exhausted as if from some dreadful punishment. I also saw the little gentleman, and the tall, stout figure of Wolstang, walk away arm in arm, and enter the wood. I was now myself again, but had at first little cause of congratulation on the change, while the unprincipled author of my calamities was moving off in his own body without a single scratch. If my frame was in bad case, however, my mind felt relieved beyond conception. A load was taken from it, and it felt the consciousness of being encased in that earthly tenement destined by Heaven for its habitation.

35

Alas, how transient is human happiness! Scarcely had an hour elapsed when a shudder came over me, precisely similar to that which occurred some weeks before on entering the college of Göttingen. I also perceived that I was stronger, taller, and more vigorous, and, as if by magic, totally free of pain. At this change a horrid sentiment came across me, and, on looking at my shadow in a well, I observed that I was no longer myself, but Wolstang; the diabolical miscreant had again effected a metempsychosis. Full of distracting ideas, I wandered about the fields till nightfall, when I returned into the city, and threw myself into bed, overpoured with fatigue and grief.

Next day I made a point of calling at my own house, and inquiring for myself. The servant said that I could not be seen, being confined to bed in consequence of several bruises received in an encounter with two highwaymen. I called next day and was still confined. On the third I did the same, but I had gone out with a friend. On the fourth I learned that I was dead.

It will readily be believed that this last intelligence was far from being unwelcome. On hearing of my own death I felt the most lively pleasure, anticipating the period when I would be myself again. That period, according to Wolstang's solemn vow, would arrive in five days. Three of these I had spent in the house, carefully secluding myself from observation, when I heard a sneeze at the outside of the door. It opened, and in stepped the little man with the snuff-colored surtout, the scarlet waistcoat, and the wooden leg. I had conceived a dislike approaching to horror at this rascal, whom I naturally concluded to be at the bottom of these diabolical transformations; I, however, contained my wrath until I should hear what he had to say.

"I wish you much joy, my dear friend, that you are going to resume your own body. There is, however, one circumstance which perhaps you have overlooked. Are you aware that you are to be buried to-day?"

"I never thought of it," answered I, calmly, "nor is it of any consequence, I presume. In two days I shall be myself again. I shall then leave this body behind me, and take possession of my own."

"And where will your own body be then?"

"In the grave," said I, with a shudder, as the thought came across me.

"Precisely so, and you will enjoy the pleasure of being buried alive; that, I suppose, you have not calculated upon."

This remark struck me with blank dismay, and I fell back on my chair, uttering a deep groan. "Is there then no hope? cannot this dreadful doom be averted? must I be buried alive?"

"The case is rather a hard one, Mr. Stadt, but perhaps not without a remedy."

"Yes, there is a remedy," cried I, starting up and striking my forehead. "I will hie me to my own house, and entreat them to suspend the funeral for two days."

"I saw the undertaker's men enter the house, as I passed by, for the purpose, I should think, of screwing down the coffin-lid. However," continued he, taking a pinch of snuff, "you may try; and if you fail, I have a scheme in view which will perhaps suit your purpose. I shall await your return."

In a moment my hat was on my head, in another I was out of the room, and in a third at my own house. What he had stated was substantially true. Some of the mourners had arrived, and the undertaker's men were waiting below, till they should be summoned upstairs to screw down the lid. Without an instant of delay I rushed to the chamber where my dear body was lying in its shell. Some of my friends were there, and I entreated them, in imploring accents, to stop for

37

two days, and they would see that the corpse which lay before them would revive. "I am not dead," cried I, forgetting myself—"I assure you I am not dead."

"Poor fellow! he has lost his senses," said one.

"I assure you I am not dead," said I, throwing myself upon my knees before my cousin, who was present.

"I know that, my good fellow," was his answer, "but poor Stadt, you see, is gone forever."

"That is not Stadt—it is I—it is I—will you not believe me? I am Stadt—this is not me—I am not myself. For Heaven's sake suspend this funeral." Such were my exclamations, but they produced no other effect but that of pity among the bystanders.

"Poor, unfortunate fellow, he is crazed. Get a porter and let him be taken home."

This order, which was given by my cousin himself, stung me to madness, and, changing my piteous tones for those of fierce resistance, I swore that "I would not turn out for any man living. I would not be buried alive to please them." To this nobody made any reply, but in the course of a minute four stout porters made their appearance, and I was forced from the house.

Returning to Wolstang's lodgings, the old man was there in waiting, as he promised. "What," said I, with trepidation—"what is the scheme you were to propose? Tell me, and avert the horrible doom which will await me, for they have refused to suspend the funeral."

"My dear friend," said he, in the most soothing manner, "your case is far from being so bad as you apprehend. You have just to write your name in this book, and you will be yourself again in an instant. Instead of coming alive in the grave, you will be alive before the coffin-lid is put on. Only think of the difference of the two situations."

"A confounded difference, indeed," thought I, taking

hold of the pen. But at the very moment when I was going to write, I observed, above, the following words:

"I hereby engage, after my natural decease, to give over my soul to the owner of this book."

"What!" said I, "this is the old compact; the one you wished me to sign before."

"The same, my dear friend."

"Then I'll be d—d if I sign it."

"Only think of the consequences," said he.

"I will abide the consequences rather than sell my soul."

"Buried alive, my dear sir—only think."

"I will not sign the compact."

"Only think of being buried alive," continued he— "stifled to death—pent up on all sides—earth above, earth below—no hope—no room to move in—suffocated, stupefied, horrorstruck—utter despair. Is not the idea dreadful?"

I gave a shudder at this picture, which was drawn with horrible truth; but the energies of religion and the hopes of futurity rushed upon my soul and sustained it in the dreadful trial. "Away, away," said I, pushing him back. "I have made up my mind to the sacrifice, since better may not be. Whatever happens to my body, I am resolved not to risk my eternal soul for its sake."

"Think again," said he, "and make up your mind. If I leave you, your fate is irrevocable. Are you decided?"

"I am."

"Only reflect once more. Consider how, by putting your name in this book, you will save yourself from a miserable death. Are you decided?"

"I am," replied I, firmly.

"Then, fool," said he, while a frown perfectly unnatural to him corrugated his brow, and his eyes shot forth vivid glances of fire—"then, fool, I leave you to your fate. You shall never see me again." So saying, he walked out of the room, dispensing with his usual bows and grimaces, and dashing the door fiercely after him, while I threw myself upon a couch in an agony of despair.

My doom was now sealed; for, on going to the windows a few minutes thereafter, I beheld my own funeral, with my cousin at the head of the procession, acting as chief mourner. In a short time I saw the company returning from the interment. "All is over, then," said I, wringing my hands at the deplorable sight. "I am the victim of some infernal agency, and must prepare for the dreadful sacrifice." That night I was supremely wretched, tossing incessantly in bed, while sleep was denied to my wearied eyelids. Next morning my haggard look was remarked by my servant, who proposed sending for a physician; but this I would not allow, knowing that woe like mine was beyond the reach of medicine. The day after was the last I was to behold upon the earth. It came, and I endeavored by every means to subdue the terror which it brought along with it. On arising from bed, I sent for my servant, an elderly woman whom I had got to supply the place of Barnabas and Louise, and gave her one hundred gilders, being all the money I could find in Wolstang's bureau. "Now, Philippa," said I, "as soon as the clock of the study has struck three, come in, and you will find me dead. Retire, and do not enter till then." She went away, promising to do all that I had ordered her.

During the internal I sat opposite the clock, marking the hours pass rapidly by. Every tick was as a death-knell to my ear—every movement of the hands, as the motion of a scimitar leveled to cut me in pieces. I heard all and I saw all in horrid silence. Two o'clock at length struck. "Now," said I, "there is but one

hour for me on earth—then the dreadful struggle be-
gins—then I must live again in the tomb, only to perish
miserably." Half an hour passed, then forty minutes,
then fifty, then fifty-five. I saw with utter despair the
minute-hand go by the latter, and approach the meri-
dian number of the dial. As it swept on, a stupor fell
over my spirit, a mist swam before my eyes, and I almost lost the power of consciousness. At last I heard
one strike aloud—my flesh creeped with dread; then
two—I gave a universal shudder; then three, and I
gasped convulsively, and saw and heard nothing further.

At this moment I was sensible of an insufferable
coldness. My heart fluttered, then it beat strong, and
the blood, passing as it were over my chilled frame,
gave it warmth and animation. I also began by slow
degrees to breathe. But though my bodily feelings
were thus torpid, my mental ones were very different.
They were on the rack; for I knew that I was now
buried alive, and that the dreadful struggle was about
to commence. I was terrified to move, because I knew
I would feel the horrid walls of my narrow prison-
house. I was terrified to breathe, because the pent air
within it would be exhausted, and the suffocation of
struggling humanity would seize upon me. I was even
terrified to open my eyes, and gaze upon the eternal
darkness by which I was surrounded. Could I resist?
—the idea was madness. What would my strength
avail against the closed coffin, and the pressure above,
below, and on every side?

Meanwhile I felt the necessity of breathing, and I did
breathe fully; and the air was neither so close nor
scanty as might have been supposed. This struck me
as very singular; and being naturally of an inquisitive
disposition, I felt an irresistible wish, even in my dreadful situation, to investigate, if possible, the cause of it.

"The coffin must be unconscionably large." This was my first idea; and to ascertain it, I slightly raised my hands, shuddering at the same time at the thought of their coming in contact with the lid above me. However, they encountered no lid. Up, up, up I elevated them, and met with nothing. I then groped to the sides, but the coffin laterally seemed equally capacious; no sides were to be found. "This is certainly a most extraordinary shell to bury a man of my size in. I shall try if possible to ascertain its limits before I die—suppose I endeavor to stand upright." The thought no sooner came across my mind than I carried it into execution. I got up, raising myself by slow degrees, in case of knocking my head against the lid. Nothing, however, impeded my extension, and I stood straight. I even raised my hands on high, to feel if it were possible to reach the top: no such thing; the coffin was apparently without bounds. Altogether, I felt more comfortable than a buried man could expect to be. One thing struck me, and it was this—I had no grave-clothes upon me. "But," thought I, "this is easily accounted for; my cousin comes to my property, and the scoundrel has adopted the most economical means of getting rid of me." I had not as yet opened my eyes, being daunted at the idea of encountering the dreary darkness of the grave. But my courage being somewhat augmented by the foregoing events, I endeavored to open them. This was impossible; and on examination, I found that they were bandaged, my head being encircled with a fillet. On endeavoring to loosen it, I lost my balance, and tumbled down with a hideous noise. I did not merely fall upon the bottom of the coffin, as might be expected; on the contrary, I seemed to roll off it, and fell lower, as it were, into some vault underneath. In endeavoring to arrest this strange descent, I caught hold of the coffin, and pulled it on the top of me. Nor was this all; for, before I could account for such a train of extraordinary accidents below ground, and while yet stupefied and bewildered, I heard a door open, and, in an instant after, human voices. "What, in Heaven's name, can be the meaning of this?" ejaculated I, involuntarily. "Is it a dream?—am I asleep or am I awake? Am I dead or alive?" While meditating thus, and struggling to extricate myself from the coffin, I heard someone say distinctly, "Good God, he is come alive!" At the same instant the fillet was drawn from my eyes. I opened them with amazement; instead of the gloom of death, the glorious light of heaven burst upon them! I was confounded; and, to add to my surprise, I saw supporting me two men, with whose faces I was familiar. I gazed at the one, then at the other, with looks of fixed astonishment. "What is this?" said I; "where am I?"

"You must remain quiet," said the eldest, with a smile. "We must have you put to bed, and afterward dressed."

"What is this?" continued I; "am I not dead? was I not buried?"

"Hush, my dear friend—let me throw this great-coat over you."

"But I must speak," said I, my senses still wandering. "Where am I? who are you?"

"Do you not know me?"

"Yes," replied I, gazing at him intently—"my friend, Dr. Wunderdudt. Good God! how do you happen to be here? Did I not come alive in the grave?"

"You may thank us that you did not," said he. "Look around, and say if you know where you are."

I looked, as he directed, and found myself in a large room fitted up with benches, and having half a dozen skeletons dangling from the roof. At last I satisfied myself that I was in the anatomical theater of the university.

"But," said I, "there is something in all this that I cannot comprehend. What—where is the coffin?"

"What coffin, my dear fellow?" said Wunderdudt.

"The coffin that I was in."

"The coffin!" said he, smiling; "I suppose it remains where it was put the day before yesterday."

I rubbed my eyes with vexation, not knowing what to make of these perplexing circumstances. "I mean," said I, "the coffin—the coffin I drew over upon me when I fell."

"I do not know of any coffin," answered he, laughing heartily; "but I know very well that you have pulled upon yourself my good mahogany table; there it lies." And on looking, I observed the large table, which stood in the middle of the hall, overturned upon the floor. Dr. Wunderdudt (he was professor of anatomy to the college) now made me retire, and he put me in bed till clothing could be procured. But I would not allow him to depart till he had unravelled the strange web of perplexity in which I still found myself involved.

"The day before yesterday," said he, "I informed the resurrectionists in the service of the university that I was in want of a subject, desiring them at the same time to set to work with all speed. That very night they returned, assuring me that they had fished up one which would answer to a hair, being both young and vigorous. In order to inform myself of the quality of what they brought me, I examined the body, when, to my indignation and grief, I found that they had disinterred my excellent friend, Mr. Frederick Stadt, who had been buried the same day."

"What!" said I, starting up from the bed, "did they disinter me?—the scoundrels!"

"You may well call them scoundrels," said the professor, "for preventing a gentleman from enjoying the pleasure of being buried alive. The deed was certainly most felonious; and if you are at all anxious, I shall have them reported to the Syndic, and tried for their impertinent interference. But to proceed. No sooner did I observe that they had fallen upon you, than I said: 'My good men, this will never do. You have brought me here my worthy friend, Mr. Stadt. I cannot feel in my heart to anatomize him; so just carry him quietly back to his old quarters, and I shall pay you his price, and something over and above.'"

"What!" said I, again interrupting the doctor, "is it possible that you could be so inhuman as to make the scoundrels bury me again?"

"Now, Stadt," rejoined he, with a smile, "you are a strange fellow. You were angry at the men for raising you, and now you are angry at me for endeavoring to repair their error by reinterring you."

"But you forget that I was to come alive?"

"How the deuce was I to know that, my dear boy?"

"Very true. Go on, doctor, and excuse me for interrupting you so often."

"Well," continued he, "the men carried you last night to deposit you in your long home, when, as fate would have it, they were prevented by a ridiculous fellow of a tailor, who, for a trifling wager, had engaged to sit up alone, during the whole night, in the churchyard, exactly at the spot where your grave lay. So they brought you back to the college, resolving to inter you to-night, if the tailor, or the devil himself, should stand in their way. Your timely resuscitation will save them this trouble. At the same time, if you are still offended, they will be happy to take you back, and you may yet enjoy the felicity of being buried alive."

Such was a simple statement of the fact, delivered in

the professor's good-humored and satirical style; and from it the reader may guess what a narrow escape I had from the most dreadful of deaths. I returned to my own house as soon as possible, to the no small mortification of my cousin, who was proceeding to invest himself with all that belonged to me. I made him refund without ceremony, and altered my will, which had been made in his favor, not forgetting, in so doing, his refusal to let my body remain two days longer unburied. A day or two afterward, I saw a funeral pass by, which, on inquiry, I learned to be Wolstang's. He died suddenly, as I was informed, and some persons remarked it as a curious event that his death happened at precisely the same moment as my return to life. This was merely mentioned as a passing observation, but no inference was deduced from it. The old domestic in Wolstang's house gave a wonderful account of his death, mentioning the hour at which he said he was to die, and how it was verified by the event. She said nothing, however, about the hundred gilders. Many considered her story as a piece of mere trumpery. She had, nevertheless, a number of believers.

These events, which are here related at full, I can only attest by my own word, except, indeed, the affair of the coming alive, which everybody in Göttingen knows of. If any doubt the more unlikely parts of the detail, I cannot help it. I have not written this with the view of empty fame, and still less of profit. Philosophy has taught me to despise the former, and my income renders the latter an object of no importance. I shall conclude by acknowledging that a strong change has been wrought in my opinions; and that from ridiculing the doctrines of the sage of Samos, I am now one of their firmest supporters. In a word, I am what I have designated myself,

"A Modern Pythagorean."

FIORACCIO.

BY

GIOVANNI MAGHERINI-GRAZIANI.

FIORACCIO.

EVERYBODY called him Fioraccio, but his real name was Antonio, and he kept a little shop for bread and macaroni just there by the bridge, where the tobacconist's is now. He was a little man, short and thick, always dressed in a striped jacket and low shoes which were never tied. He never wore a hat, summer or winter; and when the sun shone on his head, that was as bare as the back of your hand, it glittered like a brand-new tin kettle. He had yellow eyes like a cat's. He always seemed to be laughing in a sneering, scoffing fashion; and when he spoke he whistled, because he had lost his teeth; in front he had only two left, one on each side. If there ever was a rascal in this world, Fioraccio was one, and one of the first; and in his own place there was more talk of him than of Barabbas in the Passion of Our Lord. I don't mean to speak ill of him, all the same; he's dead now, and long since gone to his own place. As I said, Fioraccio had a shop where he sold bread, wine, and macaroni, and kept a sort of little inn. But the real shop was behind, where the door opened into the garden; there he kept a store of all sorts of things—wood, cloth, old iron, barrels, flasks, oil-jars, grain, wine, oil—for Fioraccio was a receiver of stolen goods; and whatever was stolen sooner or later found its way to him, and in all the years that he kept up this trade the police never once got a single chance to lay hands on him. They were after him, time and again, and hundreds of times his shop was searched, but to no purpose. When they came to look the goods were safely hidden, and Fioraccio never brought them to light until all danger was over. If he bought anything he never paid for it; nobody had ever seen the color of his money; he paid in oaths. If any one went to his shop they never got full weight.

There was a saying, "At Fioraccio's some get eight, and some get nine, but nobody gets ten." There were not the inspectors then as there are now. For that matter, in his shop nobody stopped to talk, nobody ever got the right change; and if anybody made any complaints, they got nothing but abuse. For this reason nobody who was in a hurry ever went to Fioraccio, and he troubled himself very little about his customers. "I don't care if they don't come," he said, "they only give trouble." For that shop, you see, was only the cover for the other one. But if there was anything worth while going on he was ready enough to put himself out, and often stayed up the whole night long. Otherwise, he sat the whole blessed day at the door of the shop, and had something spiteful to say to every one who passed; young or old, man or woman, married or unmarried, nobody escaped his tongue. He knew neither Easter nor Lent; one day was the same as another to him. If the holy sacrament passed by his door, he didn't even take the pipe out of his mouth or get off his stool—he smoked faster than ever, to show his disrespect. He would hear nothing about Madonna or the saints; and if the priest asked him, as he was blessing the houses,

"Fioraccio, do you want the holy water?"

"I can give it myself," he would answer.

Hardly was his old father in his grave when he cleared all the pictures and crosses out of the house; and when the old woman who swept out his rooms asked him if he wasn't afraid of the judgment, he answered,

"I don't want my wall covered with rubbish."

If he'd been content with being wicked himself! But he was always making mischief, and putting other people up to evil doings. He didn't even respect innocence, and taught little boys to lie and steal. For example, a nephew of his own, about eleven years old, whom he took to live with him—he said to the boy every morning when he sent him out,

"Now mind you don't come home empty-handed to-night."

And if he brought nothing he would give him no supper, and even beat him sometimes.

"If you want your supper you must earn it," he told him.

Near the shop of Fioraccio there was one belonging to an old aunt of his, who was nearly blind. Fioraccio used to send the boy into this shop to rob the till; and as the boy was little, and there wasn't the paper money, as there is now, he used to tell him always to bring the white money, and to take it while the old woman was at the door, but not to take too much at a time or people would find it out. And when the boy brought scudi, or other silver money, Fioraccio would give him a sou or a toy.

But one day the boy was caught, and beaten worse than a donkey. To excuse himself he told the whole story, and how he had been taught to steal, and by whom. And Fioraccio, when he heard it, beat him worse than ever, and turned him out of the house. So Fioraccio remained alone—alone in the house, and alone in the shop; and at last nobody came into the shop any more, for they didn't like to be sworn at. "Some day the earth will open under his feet," they said. They called his shop "Inferno;" and

even now, if any one is heard to swear very
hard, people say, "Holloa! has Fioraccio
come to life?" For he had become a prov-
erb, you know. And so he lived for many
years; but at last his time came, like other
people's. He began to look very old, and
to get up late, and go to bed early. The
shop would be open every other day; then
open two days and shut three days. He
grew to be a perfect skeleton, all skin and
bones, and the *scaldino** was never out of
his hands. Everybody said, "Ah! Fioraccio
isn't long for this world." And he wasn't.
The shop was always shut now. Sometimes
he'd come to the window in the middle of
the day, when it was fine, but he looked so
dreadful it was enough to frighten one. It
was old age was the matter with him, and
for that there's no cure. At last he took to
his bed; but instead of repenting and changing for the better, he went on worse and
worse. He blasphemed like a fiend. The
worse he was the worse he swore. At last

---

* An earthen pot with charcoal, to warm the hands
and feet by.

the old woman, who was the only creature that went near him, told him that if he didn't stop swearing she wouldn't come any more.

"Why not?" asked Fioraccio.

"Because I'm afraid that some day the devil will come and carry us both off," said the old woman.

"Oh, the devil! and the devil! If there was one really, he'd have made me a visit long ago," said he.

The priest, when he heard how ill Fioraccio was, said to himself, "I must go to him; there's no help for it!"

And he went; but they say he made a fast that day, though it wasn't in the calendar. He knocked, and went up-stairs. When Fioraccio recognized the priest's voice, he said, "What does that fellow want with me? I won't see him."

"How? you won't see him!" said the old woman. "It seems to me it is only polite of him to make you a visit."

"Oh yes, I dare say, but I don't care for such politeness; priests are like owls, birds of ill omen. And—"

But the old woman had opened the door by this time, and beckoned to the priest to come in.

The priest entered the room.

"But I told you not to come in," howled Fioraccio.

"Good-morning, Antonio."

Fioraccio only growled.

"I heard you were ill, and—"

"It was something that they didn't say I was dead."

"And I thought I would come and see you." So he began to talk; but as soon as he tried to bring the talk round to the point he desired, Fioraccio always changed the subject. At last the priest grew desperate, and laying his hand on Fioraccio's shoulder:

"Fiore," he said, "you mustn't be angry if I speak seriously to you. You know that we haven't only the body to look after—"

"I know what you mean; but when I want to confess I'll send for you."

"But, of course, whenever you choose—"

"Pray don't trouble yourself—"

But the priest wouldn't be content without preaching a little; so he began to talk

of repentance, and restitution, and such
things, you know. When Fioraccio heard
the word "restitution" he flew into a rage,
and called out:

"Did I ever rob you of anything?"

"I don't mean that; I mean—"

"Now, listen, Mr. Rector. You and I do
very well as long as we are apart, but if we
meet we disagree. So, if we're to have
peace, you'd better not come here any more.
Do you hear?" And he turned his back,
and not another word would he say.

"How goes it?" asked the old woman.

"He won't hear of it. If those above
don't take it up, I don't see what is to be
done. To-morrow I'll come, at all events,"
said the priest.

"The Lord and Our Blessed Lady grant
it." But before the next day Fioraccio suddenly grew worse, and before the priest could
get to him he was dead.

This happened in 1837, and there are
plenty of people living now that remember
the whole story, and can tell it you better
than I can. Scarcely was he dead when he
turned black all over, so that it was a horror

to look at him.   They rang the bell, carried him to church, and then into the church-yard, where they buried him.

The next morning, before day (it was hardly four o'clock), the priest was in bed, when he heard a knock at the door, and asked who was there, thinking some sick person wanted him.

"It's Cecco,"* said the servant.

"What Cecco?"

"Cecco from ——" (Fioraccio's place).

It was the sexton.

"What, in Heaven's name, does he want at this hour?"

"Wants to see your reverence."

"Send him in; let's see what it is."

Cecco appeared at the door, hat in hand.

"What's the matter now?"

"Something you'll hardly believe.   Didn't your reverence bury Fioraccio yesterday?"

"Of course I did.   What about it?"

"He's got up again."

"What?"

"He's got up again."

---

* Frank.

"Impossible!"

"It's the case, all the same. I was passing by on my way to work in the field.
When I was passing the burial-ground I
turned round to look in, and there, just
where we buried him, I saw something white.
I thought I must be dreaming, and as by
chance I had the key in my pocket, I went
in to look. It was he—Lord keep us from
lies!—but I turned short round, and came
away without looking back."

"So you came here and waked me."

"Who else was I to come to? The
strange thing is that the earth looks as if it
hadn't been touched."

"Some one must have done it to play
you a trick. You're sure the gate was
locked?"

"Locked and bolted. And he wasn't
very pleasant to go near, either."

"Did you bury him again?"

"Not I, indeed! And, besides, your reverence must come, for perhaps it isn't all
quite natural. I mean—you know—"

"This morning I can't manage it; I have
that affair at X——."

"You could come before that; the whole thing won't take more than an hour."

"No, no; mind what I tell you. Go and bury him again."

"But—"

"Only you put him deep enough, I'll promise you he won't come above-ground again."

The sexton turned his hat round and round. At last:

"Your reverence shall be obeyed," he said. "I'll go and get the tools." And he went out; but before he shut the chamber door the priest called him back.

"Say nothing about this, you know."

"Your reverence may depend upon me. I won't say anything. Well," said Cecco to himself, as he drew the door to after him, "at least I shall have lived to say I've buried the same man twice."

The next morning there he was again. The priest called out:

"What now?"

"Same old story."

"What story?"

"Fioraccio."

" Above ground again ?"

" Just that."

" It doesn't seem possible."

" But it's so. If you don't believe me come and see for yourself."

" I do believe you, but what can I do? You must just bury him again. Some one must have—"

" If you saw the state he's in you wouldn't think anybody 'd be likely to want to meddle with him."

" I don't know. Sometimes—"

" Well, I'll bury him this time, and then we'll see."

That same day—I remember it as if it were yesterday—I was taking some tools to the smith to be mended, when I came upon Cecco coming away from the burial-ground with the spade in his hand.

" Been putting somebody to bed?" I asked.

" If you knew !" said he.

" What ?"

" I've just buried Fioraccio."

" Only now. What did you keep him above-ground so long for? Wanted to be quite sure he was dead ?"

"I've buried him over again — twice."
And he tells me the whole story.

I wouldn't believe him, and I remember
saying: "I'm sure somebody helps him to
get above-ground."

"Somebody does, you may be sure, and
it's easy to guess who."

"I know what you mean. Somebody who
has no need of a spade. Look here," I went
on. "Let's you and I come and watch
here to-night, and see who comes. Are you
afraid?"

"No!" he answered; "not with you. I
wouldn't stay alone, though."

"Say nothing to anybody, and at nine
o'clock to-night I'll come for you, and we'll
see if I'm right."

That night at nine o'clock there I was.

"Shall we go?"

"Come along; but we'll take something
in our hands, in case it should be anybody."

So we each took a thick stick, and started
for the cemetery. It was an ugly black
night, promising rain. Outside we couldn't
stay; we should have been seen.

"Where can we go?"

"Let's go in."

Cecco opened the gate, and we went in; but we could not shut the gate when we were inside.

"Leave it ajar," said I, "if any one comes it won't be by the gate, but over the wall."

"But here we shall be seen."

"Where's he buried?"

"There, by the dead-house."

"Let's go in there, then."

"In the dead-house?"

"Where else? There's no other place."

There was a bench, and we sat down. I began to light my pipe.

"What are you doing?" asked Cecco; "if they see the light they'll know there's some one here."

"Oh yes, as if I was going to stay here all night without even smoking; I should go to sleep."

We said very little more; neither he nor I had any wish to talk. We heard nothing but the bats, which kept flying in and out; now and then a dog barked.

The clock struck eleven. I thought I heard steps on the road, but they passed by.

"It's Faustino," said Cecco. "I know
his whistle "—for he had begun to whistle
as he passed the gate, as people do when
they feel a little timid. About half an hour
later an owl flew close by my face, and gave
me a great start; but she was afraid of us,
and flew off, and we heard her hoot outside.

"It must be nearly midnight."

"We might go now. Nothing is likely to
happen to-night," said I.

"Wait till the clock strikes."

"Very well, we'll wait."

"Listen, there's the clock. One, two,
three, four, five, six, seven, eight, nine, ten,
eleven—twelve."

I felt him catch me by the arm.

"Look, look there !"

There, where Fioraccio was buried, the
earth began to heave and roll, rising slowly,
slowly, as if it were pushed up from below,
and we saw him rise out of it upright, he
remained so for a moment, and then fell
at full length on the grave. Cecco said not
a word, but strode off across the cemetery
and went out, and I after him. I wanted
to turn back and look if it were really he,

but I hadn't the courage; I passed close by
him, but I didn't look. I tell it you as it
happened. Cecco was trembling from head
to foot; I knew by his voice.

" Did you see ?" he said.

" I saw it. Won't you shut the gate ?"

" I won't touch anything. The rector must
come to-morrow and see for himself—he
wouldn't believe me. I'll go straight to him
now, and you must go with me."

" But we can't go at this hour," said I;
"to-morrow morning early, rather. I'll go
home with you to sleep. I told them at
home that I should be out all night."

In the morning early we went to the priest,
and told him all that happened.

" And what are we to do ?" he asked.

" If your reverence doesn't know who
should ?" asked Cecco.

" If you tried—"

" Tried what ? Burying him again ? You
see it's of no use."

" Certainly it is no use," said I; "in holy
ground he won't stay, that's quite plain—
such a rascal as he was."

" Hush !" said the priest. " Don't tell

any one of this—I lay it on your consciences; and, besides, we have no right to judge the dead. You, Cecco, go and put him once more underground."

"Your reverence may command me in everything, but, saving your presence, I can't and I won't go back to the cemetery again; here's the key, but go I won't—that's flat."

"Never mind, I'll send some one with you, if you're frightened. And you (to me) go to the convent of ——, with a note for the father superior."

In fact he wrote a note, and I took it to the convent. The superior read it, and said to me: "I understand; tell the rector that everything shall be done as he asks."

I took back the answer to the priest.

"Have you got him underground?" I asked.

"Yes, but I thought we never should manage it, I assure you."

"Do you want anything more of me?"

"Not now; to-night, perhaps. If I want you I'll send for you."

"You will find me at home; I'll come directly."

All the while I was at work I was wonder-
ing what the priest could want of me, but I
thought it must have something to do with
Fioraccio.   Just after sunset the priest's
nephew came to tell me I was to go to the
parsonage.   I went, and found there two
Capuchin friars, who had come to exorcise
Fioraccio.   The priest wanted me to come
with him.

"When?" I asked.

"To-night."

"Then I must go and tell my wife."

"What in the world are you doing always
out at night?" asked she.

I told her some story or other, and after
supper I went off to the priest.   He would
have it that I should sup again with him.
The friars would neither eat nor drink, and
we heard them praying aloud in the next
room, and reciting the office.   Just before
midnight one of the friars put his head in
at the door and said :

"It is time now.   Let us go."

The priest turned pale, but he was forced
to make a virtue of necessity and to come
with us.   We took a lantern, and went out

of the house by the garden-door. There
were five of us—the priest, the two friars,
Cecco, and I, all as silent as the grave; in
the dark, that way, we seemed like conspira-
tors. I was in front with the Capuchins;
Cecco and the priest came behind. When
we came to the gate I lit the lantern; plenty
of trouble it gave me, too; I thought it would
never light, but at last I found a match that
would kindle. The priest was the first to
enter the cemetery.

"What did I tell you?" whispered Cecco;
"there he is again!"

I was in front. The light fell full on the
face of Fioraccio. But why do I call it a
face? It was black as charcoal, with open
mouth and those two yellow teeth, and the
yellow eyes wide open, shining in the darkness. I turned sick and stopped short.

"Heavens! how ugly he is!" I cried.

"Hush!" said the friar who was nearest
me.

Then they put on their stoles, opened
their books, sprinkled the dead with holy
water, and recited the service of exorcism.
I held the light, the priest clung to my sleeve,

and I felt him tremble; indeed, from time to time, he gave such convulsive starts that the lantern shook in my hand, and the friars could not see to read. " Antonio ! Antonio !" called out the friar, " Antonio ! answer, in God's name."

Not a word did he say.

" Try calling him Fioraccio; perhaps he won't answer to his Christian name." This I whispered into the friar's ear.

The Capuchin sprinkled the corpse once more with holy water, then began calling, " Fioraccio, answer, answer !"

There came a deep voice, hollow-sounding, and far away, as if from fathoms underground.

" Who calls me ? What do you want ?"

It was the devil, who answered for him.

" Why do you not stay where you have been laid. What is the reason you do not rest ?"

" Because I cannot."

" Why can you not rest ?"

" Because—" And he began to tell us why. Such things ! such things ! that he had done in life. The priest put it all un-

12

der the seal of confession with us afterwards. He said "that he was damned body and soul." And saying this, he swore a fearful oath. And then he said:

"Take me away from here."

"Where do you want to go?"

"To the Arno. Under water twenty braccios* deep. There, where I can hear no bells."

"You shall have three braccios."

We heard another oath, always in that voice underground, for Fioraccio's mouth never stirred. And the friars sprinkled him again with holy water.

"For the last time; how much water must you have?"

"Five braccios."

"You shall have three, and no more."

He went on swearing. At last he said:

"Well, if I must I must, but not in too much of a hurry."

And at that moment we saw something, dressed all in red, fly up over the wall.

---

* Braccio, a measure used formerly in central Italy—a little more than half a metre long.

"We must come back to-morrow," said the friar. " God have us all in his holy keeping !"

We left the cemetery; you should have seen the priest how he trembled. The next day he sent for me and told me : " We must take him away to-night, and you must make a coffin for him."

" But I never made a coffin in my life."

" You can manage it somehow. You can generally get to the end of what you undertake. And it needn't be such a fine piece of work, you know, so long as it holds together."

" Well," said I, " I'll do my best." I went home, and looked up some chestnut planks I had, and made the coffin. Then I went to the parsonage, where I found the Capuchin friars and the priest talking together.

" The coffin is done," I said. " Shall I bring it here ?"

" What are you thinking of ? To-night, after dark, you must take it to the cemetery and put him into it; you can call Cecco, if he will go with—you, in short, do the best you can; only get him into the

coffin. Then he must be carried — somehow—"

"I understand," said I; "I am to look
after the whole business. Very well, I'll see
what I can do. Cecco wouldn't hear of
carrying him; we had better ask some of
the Brotherhood."

"No; because we must keep it as quiet
as we can."

"As quiet as you like. But it is a long
way to the Arno, and that coffin is made of
chestnut. It is heavy, I can tell you."

"Can't you find a cart?"

It was settled that I should borrow my
cousin's cart, and the priest should find
some more men. Then I went for Cecco,
who made no end of difficulty about coming,
and after dark we carried the coffin to the
cemetery. There he was again, uglier than
ever. One could see that he was damned
only to look at him.

"Here, Cecco," said I, "help me to lift
him." I turned round. No Cecco. I ran
out of the gate, and found him in the road.

"Look here," said he, "if you can't manage it by yourself, you must get some-

body else, for you've seen the last of me in
there."

I went back.   I had a great mind to run
away, too, but I had promised his reverence,
and, besides, it wouldn't have done to make a
scandal.   So I set the coffin on its side, and
rolled him into it.   B'essed Virgin ! it almost
made me faint away.   Then I had nothing
better to do than to turn round and look at
him.   It was the light, perhaps, but he looked just as if he was grinning as he used to
when he was alive.   I threw the cover on,
anyhow, and bolted—I must say I bolted—
as hard as I could go.   The priest told me
to harness the cart towards ten o'clock at
night, when there would be no one about,
and bring it to the cemetery.   I found waiting for me at the gate the priest, the two
friars, Cecco, a brother of Cecco's, and three
others whom the priest had sent for.   We
took up the coffin in silence, and put it in
the cart; then I took the donkey by the
bridle, and we set off.   It was a dark, close
night, when one could hardly breathe or see
where one was going, though we had two
lanterns.   What we went through on that

road God only knows—now we were on this
side of the road, now on that, now among
the trees, never ten paces straight ahead;
and the poor donkey tugged and tugged, as
if the coffin had been made of lead. Every
minute one or the other of the lanterns
went out. From time to time we passed
through a thick fog, so thick that we lost
sight of each other, of the east, of everything. The friars went on muttering prayers
and sprinkling holy water, and we recom-
mended ourselves to God and to the Madonna. Even I lost courage altogether.
As for the poor priest, we had to leave him
at a farm-house on the road, for he could
go no farther. But that was nothing to
what followed. Just as we passed the turning at the mill of —— a hurricane burst
over us that uprooted trees, carried off hay-
stacks, tiles off the roofs, all sorts of things.
We were surrounded by a cloud of leaves,
twigs, straw, and dust. I never remember
such a whirlwind. Two hay-stacks flew off
into the air as if they had been locks of
tow; a big pine-tree that two men couldn't
clasp round went rolling over the plain like

a twig; and along the banks of the Arno oaks uprooted, willows twisted together like yarn. Nothing to be seen of the cart or of the beast—nothing; we could not tell which way they had gone. We commended our souls to Heaven, and went on. I don't know how we found our way to the bank of the Arno, just there where it is deepest. We could hardly recognize the place. We found the donkey standing there, quite still.

" Here," said the friar.

" No," said the same voice we had heard in the cemetery. " More water—more water!" And then oaths, to make one's hair stand on end with fright.

" No; there's enough here."

Then more oaths, and more oaths.

" Here," said the friar, " I command you, in the name of God !"

All of a sudden there was a great rush and sputter of flame, as if one had thrown sulphur on a fire, and we saw a figure like a galley-slave, all in red, and heard a splash and a gurgle, and when we looked at the cart it was empty. I went home, put the beast in the stall, and turned to go to the house.

"Who's that?" cried my wife. "Wait;
I'll get up."

I didn't answer; it didn't seem as if it
was me she was speaking to.

"Will you have something to eat?" she
said. "You had no supper yesterday. I'll
make a fire and cook this bit of beef; it
will only take a minute." So saying, she
began to kindle the fire.

I looked on while my wife put a fagot on
the coals, which began to sputter and send
out sparks, and I said, without thinking,

"Just like him."

"Just like *who?*" said she.

I perceived that I had said too much, and
wanted not to say anything more; but it was
of no use, she had it all out of me. I tried
to eat, but couldn't swallow a mouthful. I
went to bed. When I was nearly asleep I
heard the house door open. I listened, and
heard a noise as if the kettle and the bucket
were rolling over the floor.

"There's somebody there," said my wife.

"Hush," said I, "I hear them," for the
noise began again.

"Get up; there's some one there."

I got up and went into the kitchen. Nobody there—the bucket and the kettle each
in its place, the door shut and bolted. I
went back to bed, but couldn't close an eye
until morning. The noise kept on all night
in the kitchen. The next morning, when I
went out, I met the old woman who had
taken care of Fioraccio. She stopped me
and asked me about what had happened in
the night, of which she had heard something. When I told her about the noise in
the kitchen, she said : " ' At that same hour
I could not sleep, and I took up my rosary
meaning to say it for him. Hardly had I
begun when I saw him appear, all dressed
in red, and he said to me :

" ' No need to say it for me ; it's of no use.
I'm damned—damned for all eternity.' "

A MYSTERY OF THE CAMPAGNA

[Ann C. Rabe]
Von Degen, pseud.

A MYSTERY OF THE CAMPAGNA.

I.

MARTIN DETAILLE'S ACCOUNT
OF WHAT HAPPENED AT THE
VIGNA MARZIALI.

ARCELLO'S voice is
pleading with me now,
perhaps because after
years of separation I
have met an old ac-
quaintance who had a
part in his strange story. I have
a longing to tell it, and have
asked Monsieur Sutton to help
me. He noted down the circumstances at the time, and he
is willing to join his share to

mine, that Marcello may be remembered.

One day, it was in spring, he appeared in my little studio among the laurels and green alleys of the Villa Medici. "Come, *mon enfant*," he said, "put up your paints"; and he unceremoniously took my palette out of my hand. "I have a cab waiting outside, and we are going in search of a hermitage." He was already washing my brushes as he spoke, and this softened my heart, for I hate to do it myself. Then he pulled off my velvet jacket and took down my respectable coat from a nail on the wall. I let him dress me like a child. We always did his will, and he knew it, and in a moment we were sitting in the cab, driving through the Via Sistina on our way to the Porta San Giovanni, whither he had directed the coachman to go.

I must tell my story as I can, for though I have been told by

my comrades, who cannot know
very well that I can speak good
English, writing it is another
thing. Monsieur Sutton has
asked me to use his tongue,
because he has so far forgotten
mine that he will not trust himself in it, though he has promised
to correct my mistakes, that
what I have to tell you may not
seem ridiculous, and make people
laugh when they read of Marcello.
I tell him I wish to write this
for my countrymen, not his; but
he reminds me that Marcello
had many English friends who
still live, and that the English do
not forget as we do. It is of
no use to reason with him, for
neither do they yield as we do,
and so I have consented to his
wish. I think he has a reason
which he does not tell me—but
let it go. I will translate it all
into my own language, for my
own people. Your English
phrases seem to me to be always
walking sideways, or trying to
look round the corner, or stand

upon their heads, and they have
as many little tails as a kite. I
will try not to have recourse to
my own language, but he must
pardon me if I forget myself.
He may be sure I do not do it
to offend him. Now that I
have explained so much, let me
go on.

When we had passed out of
the Porta San Giovanni, the
coachman drove as slowly as he
liked. The pay is more outside
the gates, and they always pretend then that their horses are
tired, and creep as slowly as
possible ; but Marcello was
never practical. How could he
be, I ask you, with an Opera in
his head? So we crawled along,
and he gazed dreamily before
him. At last, when we had
reached the part where the little
villas and vineyards begin, he began to look about him.

You all know how it is out
there; iron gates, with rusty
names or initials over them, and
beyond them straight walks, bor-

dered with roses and lavender,
leading up to a forlorn little
casino, with trees and a wilder-
ness behind it, sloping down to
the Campagna; lonely enough
to be murdered in and no one
to hear you cry. We stopped
at several of these gates and
Marcello stood looking in, but
none of the places were to his
taste. He seemed not to doubt
that he might have whatever
pleased him, but nothing did so.
He would jump out and run to
the gate, and return saying,
"The shape of those windows
would disturb my inspiration,"
or, "That yellow paint would
make me fail my duet in the
second act"; and once he liked
the air of the house well enough,
but there were marigolds growing
in the walk, and he hated them.
So we drove on and on, until
I thought we should find nothing
more to reject. At last we came
to one which suited him, though
it was terribly lonely, and I
should have fancied it very

agaçant to live so far away from
the world with nothing but those
melancholy olives and green
oaks—ilexes, you call them—for
company.

"I shall live here and become
famous!" he said, decidedly,
as he pulled the iron rod which
rang a great bell inside. We
waited, and then he rang again
very impatiently and stamped his
foot.

"No one lives here, *mon
vieux !* Come, it is getting late,
and it is so damp out here, and
you know that the damp for a
tenor voice—" He stamped his
foot again and interrupted me,
angrily.

"Why, then, have you got a
tenor! You are stupid! a bass
would be more sensible ; nothing
hurts it. But you have not got
one, and you call yourself my
friend! Go home without me."
How could I, so far on foot?
"Go and sing your lovesick
songs to your . lean English
misses! They will thank you

with a cup of abominable tea, and you will be in Paradise! This is *my* Paradise, and I shall stay until the angel comes to open it!"

He was very cross and un-reasonable, and those were just the times when one loved him most, so I waited and enveloped my throat in my pocket-hand-kerchief and sang a passage or two just to prevent my voice from becoming stiff in that damp air.

" Be still! silence yourself!" he cried. " I cannot hear if any one is coming."

Some one came at last, a rough-looking sort of keeper, or *guar-diano*, as they are called there, who looked at us as though he thought we were mad. One of us certainly was, but it was not I. Marcello spoke pretty good Italian, with a French accent, it is true, but the man under-stood him, especially as he held his purse in his hand. I heard him say a great many impetu-

ously persuasive things all in a
breath, then he slipped a gold
piece into the *guardiano's* horny
hand, and the two turned toward the house, the man shrug-
ging his shoulders in a resigned
sort of way, and Marcello called
out to me over his shoulder:

"Go home in the cab, or you
will be late for your horrible
English party! I am going to
stay here to-night." *Ma foi!* I
took his permission and left
him; for a tenor voice is as
tyrannical as a jealous woman.
Besides, I was furious, and yet
I laughed. His was the artist
temperament, and appeared to
us by turns absurd, sublime, and
intensely irritating; but this last
never for long, and we all felt
that were we more like him our
pictures would be worth more.
I had not got as far as the city
gate when my temper had cooled,
and I began to reproach myself
for leaving him in that lonely
place with his purse full of
money, for he was not poor at

all, and tempting the dark *guardiano* to murder him. Nothing
could be easier than to kill him
in his sleep and bury him away
somewhere under the olive trees
or in some old vault of a ruined
catacomb, so common on the
borders of the Campagna. There
were sure to be a hundred such
convenient places. I stopped the
coachman and told him to turn
back, but he shook his head and
said something about having to
be in the Piazza of St. Peter at
eight o'clock. His horse began
to go lame, as though he had
understood his master and were
his accomplice. What could I
do? I said to myself that it
was fate, and let him take me
back to the Villa Medici, where
I had to pay him a pretty sum
for our crazy expedition, and
then he rattled off, the horse
not lame at all, leaving me
bewildered at this strange afternoon.

I did not sleep well that night,
though my tenor song had been

applauded, and the English
misses had caressed me much.
I tried not to think of Marcello,
and he did not trouble me much
until I went to bed; but then I
could not sleep, as I have told
you. I fancied him already
murdered, and being buried in
the darkness by the *guardiano*.
I saw the man dragging his
body, with the beautiful head
thumping against the stones,
down dark passages, and at last
leaving it, all bloody and covered
with earth, under a black arch
in a recess, and coming back to
count the gold pieces. But then
again I fell asleep, and dreamed
that Marcello was standing at
the gate and stamping his foot;
and then I slept no more, but
got up as soon as the dawn
came, and dressed myself, and
went to my studio at the end of
the laurel walk. I took down
my painting jacket, and remembered how he had pulled it off
my shoulders. I took up the
brushes he had washed for me;

they were only half cleaned after all, and stiff with paint and soap. I felt glad to be angry with him, and *sacré*'d a little, for it made me sure that he was yet alive if I could scold at him. Then I pulled out my study of his head for my picture of Mucius Scævola holding his hand in the flame, and then I forgave him; for who could look upon that face and not love it?

I worked with the fire of friendship in my brush, and did my best to endow the features with the expression of scorn and obstinacy I had seen at the gate. It could not have been more suitable to my subject! Had I seen it for the last time? You will ask me why I did not leave my work and go to see if anything had happened to him, but against this there were several reasons. Our yearly exhibition was not far off and my picture was barely painted in, and my comrades had sworn that it would not be ready. I

was expecting a model for the
King of the Etruscans; a man
who cooked chestnuts in the
Piazza Montanara, and who had
consented to stoop to sit to me
as a great favor; and then, to
tell the truth, the morning was
beginning to dispel my fancies.
I had a good northern light to
work by, with nothing sentimental about it, and I was not
fanciful by nature; so when I
sat down to my easel I told
myself that I had been a fool,
and that Marcello was perfectly
safe; the smell of the paints
helping me to feel practical
again. Indeed, I thought every
moment that he would come in,
tired of his caprice already, and
even was preparing and practic-
ing a little lecture for him.
Some one knocked at my door,
and I cried "*Entrez!*" thinking
it was he at last; but no, it was
Pierre Magnin.

"There is a curious man, a
man of the country, who wants
you," he said. "He has your

address on a dirty piece of paper in Marcello's handwriting, and a letter for you, but he wont give it up. He says he must see '*il Signor Martino.*' He'd make a superb model for a murderer! Come and speak to him, and keep him while I get a sketch of his head."

I followed Magnin through the garden, and outside, for the porter had not allowed him to enter. I found the *guardiano* of yesterday. He showed his white teeth, and said, " Good day, signore," like a Christian ; and here in Rome he did not look half so murderous—only a stupid, brown, country fellow. He had a rough peasant - cart waiting, and he had tied up his shaggy horse to a ring in the wall. I held out my hand for the letter and pretended to find it difficult to read, for I saw Magnin standing with his sketch-book in the shadow of the entrance hall. The note said this : I have it still and I will copy it. It was

written in pencil on a leaf torn
from his pocket-book :

" *Mon vieux !* I have passed
a good night here, and the man
will keep me as long as I like.
Nothing will happen to me,
except that I shall be divinely
quiet, and I have already a
famous *motif* in my head. Go
to my lodgings and pack up
some clothes and all my manu-
scripts, with plenty of music
paper and a few bottles of Bor-
deaux, and give them to my
messenger. Be quick about it!

" Fame is preparing to descend
upon me! If you care to see
me, do not come before eight
days. The gate will not be
opened if you come sooner.
The *guardiano* is my slave, and
he has instructions to kill any
intruder who in the guise of a
friend tries to get in uninvited.
He will do it, for he has confessed
to me that he has murdered three
men already."

(Of course this was a joke. I
knew Marcello's way.)

" When you come, go to the *poste restante* and fetch my letters. Here is my card to legitimate you. Don't forget pens and a bottle of ink! Your

" MARCELLO."

There was nothing for it but to jump into the cart, tell Magnin, who had finished his sketch, to lock up my studio, and go bumping off to obey these commands. We drove to his lodgings in the Via del Governo Vecchio, and there I made a bundle of all that I could think of; the landlady hindering me by a thousand questions about when the Signore would return. He had paid for the rooms in advance, so she had no need to be anxious about her rent. When I told her where he was, she shook her head, and talked a good deal about the bad air out there, and said, " Poor Signorino!" in a melancholy way, as though he were already buried, and looked mournfully after us from the window when we drove away. She irritated me, and made me feel superstitious. At the corner of the Via del Tritone I jumped down and gave the man a franc out of pure sentimentality, and cried after him, "Greet the Signore!" but he did not hear me, and jogged away stupidly while I was longing to be with him. Marcello was a cross to us sometimes, but we loved him always.

The eight days went by sooner than I had thought they would, and Thursday came, bright and sunny, for my expedition. At one o'clock I descended into the Piazza di Spagna, and made a bargain with a man who had a well-fed horse, remembering how dearly Marcello's want of good sense had cost me a week ago, and we drove off at a good pace to the Vigna Marziali, as I was almost forgetting to say that it was called. My heart was beating, though I did not know why I should feel so much emotion. When we reached the iron gate, the *guardiano* answered my ring directly, and I had no sooner set foot in the long flower-walk than I saw Marcello hastening to meet me.

"I knew you would come," he said, drawing my arm within his, and so we walked toward the little gray house, which had a sort of portico and several balconies, and a sun-dial on its front. There were grated windows down to the ground floor, and the place, to my relief, looked safe and habitable. He told me that the man did not sleep there, but in a little hut down toward the Campagna, and that he, Marcello, locked himself in safely every night, which I was also relieved to know.

"What do you get to eat?" said I.

"Oh, I have goat's flesh, and dried beans and polenta, with pecorino cheese, and there is plenty of black bread and sour wine," he answered, smilingly. "You see, I am not starved."

"Do not overwork yourself,

mon vieux," I said; "you are worth more than your opera ever will be."

"Do I look overworked?" he said, turning his face to me in the broad, outdoor light. He seemed a little offended at my saying that about his opera, and I was foolish to do it.

I examined his face critically, and he looked at me half defi- antly. "No, not yet," I answered rather unwillingly, for I could not say that he did; but there was a restless, inward look in his eyes, and an almost imperceptible shadow lay around them. It seemed to me as though the full temples had grown slightly hollow, and a sort of faint mist lay over his beauty, making it seem strange and far off. We were standing before the door, and he pushed it open, the *guardiano* following us with slow, loud-resounding steps.

"Here is my Paradise," said Marcello, and we entered the house, which was like all the others of its kind. A hall, with stucco bas-reliefs, and a stairway adorned with antique fragments, gave access to the upper rooms. Marcello ran up the steps lightly, and I heard him lock a door somewhere above and draw out the key; then he came and met me on the landing.

"This," he said, "is my work-room," and he threw open a low door. The key was in the lock, so this room could not be the one I heard him close. "Tell me I shall not write like an angel here!" he cried. I was so dazzled by the flood of bright sunshine after the dusk of the passage, that I blinked like an owl at first, and then I saw a large room, quite bare, except for a rough table and chair, the chair covered with manuscript music.

"You are looking for the furni-ture," he said, laughing; "it is outside. Look here!" and he drew me to a rickety door of worm - eaten wood and coarse greenish glass, and flung it open

on to a rusty iron balcony. He
was right ; the furniture was outside : that is to say, a divine view
met my eyes. The Sabine Mountains, the Alban Hills, the broad
Campagna, with its mediæval
towers and ruined aqueducts, and
the open plain to the sea. All
this glowing and yet calm in the
sunlight. No wonder he could
write there ! The balcony ran
round the corner of the house,
and to the right I looked down
upon an alley of ilexes, ending in
a grove of tall laurel trees—very
old, apparently. There were bits
of sculpture and some ancient
sarcophagi standing gleaming
among them, and even from so
high I could hear a little stream
of water pouring from an antique
mask into a long, rough trough.
I saw the brown *guardiano* dig-
ging at his cabbages and onions,
and I laughed to think that I
could fancy him a murderer !
He had a little bag of relics,
which dangled to and fro over
his sunburned breast, and he

looked very innocent when he sat down upon an old column to eat a piece of black bread with an onion which he had just pulled out of the ground, slicing it with a knife not at all like a dagger. But I kept my thoughts to myself, for Marcello would have laughed at them. We were standing together, looking down at the man as he drank from his hands at the running fountain, and Marcello now leaned down over the balcony, and called out a long "Ohé!" The lazy *guardiano* looked up, nodded, and then got up slowly from the stone where he had been half-kneeling to reach the jet of water.

"We are going to dine," Marcello explained. "I have been waiting for you." Presently we heard the man's heavy tread upon the stairs, and he entered, bearing a strange meal in a basket.

There came to light pecorino cheese made from ewe's milk, black bread of the consistency of a stone, a great bowl of salad apparently composed of weeds, and a sausage which filled the room with a strong smell of garlic. Then he disappeared and came back with a dish full of ragged-looking goat's flesh cooked together with a mass of smoking polenta, and I am not sure that there was not oil in it.

"I told you I lived well, and now you see!" said Marcello. It was a terrible meal, but I had to eat it, and was glad to have some rough, sour wine to help me, which tasted of earth and roots. When we had finished, I said, "And your opera! How are you getting on?"

"Not a word about that!" he cried. "You see how I have written!" and he turned over a heap of manuscript; "but do not talk to me about it. I will not lose my ideas in words." This was not like Marcello, who loved to discuss his work, and I looked at him astonished.

"Come," he said, "we will go

down into the garden, and you
shall tell me about the comrades.
What are they doing? Has
Magnin found a model for his
Clytemnestra?"

I humored him, as I always
did, and we sat upon a stone
bench behind the house, looking
toward the laurel grove, talking
of the pictures and the students.
I wanted to walk down the ilex
alley, but he stopped me.

"If you are afraid of the damp,
don't go down there," he said;
"the place is like a vault. Let
us stay here and be thankful for
this heavenly view."

"Well, let us stay here," I
answered, resigned as ever. He
lit a cigar and offered me one in
silence. If he did not care to talk,
I could be still, too. From time
to time he made some indifferent
observation, and I answered it in
the same tone. It almost seemed
to me as though we, the old
heart - comrades, had become
strangers who had not known
each other a week, or as though

we had been so long apart that
we had grown away from each
other. There was something
about him which escaped me.
Yes, the few days of solitude had
indeed put years and a sort of
shyness, or rather ceremony,
between us! It did not seem
natural to me now to clap him
on the back, and make the old,
harmless jokes at him. He must
have felt the constraint, too, for
we were like children who had
looked forward to a game, and
did not know now what to play
at.

At six o'clock I left him. It
was not like parting with Marcello. I felt rather as though
I should find my old friend in
Rome that evening, and here only
left a shadowy likeness of him.
He accompanied me to the gate,
and pressed my hand, and for a
moment the true Marcello looked
out of his eyes; but we called
out no last words to each other
as I drove away. I had only
said, "Let me know when you

want me; and he had said,
"*Merci!*" and all the way back
to Rome I felt a chill upon me,
his hand had been so cold, and I
thought and thought what could
be the matter with him.

That evening I spoke out my
anxiety to Pierre Magnin, who
shook his head and declared that
malaria fever must be taking hold
of him, and that people often
began to show it by being a little
odd.

"He must not stay there! We
must get him away as soon as
possible," I cried.

"We know Marcello, and that
nothing can make him stir against
his will," said Pierre. "Let
him alone, and he will get tired
of his whim. It will not kill
him to have a touch of malaria,
and some evening he will turn up
among us merry as ever."

But he did not. I worked hard
at my picture and finished it, but
for a few touches, and he had not
yet appeared. Perhaps it was the
extreme application, perhaps the

sitting out in that damp place,
for I insist upon tracing it to
something more material than
emotion. Well, whatever it was,
I fell ill; more ill than I had
even been in my life. It was
almost twilight when it overtook
me, and I remember it distinctly,
though I forget what happened
afterward, or, rather, I never
knew, for I was found by Magnin
quite unconscious, and he has
told me that I remained so for
some time, and then became
delirious, and talked of nothing
but Marcello. I have told you
that it was very nearly twilight;
but just at the moment when the
sun is gone the colors show in
their true value. Artists know
this, and I was putting last
touches here and there to my
picture, and especially to my
head of Mucius Scævola, or,
rather, Marcello.

The rest of the picture came
out well enough; but that head,
which should have been the principal one, seemed faded and sunk

in. The face appeared to grow
paler and paler, and to recede
from me ; a strange veil spread
over it, and the eyes seemed to
close. I am not easily frightened,
and I know what tricks some
peculiar methods of color will
play by certain lights, for the
moment I spoke of had gone,
and the twilight grayness had
set in ; so I stepped back to look
well at it. Just then the lips,
which had become almost white,
opened a little, and sighed ! An
illusion, of course. I must have
been very ill and quite delirious
already, for to my imagination it
was a real sigh, or, rather, a sort
of exhausted gasp. Then it was
that I fainted, I suppose, and
when I came to myself I was in
my bed, with Magnin and Monsieur Sutton standing by me, and
a *Sœur de Charité* moving softly
about among medicine bottles,
and speaking in whispers. I
stretched out my hands, and they
were thin and yellow, with long,
pale nails; and I heard Magnin's

voice, which sounded very far away, say, " *Dieu merci !* " And now Monsieur Sutton will tell you what I did not know until long afterward.

II.

ROBERT SUTTON'S ACCOUNT OF
WHAT HAPPENED AT THE VIGNA
MARZIALI.

 AM attached to Detaille,
and was very glad to be
of use to him, but I
never fully shared his
admiration for Marcello
Souvestre, though I ap-
preciated his good points. He
was certainly very promising—I
must say that. But he was an
odd, flighty sort of fellow, not of
the kind which we English care
to take the trouble to understand.
It is my business to write stories,
but not having need of such
characters I have never particularly studied them. As I say, I

was glad to be of use to Detaille,
who is a thorough good fellow,
and I willingly gave up my work
to go and sit by his bedside.
Magnin knew that I was a friend
of his, and very properly came to
me when he found that Detaille's
illness was a serious one and
likely to last for a long time. I
found him perfectly delirious, and
raving about Marcello.

"Tell me what the *motif* is! I
know it is a *Marche Funèbre!*"
And here he would sing a peculiar
melody, which, as I have a knack
at music, I noted down, it being
like nothing I had heard before.
The Sister of Charity looked at
me with severe eyes; but how
could she know that all is grist
for our mill, and that observation
becomes with us a mechanical
habit? Poor Detaille kept repeating this curious melody over
and over, and then would stop
and seem to be looking at his
picture, crying that it was fading
away.

"Marcello! Marcello! You

are fading, too! Let me come to
you!" He was as weak as a
baby, and could not have moved
from his bed unless in the strength
of delirium.

"I cannot come!" he went on;
"they have tied me down." And
here he made as though he were
trying to gnaw through a rope at
his wrists, and then burst into
tears. "Will no one go for me
and bring me a word from you?
Ah, if I could know that you are
alive!"

Magnin looked at me. I knew
what he was thinking. He would
not leave his comrade, but I must
go. I don't mind acknowledging
that I did not undertake this
unwillingly. To sit by Detaille's
bedside and listen to his ravings
enervated me, and what Magnin
wanted struck me as troublesome
but not uninteresting to one of
my craft, so I agreed to go. I
had heard all about Marcello's
strange seclusion from Magnin
and Detaille himself, who
lamented over it openly, in his

simple way, at supper at the
Academy, where I was a frequent
guest.

I knew that it would be useless
to ring at the gate of the Vigna
Marziali. Not only should I not
be admitted, but I should arouse
Marcello's anger and suspicion, for
I did not for a moment believe
that he was not alive, though I
thought it very possible that he
was becoming a little crazy, as
his countrymen are so easily put
off their balance. Now, odd
people are oddest late in the
day and at evening time. Their
nerves lose the power of resistance then, and the real man gets
the better of them. So I determined to try to discover something at night, reflecting also that
I should be safer from detection
then. I knew his liking for wandering about when he ought to
be in his bed, and I did not
doubt that I should get a glimpse
of him, and that was really all I
needed.

My first step was to take a

long walk out of the Porta San Giovanni, and this I did in the early morning, tramping along steadily until I came to an iron gate on the right of the road, with "Vigna Marziali" over it; and then I walked straight on, never stopping until I had reached a little bushy lane running down toward the Campagna to the right. It was pebbly, and quite shut in by luxuriant ivy and elder bushes, and it bore deep traces of the last heavy rains. These had evidently been effaced by no footprints, so I concluded that it was little used. Down this path I made my way cautiously, look- ing behind and before me, from a habit contracted in my lonely wanderings in the Abruzzi. I had a capital revolver with me—an old friend—and I feared no man ; but I began to feel a dramatic interest in my undertaking, and determined that it should not be crossed by any disagreeable sur- prises. The lane led me further down the plain than I had

reckoned upon, for the bushy
edge shut out the view; and
when I had got to the bottom
and faced round, the Vigna Marziali was lying quite far to my left.
I saw at a glance that behind
the gray casino an alley of ilexes
ended in a laurel grove; then
there were plantations of kitchen
stuff, with a sort of thatched
cabin in their midst, probably
that of the gardener. I looked
about for a kennel, but saw none,
so there was no watch-dog. At the
end of this primitive kitchen garden was a broad patch of grass,
bounded by a fence, which I
could take at a spring. Now I
knew my way, but I could not
resist tracing it out a little further.
It was well that I did so, for I
found just within the fence a
sunken stream, rather full at the
time, in consequence of the rains,
too deep to wade and too broad
to jump. It struck me that it
would be easy enough to take a
board from the fence and lay it
over for a bridge. I measured

the breadth with my eye, and
decided that the board would
span it ; then I went back as I
had come, and returned to find
Detaille still raving.

As he could understand nothing, it seemed to me rather a
fool's errand to go off in search
of comfort for him ; but a conscious moment might come, and,
moreover, I began to be interested
in my undertaking ; and so I
agreed with Magnin that I should
go and take some food and rest,
and return to the Vigna that
night. I told my landlady that
I was going into the country and
should return the next day, and I
went to Nazarri's and laid in a
stock of sandwiches, and filled my
flask with something they called
sherry, for, though I was no great
wine-drinker, I feared the night
chill.

It was about seven o'olock
when I started, and I retraced
my morning's steps exactly. As
I reached the lane, it occurred to
me that it was still too light for

me to pass unobserved over the
stream, and I made a place for
myself under the hedge and lay
down, quite screened by the thick
curtain of tangled overhanging
ivy.

I must have been out of training, and tired by the morning's
walk, for I fell asleep. When I
awoke it was night; the stars
were shining, a dank mist made
its way down my throat, and I
felt stiff and cold. I took a pull
at my flask, finding it nasty stuff,
but it warmed me. Then I rang
my repeater, which struck a
quarter to eleven, got up, and
shook myself free of the leaves
and brambles, and went on down
the lane. When I got to the
fence I sat down and thought
the thing over. What did I expect to discover? What *was*
there to discover? Nothing!
Nothing but that Marcello was
alive; and that was no discovery
at all, for I felt sure of it. I was
a fool, and had let myself be
allured by the mere stage non-

sense and mystery of the business, and a mouse would creep out of this mountain of precautions! Well, at least, I could turn it to account by describing my own absurd behavior in some story yet to be written, and, as it was not enough for a chapter, I would add to it by further experience. "Come along!" I said to myself. "You're an ass, but it may prove instructive." I raised the top board from the fence noiselessly. There was a stile just there, and the boards were easily moved. I laid down my bridge with some difficulty, and stepped carefully across, and made my way to the laurel grove as quickly and noiselessly as possible.

There all was thick darkness, and my eyes only grew slowly accustomed to it. After all, there was not much to see; some stone seats in a semi-circle, and some fragments of columns set upright with antique busts upon them. Then a little to the right a sort of arch, with apparently some steps descending into the ground, probably the entrance to some discovered branch of a catacomb. In the midst of the inclosure, not a very large one, stood a stone table, deeply fixed in the earth. No one was there ; of that I felt certain, and I sat down, having now got used to the gloom, and fell to eating my sandwiches, for I was desperately hungry.

Now that I had come so far, was nothing to take place to repay me for my trouble? It suddenly struck me that it was absurd to expect Marcello to come out to meet me and perform any mad antics he might be meditating there before my eyes for my especial satisfaction. Why I had supposed that something would take place in the grove I do not know, except that this seemed a fit place for it. I would go and watch the house, and if I saw a light anywhere, I might be sure that he was within. Any fool might have thought of that, but a novelist lays the scene of his drama and expects his characters to slide about in the grooves like puppets. It is only when mine surprise me that I feel they · are alive. When I reached the end of the ilex alley, I saw the house before me. There were more cabbages and onions after I had left the trees, and I saw that in this open space I could easily be perceived by any one standing on the balcony above. As I drew back again under the ilexes, a window above, not the one on the balcony, was suddenly lighted up; but the light did not remain long, and presently a gleam shone through the glass oval over the door below.

I had just time to spring behind the thickest trunk near me, when the door opened. I took advantage of its creaking to creep up the slanting tree like a cat, and lie out upon a projecting branch.

As I expected, Marcello came out. He was very pale and

moved mechanically, like a sleep-
walker. I was shocked to see
how hollow his face had become
as he held the candle still lighted
in his hand, and it cast deep
shadows on his sunken cheeks
and fixed eyes, which burned
wildly and seemed to see nothing.
His lips were quite white, and so
drawn that I could see his gleaming teeth. Then the candle fell
from his hand, and he came
slowly and with a curiously
regular step on into the darkness
of the ilexes, I watching him
from above. But I scarcely think
he would have noticed me, had I
been standing in his path. When
he had passed I let myself down
and followed him. I had taken
off my shoes, and my tread was
absolutely noiseless; moreover, I
felt sure he would not turn round.

On he went, with the same
mechanical step, until he reached
the grove. There I knelt behind
an old sarcophagus at the entrance, and waited. What would
he do? He stood perfectly still,

not looking about him, but as
though the clockwork within him
had suddenly stopped. I felt
that he was becoming psychologi-
cally interesting, after all. Suddenly he threw up his arms as
men do when they are mortally
wounded on the battle-field, and
I expected to see him fall at full
length. Instead of this he, made
a step forward.

I looked in the same direction,
and saw a woman, who must
have concealed herself there
while I was waiting before the
house, come from out of the
gloom, and as she slowly approached and laid her head upon
his shoulder, the outstretched
arms clasped themselves closely
around her, so that her face was
hidden upon his neck.

So this was the whole matter,
and I had been sent off on a wild-
goose chase to spy out a common
love affair! His opera and his
seclusion for the sake of work,
his tyrannical refusal to see Detaille unless he sent for him—all

this was but a mask to a vulgar
intrigue which, for reasons best
known to himself, could not be
indulged in in the city. I was
thoroughly angry! If Marcello
passed his time mooning about
in that damp hole all night,
no wonder that he looked so
wretchedly ill and seemed half
mad! I knew very well that
Marcello was no saint. Why
should he be? But I had not
taken him for a fool! He had had
plenty of romantic episodes, and
as he was discreet without being
uselessly mysterious, no one had
ever unduly pryed into them, nor
should we have done so now. I
said to myself that that mixture
of French and Italian blood was
at the bottom of it; French
flimsiness and light - headedness
and Italian love of cunning! I
looked back upon all the details
of my mysterious expedition. I
suppose at the root of my anger
lay a certain dramatic disappointment at not finding him lying
murdered, and I despised myself

for all the trouble I had taken to
this ridiculous end : just to see
him holding a woman in his arms.
I could not see her face, and her
figure was enveloped from head
to foot in something long and
dark ; but I could make out that
she was tall and slender, and that
a pair of white hands gleamed
from her drapery. As I was
looking intently, for all my indignation, the couple moved on,
and still clinging to one another
descended the steps. So even
the solitude of the lonely laurel
grove could not satisfy Marcello's
insane love of secrecy ! I kept
still awhile ; then I stole to
where they had disappeared, and
listened ; but all was silent, and
I cautiously struck a match and
peered down. I could see the
steps for a short distance below
me, and then the darkness
seemed to rise and swallow
them. It must be a catacomb,
as I had imagined, or an old
Roman bath, perhaps, which
Marcello had made comfortable

enough, no doubt, and as likely
as not they were having a nice
little cold supper there. My
empty stomach told me that I
could have forgiven him even
then, could I have shared it. I
was in truth frightfully hungry
as well as angry, and sat down
on one of the stone benches to
finish my sandwiches.

The thought of waiting to see
this love-sick pair return to
upper earth never for a moment
occurred to me. I had found
out the whole thing, and a great
humbug it was! Now I wanted
to get back to Rome before my
temper had cooled, and to tell
Magnin on what a fool's errand
he had sent me. If he liked to
quarrel with me, all the better!

All the way home I composed
cutting French speeches, but
they suddenly cooled and petrified like a gust of lava from a
volcano when I discovered that
the gate was closed. I had
never thought of getting a pass,
and Magnin ought to have

warned me. Another grievance
against the fellow! I enjoyed
my resentment, and it kept me
warm as I patrolled up and
down. There are houses, and
even small eating-shops outside
the gate, but no light was visible,
and I did not care to attract
attention by pounding at the
doors in the middle of the night;
so I crept behind a bit of wall.
I was getting used to hiding by
this time, and made myself as
comfortable as I could with my
ulster, took another pull at my
flask, and waited. At last the
gate was opened and I slipped
through, trying not to look as
though I had been out all night
like a bandit. The guard looked
at me narrowly, evidently wonder-
ing at my lack of luggage. Had
I had a knapsack, I might have
been taken for some innocently
mad English tourist indulging in
the mistaken pleasure of trudging
in from Frascati or Albano; but
a man in an ulster, with his
hands in his pockets, sauntering

in at the gate of the city at break of day as though returning from a stroll, naturally puzzled the officials, who looked after me and shrugged their shoulders.

Luckily, I found an early cab in the Piazza of the Lateran, for I was dead-beat, and was soon at my lodgings in the Via della Croce, where my landlady let me in very speedily. Then at last I had the comfort of throwing off my clothes, all damp with the night dew, and turning in. My wrath had cooled to a certain point, and I did not fear to lower its temperature too greatly by yielding to an overwhelming desire for sleep. An hour or two could make no great difference to Magnin—let him fancy me still hanging about the Vigna Marziali! Sleep I must have, no matter what he thought.

I slept long, and was awakened at last by my landlady, Sora Nanna, standing over me, and saying, "There is a Signore who wants you."

"It is I, Magnin!" said a voice behind her. "I could not wait for you to come!" He looked haggard with anxiety and watching.

"Detaille is raving still," he went on, "only worse than before. Speak, for Heaven's sake! Why don't you tell me something?" And he shook me by the arm as though he thought I was still asleep.

"Have you nothing to say? You must have seen something! Did you see Marcello?"

"Oh, yes, I saw him!"

"Well?"

"Well, he was very comfortable—quite alive. He had a woman's arms around him."

I heard my door violently slammed to a ferocious "*Sacré gamin!*" and then steps springing down the stairs. I felt perfectly happy at having made such an impression, and turned and resumed my broken sleep with almost a kindly feeling toward Magnin, who was at that moment probably tearing up the Spanish Scalinata two steps at a time, and making himself horribly hot. It could not help Detaille, poor fellow! He could not understand my news. When I had slept long enough I got up, refreshed myself with a bath and something to eat, and went off to see Detaille. It was not his fault that I had been made a fool of, so I felt sorry for him.

I found him raving just as I had left him the day before, only worse, as Magnin said. He persisted in continually crying, " Marcello, take care! no one can save you!" in hoarse, weak tones, but with the regularity of a knell, keeping up a peculiar movement with his feet, as though he were weary with a long road, but must press forward to his goal. Then he would stop and break into childish sobs.

"My feet are so sore," he murmured, piteously, " and I am

so tired! But I will come!
They are following me, but I am
strong!" Then a violent struggle with his invisible pursuers,
in which he would break off into
that singing of his, alternating
with the warning cry. The
singing voice was quite another
from the speaking one. He
went on and on repeating the
singular air which he had himself called a Funeral March, and
which had become intensely disagreeable to me. If it was one,
indeed, it surely was intended
for no Christian burial. As he
sang, the tears kept trickling
down his cheeks, and Magnin sat
wiping them away as tenderly as
a woman. Between his song he
would clasp his hands, feebly
enough, for he was very weak
when the delirium did not make
him violent, and cry, in heart-
rending tones, " Marcello, I shall
never see you again! Why did
you leave us?" At last, when
he stopped for a moment, Magnin
left his side, beckoning the Sister

to take it, and drew me into the other room, closing the door behind him.

"Now tell me exactly how you saw Marcello," said he; so I related my whole absurd experience — forgetting, however, my personal irritation, for he looked too wretched and worn for anybody to be angry with him. He made me repeat several times my description of Marcello's face and manner as he had come out of the house. That seemed to make more impression upon him than the love-business.

"Sick people have strange intuitions," he said, gravely; "and I persist in thinking that Marcello is very ill and in danger. *Tenez!*" And here he broke off, went to the door, and called "*Ma sœur!*" under his breath. She understood, and after having drawn the bed-clothes straight, and once more dried the trickling tears, she came noiselessly to where we stood, the wet handkerchief still in her hand. She was a singularly tall and strong-looking woman, with piercing black eyes and a self - controlled manner. Strange to say, she bore the adopted name of Claudius, instead of a more feminine one.

" *Ma sœur,* " said Magnin, " at what o'clock was it that he sprang out of bed and we had to hold him for so long ? "

" Half-past eleven and a few minutes," she answered, promptly. Then he turned to me.

" At what time did Marcello come out into the garden ? "

" Well, it might have been half-past eleven," I answered, unwillingly. " I should say that three quarters of an hour might possibly have passed since I rang my repeater. Mind you, I wont swear it ! " I hate to have people try to prove mysterious coincidences, and this was just what they were attempting.

" Are you sure of the hour, *ma sœur ?* " I asked, a little tartly.

She looked at me calmly with her great, black eyes, and said :

"I heard the Trinità de' Monti strike the half-hour just before it happened."

"Be so good as to tell Monsieur Sutton exactly what took place," said Magnin.

"One moment, Monsieur"; and she went swiftly and softly to Detaille, raised him on her strong arm, and held a glass to his lips, from which he drank mechanically. Then she came and stood where she could watch him through the open door.

"He hears nothing," she said, as she hung the handkerchief to dry over a chair ; and then she went on. "It was half-past eleven, and my patient had been very uneasy—that is to say, more so even than before. It might have been four or five minutes after the clock had finished striking that he became suddenly quite still, and then began to tremble all over, so that the bed shook with him." She spoke admirable English, as many of the Sisters do, so I need not translate, but will give her own words.

" He went on trembling until I thought he was going to have a fit, and told Monsieur Magnin to be ready to go for the doctor, when just then the trembling stopped; he became perfectly stiff, his hair stood up upon his head, and his eyes seemed coming out of their sockets, though he could see nothing, for I passed the candle before them. All at once he sprang out of his bed and rushed to the door. I did not know he was so strong. Before he got there I had him in my arms, for he has become very light, and I carried him back to bed again, though he was struggling, like a child. Monsieur Magnin came in from the next room just as he was trying to get up again, and we held him down until it was past, but he screamed Monsieur Souvestre's name for a long time after that. Afterward he was very cold and exhausted, of course, and I gave him some beef-tea, though it was not the hour for it."

"I think you had better tell the Sister all about it," said Magnin turning to me. "It is best that the nurse should know everything."

"Very well," said I; "though I do not think it's much in her line." She answered me herself: "Everything which concerns our patients is our business. Nothing shocks us." Thereupon she sat down and thrust her hands into her long sleeves, prepared to listen. I repeated the whole affair as I had done to Magnin. She never took her brilliant eyes from off my face, and listened as coolly as though she had been a doctor hearing an account of a difficult case, though to me it seemed almost sacrilege to be describing the behavior of a love-stricken youth to a Sister of Charity.

"What do you say to that, *ma*

sœur?" asked Magnin, when I
had done.

"I say nothing, monsieur. It
is sufficient that I know it"; and
she withdrew her hands from her
sleeves, took up the handkerchief,
which was dry by this time, and
returned quietly to her place at
the bedside.

"I wonder if I have shocked
her, after all?" I said to Magnin.

"Oh, no," he answered.
"They see many things, and
a *sœur* is as abstract as a con-
fessor; they do not allow themselves any personal feelings.
I have seen Sœur Claudius listen
perfectly unmoved to the most
abominable ravings, only crossing
herself beneath her cape at the
most hideous blasphemies. It
was last summer when poor
Justin Revol died. You were
not here." Magnin put his hand
to his forehead.

"You are looking ill yourself,"
I said. "Go and try to sleep,
and I will stay."

"Very well," he answered;

"but I cannot rest unless you promise to remember everything he says, that I may hear it when I wake"; and he threw himself down upon the hard sofa like a sack, and was asleep in a moment; and I, who had felt so angry with him but a few hours ago, put a cushion under his head and made him comfortable.

I sat down in the next room and listened to Detaille's monotonous ravings, while Sœur Claudius read in her book of prayers. It was getting dusk, and several of the academicians stole in and stood over the sick man and shook their heads. They looked around for Magnin, but I pointed to the other room with my finger on my lips, and they nodded and went away on tip-toe.

It required no effort of memory to repeat Detaille's words to Magnin when he woke, for they were always the same. We had another Sister that night, and as Sœur Claudius was not to

return till the next day at mid-
day, I offered to share the watch
with Magnin who was getting
very nervous and exhausted, and
who seemed to think that some
such attack might be expected as
had occurred the night before.
The new Sister was a gentle,
delicate - looking little woman,
with tears in her soft brown eyes
as she bent over the sick man,
and crossed herself from time to
time, grasping the crucifix which
hung from the beads at her
waist. Nevertheless she was
calm and useful, and as punctual
as Sœur Claudius herself in
giving the medicines.

The doctor had come in the
evening, and prescribed a change
in these. He would not say
what he thought of his patient,
but only declared that it was
necessary to wait for a crisis.
Magnin sent for some supper,
and we sat over it together in
silence, neither of us hungry.
He kept looking at his watch.

"If the same thing happens

to-night, he will die!" said he,
and laid his head on his arms.

"He will die in a most foolish
cause, then," I said, angrily, for
I thought he was going to cry,
as those Frenchmen have a way
of doing, and I wanted to irritate
him by way of a tonic ; so I went
on :

"It would be dying for a
vaurien who is making an ass of
himself in a ridiculous business,
which will be over in a week!
Souvestre may get as much fever
as he likes! only don't ask me to
come and nurse him."

"It is not the fever," said he,
slowly, "it is a horrible nameless
dread that I have ; I suppose it is
listening to Detaille that makes
me nervous. Hark!" he added,
"it strikes eleven. We must
watch!"

"If you really expect another
attack, you had better warn the
Sister," I said ; so he told her in
a few words what might happen.

"Very well, monsieur," she
answered, and sat down quietly

near the bed, Magnin at the pillow and I near him. No sound was to be heard but Detaille's ceaseless lament.

And now, before I tell you more, I must stop to entreat you to believe me. It will be almost impossible for you to do so, I know, for I have laughed myself at such tales, and no assurances would have made me credit them. But I, Robert Sutton, swear that this thing happened. More I cannot do. It is the truth.

We had been watching Detaille intently. He was lying with closed eyes, and had been very restless. Suddenly be became quite still, and then began to tremble, exactly as Sœur Claudius had described. It was a curious, uniform trembling, apparently in every fiber, and his iron bedstead shook as though strong hands were at its head and foot. Then came the absolute rigidity she had also described, and I do not exagger-

ate when I say that not only
did his short-cropped hair seem
to stand erect, but that it literally
did so. A lamp cast the shadow
of his profile against the wall to
the left of his bed, and as I
looked at the immovable outline,
which seemed painted on the
wall, I saw the hair slowly rise
until the line where it joined the
forehead was quite a different
one—abrupt, instead of a smooth
sweep. His eyes opened wide
and were frightfully fixed, then
as frightfully strained, but they
certainly did not see us.

We waited breathlessly for
what might follow. The little
Sister was standing close to him,
her lips pressed together and a
little pale, but very calm. "Do
not be frightened, *ma sœur*,"
whispered Magnin; and she
answered in a business - like
tone, "No, monsieur," and
drew still nearer to her patient,
and took his hands, which were
stiff as those of a corpse, between her own to warm them.

I laid mine upon his heart ; it was beating so imperceptibly that I almost thought it had stopped, and as I leaned my face to his lips I could feel no breath issue from them. It seemed as though the rigor would last forever.

Suddenly, without any transition, he hurled himself with enormous force, and literally at one bound, almost into the middle of the room, scattering us aside like leaves in the wind. I was upon him in a moment, grappling with him with all my strength to prevent him from reaching the door. Magnin had been thrown backward against the table, and I heard the medicine bottles crash with his fall. He had flung back his hand to save himself, and rushed to help me, with the blood dropping from a cut in his wrist. The little Sister sprang to us. Detaille had thrown her violently back upon her knees, and now, with a nurse's instinct, she tried to throw a shawl over his bare breast. We four must have made a strange group!

Four? *We were five!* Marcello Souvestre stood before us, just within the door! We all saw him, for he was there. His bloodless face was turned toward us unmoved; his hands hung by his side as white as his face; only his eyes had life in them; they were fixed on Detaille.

"Thank God, you have come at last!" I cried. "Don't stand there like a fool! Help us, can't you?" But he never moved. I was furiously angry, and, leaving my hold, sprang upon him to drag him forward. My outstretched hands struck hard against the door, and I felt a thing like a spider's web envelop me. It seemed to draw itself over my mouth and eyes, and to blind and choke me, and then to flutter and tear and float from me.

Marcello was gone!

Detaille had slipped from Magnin's hold and lay in a heap upon the floor, as though his limbs were broken. The Sister was trembling violently as she knelt over him and tried to raise his head. We gazed at one another, stooped and lifted him in our arms, and carried him back to his bed, while Sœur Marie quietly collected the broken phials.

"You saw it, *ma sœur?*" I heard Magnin whisper, hoarsely.

"Yes, monsieur!" she only answered, in a trembling voice, holding on to her crucifix. Then she said in a professional tone:

"Will monsieur let me bind up his wrist?" And though her fingers trembled and his hand was shaking, the bandage was an irreproachable one.

Magnin went into the next room, and I heard him throw himself heavily into a chair. Detaille seemed to be sleeping. His breath came regularly; his eyes were closed with a look of

peace about the lids, his hands
lying in a natural way upon the
quilt. He had not moved since
we laid him there. I went softly
to where Magnin was sitting in
the dark. He did not move,
but only said : " Marcello is
dead ! "

" He is either dead or dying,"
I answered, ".and we must go
to him."

" Yes," Magnin whispered,
" we must go to him, but we
shall not reach him."

" We will go as soon as it
is light," I said, and then we
were still again.

When the morning came at
last, he went and found a comrade to take his place, and only
said to Sœur Marie, " It is not
necessary to speak of this night,"
and at her quiet, " You are right,
monsieur," we felt that we could
trust her. Detaille was still sleeping. Was this the crisis the
doctor had expected ? Perhaps ;
but surely not in such fearful
form. I insisted upon my com-

panion having some breakfast before we started, and I breakfasted myself, but I cannot say I tasted what passed between my lips.

We engaged a closed carriage, for we did not know what we might bring home with us, though neither of us spoke out his thoughts. It was early morning still when we reached the Vigna Marziali, and we had not exchanged a word all the way. I rang at the bell, while the coachman looked on curiously. It was answered promptly by the *guardiano* of whom Detaille has already told you.

"Where is the Signore?" I asked through the gate.

"*Chi lo sa?*" he answered. "He is here, of course; he has not left the Vigna. Shall I call him?"

"*Call him?*" I knew that no mortal voice could reach Marcello now, but I tried to fancy he was still alive.

"No," I said. "Let us in.

We want to surprise him; he
will be pleased."

The man hesitated but he
finally opened the gate, and we
entered, leaving the carriage to
wait outside. We went straight
to the house; the door at the
back was wide open. There had
been a gale in the night, and it
had torn some leaves and bits
of twigs from the trees and
blown them into the entrance
hall. They lay scattered across
the threshold, and were evidence
that the door had remained open
ever since they had fallen. The
guardiano left us, probably to
escape Marcello's anger at having
let us in, and we went up the
stairs unhindered, Magnin foremost, for he knew the house
better than I, from Detaille's
description. He had told him
about the corner room with the
balcony, and we pretended that
Marcello might be there, absorbed betimes in his work, but
we did not call him.

He was not there. His papers

were strewn over the table as
though he had been writing, but
the inkstand was dry and full of
dust—he could not have used
it for days. We went silently
into the other chambers. Perhaps he was still asleep. But,
no! We found his bed un-
touched, so he could not have
lain in it that night. The rooms
were all unlocked but one, and
this closed door made our hearts
beat. Marcello could scarcely
be there, however, for there was
no key in the lock; I saw the
daylight shining through the
key-hole. We called his name,
but there came no answer. We
knocked loudly; still no sign
from within; so I put my
shoulder to the door, which was
old and cracked in several places,
and succeeded in bursting it
open.

Nothing was there but a sculptor's modeling-stand, with something upon it covered with a
white cloth, and the modeling-
tools on the floor. At the sight

of the cloth, still damp, we drew a deep breath. It could not have hung there for many hours, certainly not for twenty - four. We did not raise it. "He would be vexed," said Magnin, and I nodded, for it is accounted almost a crime in the artist's world to unveil a sculptor's work behind his back. We expressed no surprise at the fact of his modeling; a ban seemed to lie upon our tongues. The cloth hung tightly to the object beneath it, and showed us the outline of a woman's head and rounded bust, and so veiled we left her. There was a little winding stair leading out of the passage, and we climbed it, to find ourselves in a sort of belvedere, commanding a superb view. It was a small, open terrace, on the roof of the house, and we saw at a glance that no one was there.

We had now been all over the casino, which was small and simply built, being evidently in-tended only for short summer

use. As we stood leaning over
the balustrade, we could look
down into the garden. No one
was there but the *guardiano*,
lying among his cabbages with
his arms behind his head, half
asleep. The laurel grove had
been in my mind from the beginning, only it had seemed more
natural to go to the house first.
Now we descended the stairs
silently and directed our steps
thither.

As we approached it, the *guardiano* came toward us, lazily.

" Have you seen the Signore ? "
he asked, and his stupidly placid
face showed me that he, at least,
had no hand in his disappearance.

" No, not yet," I answered,
" but we shall come across him
somewhere, no doubt. Perhaps
he has gone to take a walk, and
we will wait for him. What is
this ? " I went on, trying to seem
careless. We were standing now
by the little arch of which you
know.

"This?" said he; "I have never been down there, but they say it is something old. Do the Signori want to see it? I will fetch a lantern."

I nodded, and he went off to his cabin. I had a couple of candles in my pocket, for I had intended to explore the place, should we not find Marcello. It was there that he had disappeared that night, and my thoughts had been busy with it; but I kept my candles concealed, reflecting that they would give our search an air of premeditation which would excite curiosity.

"When did you see the Signore last?" I asked, when he had returned with the lantern.

"I brought him his supper yesterday evening."

"At what o'clock?"

"It was the Ave Maria, Signore," he replied. "He always sups then."

It would be useless to put any further questions. He was evidently utterly unobserving, and would lie to please us.

"Let me go first," said Magnin, taking the lantern. We set our feet upon the steps; a cold air seemed to fill our lungs and yet to choke us, and a thick darkness lay beneath. The steps, as I could see by the light of my candle, were modern, as well as the vaulting above them. A tablet was let into the wall, and in spite of my excitement I paused to read it, perhaps because I was glad to delay whatever awaited us below. It ran thus:

"Questo antico sepolcro Romano scoprì il Conte Marziali nell' anno 1853, e piamente conservò." In plain English:

"Count Marziali discovered this ancient Roman sepulcher in the year 1853, and piously preserved it."

I read it more quickly than it has taken time to write here, and hurried after Magnin, whose footsteps sounded faintly below me.

As I hastened, a draught of cold
air extinguished my candle, and
I was trying to make my way
down by feeling along the wall,
which was horribly dark and
clammy, when my heart stood
still at a cry from far beneath me
—a cry of horror!

"Where are you?" I shouted;
but Magnin was calling my name,
and could not hear me. "I am
here. I am in the dark!"

I was making haste as fast as
I could, but there were several
turnings.

"I have found him!" came up
from below.

"Alive?" I shouted. No
answer.

One last short flight brought
me face to face with the gleam
of the lantern. It came from a
low doorway, and within stood
Magnin, peering into the darkness. I knew by his face, as
he held the light high above
him, that our fears were realized.

Yes; Marcello was there. He
was lying stretched upon the

floor, staring at the ceiling, dead, and already stiff, as I could see at a glance. We stood over him, saying not a word ; then I knelt down and felt him, for mere form's sake, and said, as though I had not known it before, " He has been dead for some hours."

" Since yesterday evening," said Magnin, in a horror-stricken voice, yet with a certain satisfaction in it, as though to say, " You see, I was right."

Marcello was lying with his head slightly thrown back, no contortions in his handsome features ; rather the look of a person who has quietly died of exhaustion—who has slipped unconsciously from life to death. His collar was thrown open and a part of his breast, of a ghastly white, was visible. Just over the heart was a small spot.

" Give me the lantern," I whispered, as I stooped over it. It was a very little spot, of a faint purplish-brown, and must have changed color within the night.

I examined it intently, and should say that the blood had been sucked to the surface, and then a small prick or incision made. The slight sub-cutaneous effusion led me to this conclusion. One tiny drop of coagulated blood closed the almost imperceptible wound. I probed it with the end of one of Magnin's matches. It was scarcely more than skin deep, so it could not be the stab of a stiletto, however slender, or the track of a bullet. Still, it was strange, and with one impulse we turned to see if no one were concealed there, or if there were no second exit. It would be madness to suppose that the murderer, if there was one, would remain by his victim. Had Marcello been making love to a pretty contadina, and was this some jealous lover's vengeance? But it was not a stab. Had one drop of poison in the little wound done this deadly work?

We peered about the place,

and I saw that Magnin's eyes
were blinded by tears and his
face as pale as that upturned
one on the floor, whose lids I
had vainly tried to close. The
chamber was low, and beautifully ornamented with stucco bas-
reliefs, in the manner of the well-
known one not far from there
upon the same road. Winged
genii, griffins, and arabesques,
modeled with marvelous light-
ness, covered the walls and ceiling. There was no other door
than the one we had entered by.
In the center stood a marble
sarcophagus, with the usual subjects sculptured upon it ; on the
one side Hercules conducting a
veiled figure, on the other a
dance of nymphs and fauns. A
space in the middle contained
the following inscription, deeply
cut in the stone, and still partially filled with red pigment :

D. M.
VESPERTILIAE · THC · AIMA-
TOΠΩTIΔOC · Q · FLAVIVS ·
VIX·IPSE·SOSPES·MON⸴

"What is this?" whispered
Magnin. It was only a pickax
and a long crowbar, such as the
country people use in hewing out
their blocks of "tufa," and his
foot had struck against them.
Who could have brought them
here? They must belong to the
guardiano above, but he said that
he had never come here, and I
believed him, knowing the Italian
horror of darkness and lonely
places; but what had Marcello
wanted with them? It did not
occur to us that archæological
curiosity could have led him to
attempt to open the sarcophagus,
the lid of which had evidently
never been raised, thus justifying
the expression, "piously preserved."

As I rose from examining the
tools, my eyes fell upon the line
of mortar where the cover joined
to the stone below, and I noticed
that some of it had been removed,
perhaps with the pickax which
lay at my feet. I tried it with
my nails and found that it was

very crumbly. Without a word,
I took the tool in my hand,
Magnin instinctively following
my movements with the lantern.
What impelled us, I do not know.
I had myself no thought, only an
irresistible desire to see what was
within. I saw that much of the
mortar had been broken away,
and lay in small fragments upon
the ground, which I had not
noticed before. It did not take
long to complete the work. I
snatched the lantern from Magnin's hand and set it upon the
ground, where it shone full upon
Marcello's dead face, and by its
light I found a little break
between the two masses of stone
and managed to insert the end
of my crowbar, driving it in with
a blow of the pickax. The
stone chipped and then cracked
a little. Magnin was shivering.

"What are you going to do?"
he said, looking around at where
Marcello lay.

"Help me!" I cried, and we
two bore with all our might upon

the crowbar. I am a strong man,
and I felt a sort of blind fury
as the stone refused to yield.
What if the bar should snap?
With another blow I drove it
in still further, then using it as a
lever, we weighed upon it with
our outstretched arms until every
muscle was at its highest ten-
sion. The stone moved a little,
and, almost fainting, we stopped
to rest.

From the ceiling hung the
rusty remnant of an iron chain,
which must once have held a
lamp. To this, by scrambling
upon the sarcophagus, I con-
trived to make fast the lantern.

"Now!" said I, and we heaved
again at the lid. It rose, and
we alternately heaved and pushed
until it lost its balance and fell
with a thundering crash upon
the other side; such a crash that
the walls seemed to shake, and
I was for a moment utterly
deafened, while little pieces of
stucco rained upon us from the
ceiling. When we had paused

to recover from the shock, we leaned over the sarcophagus and looked in.

The light shone full upon it, and we saw—how is it possible to tell? We saw lying there, amid folds of moldering rags, the body of a woman, perfect as in life, with faintly rosy face, soft crimson lips, and a breast of living pearl, which seemed to heave as though stirred by some delicious dream. The rotten stuff swathed about her was in ghastly contrast to this lovely form, fresh as the morning! Her hands lay stretched at her side, the pink palms were turned a little outward, her eyes were closed as peacefully as those of a sleeping child, and her long hair, which shone red-golden in the dim light from above, was wound around her head in numberless finely-plaited tresses, beneath which little locks escaped in rings upon her brow. I could have sworn that the blue veins on that divinely perfect bosom held living blood!

We were absolutely paralyzed,
and Magnin leaned gasping over
the edge as pale as death, paler
by far than this living, almost
smiling face to which his eyes
were glued. I do not doubt that
I was as pale as he at this inexplicable vision. As I looked,
the red lips seemed to grow
redder. They *were* redder! The
little pearly teeth showed between them. I had not seen
them before, and now a clear
ruby drop trickled down to her
rounded chin, and from there
slipped sideways and fell upon
her neck. Horror-struck I gazed
upon the living corpse, till my
eyes could not bear the sight
any longer. As I looked away,
my glance fell once more upon
the mysterious inscription, half
Latin, half Greek, and the awful
meaning of the words flashed
upon me suddenly as I read
them this second time. "To
Vespertilia"—that was in Latin,
and even the Latin name of the
woman suggested a thing of evil

flitting in the dusk. But the full horror of the nature of that thing had been veiled to Roman eyes under the Greek *τῆς αἱματο-πωτίδος*, " The blood-drinker, the vampire woman." And Flavius —her lover—*vix ipse sospes*, " himself hardly saved " from that deadly embrace, had buried her here, and set a seal upon her sepulcher, trusting to the weight of stone and the strength of clinging mortar, to imprison forever the beautiful monster he had loved.

" Infamous murderess ! " I cried, "you have killed Marcello ! " and a sudden vengeful calm came over me.

" Give me the pickax," I said to Magnin. I can hear myself saying it still. He picked it up and handed it to me as in a dream ; he seemed little better than an idiot, and the beads of sweat were shining on his forehead. I took my knife, and from the long wooden handle of the pickax I cut a fine, sharp stake.

Then I clambered, scarcely feeling any repugnance, over the
side of the sarcophagus, my feet
among the folds of Vespertilia's
decaying winding - sheet, which
crushed like ashes beneath my
boot.

I looked for one moment at
that white breast, but only to
choose the loveliest spot, where
the network of azure veins shimmered like veiled turquoises, and
then with one blow I drove the
pointed stake deep down through
the breathing snow and stamped
it in with my heel.

An awful shriek, so ringing and
horrible, that I thought my ears
must have burst ; but even then
I felt neither fear nor horror.
There are times when these cannot touch us. I stooped and
gazed once again at the face,
now undergoing a fearful change
—fearful and final !

" Foul vampire !" I said, quietly,
in my concentrated rage. " You
will do no more harm now !"
And then, without looking back

upon her cursed face, I clambered out·of the horrible tomb.

We raised Marcello, and slowly carried him up the steep stairs— a difficult task, for the way was narrow and he was so stiff. I noticed that the steps were ancient up to the end of the second flight ; above, the modern passage was somewhat broader. When we reached the top, the *guardiano* was lying upon one of the stone benches ; he did not mean us to cheat him out of his fee. I gave him a couple of francs.

" You see that we have found the Signore," I tried to say in a natural voice. " He is very weak, and we will carry him to the carriage." I had thrown my handkerchief over Marcello's face, but the man knew as well as I that he was dead. Those stiff feet told their own story, but Italians are timid of being in- volved in such affairs. They have a childish dread of the police, and he only answered, " Poor Signorino ! He is very ill; it is better to take him to Rome," and kept cautiously clear of us as we went up to the ilex alley with our icy burden, and he did not go to the gate with us, not liking to be observed by the coachman, who was dozing on his box. With difficulty we got Marcello's corpse into the carriage, the driver turning to look at us suspiciously. I explained we had found our friend very ill, and at the same time slipped a gold piece into his hand, telling him to drive to the Via del Governo Vecchio. He pocketed the money, and whipped his horses into a trot, while we sat supporting the stiff body, which swayed like a broken doll at every pebble in the road. When we reached the Via del Governo Vecchio at last, no one saw us carry him into the house. There was no step before the door, and we drew up so close to it that it was possible to screen our burden from sight. When we had brought him into his room and laid him upon his bed, we noticed that his eyes were closed; from the movement of the carriage, perhaps, though that was scarcely possible. The landlady behaved very much as I had expected her to do, for, as I told you, I know the Italians. She pretended, too, that the Signore was very ill, and made a pretense of offering to fetch a doctor, and, when I thought it best to tell her that he was dead, declared that it must have happened that very moment, for she had seen him look at us and close his eyes again. She had always told him that he ate too little and that he would be ill. Yes, it was weakness and that bad air out there which had killed him; and then he worked too hard. When she had successfully established this fiction, which we were glad enough to agree to, for neither did we wish for the publicity of an inquest, she ran out and fetched a gossip to come and keep her company.

So died Marcello Souvestre and so died Vespertilia, the blood-drinker, at last.

There is not much more to tell. Marcello lay calm and beautiful upon his bed, and the students came and stood silently looking at him, then knelt down for a moment to say a prayer, crossed themselves, and left him for-ever.

We hastened to the Villa Medici, where Detaille was sleeping, and Sister Claudius watching him with a satisfied look on her strong face. She rose noiselessly at our entrance, and came to us at the threshold.

"He will recover," said she, softly. She was right. When he awoke and opened his eyes he knew us directly, and Magnin breathed a devout "Thank God!"

"Have I been ill, Magnin?" he asked, very feebly.

"You have had a little fever," answered Magnin, promptly;

"but it is over now. Here is Monsieur Sutton come to see you."

"Has Marcello been here?" was the next question. Magnin looked at him very steadily.

"No," he only said, letting his face tell the rest.

"Is he dead, then?" Magnin only bowed his head. "Poor friend!" Detaille murmured to himself, then closed his heavy eyes and slept again.

A few days after Marcello's funeral we went to the fatal Vigna Marziali to bring back the objects which had belonged to him. As I laid the manuscript score of the opera carefully together, my eye fell upon a passage which struck me as the identical one which Detaille had so constantly sung in his delirium, and which I had noted down. Strange to say, when I reminded him of it later, it was perfectly new to him, and he declared that Marcello had not let him examine his manuscript. As for the veiled bust in the other room, we left it undisturbed, and to crumble away unseen.

The Green Hands
A Story About a Duet

George Augustus Sala

TERRIBLE TALES.

NO. 1.—THE GREEN HANDS.

A STORY ABOUT A DUET

THERE is nothing more ridiculous, of course, than the superstition which stigmatizes such and such a thing, such and such an action, or such and such a colour—for superstition goes as far as the prismatic range—as being "unlucky." Why should we have a horror of being thirteen at the dinner-table? Why should it be unlucky to spill, or to help your next neighbour to salt? Why should inexorable tradition forbid you, under the penalty of "sorrow" following, to make a present to, or to accept from any one, a knife, or a pair of scissors, without giving or taking some money payment, however trifling, in return? Why should Friday be an unlucky day?* A boy's misfortunes usually begin on Monday, when he goes to school; yet the smallest urchin will tell you that Friday is "un-lucky." The Americans, whose rise and progress as a nation have been so surprisingly contradictory of all known superstitions, traditions, and prece-dents, once tried to put the unluckiness of Friday to the test. At least, a worthy citizen of Salem, in the State of Massachusetts—and every individual American wisely considers himself to be, and in no small degree, a representative of the United States—determined that Friday should no longer be reck-oned among the ill-omened days of the week. He was a ship-owner. He called a cunning shipwright, and bade him take chalk in hand, and lay down the lines of a trim sloop, on a Friday. The craft was, in due time, built; and it was on a Friday that the last piece of caulking to her deck was finished. She was launched on a Friday. The owner, by dint of sedulous searching among the ship-brokers' offices of Salem and Boston, secured a skipper, whose name was Friday. As to his first

mate, he had been born, while the boatswain had been christened, and the cook married, on a Friday. To complete the special nature of the transaction, the ship was named the "Friday;" and a bottle of right Bourbon whisky was, to that intent, broken over her bows. Were there any hot cross-buns in America, she might have been freighted with those dainty, but indigestible cakes. In default of buns, the "Friday" carried a neatly-assorted cargo of New England's "notions." She was despatched to the port of Charleston, South Carolina; and she set sail on a Friday, much to the distaste of the ship's company—for the sailor's motto is, "Six days shalt thou do all that thou hast to do, and go to sea on a Sunday." Of course, you have guessed the end of the story ere this. The good ship "Friday" was wrecked in a gale, off Cape Hatteras, and went down, with all hands—on a Friday! Her owner never held up his head again; but he was wont to declare that the misfortune which had happened to the "Friday" was due to his over zeal in shipping the cook—a black man, by the way—who had been married on a Friday. "There it is," the owner would complain, dolefully; "it was all along o' that darned nigger being married at all!" It must be explained that the unlucky owner was the crustiest of old bachelors.

All the world, fortunately, are neither crusty old bachelors nor acidulated spinsters; and, among the majority of humanity, to be married is looked upon as one of the luckiest of events, and not one fraught with evil fortune. Yet I question whether many of my fair readers would care about going to Han-over Square on the fifth (although some call it the sixth) day of the week. Everybody knows that it is unlucky, in connexion with matrimony, to pass under a ladder—why, I am unable to determine; unless, indeed, it be for the reason that, in old times, criminals sentenced to be hanged were pushed off

---

* The cause of the aversion from Friday, from thirteen guests at table, and from spilling salt, is, among Christians, at least, obvious. There were thirteen guests at the Last Supper; and Judas Iscariot is said by tradition *to have over-turned the salt-cellar.*

the ladder by Jack Ketch, and that marriage and hanging are generally said to go together. You must not buy tripe on a Friday, either, so an old song says. I suspect the song was written by a butcher, who wished to spoil the tripe-dresser's trade, for epicures declare that Friday is the very best day in the week for tripe. I know it is for sprats.

There are hundreds of superstitions more preposterous than those I have noted, and a furtive, shamefaced belief in which is not by any means confined to what are insolently termed the uneducated classes. The most cultivated and refined persons are frequently as grossly superstitious as the crassest clodhopper in Somerset or Dorset; nor is it unworthy of remark, that your strong-minded folks, your positivists, your materialists, your philosophers, who laugh at Adam and Eve, and scorn Noah's ark, and refuse to admit anything that cannot be proven by reason and justified by fact, are precisely the kind of people who are often most addicted to placing faith in the silliest and most irrational superstitions. Were Tom Paine alive now, I should not be at all surprised to hear that he was a member—with Condorcet, Volney, and Dr. Priestley—of a "Spiritual Athenæum;" or that M. Arouet de Voltaire had adopted Mr. Home as his son, and given him fifty thousand pounds to buy lollipops with.

In Italy and the East, legends concerning the baleful tendency of certain actions or things are merged and absorbed in the great superstition of the Evil Eye. Certain persons among the Italians are said to be born with the mal'occhio, and to have the sinister power of the gettatura, or of casting ill luck to those on whom they look; and to avert those ominous glances, almost every Italian, male or female, wears, from the cradle upwards, a bit of coral about the person. You shall scarcely pass an Italian dandy, whether from the northern or southern part of the Peninsula, without observing among the trinkets hung to his watch-chain, a tiny crooked branch of coral. This is to ward off the Evil Eye. The idea is carried to an almost incredible extent. Such a preacher cannot get any congregation to listen to his sermons; such a schoolmaster is bereft of scholars; such a tradesman of customers, through an insensate belief that the poor devil has the mal'occhio. The highest personages in the land are not exempt from the aspersion of being able to cast ill luck. I remember once travelling by railway between Venice and Milan; and when we were about two miles from Camerlata, the train broke down. We were delayed a good hour and a-half; and the five Italian gentlemen who were in the compartment I occupied were unanimous in ascribing the disaster to the presence in the train of "that maladetto, Ratazzi." The ex-Prime Minister of the kingdom of Italy was one of our fellow-passengers, and his countrymen universally credit him with the possession of the mal'occhio. He has certainly been the unluckiest of premiers. In the East, belief in the Evil Eye is as fundamentally impressed on the popular mind, as faith in the mission of Mahomet, and the canine extraction of giaours. Every Oriental baby has an amulet—not necessarily of coral—hung round its little neck, to undo the spells woven by evil-eyed enchanters. Over the door of every Moorish house is sculpt or painted an outstretched hand—always with a view to the Evil Eye; and every felucca that puts out from a port on the Barbary coast has a human eye painted on the prow, or some other conspicuous part of the vessel. So long as they "mind their eye," the Arab mariners are morally certain of not coming to grief.

I will not detain you over the vexed question as to which is the unluckiest card in the pack—the four of hearts or the nine of diamonds; which is the unluckiest letter in the alphabet—some say it is Y; and which the unluckiest coin to toss with. Professed tossers say it is a half-sovereign. I will mention only one more superstition, and I will own that I have been somewhat reluctant to name it, and have beaten about the bush a good deal before coming to it, for the reason that I happen to be strongly impregnated with the superstition myself. As firmly as sailors set their faces against Friday as a day for going to sea upon—as strongly as Italians and Orientals hold that the Evil Eye can be averted by crooked bits of coral, or by the effigy of an outstretched hand, do I believe that Green is an unlucky colour. I don't know why—I am not bound to tell you why: it is sufficient that I believe in its unluckiness, and that my grandmother believed so before me. She had a magnificent dress of Turkish poplin once given to her by a great lady who had been ambassadress at Constantinople; but the robe was a bright emerald green, and my grandmother gave the dress away. This was quite according to the way of the world. My grandmother didn't care much whether the person to whom she gave the dress was exposed to misfortune through its hue. With regard to my own personal experience, the number of scrapes into which I have fallen through green are infinite. I wouldn't live in Green Street, Leicester Square, for a trifle, or have a greengrocer as my landlord, I assure you; and, indeed, I never inhabited a room of which the wall paper was of a verdant tinge, without quarrelling with the landlady, or having the brokers in, or undergoing some analogous inconvenience. Nor do I think that I should like to go to sea in one of Mr. Green's East Indiamen, sumptuous as the accommodation on board those vessels is said to be. Everybody knows that green tea plays the deuce with your nerves, and that jealousy is a green-eyed monster of which we should all beware. I might, perhaps, except the "Green Bushes," which is a capital play, from my catalogue. But take green, under most of its aspects, and no good will be found to come out of it. What is the colour, pray, of the billiard and the roulette table? Why, green. The unwholesomeness of green gooseberries and green apples, is notorious. As regards personal attire, I never knew a man who habitually wore a green coat who wasn't a villain; I never knew a lady in a green silk dress whom I could like. Green spectacles have upon me a most disagreeable effect. I cannot even endure a green parasol. If ever I chanced to buy a plaid scarf, and I found there was green in the pattern of the tartan, I forthwith discarded it. I wouldn't buy a set of malachite shirt-studs or wrist-buttons for any money; although I am not prepared to state exactly what I should do if his Majesty the Emperor of Russia sent me a snuff-box of malachite set with diamonds. I might take the diamonds out, and bestow the green casket in charity.

This superstitious dislike to a particular colour is no doubt exceedingly nonsensical; but have the parallel superstitions I have quoted above, and in one or another of which most of us have some lurking kind of faith, any more sense in them? I think not. Touching my own peculiar weakness, I know that I have lost money, friends, sweethearts, and chances of advancement in the world enough, through that accursed hue of green; and that if I ever partake of an alcoholic stimulant which does me harm, it is sure to be that deadly green and most perilous stuff, absinthe—the Fairy with the Green Eyes, as the French call it. I am not alone, I daresay, among those who can tell Terrible Tales of misfortunes which have happened to themselves, their relations, friends, and acquaintances, all in consequence of green. And these reflections may serve as a preface to the first of the Terrible Tales which I am about to narrate to you.

Mind this: that the persons who acted in this brief drama are all dead; and that I am, therefore, committing no indiscretion, violating no confidence, in telling a story which, I give you my word and honour, is as true—as most ghost stories are.

You know the nature of what, in sweethearting parlance—the most ungrammatical, but most charming, dialect with which I am acquainted—is termed a "long engagement." Well, there had been such an engagement for ever so long between Basil Olifaunt and Virginia Lyle. It seemed to have been settled almost since they were children, and played (and sometimes fought) together, that they were to be, in the fulness of time, man and wife. Their respective parents had a comfortable understanding on the subject; and Basil and Virginia seemed, on their part, tacitly to acquiesce in the arrangement. Although, as I have hinted, their juvenile disputes, in respect to plum-cake, picture-books, and pet rabbits, occasionally ended in fisticuffs—encounters in which, I promise you, Basil Olifaunt was not always the victor, for Virginia had a very quick eye, and a very long arm—they loved each other very dearly, as all good children should do. When Basil was corporeally chastised by his papa, for going out fishing with salmon flies in the poultry-yard, and catching an elderly hen in lieu of a salmon, Virginia tried hard to beg him off his whipping; and, failing in that, cried as though her heart would break. When Virginia, for the dire offence of spilling a bottle full of ink over a beautiful new green muslin frock,—mind, it was a *green* one,—was sentenced by her mamma to her bed-room, and bread and water, for forty-eight hours, Basil bribed the housekeeper to unlock the door of the captive's dungeon—which the good ,woman, nothing loth, would have done without a bribe — and conveyed therein substantial consolation, in the way of tarts, apples, and the "Arabian Nights' Entertainments." When Basil went to Rugby, it was Virginia who packed his play-trunk; when he obtained his commission as cornet in the Twenty-fifth Hussars, it was Virginia who insisted on making his grand new cavalry officer's sash, and who wept with vexation when she was informed that its pattern was not in accordance with the Queen's regulations, and that it must be replaced by one provided at the moderate price of twelve pounds twelve, by Messrs. Sabretash and Co., army tailors. Nor was Basil remiss in reciprocating the attentions of his betrothed. He wrote her letters in a big schoolboy hand; he spoke of her habitually as "his little wife;" and he had not been six months in India, whither his regiment had been ordered very soon after his entrance into the army, before he sent her a Trichinopoly chain, a pair of filigree bracelets, and a cashmere shawl, with gold woven into the "palms," fit for a Lallah Rookh to wear.

The estates of General Olifaunt and Lady Alice Lyle, the widowed mother of Virginia, adjoined each other. Both were in the pleasant county of Bucks, not far from Reading. Some said that the long engagement between Basil and Virginia might have been paralleled by a longer engagement between the General, who was a widow, and Lady Alice; and that they all could not have done better than to have made a four-cornered match of it, had it not been for those uncomfortable but hazy prohibitions in the Prayer-book. At all events, General

Olifaunt was always jokingly addressed at quarter sessions as Sir Roger de Coverley, and his brother justices seldom omitted to ask him how her ladyship, the perverse widow, did. There was a happy equality of fortune between the two, and both were wealthy. Lady Alice was absolute mistress of the estates left her by her husband, and Basil was the General's only son.

As I have said, he became a cornet of hussars, and went to India. He became a very dashing cornet indeed; and, by virtue of a certain round sum of money paid in to his agents in Craig's Court, Charing Cross, was to be a more dashing lieutenant. He was known as "handsome Olifaunt" in his regiment. He was the boldest rider imaginable, and a sure hand at tiger-hunting and pig-sticking. He was a capital waltzer, which made him an astonishing favourite with the ladies; and played a very careful game of whist, which caused him to be looked upon with approving eyes by his commanding officer. Even the Scotch surgeon liked him, for he was blessed with good temper and great patience, and was the only man at the great up-country station of Hum-Drum who would listen to the medico's long stories. He was the pet of his brother officers, for he had plenty of money, spent it liberally, did not shirk the claret at mess, paid his bets punctually, and never bothered impecunious subalterns for payment when he won. Hum-Drum, as regards the social life of the cantonment, was true to its name. It was the dullest of Indian military stations. The days I speak of were long prior to the Indian mutiny; and the Twenty-fifth Hussars, when they had gone through morning parade, and groomed their horses (or, the rather, saw them groomed by Indian syces), had literally nothing to do. The privates were as idle as the officers. The men went down to the bazaar, drank bad liquor, married native women on the sly, and otherwise got into mischief. The commissioned officers and gentlemen did not do much better. Doctor MacToomickey, from Aberdeen, nearly bored the mess to death. The lieutenant-colonel turned pious, talked about the battle of Armageddon and the Number of the Beast, and would always exempt a defaulter from punishment drill if he would undertake to learn a tract by heart. The major took to drinking, and the senior captain to beating his wife. The adjutant bought a turning-lathe, and made wooden rolling-pins and washing-bowls. Lieutenant Muggins, who was always of a studious turn, tried to read Cæsar, Ségur, and Jomini, to perfect himself in the art of tactics, but eventually subsided into opiated cheroots and brandy pawnee. The riding-master became literary, and was continually writing sporting articles for *Bell's Life*, which that popular journal as consistently declined to print, and the sergeant-major turned bird-stuffer. As for the married ladies' they slept half their time, and devoted the remainder to scolding their servants, squabbling among themselves, and talking scandal against their neighbours. Indeed, had it not been for these scandals and an occasional court-martial, the Twenty-fifth Hussars, hussaresses, camp-followers and all, must have died of sheer *ennui*.

The gallant corps was at the very lowest pitch of boredom when Cornet Olifaunt arrived out; but he speedily contrived to infuse life and merriment into the *blasé* Indian circle. He played whist with the colonel, single-stick with the riding-master, and backgammon with the adjutant. He worked at the turning-lathe, he tossed for rupees with the youngsters, and he made love to the ladies all round in a perfectly harmless way, *bien entendu:* was he not engaged to Virginia Lyle? The husbands of the respective ladies did not in any manner object to Cornet Olifaunt's love-making. They had been too much bored to object to anything. But Basil Olifaunt had another claim to the suffrages of the ladies. He was a capital musician, had a rich bass voice, possessed much taste and feeling, and played the pianoforte admirably. Thenceforth musical parties grew into tremendous vogue at Hum-Drum, and even among the privates there was formed a tonic sol fa association. It was a sight to see the brown-skinned camp-followers gathering in the barrack compound, and staring in mute astonishment on the gallant Twenty-fifth Hussars thundering forth the "Old Hundredth," or the Jager chorus from "Der Freischutz."

It must be owned, however, that the pace at which Cornet—now Lieutenant—Olifaunt went, became at last too rapid, and began to tell upon him. Whether it was incessant singing, pianoforte-playing, and whist, or flirting, smoking, and taking his share of the claret-cup, may be open to doubt; but it is certain that when he had been at Hum-Drum about eighteen months, he began to hint that he felt a little "seedy." About a month afterwards, he declared that he was "shaky." Six weeks subsequently, it was the unanimous opinion of the men, that if Handsome Olifaunt didn't ask for leave, he would "go to the bad." Dr. MacToomickey — who, as he was his solitary listener, was very loth to part with the lad — was fain at last to admit that the Lieutenant's complaint was liver, and that although Europe might do him some good, calomel would not. He applied for leave at last—long leave,—and easily obtained it, being so deservedly a favourite with his superiors. I dare say his liver was not quite so sound as it should have been; but I have heard that Lieutenant Olifaunt, on the evening before the answer to his application for leave arrived, expressed to Captain Tasselbraid, his great crony, that if he did not go to England and see his Virginia, or have a little fighting, by way of a change, he should be bored to death at Hum-Drum.

A long sea voyage—for he came round the Cape, for his health's sake—very speedily made right all that which had been wrong in Lieutenant Basil Olifaunt's liver. There is no need for me to dwell on the nature of his reception at home, save to remark that "it left," as the French penny-a-liners say, "nothing to be desired." He found Virginia, whom he had quitted just emerging from the bread-and-butter stage of schoolgirlhood, grown into a most beautiful and accomplished young woman, graceful and dignified; yet, when the humour seized her, very sprightly, and slightly mischievous. She seemed as fond of him as ever, and it is certain that the Lieutenant loved her with all his heart and with all his soul.

As he had passed so long a time in India, away from the amenities and recreations of English society (and, indeed, the Lieutenant told most piteous stories of the way he had been bored at Hum-Drum), his affectionate relatives, wedded, as they usually were, to country life, determined to pass the whole season in town for Basil's special gratification; and I fancy that this determination was by no means displeasing to Miss Virginia Lyle; who, since Basil's departure, had undergone an English edition of Hum-Drum *ennui*, in a highly picturesque, but decidedly dull, Tudor mansion, seven miles from a railway station. So General Olifaunt came to town, and put up at Hatchett's; and Lady Alice came to town, and took apartments in Piccadilly; and one day the Olifaunts dined with the Lyles, and the next day the Lyles dined with the Olifaunts; and at night they shared the same private box at the opera or the play; and all went "merry as the marriage bell" which was to ring at no very distant date for the young couple. For it had been settled, between the high contracting parties, that Basil, at the expiration of his twelvemonths' leave, should return to India for a year, get his captaincy, exchange into a regiment on home service, and then proceed with Virginia to the altar of St. George's, Hanover Square, as aforesaid.

It was a halcyon time. It was all opera and play, when it was not morning concert, or Ascot Cup day, or fancy fair, or excursion to Richmond or Greenwich. And the old people seemed as happy as the young ones. It was the height of the season. The General had strolled down to his club one morning,—he was a member of the Oriental, of course—and Lady Alice had gone to pay a visit to an old dowager acquaintance in Belgravia. Basil and Virginia—as "engaged ones," they were free to do as they pleased—had elected to visit the Exhibition of the Royal Academy, and thither they proceeded

in the neat open barouche and pair, jobbed from Mr. Quartermaine for the season. Just as they were passing the Burlington Arcade, Miss Lyle gave a little cry of vexation.

"How stupid—how silly that Bowring is!"— Bowring was her maid—"or, rather, I am," she said. "Now just look at these rumpled, worn-out gloves. Are they not disgraceful? I don't know what I could have been thinking of when I took them from my toilet-table."

Of course, Lieutenant Basil Olifaunt bent low over the tiny hand extended for his inspection, and whispered that he should like to kiss it; and that he would, were there not a policeman leaning against a lamp-post at the corner of Dover Street, and warning him with his municipal glance. His whisper, however, was not so low but that it could be heard by John Thomas, in the rumble, who grinned, even to the shaking of his broad shoulders.

"Don't be naughty, sir!" Miss Lyle observed, giving the broad, buck-skinned paw of the dragoon a warning tap with the tiny hand; "but, there's a dear old Basil, get out at the Burlington Arcade; stop at the shop at the right-hand corner, and buy me a pair of gloves—six and a-half, you know."

He knew perfectly well. As an engaged one, was it not his duty to fetch and carry? And wouldn't he have brought her one of the tigers from the Zoological Gardens if she had asked for it? The carriage drew up at the Arcade, and Lieutenant Olifaunt alighted.

"What colour?" he asked, twisting his long moustache.

"Any colour; only make haste," replied Virginia.

In a couple of minutes he had returned with a little packet enclosed in silver paper. When Miss Lyle opened it, she gave another little cry.

"Was there ever such a dear old simpleton?" she exclaimed. "Don't you know, Basil, that I hate this colour? Don't you know that mamma declares it to be unlucky? What on earth could have prompted you to bring me a pair of green gloves?"

The dragoon, who had no prejudice whatever against the colour in question, and happened to be wearing at the moment a very handsome necktie, grass-green in hue, replied somewhat sulkily, "That if Miss Lyle desired it, he would return to the Arcade, and change the gloves." I believe he qualified it as the "infernal" Arcade. But Miss Lyle gave him another tap, punitive, this time, with the little hand, and forbade him, for a wicked boy as he was, to swear. It was too late to go back, she added, and the gloves would do very well. They certainly fitted her like wax, and her hands looked tinier and prettier than ever.

Lieutenant Oliphant was pleased to say that "green gloves were rather uncommon, and that he must have been a fool to take them from the shopman; but, that, by Jove, Vergy"—which was his pet name for Virginia—"looked 'stunning' in them." Whereupon he was again tapped, and reprehended—but not with much severity—for using vulgar language.

I think it was in that year's Royal Academy that Mr. Holman Hunt's famous picture of the "Awakened Conscience" was exhibited. You know the piece of music which lies on the pianoforte in that picture. It is Bishop's duet of "Oft in the Stilly Night," a composition of which Basil and Virginia were passionately fond. After an hour's stroll through the crowded saloons of the exhibition, they drove home to Piccadilly, and to lunch; and after lunch, and a little quarrel, and a little making up; and after the Lieutenant had been permitted to smoke his afternoon cheroot in the balcony, Lady Alice, as was her wont, went to sleep in the front drawing-room; while the engaged ones, as was also their wont, retired to chatter in the back salon.

Virginia had partially contributed to her mamma's somnolence by softly passing her fingers over the keys of the piano. Her head was full of Mr. Holman Hunt's picture; and she was playing, almost unconsciously, the air of "Oft in the Stilly Night."

"I wish you'd take your gloves off," said Basil. "Somehow, I don't like those confounded things I bought for you this morning!"

But his affianced one told him that he was a darling old simpleton: and she went on carelessly playing the beautiful melody. All at once she started to her feet, with a piercing shriek.

"Merciful heavens!" she cried, "the hands—the green, green hands!" As she spoke, she covered her face, as if to hide some horrible object from her with her hands, clad in those accursed green gloves.

Lady Alice woke up, and rushed alarmed to the piano. Virginia did not faint; but she shuddered and shook, as one in the ague. And all that she could utter—all that she could repeat, was, "*There was another pair of hands, and they were green!*"

For an entire week following this curious incident Miss Lyle was exceedingly indisposed. She was nervous, preoccupied, irritable. Both her mamma and her lover strove to reason her out of the strange hallucination with which she had become possessed; but she shook her head and sighed, declaring, in tremulous tones, and with a scared look, that she had seen what she had seen; that another pair of hands had appeared on the key-board of the piano, and that the colour of those hands was a horrible, sickly, "damp-look-

ing" green. By degrees she grew calmer, and at length acknowledged that she might have been deceived, or that the illusion at most, was an optical one. The sun had shone too brightly that day; she had been careless in using her parasol; she had passed too long a time in the hot and crowded rooms of the Academy. Sir Paracelsus Flum, F.C.P., who was called in to prescribe for Miss Lyle, smiled, and whispered softly, "Liver." He made her up some very nice little medicines, and gradually Virginia forgot all about that evil afternoon; or, if she recalled it, would joke about the intrusive Green Hands, and wonder that she could have been so foolish as to fancy she saw them.

But it was time for the lieutenant to go back to his regiment, and get his captaincy, and come home, and be married. Man proposes, and heaven disposes. Lieutenant Basil Olifaunt never became a captain in the Twenty-fifth Hussars, nor in any other regiment, horse or foot, in her Majesty's service. He never came home again. He was never married. He started for the East by the Overland Route. He made Marseilles, Malta, Alexandria, in safety; but the Peninsular and Oriental Company's steamer, Tippoo Saib, which was conveying him from Suez to Aden, struck on a coral reef, in the Red Sea. The noble vessel went down with all hands; and Lieutenant Basil Olifaunt was drowned.

In three-volume novels, girls who have endured so terrible a bereavement as that which fell to the lot of Virginia Lyle, are usually inconsolable. Until their dying day they wear mourning for the lost dear one. If they are Romanists, they take the veil; if they are Protestants, they devote the remnant of their blighted existence to the missionaries, to the ragged schools, or the tract societies. In real life, women who have suffered a grief so dreadful do this kind of thing sometimes. But not always. Occasionally—especially if they are wealthy, and of high rank—they consent to be consoled. There are Ephesian virgins as well as Ephesian matrons. The heroine of Washington Irving's "Broken Heart"—the beautiful Irish girl who was betrothed to Robert Emmett—married, although she was frank enough to tell the man to whom she gave her hand, that her heart was in Emmett's grave. This was fact. But the beauteous maiden in Shenstone's ballad of "Jemmy Dawson" expires in the very mourning-coach in which she has followed her lover to the scaffold. This was fiction.

Virginia Lyle grieved long, passionately, and sincerely for the drowned Basil. But she was in the world, and of it; and the world could not go on if all bereaved lovers were to grieve for ever. She had a duty to perform towards her parent, towards the world, towards herself—what you will. She mourned for the dead man four long years. But she was still young, still beautiful, still wealthy. General Olifaunt was dead. The mother was growing very aged and feeble. Virginia had not forgotten Basil ; but the mind-picture of her loss had no longer a dreadful ghastly vividness. It was growing softened ; it was fading into the realms of long, long ago. So long ago did it seem since the news came that the lieutenant was drowned, that his phantom was quite laid in the Red Sea, and Virginia consented to enter a gilded barge, which was to waft her over the happy lake of matrimony. She accepted a man's hand, and made the usual vows and promises at the altar-rail of St. George's, Hanover Square. It was a prudent marriage—a capital marriage, in fact. The Honourable and Reverend Gerald Daubeny was the son of a bishop, and had two benefices and a prebendal stall. He was accomplished, affluent, and pious. According to the way of the world, there could not have been a more commendable marriage.

The Honourable Mrs. Daubeny resided now at one or another of her husband's rectories ; now in the cathedral city in which he held his stall, and now at her mother's house, in Buckinghamshire. She was not blessed with children, but she was tolerably cheerful. It was remarked, however, as a very curious circumstance, by her friends, that she, who had hitherto been passionately devoted to the practice of music, never touched the piano-forte—with one solitary exception—after her marriage. The exceptional occasion was one when, at an evening party, her husband, who was proud of her talents, had implored her to play. She yielded, at last, to his entreaties—sat down before the instrument—and swept her fingers carelessly over the keys. But she suddenly arose, uttered an appalling shriek, and swooned. For many weeks afterwards, she remained in a pitiable state of nervous excitement, continually declaring *that she had seen on the key-board, beside her own, a pair of green hands; that those hands were not clad in gloves, but were as the hands of a corpse that had been drowned ; and that on the forefinger of one of the hands was a signet-ring, such as Basil Olifaunt had been known to wear.*

GHOSTS

Ivan Tourguéneff, [Turgenev]

GHOSTS.

[From Ivan Tourguéneff.]

— —

I.

I COULD not sleep, and tossed on my bed from one side to the other. "The devil, himself," thought I, "must be in this table-turning to excite one's nerves like this."

After a while, however, I had begun to grow more calm, when, suddenly near me I heard a low sound like some stringed instrument; a sad, sweet note.

I lifted my head. The moon had just risen and its rays shone full upon my face. One bar of light, white as chalk, fell across the floor.

The sound was renewed, and this time more distinctly. I raised myself on my elbow; my heart beat quickly. One minute passed, and then another. . . Somewhere in the distance a cock crew, answered, farther off, by another.

My head fell back upon the pillow. "This is pleasant," said I to myself; "will my ears never stop ringing?"

At last I fell asleep, or I thought I slept. I had strange dreams. I seemed to be in my room and in my bed, without the power to close my eyes.

Again the same sweet sound! I turned my head. The ray of moonlight crossing the floor slowly gathered itself together. . . Before me, light as a mist, stood the light apparition of a woman. "Who is there," I asked with an effort. A voice soft as the rustling of leaves answered me, "'T is I; I come to see thee." "To see me! what art thou?" "Come to-night—to the edge of the woods under the old oak tree; I shall be there."

I must see the features of this mysterious being. I shuddered involuntarily and felt chilled through. I found myself no longer lying down, but sitting up in bed; and where I thought I had seen a ghost, I saw only the white bar of moonlight strike across the black floor.

II.

The day passed very slowly. I tried to read; to work: I could do nothing. At last it was night; my heart beat strongly as I waited for what might come. I lay with my face turned to the wall.

"Why didst thou not come?" murmured a voice soft and low, but distinct. It was in the room close behind me. It is she! The same mysterious vision, with its motionless eyes; its motionless face, so full of sadness.

"Come," murmured she again. "I will," said I, without fear. The phantom seemed to move towards me; it trembled; its form became confused and agitated like a vapor. In another moment there was nothing there but the polished floor and the white moonlight upon it.

III.

I spent the whole of the next day in the most violent agitation. At supper I drank nearly a bottle of wine. For a moment I went out upon the lawn, but immediately came in again and threw myself upon my bed, with my pulses throbbing.

Again the vibration sounded in my ears. I trembled and did not dare to look round. Suddenly I felt as if some one from behind laid a hand on each of my shoulders and murmured in my ear, "Come, come, come!" I tremblingly answered with a sigh, "I will come," and raised my head. The white lady was there leaning over my couch. She smiled sweetly and immediately disappeared. I had gained one good look at her face and it seemed to me I had seen her before somewhere; but when and where? The next morning I rose

very late and all day I walked about the fields.
I went to the old oak-tree at the edge of the
woods and looked carefully all around it.

As evening fell, I seated myself at the window of my study. My old housekeeper
brought me a cup of tea, but I did not touch
it. I could not make up my mind what to do,
and felt almost as though I were going mad.
The sun slowly sank; in the sky there was not
one cloud. Suddenly the landscape was
flooded with a purple light that seemed almost
supernatural; the trees, the grass, the hills, all
looked petrified and covered with a brilliant
glaze. This glaze and immobility, the sharp
and brilliant distinctness of every object, and
the solemn stillness, all seemed in strange and
incomprehensible contrast. Without the least
noise a large brown bird flew suddenly to my
window-sill, and as I looked at him, returned
the glance with his round, deep eyes. "No
doubt," thought I, "you are sent to me that I
may not forget my rendezvous." At once the

bird flapped his downy wings and flew away with as little noise as he had approached.

For some time after I remained seated at my window, but all doubt or irresolution was gone. I felt powerless, as though drawn into some magic circle. Resistance was useless, dragged on as I was by some secret power, as a boat is carried along by the rapids inevitably towards the cataract.

At length I rose; the purple color of the landscape had vanished, the brilliant hues had died away and all objects were fast becoming lost in obscurity. The magic immobility had also ceased, a wind began to blow gently and the moon rose bright in a clear blue sky, and under her cold glance the leaves of the trees trembled and rustled, now silver, now black.·

My housekeeper came in with a lighted candle, but a puff of wind extinguished it. I rose quickly, crushed my hat down over my eyes and walked rapidly to the corner of the forest where the old oak-tree stood.

IV.

Many years ago this oak had been struck by lightning. Its shattered top was dead, but the rest had still life enough for several centuries. As I approached it a little cloud, passing over the moon, made the shadows under the foliage nearly black. At first I could make out nothing noticeable, but on looking to one side, my heart suddenly stopped, for I saw a white figure motionless, near a bush which grew between the oak-tree and the forest. My hair stood on end, I could scarcely breathe, but I kept on advancing toward the wood.

It was indeed she—my nocturnal visitor. Just as I came near to her, the moon emerged from behind the cloud. The apparition seemed to be made of a milky-white mist half transparent, for while gazing at her I could just discern through her head a branch waving in the wind behind her. Only her eyes and hair seemed darker. I saw, too, that on one of her fingers, as she held her hands crossed before her, there gleamed a little gold ring, pale but brilliant.

Within two steps of her I stopped and wished to speak, but my voice stuck in my throat; still the feeling I had was not terror exactly. She turned her eyes toward me, her gaze expressing neither sadness nor gayety, only pensive attention. I waited for her to speak, but she remained silent, motionless, looking at me with a glance fixed and dead.

"Here I am!" I said finally, with a supreme effort. My voice sounded harsh and strange.

"I love thee!" said she, with her still soft voice.

"You love me!" cried I, stupefied. "Give thyself to me," she whispered. "Give myself to thee! Why, you are a spirit—you are only a ghost!" My brain was in a whirl. "What are you? A vapor? A mist? A form of air? Give myself to you! First tell me who you are. Have you ever lived upon the earth? Where do you come from?"

" Give thyself to me. I will not harm thee. Say only these two words : ' Take me.' "

" What does she say ?" I thought. " What does all this mean? Shall I venture ?" "Well," cried I, suddenly and with unlooked for courage, as though something had pushed me on from behind, "take me!" The words were scarcely spoken, when the mysterious figure, with a silent laugh which made it quiver all over, advanced toward me as she unclasped her hands and spread out her arms. I longed to spring back, but already I was in her power, and she held me in her arms.

I felt myself lifted from the ground and together we flew, moderately fast, over the top of the motionless grass.

V.

At first my brain reeled and I closed my eyes. When I opened them a moment after, we were still flying and already the woods were left behind. Below us lay a vast plain, and I saw with horror that we were at a prodigious height from the ground.

The thought struck me like lightning. "I am in the power of a demon!" Up to this time the idea of evil or of my own possible destruction had not crossed my mind. And still we flew along and it seemed to me we rose still higher. "Where are you taking me?" I cried at last. "Where thou wilt," answered my companion, clasping me yet more firmly in her arms. Her face touched mine, yet I could scarcely feel the contact. "Take me back to the earth," I faltered, "I am dizzy at this height."

"Well, but close thine eyes and hold thy breath."

I obeyed and at once felt myself falling like a stone. The wind lashed my hair. When I got my breath I found that we were flying along the ground just touching the tops of the long grass.

"Put me down here," I said, "I don't like to fly; I am not a bird."

"I hoped to give thee pleasure. As for us, we do nothing else."

"Us! Yes; but, who are you?" No answer. "You do not dare to tell me!"

A plaintive sound like the sad note which had revealed her presence the first night, sounded in my ear as we flew along through the moist air near the ground.

"Put me down, I tell you," said I. She inclined her head in token of obedience, and I found myself once more on my feet. She stood before me and again joined her hands as though waiting. As at first, her expression seemed to me one of quiet resignation.

"Where are we?" I asked, not recognizing the place where we had alighted. "Far from thy house, but we can reach it in a moment," was the answer. "How can that be; must I trust myself to you again?"

"I have not harmed thee, nor will I. We can fly about together until dawn; that is all. Any-where thy thoughts or wishes lead thee I can take thee—in every country on the earth. Give thyself to me. Say again, 'Take me.'"

"Very well, take me," and her arms once more closed round me. Again we left the earth and began our flight.

VI.

"Where wouldst thou go?" said she.

"Straight ahead of us."

"But here is a forest."

"Let us pass over it, but not so fast."

Immediately we rose, whirling as a woodcock flies; and then flew straight on again. No longer grasses and shrubs, but the tops of majestic forest-trees seemed slipping away from under our feet. A strange sight was this forest, viewed from above, with here and there the moonlight striking through its dense foliage. It seemed like some great animal asleep, and breathing with an indistinct muttering noise. Now and then we would cross a clearing, and I could see the shadows of the trees,

sharply outlined. From time to time we could
hear the hare's plaintive cry from the brush-
wood, or the hoot of the screech-owl, which
flapped its wings close beside us. The night
breeze wafted up to us odors of mushrooms,
wild parsley and the swelling buds of the wild
rose. Cold and severe shone round us the
moonlight, and right above our heads gleamed
the Great Bear. Soon the forest was left behind, and we saw a plain, through which a
long ribband of gray mist marked the course
of a river. We followed one of its banks lined
with bushes weighed down with the heavy dew.
The current shone with a bluish lustre, and
then again swept round and round in dark and
threatening whirlpools. Here and there in
spots little wreaths of mist played above the
surface; and again I could see, where the water
ran quieter, white water-lilies opening their
petals and bathing themselves in the moonlight, like naiads who think themselves shel-
tered from every eye. I sought to pluck one,
and stooped so low as almost to touch the clear

mirror of the stream, but a damp, unpleasant odor was flung into my face as I grasped its slippery stem.   Now we began to fly from one bank across to the other, like the curlew, and in fact roused some real birds every minute. More than once we passed over pretty flocks of wild ducks, gathered in little groups among the foliage of the rose-trees.   They did not fly; one would quickly draw his head out from under his wing, and look and look; and then, as if satisfied, would hide it again in the silky down, while his comrades would utter a feeble "quack, quack."   From a cytisus bush we started up a heron, and when I saw him struggle on his long legs and awkwardly shake his great wings it made me think of a German professor more than ever.*   But as to fish, we did not see one; they must all have been asleep at the bottom.   By this time I began to become accustomed to flying, and even to enjoy it.

---

* In Russia, the common nickname given to Germans is "herons."

Whoever has dreamed of it can understand my feelings. Completely reassured, I could observe more closely the strange phantom who was my companion in this incredible adventure.

VII.

She appeared to be a young woman, with features with nothing of the Russian type about them. Her form, grayish-white and semi-transparent, reminded me of the figures we see carved on alabaster vases and lighted from within by a lamp. It seemed to me again that her features were not entirely unfamiliar.

"May I speak to you?" I asked.

"Speak."

"You have a ring on your finger. Have you lived on earth? Have you been married?" I stopped; she did not answer.

"What is your name; or what was it?"

"Call me Ellis."

"Ellis! That is an English name! Are you English? Have you ever known me?"

"No."

"Then why is it to me that you come?"

"I love thee."

"Are you happy?"

"Yes. To fly, to soar aloft with thee in the pure air!"

"Ellis," cried I, suddenly, "are you not a lost spirit? Are you not a soul in torment?"

"I do not understand," she murmured, lowering her head.

"In the name of God, I beseech you"—began I, but she interrupted me.

"What sayest thou?" said she, as though she did not at all understand me; "I know not what it means;" and I seemed to feel a feeble pressure from the arm that encircled me like a cold band. "Fear not," she continued; "fear nothing, my friend!"

Her face bent down to mine; on my lips I felt a strange sensation as of the prick of a blunt needle, or the first touch of a leech that has not yet drawn blood.

VIII.

We were flying at a considerable height, and looking down I saw we were passing over a town, which I could not recognize, built on the side of a hill. Church spires rose above a mass of shingled roofs and dark orchards. At one of the bends of the river I could see the black outline of a bridge. Gilded cupolas and metal crosses shone with a subdued brilliancy. Silently outlined against the moon-lit sky, I could see long well-sweeps amid the clumps of willows. Silently, too, the white high-road ran straight as an arrow into one end of the town, and emerged at the other as silently, to be lost in darkness and the monotony of an endless plain beyond.

"What town is this?" I asked of Ellis.

"N——."

"In the province of J——?"

"Yes."

"We are very far from my home!"

"For us, not far."

"Really!" I suddenly became audacious. "Take me to South America."

"Impossible. It is day there."

"Ah, we are night-birds, are we? Well, never mind where; only far away."

"Close thine eyes and do not breathe," answered Ellis; and we set off swift as the storm-wind.

The air whistled in my ears with a deafening noise. Soon we stopped, but the roar continued, indeed it increased. It was like a horrible tempest, an unearthly struggle.

"Now open thine eyes," said Ellis.

IX.

I obeyed. "Great heavens, where am I?" About our heads crowded heavy thunder clouds, black, pushing and pressing on like furious monsters. Below us another monster, the tossing, raging ocean. Great mountains of boiling foam were shattered against crags as black as jet. The howl of the tempest; the cold blast from the seething abyss; the hoarse sound of the surf grinding upon the beach! Above these I seemed to hear cries of distress, the distant discharge of cannon and the tolling of bells; boats grating upon the land; the scream of an unseen sea-gull; and by a sudden gleam of lightning there flashed across me the uncertain outline of a ship! Everywhere death and destruction! Again I shut my eyes overcome with horror.

"What is this? Where are we?"

"On the southern coast of the Isle of Wight, at the Black Gang Rocks, where many a vessel is wrecked," answered Ellis, with what seemed to me an expression of malignant joy.

"Take me away, far from here! Take me home!"

I covered my face with my hands. We seemed now to fly faster than ever. The wind no longer whistled. It howled and tore at my clothing and at my hair. I could not breathe.

"Stand up!" said Ellis.

I tried to get my wits again about me. I

felt the ground under my feet, and the noise
had ceased. All around me seemed dead;
but the blood throbbed violently in my temples; my brain reeled, and in my ears was a
feeble ringing sound. Gradually I overcame
my faintness, stood up and opened my eyes.

X.

We were on my own carriage-road. Straight
ahead of us through the pointed leaves of a
row of willows we could see a large pond,
above which hovered the mist as though clinging to the surface; on the right the pale green
of a wheat field; and on the left, looming out
of the fog, my orchard with its great motionless trees covered with moisture. The breath
of the morning had just touched them. Across
the pale sky were scattered some white clouds,
tinged with a faint golden light which announced the coming of the day; though from
what point of the horizon the light came I
could not tell. In the uniform paleness of the

sky no one could say where the sun would rise. The stars had disappeared; nothing was stirring, but every thing was at the point of awakening at the touch of the approaching dawn. "Day is coming," whispered Ellis in my ear. "Farewell until to-morrow."

I turned towards her. She was rising slowly in the air before me. Suddenly I saw her hold her two hands above her head. Her head, her hands, her shoulders, assumed all at once the color of flesh; in her dark eyes flashed a gleam of light; a singularly gentle smile drifted over her lips, now ruddy; she appeared a charming young woman. This sight lasted but an instant. As though suddenly overcome, she threw herself backward and quickly dissolved in air. For some time I remained stupefied and motionless. When I could look about me, it seemed as though the delicate rosy flesh tints that had so suddenly lighted up the apparition had not vanished, but filled the air all around. It was the sunrise. I felt all at once overcome by fatigue and weakness, and turned toward the house. As I passed through the poultry-yard I could hear the fowls cackling; they are the first birds to awake. Along the edge of the thatched roof, like sentinels, perched the rooks, all busy with their morning toilets, strongly and sharply outlined against the milky sky. From the woods near I could hear the querulous note of the grouse, already up and in search of wild berries through the wet grass. As for myself, feeling a chill creep over me, I threw myself upon my bed and soon fell into a heavy sleep.

XI.

The following night, as I approached the old oak, Ellis came to meet me quite like an old acquaintance. On my side all fear was gone, and I greeted her almost with pleasure. I had ceased to try to comprehend anything in this strange experience and, simply to satisfy my curiosity, was willing to let myself be carried flying through the air.

Soon I felt her arm embrace me, and we rose from the ground.

" Let us go to Italy," I said in her ear.

" Where thou wilt, friend," answered she, with quiet earnestness, and gently and gravely she bent down her head toward me. It seemed as though her face were less transparent than the night before, her features more feminine and less vaguely outlined; she recalled to my mind the beautiful vision which I had beheld that morning just as she disappeared.

" To-night," said Ellis, " is the Great Night. It comes rarely when seven times thirteen " .

. . Here I lost a few words : . . " then," she continued, " can be seen what at other times is hidden."

" Ellis," said I, in a suppliant tone, " who are you ? Tell me at once !"

Without answering me she stretched out her long white hand; with her finger she pointed out far off on the sombre sky the dull red light of a comet shining among some small twinkling stars.

"How am I to understand you? Do you live as that comet wanders, between the planets and the sun? Do you wander among mortals? And what? and where?"

The hand of Ellis was suddenly laid upon my eyes. A heavy white mist, such as rises from damp valleys, surrounded me. "To Italy! To Italy!" she whispered. "To-night is the Great Night!"

XII.

The fog was lifted, and I saw beneath us a boundless plain, and the warm air soft on my cheek told me we were no longer in Russia. The plain, too, did not look like our own; it was an immense desert tract without tree or shrub. Here and there on every side, like fragments of a broken mirror, shone pools of stagnant water. Further on I could just discern a noiseless, motionless sea. Between the masses of cloud the gleaming stars shone large, and on every side sounded the incessant, con-

tinuous hum and trill of a thousand voices.
These sounds, at once dull and penetrating,
were the voice of the desert.

" The Pontine Marshes !" said Ellis. " Hear
the frogs ! Can'st thou not smell the sulphur ?"

The Pontine Marshes ! A feeling of solemn
sadness fell upon me.

" Why do you bring me to this melancholy,
deserted place ? We had better have gone to
Rome."

" Rome is near," said Ellis; " be ready."

We flew along just above the old Via Latina.
Standing knee-deep in the swamp a buffalo
raised his great head, with shaggy tufts of hair
between his wide spreading horns. He shewed
the whites of his stupid, wicked eyes and
snorted loud through his wet nostrils, as if he
scented us.

" Rome ! Here is Rome," said Ellis. " Look
ahead !"

What bleak mass is this looming above the
horizon ? Are they the arches of some giant's
bridge ? What river can it cross ? Why is it

in ruins here and there ?   No, it is no bridge,
it is an aqueduct, and this is the sacred Campagna !   There rise the Alban Mountains !
Their tops and the grey-brown of the old aqueduct are feebly lighted by the first rays of the
rising moon.   On we rushed swiftly, and found
ourselves hovering over a detached ruin.   No
one could tell what it had once been : a tomb,
a palace or a temple.   A dark ivy-vine clasped
it with its mournful foliage ; and below, like a
gaping mouth, opened the black entrance to a
subterranean vault.   A rank, earthy smell of
decay rose from every ivy-covered stone, from
whose rough surface the polished marble facing had long ago crumbled away.

 " Here !" whispered Ellis, stretching out her
hand.   " Call loudly, three times, the name of
a great Roman."

 " What will happen ?"

 " Thou shalt see."

 I thought a moment, then cried: " Divus
Caius Julius Cæsar ?"   .   .   .

 " Divus Caius Julius Cæsar !"   .   .   . and

with an effort prolonging the sound, . .
'' Cæsar ?''

XIII.

The last echo of my voice had not died
away, when I heard—I despair of describing how I felt or what came over me. First
there was the murmur of a confused noise,
hardly perceptible to the ear, but constantly
repeated and increasing; blowing of trumpets
and clapping of hands. Then I heard as
though far away in the distance, or from some
bottomless abyss, a clamor and confusion of
many voices that came up to me in swelling,
always swelling waves of sound. There were
cries, stifled shrieks, like those of a woman in
some fearful nightmare: and then the air
around the ruin became troubled and dark. I
thought I saw myriads of shadows surging up
from the door of the vault and defiling in
every direction. Some rounded at the top as
though wearing helmets; others sharply pointed
as though carrying spears. The light of the moon

in thousands of blue rays glinted upon these casques and lance-heads, and all this army, all this multitude pressed on and pushed each other and grew in number. I could feel—I was suffocated and crushed by it—the wild, wierd, nameless force and energy that filled and animated the mass. Yet not one single shadow was distinct. Suddenly a swaying movement agitated the whole crowd; as great billows rush on and then backward: "Cæsar! Cæsar venit!" was the roar of ten thousand voices, like the sound of the storm-wind in the forest. A dull reverberation—as though, were we touching the earth, I should have felt it tremble; and there rose slowly from the ruin a pale, severe head, crowned with a wreath of laurel, the eyes closed. It was the head of the Emperor!

No human words can describe the horror that seized upon me at this sight. If those eyes or lips should open, I felt I must die on the spot. "Ellis!" I cried frantically, "Ellis, I will not! I can not! Take me away from

Rome, this brutal, terrible Rome! Take me away. Away!"

"Faint heart," she whispered, and we resumed our flight. Behind me I heard, this time high and loud, the cry of the Roman legions. Then all was hushed.

XIV.

"Look," said Ellis, "and be calm!"

I remember that my first feeling was so quiet and peaceful that I could only take in long breaths of the soft air. A blue vapor, half light, half mist, enveloped me in its silvery radiance. At first I could distinguish nothing —the blue light blinded me—but gradually I discerned the outline of wooded hills. A lake lay beneath us with the reflections of the stars shimmering on its deep waters. I heard the murmur of the gentle waves breaking on the strand. The perfume of orange-flowers was on the breeze, pure and strong, and with it as pure and strong floated the sound of a young, fresh, woman's voice.

Led on, fascinated by the perfume and the voice, I desired to descend, and, floating lower and lower, we came toward a splendid palace of marble, girt in with great cypress-trees. From one of the upper windows came forth the voice: . . . Right against the foot of the palace walls broke softly the waves, glistening with the bright, dusty pollen of flowers; and directly opposite in front of us rose an island from the waters, dense with orange trees and laurels, and enveloped in a downy mist through which gleamed white the marble of porches, columns and statues.

"Lago Maggiore!" said Ellis, "and this is Isola Bella!" and I could answer only with a long breath of delight as we descended. The voice sounded always nearer and irresistibly drew me on. I must see the face of her whose voice made such music on such a night; and we neared the window.

In the middle of a room, decorated like a

villa of Pompeii, more like a museum of an-
tiques than a modern apartment, crowded with
Greek statues, Etruscan vases, rare plants and
gorgeous draperies, lighted from above by two
crystal globes for lamps, sat a young woman
at a piano. With her head thrown back
lightly, her eyes half-closed, she was singing
an Italian song. She sang and smiled. She
smiled, and from a marble niche across lazy
wreaths of blue smoke slowly rising from a
bronze incense burner, a faun of Praxiteles,
young and careless as she—and, like her, soft
and voluptuous, smiled too, I thought. The
young woman sat and sang alone. Enchanted
by her voice, her beauty, intoxicated by the
light and the perfume, and my whole being
stirred at the sight of her youth, her freshness
and her rapture, I altogether forgot my shadowy companion. I forgot the strange means
by which I had been thrust into the privacy of
this life so foreign and so distant from my own.
I tried to climb through the window and to

speak. . . . Suddenly my whole frame
felt a shock, and quivered as though I had
touched a Leyden jar charged to the utmost.
Through the mist and cloud of Ellis' features
her expression showed dark and threatening.
Into her wide-opened eyes had come a look of
fierce and deep malignity. "Away!" said she
roughly; and again the rush of the wind, the
roar, the giddiness, but this time, instead of
the cruel cry of the triumphing legions, it was
the last sweet note of the song I had heard,
that long vibrated in my ear.

We stopped, but this sound still lingered,
though I felt round me a far different atmosphere. Then louder and more shrill rose the
note, and a fresh breeze sprang up as from
some great river, with smells of hay and thatch
and smoke. A second note sounded and then
a third, but in so different a style, in one so
familiar to me, I at once recognized a Russian
song—a Russian singer. And then every
thing around me grew distinct.

XV.

We were on the banks of a great river. On our left the long, flat steppe from which here and there loomed up large wind-mills; on the right, far as the eye could reach, the river ran. Near the bank long boats at anchor, nodding with the current, floated up and down at the end of their cables, their masts pointing and moving like fingers making mysterious signs. In one of these boats, from which the singing came, gleamed a little fire, the light of which reflected in long lines of red, trembled on the ripples of the dark water. On every side shone similar fires, in the boats and on the shore. Were they far off or near? I could not tell. Now they would all of a sudden sink down, and then blaze up again. Countless crickets, busy as the incessant frogs on the marshes of the Campagna, chirped in the grass. The sky was without a cloud and here and there and now and then around us in the air

I heard the plaintive cries of birds I could not see. "Are we not in Russia?" I asked.

"This is the Volga," answered Ellis, as we flew along above the river.

"Why did you take me away from that beautiful spot?" said I. "Did it displease you? Perhaps it was jealousy you felt!"

Ellis's lips trembled. Her look grew threatening; but almost immediately her feat··res assumed their usual impassive quiet.

"I should like to go home," I said.

"Wait! wait!" she cried. "To-night is the Great Night! It will not come soon again. Thou may'st be of help. Wait!"

We crossed the Volga, darting obliquely on this side and that in short, sharp turning flights, as swallows fly before a storm. The deep waters murmured on beneath us, a cold wind struck us and beat against my face. Soon the right bank of the river could be seen and through the half darkness we perceived rough cliffs with crevices and caves seaming their steep sides. "Cry 'Saryn na Kitchkou,'" said Ellis in a low voice.

I had but just recovered from my fright at seeing the Roman spectres, and besides was tired and felt strangely sad. In short, I lacked courage. I wished not to speak those terrible words, sure that they would summon—as in the Wolf's Glen in "Der Freischütz"— some frightful apparition, but in spite of myself my lips opened and in a stifled voice I cried, "Saryn na Kitchkou."*

XVI.

As at the Roman ruin, at first all was silent. All of a sudden, right in my ear, I heard a brutal laugh, followed by the sound of a body falling and struggling in the water. I peered about me; there was no one; but soon I heard

---

* These words of a Tartar dialect were the war-cry of the pirates of the Volga. At this sound the crews of vessels boarded by these outlaws would throw themselves on their faces on the deck on pain of having their throats cut.

the same sounds echoed along the cliffs; and
there rose a fearful and ghastly tumult. It
was a chaos of sounds; cries of agony, blows,
furious imprecations, and laughter more terrible and hideous than all the rest; the plash
of oars in the water; blows of hatchets; the
sound of splitting open doors and chests;
the creak of the rigging; the noise of wheels
upon the sand; the tramp of many horses;
the clanking of chains; the crackling and
roaring of mighty fires; drunken songs; grinding of teeth and fearful curses; lamentations;
entreaties; military orders; groans of the dying, all mingled with the shrill blast of the
fife and savage yells of triumph. I could
hear and distinguish cries of "Kill him!"
"To the water!" "Burn them!" "To work!"
"No quarter!" I could even hear the la-
bored panting of the exhausted and the dying. And yet I could see nothing. The
landscape remained unchanged. Beneath us
rolled the river, dark and silent. The banks
seemed wilder and more deserted than before.

I turned to Ellis. She placed her finger upon my lips.

"Stepàn Timoféitch! Here comes Stepàn Timoféitch!"* The fierce cry rang all over the plain. "Long live our little father! Our Ataman! Our leader!" All at once, though I still saw nothing, I seemed to feel the approach of a gigantic form, and a terrible voice shouted: "Frolka! where art thou, dog? Set fire to every thing! Here, give a stroke of the hatchet to those white hands! Make mince meat of them all!"

I felt the heat of a fire not far from me; the pungent smell of burning wood choked me; warm drops like blood fell on my hands and face. Peals of savage laughter echoed around me.

---

* Stepàn or Stenka Razine, a Cossack ; first a pirate on the Volga and Caspian Sea, then chief of a formidable insurruction of serfs. He captured Astrakhan and devastated the central provinces or Russia in the middle of the 17th century, and was afterward taken and broken on the wheel.

I lost consciousness, and when I had again come to myself I was flying with Ellis over my own forest near the old-oak tree.

"See'st thou that pretty little path," she asked; "there where the moonlight falls and those two birch-trees are moving? Shall we go there?"

I was so overcome and worn out, body and mind, that I could only utter the word "Home!"

"Thou art at home," said Ellis's voice. I was standing alone at my own door. Ellis had vanished. The watch-dog came up, looked at me suspiciously and ran away howling. I dragged myself up stairs, and without undressing, flung myself upon the bed and dropped asleep.

XVII.

The next day—all the morning—I was wretched. I could scarcely move, but my physical pains did not trouble me most; I was ashamed of my conduct and disgusted with

myself. "Faint heart!" I repeated. "Yes,
Ellis was right; why should I have been
afraid? Why not have used my opportunities? I might have seen Cæsar; and fear
took away my senses, and I fled like a child
from the rod! As to Razine, that is a different thing. In my position as a gentleman and
landed proprietor—but even then, why have I
been afraid? Faint heart! Faint heart?"

"All this — may it not have been all a
dream?" I said to myself, at length. I called
my old housekeeper.

"Marfa, what time was it when I went to
bed last night? Do you remember?"

"Why, how can I tell, my master? Late, I
should think. When it began to grow dark
you went away from the house, and I could
hear the heels of your boots on the floor of
your room long after midnight—about morning. Yes, about morning. And this has been
the way for two nights, now! Does any thing
trouble you?" . . . "Good! These
flights," thought I, "these flights through the

air — how can I doubt their reality now?
Marfa! How do I look to-day?" I asked.

"How? Let me look at you. Your cheeks
are hollow. Yes, and you are pale, master.
Why, you are as yellow as wax, too!"

A little out of countenance, I sent Marfa
away.

"I shall die of it, or else lose my wits," said
I to myself, as I stood at the window. "This
must end! It is terrible! My heart beats so
strangely! While I fly, it seems as though something was drinking my heart's blood, or as
though it were oozing away, drop by drop, as
the birch-tree loses its sap, when its bark is
pierced by a hatchet. All this is not natural.
And Ellis! She plays with me as a cat with a
mouse, and yet she does not appear to wish
me any harm. Well, this shall be the last time
that I trust myself with her. To-night I will
see as much as I can, and then— But, what
if she should be drinking my life-blood; absorbing my vitality! What a horrible thought!
To fly so very swiftly must be injurious! They

say that in England it is against the law to
travel faster on the railways than 120 versts an
hour."

I thought it all over for a long time, but at
ten o'clock in the evening I was standing again
by the old oak-tree.

XVIII.

The night was dark and cold; the air felt
damp. To my great surprise, I found no one
under the oak. I walked about for a little
while; I went as far as the woods; I came
back, always trying to penetrate the gloom.
No one! I waited awhile, and then called
" Ellis !" several times, raising my voice more
and more, but all in vain. I felt disappointed,
almost sad. Already I had forgotten the possibility of all those dangers that had troubled
me so much a short time before. I could not
make up my mind not to see Ellis again.

"Ellis! Ellis! Come! Will you not come ?"
I cried for the last time. Roused by my voice,

a crow suddenly took flight from the top of a neighboring tree, flapping his wings and making a noise through the branches. Ellis did not appear, and with hanging head I went back toward the house. I was already on the carriage road, and could see the light shining from the window of my room, now bright, now obscured by the foliage of the intervening apple-trees. It seemed like an eye that was watching and guarding me. Suddenly I heard a little rustling sound behind me, and felt myself lifted from the ground just as a quail is seized by a sparrow-hawk. It was Ellis. Her cheek touched mine, and I felt her arm embrace me tightly. She spoke, and her voice, always low and soft, fell on my cheek like a cold breath.

"It is I!" she said. I felt at once pleasure and fear. We were flying close to the ground.

"You did not wish to come to-night then?" I asked.

"Thou wert sorry not to find me? Oh, thou lovest me then! Thou art mine!"

These last words troubled me. I did not know what to say.

"I was kept back," she said. "I was watched."

"Who has the power to control you?" I asked.

"Where shall we go?" asked Ellis, as usually, without answering my question.

"Take me to Italy — to that lake. You know!"

She shook her head. At this instant I noticed for the first time that her face was no longer transparent. It seemed as though a faint rose-color had spread over its milky whiteness. I looked into her eyes, and their expression gave me an unpleasant feeling. There was, deep down, a sinister look, hardly visible, yet decided; like the eye of a frozen snake that the sun is just beginning to warm into life.

"Ellis!" I cried, "who are you? Tell me, I conjure you!"

She shrugged her shoulders in silence. I

was piqued, and thought I would give her a lesson. The idea struck me that we should go to Paris. "There," thought I, "she will have chance enough to be jealous."

"Ellis, you are not afraid of large cities? Of Paris, for instance?"

"No."

"No? Nor of the brightly-lighted places like the boulevards?"

"It is not the light of day," said Ellis.

"Very well. Take me, then, to the Boulevard des Italiens!"

She threw the end of her long sleeve over my head. At once I felt myself surrounded with the same white mist, with an odor of poppies in the air. Every thing vanished, light, sound, almost all sensation. I was scarcely conscious of life, and this state of almost annihilation brought me rest and pleasure. Suddenly the fog was lifted; Ellis took her sleeve from before my face; I saw below me vast buildings and a blaze of light and motion. It was Paris.

XIX.

I had been to Paris before, and at once recognized the place to which Ellis had brought
me. Here was the Tuileries Garden, with its
old Indian chestnut-trees, its grated windows,
its moats, its Sentinel Zouaves looking like wild
animals. We passed in front of the palace and
of St. Roch and stopped at the Boulevard des
Italiens. Throngs of people, young and old,
workmen in their blouses, ladies in gorgeous
raiment, streamed along the sidewalks. From
restaurants and cafés, lavishly gilded, shone
innumerable lights. Omnibuses, fiacres, ve-
hicles of all kinds crowded each other through
the street—every thing gleamed and glittered,
until the eye was dazzled, and yet, strange as
it may seem, I was in no wise tempted to quit
my airy post of observation—so lofty, so pure,
to mingle with and lose myself in this human
ants' nest. I felt mounting up towards me a
heavy, red-hot vapor of a dubious smell. Too
many human lives were mixed up in this

crowd! I was yet hesitating, when sharp and
harsh, like the rasp of a file, there squeaked up
to me the voice of a Lorette: the brazen tone
penetrating me like the bite of some reptile.
My imagination saw a stony face, flat, expres-
sionless, a real Parisian face, white, red, with
the eyes of a usurer, frizzled locks—a shrill
bouquet of artificial flowers on an audacious
hat: nails cut like claws and ample crinolines.
I imagined at the same time I saw one of my
stupid, good-natured countrymen fresh from
the Steppes and just turned loose in Paris,
trotting in meek admiration at the heels of this
wretched venal doll. I could see him trying
to hide his awkwardness under an air of effront-
ery, rolling his "r's," talking in a falsetto
voice, endeavoring to imitate the manners of
the waiters at Véfour's, talking platitudes, bowing and cringing. In utter disgust I turned
away. "Ugh!" said I, "Ellis need not feel
jealous here."

I noticed, however, that we had begun to

descend. All the noises and smells of Paris came up to meet us.

"Stop!" I said. "Don't you feel, Ellis, that it is stifling here?"

"It was thine own wish to come to Paris."

"I was wrong; I have changed my mind. Take me far off from here, Ellis, I beg of you! Why, there's Prince Koulmametof trotting along the Boulevard, and his friend, Serge Varaxine, waving his hand to him and crying, 'Ivan Stépanitch! Sup with me! I have engaged Rigolboche himself!' Take me away, Ellis, far away from Mabille, from the Maison Dorée, from the Jockey Club; far off from the soldiers with their shaven foreheads and gorgeous barracks, from the sergents de ville with imperials on their chins; from the glasses of absinthe, the gamblers at dominoes and at the Bourse; from the knots of red ribbon in coat and overcoat button-holes; far from M. de Foy, inventor of the Marriage Bureau; from courses of lectures on literature and from political pamphlets; far from Parisian Comedies,

Parisian Opera Bouffe, Parisian politeness and
Parisian ignorance! Away! away! away!"

. . . . I opened my eyes. A dark plain,
with lighter lines cut across it here and there,
by the many roads, was rapidly slipping away
beneath us, and far off on the horizon, with a
glare as of some great conflagration, gleamed
the million lamps that light the Capital of the
world.

XX.

Again the sleeve of Ellis fell across my
eyes; again I lost consciousness—and then
again the cloud dissolved.

What is this? What park is this with its
formal avenue of lindens cut trim and stiff
like a wall, small trees looking like umbrellas,
with porticos and temples in the Pompadour
style; statues of rococo; tritons and nymphs
in strangely shaped fountains, surrounded by
balustrades of smoky marble? Can it be Versailles? No, it is not Versailles. It is another and smaller palace in rococo, that is

built near by under a group of oak-trees. The
moon is veiled hy a thin cloud, a smoky vapor
seems to rise from the ground. The eye can
not distinguish what it is. Is it really smoke,
or only the misty moonlight? Further on, in
one of the basins, floats a sleeping swan; its
rounded white back recalls to me the frozen
snow of the Steppes. Here and there glow-
worms are shining like diamonds in the grass
and on the pedestals of the statues.

" We are near Mannheim," said Ellis. "This
is the park of Schwetzingen."

"Ah, we are in Germany," I thought, and
began to listen. All was still except an unseen
spring, whose waters dropped into some hidden pool. It seemed as though the water were
always repeating the same words: " There,
there, always there!" In the middle of a
path, between two formal walls of trees, I perceived a gentleman with a braided coat, red
heels and lace cuffs, his sword dangling against
the calves of his legs, who gave his hand with
an exquisite grace to a beautiful lady, puffed

and frizzled and powdered. Pale, strange
phantoms! I wished to see them closer, but
they vanished, and I could hear only the bab-
ble of the spring.

"Those," said Ellis, "are dreams out walking. Yesterday we could have seen very different things—strange things. To-night even
the dreams fly from human sight. Away!
Away!"

We rose and flew so straight ahead that I
was hardly conscious of any motion, and the
country beneath seemed flying from under us.
Sombre, rocky mountains, covered with trees,
came and went, followed by other mountains,
with their rocks and ravines. Here and there
were clearings, and the light gleams that came
from some cottage beside a lake or stream;
and still mountain succeeded mountain. We
were in the midst of the Black Forest.

More mountains, more forests—grand forests with vigorous old trees. The night is
clear; I can distinguish the different kinds of
trees, and can see, above all, the great pines,

with their long, straight, white trunks. Now
and then, at the edge of the woods, I see a
fawn, motionless on his slender legs, now looking about him vigilantly, his small ears turning
from one side to the other. I see the ruins of
an old tower on top of a bare crag, its ragged
outlines looking stern and sad against the sky.
A star shines peacefully just above its crum-
bling walls. From a little, dark lake rise the
complaining voices of croaking frogs. Other
sounds as melancholy and prolonged as the
tones of an Æolian harp strike upon my ear.
We are in the land of legends and fairy tales.
Here, too, the thin vapor just touching the
ground, that I had noticed at Schwetzingen,
covers the earth. It is thickest in the valleys. I can count five, six, ten different clouds
of this vapor marking the watercourses along
the mountain side, and over all the landscape
the moon shines peacefully. The air is light
and clear; I feel light myself, and am singularly calm.

"Ellis," I cry, "you must love this land!"

"I! I love nothing!"

"How? Not even me?"

"Ah yes, you," she answered carelessly; and I seemed to feel her arm grasping me with renewed force.

"On! On!" she cried, with a sort of cold passion.

XXI.

A sharp cry, a prolonged rattling sound arose suddenly above our heads, and was repeated in front of us. "It is the rear-guard of a flock of cranes traveling to the North," said Ellis; "shall we join them?"

"Yes; let us fly with the cranes."

Thirteen large and handsome birds flying in a triangle advanced rapidly, flapping their tufted wings. With heads thrown back and their strong breasts forward, they flew so fast that the wind whistled behind them. It was strange to see, at this height in the air, far from other living creatures, this bold, vigorous courage, this irresistible will. Without halting or slackening the swiftness of their flight, they exchanged from time to time, as they clove the air, shrill cries with their comrade at the forward point of the triangle. There was something earnest and grave, like a feeling of unshaken confidence in a friend, in this aerial sociability and conversation. " We will hold out to the end, in spite of fatigue," they seemed to say, encouraging one another. And it crossed my mind that in Russia or in the whole world how few men were fit to be compared to these birds.

"Yes, we are in Russia now," said Ellis. I had noticed before that Ellis could nearly always read my thoughts.

" Wilt thou go elsewhere?" she asked.

" Elsewhere? No! I come from Paris. Take me to St. Petersburg."

" Now?"

"At once; only cover my head with your sleeve to protect me."

Ellis stretched out her hand, but before the mist closed round me, I felt again upon my

lips the leech-like touch I had noticed once
before.

XXII.

"Beware! Beware! or, or"— This cry
resounded in my ears. "Beware! Beware!
or"— echoed in the distance. "Beware! Beware! or"— the cry died away somewhere
near the end of the earth. I shook myself.
Right in front of me shone a great gilded
arrow. I recognized the fortress of St. Petersburg.

Pale night of the North! Is it really night?
Is it not rather a faint sickly day? I have
never liked the night in St. Petersburg, but
now I was almost frightened at it. Ellis had
entirely vanished, dissolved like the morning
mist in the July sun, and yet I could distinctly
see my own body hanging heavily in the air at
the height of the column of Alexander.

So this was St. Petersburg! There could be
no doubt about it. The wide, deserted, ash-
colored streets; the houses, yellow gray, blue

gray, grayish white, covered with thick stucco;
the windows sunk deep in the walls, with
gaudily painted signs and iron balconies above
the doors! The dirty fruit stalls, the white-
plastered Grecian columns, the sign-posts, the
troughs for hack-horses, and the swarms of
police guards! ' Here is the guilded cupola of
St. Isaacs; the Bourse with its motley colors;
the granite walls of the fortress, and the
broken, worn out, wooden pavement. I recognize these boats loaded with hay and wood.
I recall the odors of dust, cabbages, straw, and
stables. I can see the porters standing in their
long coats as if turned to stone, and the hack-
men curled up asleep on the boxes of their old
droschkes. Yes, this certainly is our modern
Palmyra. In this pallid light every thing is
seen with a painful distinctness that makes one
sick at heart, and every thing is asleep in the
mournful surrounding of this troubled and
sickly atmosphere. The pink of yesterday's
twilight, that consumptive pink, has not yet
died away; it will last until morning comes

with its white, starless sky.   In long lines upon
the waters of the Neva its reflection is cast—
the Neva, blue and cold, flowing slowly on toward the sea.

"Let us fly!" cried Ellis; and without waiting for my answer she carried me to the opposite bank of the river, the other side of the
Place de Palais, near the Foundry.   Beneath
us, I could hear footsteps and voices.   Through
the streets passed a group of young men talking over some riotous ball they had just quitted.

"Second Lieutenant Stolpakof, No. 7!"
cried out a sentinel, just roused from sleep
near a pile of rusty cannon-balls.   A little
further on, through an open window of a large
house, I saw a young woman in a tumbled,
soiled silk dress, with bare arms, a band of
pearls in her hair and a cigarette in her mouth,
absorbed in a book: a volume of some very
modern journal.

"Come away, quick!" I cried to Ellis.

In an instant the forests of stunted saplings

and the mossy marshes that surround St. Petersburg had vanished from beneath us. We
were flying straight south. The sky and earth
gradually grew darker as we flew. Sickly
night; sickly day; sickly town; we left them
all far behind! . . .

XXIII.

We flew more slowly than usually, and I could
easily follow with my eye the changes in the
surface of my native land. It was a boundless
panorama. Woods, fog, fields, valleys and
rivers; further on towers and churches, and
again beyond, fields, valleys, rivers, fog.

I was in a bad humor, indifferent and bored;
but not uninterested, and bored simply because
we were flying through Russia. No; the
countries of the whole earth, with their short-
lived populace, so full of petty cares and troubles and diseases, hanging on to this wretched
ball of clay—this fragile red crust which has
grown above the sand of our planet and been

covered by the thin moss-like growth which
we dignify by calling it the vegetable kingdom—these human flies, infinitely more con-
temptible than the insects, the slight traces of
their tiresome, miserable quarrels, their absurd
battles against the immutable and the inevitable!
Ah, how small this all seemed to me! My
heart swelled within me; I no longer wished
to gaze at so insignificant and absurd a carica-
ture. I was disgusted. I even ceased to feel
any pity for my kind. All my feelings were
merged into one of which I myself was
ashamed,—utter disgust, and worse still, disgust with myself.

"Stop!" said Ellis, "Stop! or I can not
support you. You are growing heavy."
"Home," I said to her, in the same tone that
I might have used to a coachman at four in
the morning, on leaving the house of some
friend where I had been dining and talking
over the future of Russia and the meaning of
the Communistic principle.

"Home!" I repeated and closed my eyes.

XXIV.

I soon opened them, for Ellis pressed close
to me in a strange manner, almost pushing
me. I looked at her and the blood froze in
my veins. Who ever has seen the human face
expressing the most abject terror without apparent cause, can faintly appreciate my feeling.
Horror, the most real and wildly expressed,
convulsed the face of Ellis. I never had seen
the like on a mortal countenance. This bloodless phantom—this spirit of the air—this
shadow—and yet such a look of horror!
"Ellis! what is the matter?" cried I. "It is
He! It is He!" gasped Ellis, with an effort.

"Who? He?"

"Do not speak his name! Don't speak it,"
she whispered. "We must fly! All will be
over—forever! Look! There He is!"

I turned my eyes in the direction her trembling hand indicated, and I saw something—a
horrible something!

It was all the more fearful because it had no
distinct form. It was a heavy dark mass of a
blackish yellow—spotted and writhing like the
belly of a lizard. It was neither a cloud nor
a mist. It crept slowly along the ground like
a reptile; then with quivering leaps; now up,
now down, with regular movements like the
flapping of the wings of a bird of prey, ready
to seize its victim. Now it would crouch close
to the earth before making a hideous bound,
as a spider throws itself upon a fly caught in
its web. At its approach I could see it and
feel it; every thing was destroyed and over-
whelmed. A pestilent, venomous, cold breath
spread around, and at its chill touch the heart
stopped, the eye became blind, the hair stocd
on end. It was a moving, irresistible force,
that nothing could stop; which, without form,
without sight, without thought, could still see
every thing and know every thing. As fierce
as the vulture in seizing its victim; as cunning
as the snake and like him slowly covering its

prey with the cold breath of its poison. "Ellis!" I screamed, shuddering, "I know Him! It is death!"

The plaintive sound I had first heard from her, came from the parted lips of Ellis; but this time it was more like a cry of human despair. We rushed on blindly in our flight. Ellis would whirl and plunge in the air, turning wildly from one side to the other like a wounded bird, or the quail trying to decoy the hunting-dog away from the nest.

And now from the horrible mass there stretched themselves long hairy tentacles, like those of the devil-fish, that spread out in the air toward us like claws. . . Ellis desperately struggled on. "He sees us! All is over! I am lost," she cried, gasping, "Wretched me! I might have succeeded; life might have been mine! And now! Destruction! Annihilation!"

As I heard these last words my senses forsook me.

XXV.

When I came to myself I was lying on the
grass, and in all my limbs was a racking pain,
as though I had fallen from a height. Day
was dawning and things were already growing
distinct. At a little distance a road, bordered
with willows, wound along toward a forest of
birch-trees. I knew the place well.

I began to recall the events of that terrible
night, and I shuddered at the thought of the
dreadful apparition that my eyes had beheld.
"But why," I asked myself, "was Ellis so overcome by fear? Is she, too, subject to his do-
minion? Perhaps she is not immortal; perhaps she is destined to annihilation. But how
can that be possible?"

A faint sigh close to me made me turn my
head. About two steps away, stretched upon
the ground, lay the body of a young woman,
clothed in a long white robe. Her dark hair
was dishevelled and one shoulder bare. Her
left hand was behind her head, the other

across her breast; her eyes were shut and about her lips I saw a faint stain of bloody foam. Was it Ellis? But Ellis was a phantom, and before me lay a woman of flesh and blood!

I dragged myself toward her, and leaning over her cried, " Ellis, can this be you?" Suddenly, with a slight quiver, her eyelids opened and her great black eyes were fixed upon me. I was transfixed by her gaze, and at the same instant I felt upon mine, her lips soft and warm, but with a faint odor of blood. I felt her burning bosom pressed against my breast as she clasped her arms about my neck. "Farewell, farewell, forever!" she murmured, in a dying voice, then all disappeared. . . I rose, staggering like a drunken man; and I looked about me for a long time, passing my hands across my eyes. At last I found the road to N——, two versts from my own house. The sun was up when I reached my room. . . . The next night I waited, I must confess, not without fear, the return of the phantom, but she did not come.

Once I went, at night, out under the old oak-tree, but saw nothing unusual. I could scarcely regret this. For a long time I had thought over my adventure, and felt sure that science could not explain it, nor legend or tradition furnish its parallel.

Who or what could Ellis have been? A ghost; a soul in torment; a demon; a vampire? Often it seems as though she were some woman I had known formerly. I have tried with all my might to recall where I could have seen her. Once—to-day—just now, I remember—no, all is confused in my memory, as in a dream.

Yes; I have thought it all over and over, and no one will be astonished when I say that I can come to no conclusion. I did not like to speak of this to my friends; they would think I was mad. At last I concluded to banish it from my mind. I had many things to occupy me. The emancipation of the serfs came, and arrangements about the property had to be made. Besides, my health was seriously affected. I suffer from weak lungs, sleeplessness and a dry, hard cough. I have become emaciated; my face is as pale as a dead man's. My physician tells me my blood is poor. He calls my sickness anæmia. He sends me to Gastein. My steward says that without me he can not manage my affairs with the peasants. Well, let them manage themselves, then!

But what can be the meaning of those strange sounds, clear and distinct as the notes of a harmonica, that I hear whenever they speak to me of the death of anybody? They become stronger and stronger and wilder and wilder.

And why do I feel this terrible chill creep over me at the mere thought of annihilation?